PANIC ROOM

"WHAT ON EARTH IS A PANIC ROOM?"

The two realtors entered the room, but Meg lingered near the door, her eyes doing a quick and thorough inventory of the interior. There were several large gray plastic crates that opened down the middle, displaying in block print their contents: survival supplies, including water, batteries, flashlights, tools, both metric and nonmetric, clothes, blankets, army-type K rations, medical supplies, cooking utensils, canned goods and various forms of powdered foods.

Meg felt a chill go through her as she reluctantly stepped just inside the room. What kind of mind needed a room like this? What did this room say about the previous owner? She was a believer in signs and portents, and she could feel the man's ghostly presence looming near her at that moment—dark and smothering. Was he saying something to her? Warning her? She could almost feel his touch on her skin.

PANIC ROOM

A novel by James Ellison

Based on the screenplay written by David Koepp

POCKET BOOKS
NEW YORK LONDON TORONTO SYDNEY SINGAPORE

James Ellison would like to thank Francine Hornberger, whose writing skills and mastery of the "big picture" cannot be learned in any writing class.

An *Original* Publication of POCKET BOOKS

POCKET BOOKS, a division of Simon & Schuster, Inc.
1230 Avenue of the Americas, New York, NY 10020

ISBN: 0-7434-5154-6

First Pocket Books printing February 2002

10 9 8 7 6 5 4 3 2

For information regarding special discounts for bulk purchases,
please contact Simon & Schuster Special Sales at 1-800-456-6798
or business@simonandschuster.com

Printed in the U.S.A.

PANIC ROOM

— CHAPTER —

1

M eg found it hard to believe that at this time only last year, she was happily married to pharmaceutical giant Stephen Altman, living the blissful Greenwich, Connecticut, life in her palatial suburban home, lunching with various neighbors, and going back-to-school-shopping with her daughter, Sarah.

Of course, living in Manhattan would mean doing all these things, in time, but in an entirely different way.

And while life in suburban Connecticut was in many ways idyllic, Meg was looking forward to getting away. She needed to get away. She craved a fresh start. She was starting to resent the pitying looks of women acquaintances who knew her situation, but not nearly as much as she resented the venomous revenge fantasies of the other recently jilted middle-aged housewives, whose husbands had left for greener pastures, or for women whose breasts didn't yet understand gravity. While she appreciated their support, after a while it just became exhausting to be expected to rehash the events of the breakup every time she saw these friends.

It wasn't as if Stephen had always been a bad man. In fact, he was the last person she had ever expected would run out on her—and take up with a twenty-something supermodel. Steve had always been the type to prefer the mousy, bookworm type, which is exactly the type Meg had been when they met in college.

She was busy poring over art history books in the library, cramming for her Masters of the Renaissance midterm, when he bounded in with a few of his fraternity brothers. She hated the type, and only looked up for a moment to shoot the boisterous group a look fit to kill. She hadn't even noticed him. But he noticed her. And for the next three months, he pursued her relentlessly until she finally gave in and agreed to a date. He was immediately smitten; she warmed up to him over the course of a couple of years. And a year after graduation, she married him. She still wasn't convinced that she had done the right thing, even as she stood at the altar prepared to say "I do," but he was a good man. Dedicated to her. Devoted to making the relationship work. And like anything else that Meg did, she threw everything she had into this life. She would make it work. She was determined to make it the best marriage that had ever existed.

For the next twelve years, she put her career on hold to help him further his; devoted herself to her marriage and to raising the best product of it, their daughter Sarah. She had wanted more children, but he was satisfied with "his two girls." Was this a clue that she had somehow managed to miss? As she mulled over the failure of their marriage, she wondered if his not wanting a second child was a sign that he had already begun to cool on their relationship.

And now she was moving to Manhattan, a place she had never dreamed she would live, mostly because of her deep-seated fear of confined, enclosed spaces. She much preferred the wide expanses of yards and spread-apart houses where there was enough air for everyone to breathe. But Manhattan, with its tall buildings and congestion, people within inches of each other, cars and noise everywhere, frightened her. Every time she thought of leaving Greenwich her stomach knotted with terror. But she had decided it was time to quash the fear that always governed her every action and to take her life back.

A large part of the reconstruction of Meg Altman involved getting a Master's degree in Art History. She had applied to Columbia nine months earlier on a whim, before she was aware that her life with Stephen was about to end. But when she was accepted, she took it as a sign that she had instinctively made the right move, that graduate school was ordained. It was high time to do something for herself for once.

Sarah wasn't happy with the move. She wanted to stay with her friends, at *her* school, and even though she accepted that it was her father's fault that things were changing, at ten she had already begun to question her mother and all that she stood for. She had begun to cast a critical eye on everything her mother said and did and was not shy about expressing herself. She was turning from girl to woman far too early. Meg tried to accept the changes in Sarah with grace and a measure of patience; she had always known her daughter to be years ahead of her actual age. She was never a baby; the cute doll phase simply passed her by. She talked in full sentences before her first birthday. She already knew things a ten-year-old could not possibly know. Meg wanted to blame it on the generation—on TV and movies and the various messages these media fed young minds. But she knew better. Sarah was Sarah, and if she never watched even one hour of TV, she would still be the insightful, perceptive, and wise-before-her time child her mother could not possibly live without. And for these qualities, Meg not only loved her daughter but truly admired her.

Meg was still very much the mother, though. She was still in charge and she was primed and ready for a change. One thing she knew for certain: she needed to be around a different class of women—women who didn't define themselves by their homes and their children's accomplishments, and their husbands' achievements. She wanted to be around women who made it happen for themselves: women not afraid of plain speech and power.

That was what had attracted her to the realtor she was working with in the agonizingly slow process of finding a new home. She had called around and interviewed many agents. But when she got Lydia Truman on the phone with her sassy, take-no-prisoners attitude, Meg knew that this was a woman who was going to help her take the first step in making her life happen.

Lydia had made a great career for herself selling real estate in New York City. Married and divorced twice, she was not one to define herself through the successes and failures of her husband. Her identity was all her own, and to make sure this was understood by family, friends, and professional acquaintances she had insisted on keeping her surname. Lydia had a boundless energy and a zest for living that Meg so desperately craved at this point in her life, though she knew that spending too much time with Lydia would exhaust all possible energy reserves—both emotionally and physically. Like right now.

Lydia vaulted ahead of Meg and Sarah, on a clear and cloudless day in early September, taking wide, determined strides and talking in a husky, tobacco-laced voice as she read from a Post-it note stuck to her right index finger.

"Forty-two hundred square feet, four floors—absolutely ideal. Listen to this: courtyard in back, south-facing garden. *Per*fect. This is absolutely—"

Meg, struggling to stay abreast, yelled to Sarah, who was gliding down the sidewalk on a Razor scooter, one of Stephen's many recent guilt gifts to his daughter. His largesse was just another way to make Meg crazy and feel completely alone and inadequate in child-raising. "Honey, don't you go *near* that curb, you hear me?"

"Yeah, yeah. Loud and clear, Ma."

Sarah weaved in and out between the two women and was doing loops right to the edge of the curb. She flashed her mother a wide smile, composed in equal parts of mischief and keen intelligence. She was tall and skinny, and her energy could barely be contained.

Meg said to the real estate agent, "Why don't we grab a cab? We've got ten blocks to go and we're late."

"No, no. We'll be sitting in traffic forever. And I know those people from Douglas Elliman. One minute late, they swoop down and it's off the market."

"You're just trying to scare me, Lydia," Meg said with a grin. "My new life philosophy is, if it's gone, it's gone. Things have a way of working out. Life happens—you can't force it. Can I at least see the listing sheet?"

Ignoring Meg's last question and sneaking a look toward Sarah to see whether she was within earshot, Lydia said, "The philosophy of the bereaved and the jilted. In my opinion, for what it's worth, you're well rid of the bastard. Isn't the male mid-life crisis the most boring act on earth?"

Meg to herself: *Okay. Just don't ask me to plot out how vindicated I would feel if I filled Stephen's car with horse manure or sewed dead fish into the hems of his drapes. . . .*

Meg out loud: "Sarah? Pick that scooter up and walk with us, okay? You're making me very, very nervous."

The girl grinned, but continued to race along, perilously close to the traffic.

"Lydia—the listing sheet. May I see it, please?"

"Listing sheet?" said Lydia. "There's no listing sheet. This property's not even on the market. I heard about it this morning; it'll be gone this afternoon."

"You must have quite a network, I must say. Very impressive."

"This is a tough town. You have to be on top of every single thing. The race is definitely to the swift."

Meg was not going to let the air go out of her balloon. No matter how cool she appeared to play it, she just had to find something today. She needed to settle. She needed a way out of the limbo her life had become over the past few months and she wanted it quick.

"How many more places do we have after this?" she said. "I'm exhausted and Sarah is driving me—" Meg swung around and spotted her daughter skating on the very edge of the curb, flirting with disaster in the form of oncoming taxis and buses. "Sarah! *Do not ride out there!*" she shouted.

"Chill, Ma."

"Yeah, chill, Ma," Lydia told her client, "and listen to me very, very closely. In words of one syllable, this is *it*. There is nothing else to see. Nada. Zilch. Nothing that's remotely suitable. You must know how tight the market is." Meg simply shrugged her shoulders.

Sarah swung up beside Lydia and said, "Who wants to live in this dirty, smelly city anyway? It sucks."

"You should be wearing a helmet, young lady," said the real estate agent, affecting sternness. "Where is it?"

"Don't know," said the girl.

"She loses everything," Meg said.

"I'm an absentminded genius," Sarah piped in, "in case you didn't know."

Her mother shot her a sharp look. "You're not funny."

They turned the corner, south of the Museum of Natural History, and rapidly approached the property for sale. A man, dressed in a pinstripe suit and a severe blue striped tie, was coming down the stairs from a four-story townhouse fronted by a postage stamp-size garden and a single *Ginkgo biloba* tree.

Lydia pointed at the tree, a handful of flowers and a few square feet of grass. "By Manhattan measurements this piece of dirt is priceless—practically a pasture," she explained to Meg.

She came to a sudden stop and stared, her hand to her mouth. "Oh, shit. That miserable little prick is already leaving."

"Who is he?"

"Evan Racine," Lydia said. "It's his exclusive and I'll have to share the commission with him."

"If he has the exclusive, why does he want to share it with you?" Sarah asked.

Lydia narrowed her eyes. "Well, little one, the reason is, I have the perfect client in your mother. I do the work, he gets richer."

Evan Racine approached them, his mouth below a wispy mustache an angry snip of wire.

"One day you'll learn to respect people's time, Lydia. One day you'll realize that the world does not stop and start at your convenience."

"Evan—I am so, *so* sorry. . . ."

"My schedule calls for Arthur Digby Laurence in"—he scowled at his watch—"exactly twenty-six minutes. And if you think Arthur Digby Laurence is the kind of man who tolerates being kept waiting, you are sadly mistaken."

"Arthur Digby Laurence is a ridiculous name," Lydia observed.

"I will ignore that comment."

"He's not going to buy anyway, Evan."

"What?"

"He's filthy rich, owns a glut of houses already and is more likely to sell than buy. Also, he has a reputation as a professional looker. A real house-browsing prick tease. He loves to waste your time."

"Listen, I don't have to stand here and—"

"You were a *saint* to wait for us, Evan dear," Lydia said as she blew right past him. "I've told my client about this house and she is very, very excited. Isn't that true, Meg?"

"I'm certainly interested in seeing it," Meg said weakly. Even as the words left her mouth, she could tell that this man would never take her seriously. She was glad she had Lydia by her side. She sensed that her toughness and aggression were a match for any man. Evan Racine sullenly marched up to the front door and unlocked it again, revealing a spacious and airy foyer. The two women followed him in. Sarah rode her scooter across the polished pine floor as the broker glared at her.

"It's kind of a cross between a townhouse and a brownstone," he said, quickly locking into his tour mode. "We like to call it a townstone. It was built in eighteen seventy-nine. This is the middle of the house—the parlor floor. The living room is directly ahead and the formal dining room is in the back. Casual dining is below, on the kitchen level, which was renovated five years ago, with all the expected amenities." His tiny chest swelled as he added, "I can't stress enough how rare it is for a house of this pedigree to come on the market."

"You're so right, Evan," Lydia said sweetly.

Meg was torn between listening to the broker and making frantic hand signals to tell Sarah to stop riding the scooter in the house.

"There are two bedroom floors above," the broker continued.

"My God, this place is simply huge," Meg said in wonder.

Racine nodded, and said with a note of condescension, "I don't have to tell you, this amount of living space is extremely uncommon in Manhattan. Rare as hen's teeth."

"Sarah," Meg whispered out of the corner of her mouth, but her daughter ignored her, doing loops into the living room.

"No scooter, kid," Lydia said sharply.

Sarah reluctantly came to a stop. She picked up her scooter and wandered into the solarium. She peered through big French doors that looked out over a courtyard area. A row of brownstones lined the next block, and all of the patios backed up to one another. With a sigh, her breath fogging the window, she leaned up against the door. She did not look happy. This move into the city would mean leaving all her school friends behind. No more horseback riding, although her father had promised to look into riding at the Claremont Stables, which were situated nearby. No more ice skating on the pond near their house in Greenwich. No more hikes in the woods with Grace and Maureen, her best friends. All of that on top of her parents' divorce was a heavy burden to carry.

"Well," she said, more to herself than the others, "at least there's a yard." She shook her head. "Sort of a yard."

The broker, throwing Sarah a dark look, said to Lydia, still ignoring Meg, "Quite honestly, the courtyard is in a state of disrepair, but the potential is simply enormous. It's a twenty-one foot lot, fifty-three feet deep, which does allow for an expansive garden."

"My mother doesn't have a green thumb," Sarah said, with an impish grin, glancing at the small angry man for the first time.

"Sarah!"

Evan Racine quickly strode across the room and flung open the door of an old-fashioned, cage-style elevator.

"*This* you don't see often," he announced grandly. "A working elevator of this vintage is priceless. You probably won't find one in ninety percent of the townhouses in this city."

"Cool," Sarah said, staring at the elevator with interest.

"How *won*derful," Lydia exclaimed. She nudged Meg. "I've always dreamed of having one of these."

Meg made a noncommittal sound, keeping a wary eye on her daughter.

"I'll grant that this building is something of a fixer-upper," Racine said, sliding an appraising glance at Meg. "But we anticipate an enormous amount of interest. Quality is so rare these days—simply priceless. This is a very . . . *emotional* property."

Meg turned to him, her eyebrows raised in a question. "Emotional?"

"It resonates with feeling," he said, pain or impatience furrowing his forehead. "I can sense the past in the air."

As he started up the stairs two at a time to the next level, Lydia whispered to Meg, "You should offer immediately. This will *not* stay on the market."

"Do you mind if I see it first, please? You're rushing me, and I don't like to be rushed." Meg smiled to herself, proud to have stood up to this powerhouse of a woman.

"It's emotional, Ma," Sarah said, imitating Evan Racine's fruity tones. "*Emotional*."

Ignoring the child, Lydia said, "I'm telling you, there is nothing *remotely* like this around right now. You have to set your sights realistically, Meg. You can't move from Greenwich to the Upper West Side and expect to still have a house, a garden, and space to spare—but *here it is*. Plus an elevator. It's got everything you wanted, and more. Think of the fun you can have fixing this up, decorating, haunting the antiques shops for just the right pieces. You can make this an incredible showpiece. I can just see the dinner parties right now."

"Pizza for two," Sarah muttered. "That's what *I* see."

"It will cost a fortune," Meg said.

"Well," Lydia said, "luckily for you that's not an issue, is it?"

"This isn't Barney's, Ma," Sarah put in. "You don't have to pay the sticker price, you know."

Lowering her voice, Lydia said, "From all you've told me, that runaway husband of yours can damn well afford it. And he owes you, big time."

"Ex-husband, Lydia."

Overhearing this exchange, Sarah gave the real estate woman an evil stare. She marched into the elevator and rattled the door shut with a metallic clang.

"Please!" Evan Racine called from upstairs. "It would be lovely if I could show this property in the few minutes we have remaining."

The two women glanced at each other.

"Emotional." Meg imitated her daughter's put-on fruity accent with a slow grin.

"He's a jerk," Lydia said, rolling her eyes.

They walked up a flight of winding stairs and joined the broker. They then followed him up another flight of stairs.

"Top floor," he announced, flushed and breathing heavily. "Two bedrooms, one on either end. They share one small bath, but there's room for expansion. Originally, this would have been the servant's quarters. The previous owner kept a small nursing staff, but as you can see, it's perfect for a live-in."

"Just perfect," Lydia echoed.

From the hallway they could hear the metallic groaning of the elevator as it slowly ascended. Evan Racine batted his eyes and pursed his lips in annoyance, but managed to hold his tongue.

He turned a chilly glance on Meg.

"I assume you have live-in help."

"Actually, no. It'll just be the two of us."

He nodded as though that was what he had

expected to hear. Frowning at Lydia, he led the way down to the third floor.

"This is the spare bedroom-den-what-have-you," he said, waving a limp arm at a vast empty room. "Mr. Pearlstein used it as an office. But it would make a lovely library." He paused, waiting for a response.

Lydia nudged Meg's arm. "He's talking about Sidney Pearlstein," she said, a touch of awe in her voice.

Meg shook her head and shrugged.

"The financier?" Lydia said impatiently.

"Oh, yes," Meg said. But it was clear from her vague tone that she had never heard of the man.

Evan Racine cleared his throat and, gazing directly into Meg's eyes for the first time, said, "May I ask what you do, Mrs. . . . ?"

"Altman," she answered too quickly. "I'm going back to school—Columbia. For my master's—"

"Ah—how interesting." He cut Meg off and exchanged a quick glance with Lydia, and his expression was easy to read: Why the hell did you bring a student to look at *this* house? Are you out of your mind?

"Her husband's in pharmaceuticals," Lydia explained in a rush. "Stephen Altman."

After a quick beat the broker's face brightened with a smile. He practically gushed as he said to Meg, "So you're Stephen *Altman's* wife. I didn't realize. I was fascinated by the piece on him in the *New Yorker.*"

"I was, until recently."

"What? You were fascinated?" He stared at her in puzzlement.

"His wife. We're recently divorced. That's why I'm here looking at this house."

"Oh, I see." He cleared his throat and his busy eyes darted away from hers. He nodded several times, staring intently at his feet. "I see. . . ."

He showed them the master bath, which was huge and done in marble.

"Pearlstein's in all the papers since he died," Lydia said to Meg. "It's a juicy scandal. His kin are suing each other over his estate and it's gotten really vicious. Haven't you been reading about it?"

"No."

"It's covered by Page Six nearly every day."

"I don't read the *Post,*" Meg said with the hint of a smile. "Actually I don't read the *Times,* either."

"He was a recluse," Lydia told her. "Rich as Croesus and paranoid as hell. And now it turns out they can't find a huge chunk of his money. Probably in tin cans and mattresses."

"Lydia, really," Racine said sharply. "I hardly see how family gossip is germane to showing the property."

" 'Really,' yourself, Evan. And would you

please stop calling it 'the property'? You sound like a talking lease."

He turned his back on her and said to Meg, "This is the master closet. As you can see, it's roughly the size of your average studio apartment in the West Village, without the Village, ah, divertissements." He giggled at his little witticism, then winced as the elevator came to a groaning, shuddering halt and Sarah emerged screaming with delight. Speaking as though his mouth hurt, Racine said to Meg, "Could the little one please stop that?"

"Sarah, babes, *no elevator,*" Lydia said firmly. She winked at Meg. "Who's the mother here, anyway?"

"I'm beginning to wonder."

"And now," said Evan Racine, coughing into his hand for attention, "the *pièce de résistance.* Here is the master suite—grand, to say the least." He made a flourishing gesture with his arm, then quickly checked his watch and frowned.

Meg looked around, taking in the dimensions of the room. After glancing at the far wall, the one that bordered the house next door, she backed up a step to study more carefully the wall that cornered it. She took pride in her eyes. She was a gifted watercolorist, who had had a successful show of her work in a Greenwich gallery two years earlier, one of the first and last things she had accomplished for herself since she graduated college with summa cum laude honors. Stephen had often boasted of her that she had the vision of a master detective. "She has this way of seeing what the rest of us fail to see," he was fond of saying, to her embarrassment and slight annoyance. "The smallest details, she notices them."

She shook her head slightly, still scrutinizing the wall. "That's really odd," she said.

Lydia swung around to her. "What?"

"There's something funny," Meg said. "This room seems smaller than it ought to."

Lydia, who was seriously myopic but refused to wear glasses and often lost her contact lenses, squinted into palpable mist. "What's wrong with it, Meg? It looks just fine to me."

Evan Racine pointedly glanced at his watch as he tapped his foot. To make his point, he breathed an audible sigh.

"No—no, look." Meg pointed to the far end of the wall, near the entrance to the closet. A mirrored door led to the closet and there was a mirror on the wall alongside it. "Don't you see? The mirrors are tilted just slightly—just enough to cause an optical illusion. The corner of the room appears closer to the door than it actually is."

Lydia continued to squint. "I don't see it."

Meg looked at Racine, who stepped forward, shaking his head in agreement. "You're quite right, Mrs. Altman. I was waiting to see if you'd notice. No one from our office had the slightest idea this existed when we accepted the listing."

"That *what* existed?" Lydia asked, clearly upset to be left in the dark.

Racine ran his hand along the top of the wall mirror until it gave a faint click, which caused it to open a few inches off the wall. He then pulled the mirror toward him, one hundred eighty degrees, until it fastened itself magnetically to the back of the closet door. On the smooth wall where the mirror had been was a faint vertical crack. Racine pushed against the wall, first at the top, then at the bottom, and the wall slowly came ajar. He pulled it wide open. Meg and Lydia took a few steps forward, fascinated. He hit a switch and a row of fluorescent bars flicked on bluely overhead.

"This is called the panic room," he said. Meg noticed that his voice was flat and lacked its usual enthusiasm. She sensed that he would not have brought it up if she hadn't noticed the unusual dimensions of the room, and she wondered why.

"Goodness," Lydia said, grinning. "How exciting. This house is full of surprises. First the grand old elevator, now this."

"A panic room," Meg said, studying Racine. While the others moved toward the wall, she hung back, her hand to her throat. "How odd. What on earth is a panic room? It sounds frightening."

"A safe room," the broker answered quickly. "In medieval times I imagine it would've been called a castle keep."

"You know, I think I've seen one of these," Lydia said. "I was showing a place on Fifth Avenue, in the upper sixties. This was eight, maybe ten years ago, and my memory is a little vague, but I *think* it might have been some sort of secret room."

Lydia and Racine entered the room, but Meg lingered near the door, her eyes doing a quick and thorough inventory of the interior. There were several large gray plastic crates that opened down the middle, displaying in block print their contents: survival supplies, including water, batteries, flashlights, tools, both metric and non-metric, clothes, blankets, army-type K rations, medical supplies, cooking utensils, canned goods and various forms of powdered foods.

Meg felt a chill go through her as she reluctantly stepped just inside the room. What kind of mind needed a room like this? What did this room say about the previous owner? She was a believer in signs and portents, and she could feel the man's ghostly presence looming near her at that moment—dark and smothering. Was he saying something to her? Warning her? She could almost feel his touch on her skin.

"This is so absolutely *winning*," Lydia enthused. "Imagine the alarm goes off in the middle of the night. What are you going to do? Call the police and wait around for hours and hours till they quit cooping or whatever they do? Traipse around downstairs in your underthings to check it out? *I think not.* You have *this.*" She waved her arms dramatically, encompassing the room.

Racine nodded, warming to her enthusiasm. "It is definitely state of the art. Solid steel-core walls. A buried phone line, *not* connected to the house's main line—you can call the police and nobody can cut you off. Your own ventilation system, surveillance monitors—" he hit a switch next to a bank of small video monitors—"covering nearly every corner of the house." His smile was more of a self-satisfied smirk than a genuine smile. "Talk about being armed against any contingency, well, this is the ultimate in protection." He turned to Meg. "What do you think, Mrs. Altman? You have a child, and this is the last word in child protection."

She felt a drop of sweat trickle down her forehead; she swiped at it with her hand. "It makes me nervous."

"Why?" Lydia said. "It should give you a sense of security."

"Well, it doesn't." There was a slight edge to Meg's voice. "I can't help thinking of Edgar Allan Poe."

"Poe? What about him?"

"This has a Poe feeling to it."

Evan Racine stared at his watch with a deep sigh.

"Oh, really, Meg. That's just silly."

"Is it? What's to prevent someone from prying open the door?"

Racine reached past Meg and pushed a red button on the wall behind her. With a sudden slapping sound, a heavy steel door slid out of a slot in the wall and slammed shut. A series of metal latches clicked into place inside it, from top to bottom, securing it.

"There's your answer," he said. "Steel. Very thick steel. With a full battery backup. Even if the power's out, it's still functional. You can keep an entire army at bay."

Lydia laughed. "Old Sidney didn't miss a trick, did he? I guess with his millions he figured someone would be after him. And the relatives he was saddled with, no wonder he needed a place to hide."

"That's highly inappropriate, Lydia," Racine said, scowling at her.

"Open the door, please," Meg told him. "I don't like it in here. I feel as though I'm suffocating."

The broker shrugged. "As you please."

He hit a green button and the door groaned open, recoiling its massive spring and revealing Sarah standing in the entryway grinning. She stepped inside, took a quick glance around and said, "My room. *Definitely* my room. Wait till Maureen sees this, Ma. It's too cool."

"Come out right now," Meg hissed as she left the panic room.

"But this is great," Sarah insisted. "What's wrong with it?"

Meg breathed in deeply, trying to regain her composure. What was wrong? Easy answer: everything was wrong. The shadow of Stephen hung over her, but there was also the shadow of the Harrison Caves in Barbados. She was down in them all over again. Sarah was seven and Meg and Stephen were still in love and planning a lifetime together, and they had taken the trolley deep down, nearly one hundred eighty feet, into the caves, past stalagmites and stalactites posted like pale silent sentries on ground and ceiling as they descended. The depth of the darkness and the silence, profound as death itself, had covered Meg like a shroud. Suddenly she couldn't breathe, she had wanted to scream but her throat was constricted with panic. Gripping the trolley rail, she had prayed to God that He would return her to the surface safe and sane and that the entire experience would soon fade into nothingness. It had taken months for the fear of that hour in the cave to begin to fade (Stephen had not taken her panic seriously, for which she had never forgiven him). She felt some of that same degree of fear again now, washing over her like a drug flashback.

"This door seems like a hazard," Lydia halfasked, half-accused Racine.

"No, not at all."

He pushed the button again, but just before the door closed he slid a hand into a tiny red beam that shone across the doorway at shoulder height. The beam broke, the door stopped halfway shut and groaned open again. "You see? Infrared—just like an elevator. The door can't close if the beam is blocking it. There's another one at your ankles. The system couldn't be designed for greater safety."

"Unless you're being chased," Lydia said with a grin at Meg, who regarded her without expression.

The broker did not find the remark amusing. "Voilà!" he said, reaching up to push the button again. The metal door rocketed shut with a whang!, the metallic thunder reverberating in the room. Almost immediately the fake piece of wall hummed shut of its own accord, followed an instant later by the mirror, which detached itself from the back of the closet door and slid silently back into place, closing over the hidden door. Now the corner of the room looked like an ordinary corner again.

It took some ardent persuading on the part of Lydia Truman, but by the following evening Meg, with Sarah going along unenthusiastically, agreed to the asking price ("You've got to *stick* it to that husband of yours," Lydia admonished her).

She was also able to persuade the Pearlstein estate to close quickly, giving the family more liquid assets to feud over, and allowing Meg and Sarah an opportunity to move into the house sooner than anyone could have dreamed possible. It wasn't soon enough as far as Meg was concerned.

Two weeks later a huge moving van—an eighteen-wheeler only half-full—pulled up to the townhouse and began to unload the Altman belongings. Meg directed the moving men while Sarah drove her scooter from room to room becoming acquainted with every nook and cranny of the huge house. She was a girl who lived a large share of her life in her imagination, and now that she was deprived both of her friends and her father, she began making up stories of spooks and goblins that haunted the house. Not that she really believed in spooks and goblins, but the idea of them amused her. She gave one ugly little boy creature with triangular green eyes and three horns the panic room as his haunting headquarters. As always, in the full swing of her fantasies, she magically made herself healthy. No more diabetes for you, Sarah. No more pills, no more pulse regulator. No more fears of coma. You are *healthy as a horse*.

At the end of their first day in the new house Meg lay sprawled out in the middle of the black-and-white tile floor in the entryway, which was still piled high with moving boxes. She stared at the ceiling, bone weary. She had worked steadily all day, not even stopping for lunch, and it seemed to her that she had barely made a dent in the chaos surrounding her.

Sarah, not nearly so tired as her mother, was busy dribbling a basketball the length of the entryway. She was perfecting her ball handling by dribbling through her legs and behind her back. On her head she wore a New York Knicks cap, with the bill turned backward. "Spree" was stenciled in red on both sides. When she brought the ball up close to her mother, Meg slapped the ball away. "Watch it."

"Quick hands, Ma."

"I'm not in the mood."

"Oh, my. Are we having an attitude problem, Mother Dearest? Or are we PMSing?"

"Don't be smart. I just have an incredible headache."

Sarah tucked the basketball under her arm. "You know something? This place has too many stairs."

"Tell me about it. I've been up and down them all day carrying things."

"That's what the elevator's for." Sarah gave her mother a quick glance. "Uh oh, I forgot. Enclosed spaces." She smiled. "Just like those caves in Barbados, right, Ma? Daddy said you really freaked out. I kind of half remember."

"I ride elevators all the time," Meg said defensively.

"But if there are stairs, you take them, right?"

Meg opened one eye and studied her daughter. "Listen Miss Smarty, Miss Know-It-All. I didn't see *you* carrying any boxes up the stairs. You left all the heavy lifting to your poor old mother."

"Thirty-six isn't exactly old, Ma." Sarah flopped down beside her mother, effortlessly assuming the lotus position, and let out a deep sigh. "We should've got an apartment. This place is too big for the two of us."

"You were crying about how much you loved it when I signed the papers. You couldn't live without it."

"That was then, this is now. I have a right to change my mind."

"Well, you'd better change it right back. Because we're here to stay."

In a soft voice, a touch babyish, Sarah said, "I miss Greenwich. I miss my friends. I'm sorry, Ma, but this just sucks."

"I'm sorry, too," Meg said, running a hand through Sarah's light silky hair. "Believe me, I'm sorry. But this is life. We have to accept it."

Sarah chewed on an already thoroughly chewed thumbnail as she studied her mother.

"Will Daddy come to visit?"

"Sure."

"When?"

"We'll make arrangements."

"When?"

"Don't pester me right now, Sarah. I have a terrible—"

"I'll call him tonight. I'll find out when he's coming."

"Do that."

Sarah flopped onto her stomach, her face inches from Meg's. "I've been through all the boxes. There's a whole lot missing. Where's all our stuff?"

"We didn't bring everything."

"What did we do with it?"

"We gave a lot of stuff away. We had tons of things we didn't need. It's so much easier to collect things than to get rid of them."

"Daddy doesn't hold onto things like you do."

"I know." *He didn't hold onto us. He just threw us away.*

"I'm surprised you didn't keep everything."

"This is a new start for us. Make way for the new, that's my motto."

"But what if I *wanted* things you gave away?"

"Well, *I* didn't want them. There was planning to do, decisions to make, and I made them."

"So what are we supposed to do? About half of my clothes are missing, for one thing."

"Listen, sweetie, I'm very, very tired. Frankly, I feel lousy at the moment and I'd appreciate it if you'd cut me a little slack. Okay?"

Sarah suddenly gave her mother a loud smacking kiss on the ear.

"Don't *do* that. You'll deafen me."

"I'm hungry, Ma."

Meg groaned as she rose to a sitting position. "I filled the refrigerator. I'll see what I can whip up."

"Try five-seven-nine-three thousand. They'll whip it up faster and deliver it to us. Somebody left menus on the kitchen table."

"Oooh-*kay*."

Meg reached for her purse and fished out her cell phone. She pressed the "on" button and shook her head. "Battery's dead."

Sarah helped her mother to her feet. "There's a phone in the kitchen. It works."

"How do you know?"

"How do you think? I picked up the receiver to check for a dial tone. It just needs to be hooked to the thingy on the wall."

Sarah bounced her basketball down the stairs to the ground floor and sat at the table, her head cupped in her hands, watching her mother slide the telephone into a slot on the wall. Meg picked up the receiver, held it to her ear, and smiled.

"Hey, I hooked up the phone. It works."

"I *told* you it works, Mother Dearest," she said. "Do you not listen to me?"

Meg started to dial. "Five-seven-nine . . . ah . . ."

"Three thousand," Sarah said.

An hour later, mother and daughter sat at the kitchen table, four slices of pepperoni pie left in the box. As Sarah's hand shot out for one of them, Meg reached out and covered hers.

"Two slices is enough, Miss Piggy."

Sarah then started to pour herself another glass of Coke.

"Hey, *enough*, Sarah."

The girl shrugged her shoulders resignedly.

"I'm eating and drinking away my sorrows, Ma. Do you mind?"

Meg studied her daughter's features carefully to see if this was one of her ironic statements or whether this had to be taken at face value. It was Meg's belief that she was in possession of the only ten-year-old on the planet capable of irony.

"Are you feeling sad?" she asked.

"Just kidding." She burped. "Sorry."

"Cover your mouth, please."

Sarah clapped a hand over her mouth.

"I mean when you *burp*." She continued to regard her daughter. She said at last, "Was it okay that we had pizza?"

"What do you mean?"

"I don't know. It's just—well, it's not what I planned for our first night here. I figured we'd do something special."

Sarah shrugged. "What's wrong with pizza, anyway? It's got most of the food groups."

"I guess."

Meg finished her glass of Chardonnay and looked away, blinking rapidly. Stephen and that tramp of his were probably dining right now at one of his favorite midtown restaurants, probably at the Four Seasons near the pool, drinking champagne and chatting up the owner, a friend of Stephen's. Moisture filled her eyes.

She felt Sarah's hand on hers.

"You still love him, Ma."

"Well, you can't just turn it off."

"I love him, too."

"I know."

"But fuck him."

Meg shook her head. "Don't."

"He's my dad—I love him. And just like you I can't stop loving him. But fuck him."

"Please, Sarah. I didn't bring you up to talk this kind of talk."

"Cut the crap. You talk like a truck driver when you're pissed."

"That doesn't give *you* license to."

"And while we're on the subject, fuck *her*, too."

Meg managed a weary smile. She squeezed her daughter's hand. "For once I have to agree with you."

Mother and daughter locked glances for a moment, smiling into each other's eyes. Then Sarah grabbed another slice of pizza and, with one hand, deftly folded it in two. "Gotta feed the savage beast," she said.

It was nearly midnight by the time Sarah had showered and she and her mother had set up her twin bed in one of the fourth-floor bedrooms. For the first time all day Sarah was feeling exhaustion. Hair wet and wearing cotton pajamas featuring Pooh and Piglet, she plumped down on her bed, her knees pulled up to her chest. She watched Meg move around the room, unpacking clothes, putting them neatly in drawers.

"You never really asked me what I thought of this house."

"I know."

"It might have been a good thing to do."

"You told me you like it, now you hate it. You're always changing your mind."

"I don't *hate* it. I agree with that Lydia woman, it's better than the other places we saw—either dumps or too shiny and unreal." She sighed. "I like our old house."

"We've been over that."

"But I *loved* it."

"So did I."

Their words hung in the air as Meg continued to unpack and Sarah continued to watch her.

"I was born in that house," Sarah said, breaking a long silence. "I planned on living there till I went off to college."

"Plans change, sweetie. That's life."

"Well, I guess life sucks."

Meg looked up and said with a forced note of enthusiasm, "You know what I think I want to do on this wall? Stencil the whole thing. Wouldn't that be neat? We could do it ourselves."

"Go ahead, Ma. Be my guest. And please drop the word 'neat.' It's over."

Meg snapped her fingers. "Oh, shoot. I forgot to set up a tour of your school."

"I know," Sarah said, her voice flat. "Daddy already did it. I'm going with him on Sunday."

"Oh." Meg yanked a handful of sweaters out of a suitcase, dropping them on the floor. "You didn't tell me."

"I forgot. I'll just take a cab and meet him there."

"Was that his idea?"

"Well, isn't that what's supposed to be great about Manhattan? You don't have to drive everywhere?"

"I'll ride down with you."

Sarah flopped over on her stomach and posted her chin on her fists, giving her mother a baleful look. "Why did you bring me to the city if I can't go places by myself?"

"I quit. I can't fight you anymore today. I'm drained."

Meg bent down to the mini refrigerator, which served as a nightstand, opened the door and removed a bottle of Evian water. She unscrewed the top and left the open bottle on top of it for Sarah. Meg leaned forward and kissed her forehead and pulled her blanket up to her chin.

"I really love you," she said.

"I know."

Meg flicked off the light and headed for the door.

"Too dark," Sarah said.

Meg opened the closet door, turned on the interior light and left the door slightly ajar. She looked down at Sarah. "Better?"

"Yeah. Hey, Ma?"

"Yes?"

"What about my song? My good-night song."

Meg sat on the side of the bed and held her daughter's hand. "You want me to sing it to you? It's been six months, maybe more. You told me you'd grown too old for it."

"Well, I don't feel too old for it tonight." A childish singsong note had crept into Sarah's voice.

Meg leaned close to her and sang in a husky whisper, "Good night my little baby, good night my little girl. You're Daddy's girl, you're Mommy's girl. Good night my little baby, good night my little girl. You're Daddy's girl, you're Mommy's girl. Good night, my little baby—good night, good night, good night. . . ."

She kissed Sarah's eyelids, waited for a moment to make sure she was sleeping and then tiptoed from the room.

As late as it was, Meg still had items on her list before she was ready to call it a night. She made up her bed in the master bedroom, then took a box down from a table right outside the panic room; the door to the panic room was held ajar by blankets Sarah had left there earlier. Meg slit the tape with her Red Cross knife and dug through the wads of newspaper stuffing and pulled out a box with a new phone in it. She set it on the table in front of a phone jack. Continuing to dig inside the box, she fished out a clock radio and the charger for her cell phone, along with a framed picture of an eight-year-old Sarah.

She plugged in the charger as she hummed

"Strawberry Fields" slightly off-key, placed the phone in its cradle, on a box she was using for a night table next to the bed. The phone beeped and a readout said: "Charging." She set the digital clock and placed that on the makeshift table too, next to the picture of Sarah. It was 12:26.

Switching to an off-key rendition of Blondie's "Rapture," one of her favorite songs, she poured herself a full glass of wine from the bottle she had carried up from the kitchen and ran a hot bath, splashing in a liberal amount of lilac-scented bubbles. She was so very tired, deep-down sad, and craved comfort. She sank into the bubbly water with a sigh and stared ahead at nothing. She performed her eye rolls, her method of preventing unwanted thoughts from invading her mind. But her meditation didn't work tonight. There was Stephen, there was the loathsome Marci Haynes, all of twenty-four, there was a needy child, and an abandoned woman. There was an uncertain future. A few tears rolled down her cheeks, and the tears made her angry. *What a wimp you are. Your daughter has more guts than you do.* Meg picked up the washcloth and rubbed her face until it burned. She reached for her wineglass and emptied it in a single gulp. Stretching for the bottle, which she had set on the floor next to her, she refilled her glass.

Half an hour later, feeling a definite buzz from the wine, she toweled herself dry and walked unsteadily into the master bedroom. Standing in front of the alarm panel, she read from an instruction manual, trying to figure out the alarm system. The directions were densely phrased, as directions always are, and she slurred a few curses.

"Bypass non-ready zones," she muttered aloud. "Shunt . . . enter . . . zone number . . . Okay, girl, here goes nothing. . . ."

Her fingers danced over the alarm panel and a small red light flashed on. As she set the alarm system for the home, she had no way of knowing that the action also caused the dozen small video cameras in the panic room to come to life. The inactivity of the house was captured on the screens while a series of VCRs underneath the screens taped whatever ran across them.

"Whow, dammit . . . how'm I gonna turn this off," she slurred. But at this point, she didn't care. At least she and Sarah would be safe with the alarm set for the night. Meg carelessly tossed the instruction book to the floor and stumbled over to the bed. She climbed under the sheets, moved to the center of the bed—a practice she had been forcing herself to do every night instead of sleeping alone on the left side of the bed—and closed her eyes hoping sleep would come.

But sleep did not come easily. For as much as she was training herself to sleep alone, it was still hard for her to drift off lying in the middle of the bed. She longed to flip to her side and drape her feet over it. Because when she used to do this, Stephen would spoon her and softly massage her shoulders and neck and she would fall instantly asleep. Everything was all right in the world when they were cupped that way, warm skin to warm skin. And now her job was to convince herself that everything was going to be all right again—*and then make it happen.* Her days of depending on men for inner sustenance were over. *This is a new world, Meg, and you're going to grab it by the neck and make it work for you and Sarah.*

Within an hour or so, she had fallen into a drunken slumber, and in her sleep, had managed to pull herself over to her side of the bed, where she slept with her hand dangling off the side panel, just missing the floor. She told herself that tonight she would not dream of Stephen.

"You're a loser, Frank Burnham. You're a fucking dreamer. You always have been and always will be. I can't take any more of this. Get the hell out of here!"

"Alison, come on. I'm trying, baby."

"No, Frank. You have been *trying* for years. You're never going to get over this goddamn gambling habit of yours, and to be honest, I really don't want you around the children until you get your act together."

"Come on . . . I've been going to the meetings, and—"

"And nothing! You still never seem to have enough money to pay child support or even take these poor kids for a goddamn ice cream once a week. I'd rather they had a dead father than a deadbeat—and that's what you are. *That's exactly what you are, Frank.* Now just stay away from me, stay the hell away from the house, and especially, *don't try to get in touch with my children."*

Her children? Frank Burnham thought about Alison's words over and over again as he rode the 6 train back to his small Lower East Side apartment, the one she had forced him to move into when he had gambled away their savings and they had come close to losing the house. The apartment was a small box of a place he had to share with his brother, Ralph, an itinerant house painter who had a drinking problem and had also been kicked out of his house. Frank hadn't meant any harm. No one but an addict could ever understand the thrill of the roulette wheel, the dance of dice as they tumbled over felt. Sure, you wanted the seven, you wanted to hit the number, but if you did you didn't stop and if you didn't win you didn't stop either. Gambling was about gambling, not winning and losing. He had never been able to get enough of it. He almost wished he could be like Ralph. Drinking was almost easier to quit and maybe even did less damage to those you loved.

He was desperate to quit gambling because he loved his children, and he loved his estranged wife with a passion that had never grown stale; he loved them more than anything else in the world and always tried to do the best for them. He wanted to win them back, and he was willing to do anything to make them a family again. He would never, never repeat the disaster of using the mortgage money to win a high-stakes poker game. Six months ago he had lost their last few hundred dollars of savings in an all-night game and had tried to borrow from his company, but he was already in debt to them. When he confessed to Alison, it was the last straw. She threw him out. His last appeal had been to Alison's father, but the two men had never gotten along. The old man was more than happy to hammer a nail into the coffin of that marriage at any opportunity.

It was in this state of mind that Burnham happened to meet up once again with Junior Pearlstein, grandson of the late eccentric Sidney Pearlstein, a member in good standing of the *Fortune* 500. Junior was the kind of guy that Burnham, in his younger days, would have kicked the crap out of just for walking down the street and looking at him the wrong way. He was one more in a long line of world-class, rich white boys, ne'er-do-well assholes, as far as Burnham was concerned. And dumb as a stump. Junior had flown the "entitled" ticket through life: his family money bought him his college education and MBA degree. And while poor bastards with the wrong skin color, guys like Burnham, struggled as dishwashers and security guards by night to pay for their own community college educations, fuckers like Junior coasted through the hallowed halls of Ivy League schools without a hitch. They collected their gentleman C's while they learned more about exotic beers and porno flicks than economics and the fine points of grammar.

"Don't use your blackness as an excuse," Alison was forever lecturing him. "But it's not an excuse," he would argue with her. "It's reality. A black man in America has to watch his ass every second of the day. Somebody's always out there watching you. Judging you. Waiting for you to make a wrong move. They all know damn well you're going to make that wrong move, and when you do there's no mercy." "Don't *expect* any," she would rail at him. "Self pity is like a cancer, Frank. It eats away at you and before you know it you're dead inside. You're black and you've got to deal with it—find some way to make it work for you." These arguments were never resolved and usually ended in sullen silence. At least until they got into bed. Until very recently they had always found a way to make up all their differences in bed.

It was just by chance that Burnham had attended the Pearlstein funeral. He had seen the segment on the news that the old guy had died, but it had been quite a while since he had had any contact

– 44 –

with him. In fact, he was on the Upper West Side that day just by coincidence. Burnham had been sent out by his boss to check out a potential opportunity for installing a safe room in an apartment building on West End Avenue. When he caught sight of the crowd of mourners outside Riverside Funeral Home on Amsterdam Avenue, he realized they were there to pay their respects and decided as long as he was there, he might as well join them. After all, he had always liked the old guy. He was one of the good white guys, and Frank had to admit that there were some—few and far between, maybe, but they did exist. Mr. Pearlstein had been nothing but nice and respectful to Burnham during the weeks he had worked in the man's apartment. Pearlstein had commissioned All-Tight Security Systems, the company that employed Burnham, to install a safe room in his Upper West Side mansion. He always greeted Frank with a warm handshake and an offer of thirty-year-old Scotch late in the afternoon. Burnham would usually accept one drink (but always refused a refill) if the day's work had gone smoothly and it was not a day he had to pick up his daughter from her dance lesson before dinner.

Junior, the old man's grandson, on the other hand, was a piece of work. The kid was like a shadow in his grandfather's house. He had never settled on a profession or a trade and spent most of his time hanging out with his college cronies—those, like him, who had shunned the growing-up process and were committed to nothing more than continued good times. He was skilled at ordering the right wines in good restaurants, at picking up gullible women, at dressing in the fashion of the moment, and at cozying up to rich friends. He was clearly the family's resident black sheep. Junior was aware that even though he had once played nursemaid to his grandfather for a brief period, the only way he was going to see any kind of sufficient inheritance when his grandfather kicked the bucket was to buddy up to him. But he was a smarmy bastard, as Frank Burnham, a pretty good judge of character, easily detected. He was too obvious; and the old guy had to be too smart to buy his act. The kid oozed sleaze and it was pathetically obvious why he hung around the old man at all. However, judging family dynamics was not part of Burnham's job description, so he went about his task, trying to have as little contact with Junior as possible.

Except that Junior seemed particularly interested in Burnham and what he was doing in his grandfather's home. Because the elder Pearl-stein was a known eccentric, Junior had been able to piece together that the old codger didn't keep all his liquid assets in banks, and had somehow been planning to hide them in this room. He was very interested to know where and how.

Soon after Burnham began the complicated installation at the Pearlstein mansion, Junior invited him for a drink at a neighborhood bar. The invitation surprised Burnham. What did this young white rich kid want with him? He obviously wanted something. Although Burnham instinctively distrusted Junior, he was also curious and he accepted a beer at a noisy bar on Columbus Avenue.

Junior started a meandering monologue about the year he had spent in Mexico. "It's the greatest, Frank," he said, putting his hand on the older man's shoulder. Burnham tried not to shrink away from his touch. "I was in Guadalajara. The women are bitching, man, those tropical drinks are outstanding, and you can't beat the climate. You speak a little Spanish and the pussy flocks to you." He leaned forward and said confidentially, "This is my plan—I want to move there. Get the fuck out of this cesspool. The city has had it, man, as far as I'm concerned. It's full of phonies and weirdos and you can hardly breathe the air."

What is he getting at? Burnham wondered. *What does he want from me?*

"If you feel that way, you should go," he offered.

Junior stared at him, his gray eyes slits.

"There's just one problem, man. At the present time my money is funny."

Burnham nodded. "I hear you."

"You got the same problem?"

"Who doesn't?"

Junior sipped his Scotch, Johnnie Walker Black Label. "It's a bummer, isn't it? We all have dreams and the only thing standing in our way is money. You want to travel? You want to buy a nice car—a Porsche maybe? A Mercedes? You want to feel you can do any fucking thing you want and not have to worry about how you're gonna pay for it. And what stands in your way? Money. Lack of same. End of story."

"Tell me about it." Burnham took a small sip of his beer. The kid already owned a Mercedes. What the fuck was his problem?

After a decent interval Burnham managed to make his excuses and leave the bar. But he left with the uneasy feeling that he hadn't heard the last of this youngest, and most problematic, of the Pearlstein clan.

At the memorial service, Junior made a straight line for Burnham, although Burnham, who had spotted him first, pretended not to see him. His sweaty hand outstretched, the young heir shouted, "Hey, Burnham, my blood!" Then, as though suddenly aware of the setting, he said with an appropriately grave expression, "A tough thing, you know. My grandfather was a great man. You won't see the likes of him again any time soon."

Burnham nodded as he stared at Junior. The man's hair covered his ears to the lobes and he was wearing some weird slick-back gel crap. *Little punk couldn't be bothered to even get a haircut for the old man's funeral. My blood! Asshole.*

With skin crawling and yet with a perfectly blank expression, Burnham replied: "Junior, I know how you feel. My sympathies to you and your family for your loss." He paused and added slowly, "Your grandfather had a lot of heart. He was a very learned man and I believe he cared about people. You're right—you won't see the likes of him again soon."

"Ah, yeah, well. You know . . . when it's your time I guess it's your time. And the good thing is, he's not suffering anymore and all that." Junior shook his head and bit his lower lip. "Whatever. The thing is, he had a good life. And a long one. What more can you ask, right?"

Then he winked as though this was all preamble and now the serious business was at hand.

"Listen, man. I have sort of like a business proposition I want to discuss with you. Can we split from here for a few minutes? Grab a beer or something?"

Burnham was skeptical, but his financial woes and desire to get back on the good side of his family had upped the ante of his desperation. He was willing to try anything and listen to anyone—even Junior Pearlstein. He couldn't continue to live as he was, out of a suitcase stumbling over his drunken brother, not seeing his kids and out of the good graces of his wife. Something had to give, and soon.

"You know, I don't have a lot of time. . . ."

"It'll only take a minute—and I promise, it will be well worth your while."

"Yeah, okay. There's a coffee shop a couple blocks down where we can sit and talk."

The two men worked their way through the large crowd of mourners. Sidney Pearlstein had been an eccentric and pretty much a recluse in his later years, but he was a famous financier and famous men tended to attract large followings when they died. The curious far outnumbered the concerned.

Sitting in a booth in the back of the coffee shop, Junior laid out his plan. As he listened carefully, offering nothing, Burnham had to reluctantly revise his opinion of Junior. The kid was crass, he was offensive, he was probably totally amoral and rotten to the core, but he did possess imagination. Burnham had underestimated him, and he knew how dangerous it was to underestimate anyone.

He listened without comment or expression, and when Junior paused and stared at him, waiting for a reaction, he said, "It can't work."

"Why not?"

Burnham named his objections and outlined the problems. Junior methodically answered them one by one. He had obviously done his homework.

"There's a bigger problem," Burnham said.

"What's that?"

"I won't do it. This is criminal stuff, and I'm not a criminal."

"I'm not either. But I have a feeling I've been shafted out of my share of the estate. You see— my grandfather never really warmed up to me. The way I look at it is, he owes me. I'm family. I'm only going to take what I feel is rightfully mine."

"It's wrong," Burnham persisted. "Besides, I liked your grandfather. I wouldn't want to do this to his memory."

Junior's smile was tight as he regarded Burnham. "He has no memory, Frank. The man is dead."

"It's just wrong," Burnham said again.

Junior sipped his coffee and lit a cigarette. He puffed at it and said finally, "Look at it this way. You're only given so many chances in life. Some people are really unlucky—they get no chances at all. All the talk about the brass ring, the shot at doing what you want with your life. It's usually just bullshit. A way of getting through the day, dreaming your ship will come in, that kind of shit. But you *do* have that shot, man." He put his face close to Burnham's. "I'm giving you that shot. How old are you—forty-two? Forty-three?"

"Around there."

"Well, this is your chance, man. And it may be the only one you'll ever have."

Now, dressed all in black, Burnham, with Junior, wearing a black knit cap pulled low over his eyes, jumped out of a van parked outside the former home of Sidney Pearlstein. The irony of his being an expert in home security did not escape him while he headed to the front door to break into the house. Home security had brought him into contact with Mr. Pearlstein, a man he respected. Home security had also introduced him to the man's grandson, a man he disliked but was now partnering up with to rob the older man. He wondered why he was here exactly. Was it to salvage his relationship with Alison? To bring his children back into his life? Or was it possible that he wasn't really all that different from Junior, and that his principal motivation was greed. It was best not to think about it. He had to keep his mind clear.

Junior was really getting to Burnham, and the job hadn't even started yet. He was a nonstop talker and most of his talk was nasty. Creepy sex stuff with women. Bragging about everything. If you could believe him (and Burnham didn't for a moment) he had been a terrific college athlete, a prize-winning debater, and a world-class mountain climber. What he was, was a world-class liar. The only good thing about this job was that once it was over Burnham would never have to lay eyes on him again.

Burnham quickly approached the house, the younger, shorter man easily keeping pace with him. When the two men arrived at the front door, Junior reached into his pocket and pulled out a key, which he immediately handed to Burnham. They exchanged glances, and Burnham sensed that it was the first move in their relative positions of power. He shot Junior a look as if to say, "Why do *I* have to open the door?" and Junior shot back a look that said, "I'm in charge, I have the money. Therefore *you* obey *me.*" It was a look that Burnham wanted to knock right off his snotty little face, but he kept his cool. Round one to Junior. But the game had only begun.

He slid the key into the lock. It went in smoothly, but he couldn't get it to turn either to the left or the right. He jiggled it back and forth, but nothing. He could feel his annoyance mounting and was about to lash out at Junior and call it a night. There had to be a better way to get the money he needed. He had very bad feelings about this. With Junior as a partner, how could things go right?

"Why don't you try—"

"Jesus Christ, man, you're the mechanical genius. Just open the fuckin' *door.*"

Burnham kept trying. Nothing.

"Here," Junior said. "Try this." He handed Burnham a second key. It didn't even fit into the lock.

"What are you—some kind of idiot?" exclaimed Burnham, turning to Junior, his face tight with anger.

"Hey, it worked a few days ago."

"Which key?"

"I think—both of them." But he sounded uncertain.

"Let me tell you one thing, Junior. One more fuck-up and I'm out of here. You understand what I'm saying?"

"It was a mistake, man. Mistakes happen."

"We can't afford mistakes. Not even one."

The two men decided to split up, looking for another means to gain entry. Junior headed for the kitchen, while Burnham went around to the back of the house.

While Burnham made his way around the side of the building, he was aware that he had reached the point of no return. The moment he entered the house, he was committed. As of this moment no damage had yet been done; it wasn't too late to turn back and take a subway down to his crummy box of an apartment. That was the problem—the crummy box of an apartment.

That and his drunken good-for-nothing brother. That and a wife who wouldn't let him come home, and children he couldn't see. He had to do this. What other option did he have? The money was here, in this house, and he desperately needed the money. There was no way out: he had to go through with this job.

He studied the back door. Maybe one of the keys Junior had given him would work in this lock. He didn't trust Junior; the guy was flighty, full of himself and definitely light on intellect. Maybe the keys were meant for this lock, but when he tried them they couldn't even be inserted, much less turned.

"Fuck this," he muttered furiously to himself. "If I'm in this, I'm in this all the way. Let's get this show on the road."

Just as he was about to put his gloved fist through the glass-enclosed French doors, he looked up and spotted the fire escape. He sensed the possibility. There was the chance that a careless realtor might have left a window open somewhere in the house. Or even better, maybe the roof access panel was still unlocked or could easily be broken into.

He jumped up to grab the ladder and missed twice, scraping his hand on the second attempt. Finally, on the third try, he grasped the ladder and pulled it down. He climbed all the way to the top of the house, puffing from the unaccustomed exertion. He passed over the skylight in the ceiling of Meg Altman's new bedroom, but did not glance through the window where she was lying in restless sleep. If he had, he would surely never have entered the house. He located the panel at the far end of the roof, removed it, and jumped in onto the fourth floor. What he didn't notice when he landed were the many brown cardboard moving boxes that littered the hallway. In fact, it wasn't until he barreled down the stairs to the next level that he realized that the situation had just gone from passably wrong to potentially dangerous.

"Oh, fuck," he muttered half to himself, half out loud. He looked into the master bedroom and saw Meg lying there. What he didn't realize was that she was awake; what she didn't realize was that there was a strange man in her house, hovering in front of her bedroom door. Burnham quickly, but quietly now, crept upstairs to see Sarah fast asleep in her bed. He had left the entrance to Meg's bedroom just in time, as she flipped over a few seconds later and faced the door right where he'd been standing.

"A bummer," he grumbled. "What a moron that asshole no-good rich kid is. First we can't get in. Now this." The point of no return had now been passed and Burnham wasn't sure there were any instruments that would see them through the storm ahead.

5

H e headed down the stairs to the kitchen. He disabled the alarm with the code that he had suggested to the old man more than a year ago (it seemed now like a lifetime ago) and let Junior in through the kitchen door.

"We've got a problem," he said. "We've gotta talk, man."

The young man stalled at the entrance. "Not now."

"Now, Junior. We're fucked."

Right behind him, another guy walked up, but stayed outside the door, which Junior slowly closed on him. He was tall, lanky, with burning eyes. He was white, really pale-skinned, but wore dreadlocks. Burnham was immediately suspicious of white guys who wore dreadlocks. They were generally fuck-ups, deadbeats, in his opinion. Guys trying to be tough and with it. Burnham had him pegged right away. He didn't even have to speak before Burnham understood exactly who he was. They had started at about the same place, except he was black and this guy was white; he had made an effort to pull himself up and be a decent citizen; this guy had not. Burnham quickly picked up on the toughness and the obvious resentment this guy felt for Junior, just by the way he stared at him. Burnham understood the guy in a kind of instinctive flash but that didn't mean he liked him—and it certainly didn't mean that he would dare trust him.

"What's this guy doing here?" Burnham demanded, staring hard at Junior. "Who is he?"

"Raoul," Junior replied.

"Yeah? And just who is Raoul? You didn't mention a third party." Burnham leaned close to the younger man, who neither blinked nor backed up. "You're fucking up, Junior. I don't like it."

"Raoul's okay. Don't you worry, Frank. Raoul has *experience.*"

"You mean he does jobs. Right?"

"He does a whole lot of things, man. He's cool, trust me."

"Where'd you get him?"

"Through some people."

"You bought drugs from him, is that it? I'll bet that's it."

Raoul pounded on the door. "Let me the fuck in, man."

Burnham sighed. If that woman and the girl had not already made this adventure take a wrong turn, this creep would have accomplished it all by himself.

Junior turned to the door and let Raoul in. The creep immediately tried to outstare Burnham, wanting to mentally outmuscle the older black man from the get-go.

"Raoul, this is Frank Burnham," Junior said. "Frank, Raoul Avila."

"Peace," Raoul muttered, squinting hard at Burnham.

Burnham nodded. It was clear to him that peace was not in Raoul's voice or attitude, but he would let that slide for now.

He moved closer to Junior. "We've stepped in shit here," he said. "Look around you, man."

Junior stared at the boxes in the kitchen and the dirty glasses in the sink. He shook his head, cleared his throat. It finally dawned on him that they were not alone.

"What the fuck. . . ."

"No shit," Burnham said with a sigh.

"Who's here? There's not supposed to be anybody here."

"Little girl on the top floor. Woman on the third—both asleep."

"They're not supposed to be here," Junior repeated. He continued shaking his head.

Burnham poked a finger in the younger man's ribs. He backed away.

"This was your department, Junior. The key was your department. The two of us doing this job together was the agreement. So far you're batting zero."

"They're not supposed to be here," Junior said a third time. "I don't get it. This wasn't supposed to happen."

Burnham shrugged. "There's another problem. A big fucking problem. It's called videotape."

"What?"

"We're on videotape," he said. "And we've been on it since we got within ten feet of this place, and the tapes are upstairs. You fucked me, man. We should just walk right out of here now and count our blessings."

Raoul turned to Junior. "What the fuck's he sayin', man. I came to do a job here, not listen to all this bullshit."

Junior ignored him. Looking clearly perplexed, he said to Burnham, "Fourteen-day escrow. That's almost three weeks! They shouldn't be here for another week!"

Burnham rolled his eyes. Certainly he couldn't

produce an Ivy League degree, but simple math did not escape him. "Exactly how is fourteen days almost three weeks, Junior?"

"Fourteen *business* days," Junior replied. "Escrow is always business days. Five-day weeks. Always. I mean, right?"

"You may be right. If you are, it's the first time today. All I know is, I'm outta here. This is disaster waiting to happen."

Burnham headed for the door.

"Wait a minute—just wait a minute. We can handle this." He looked over at Raoul. "Can't we still handle this?" Certainly his hired hand would back him up.

Raoul leveled his dark stare on Burnham. "Just the woman and the kid?" he asked.

"Far as I know. Unless Daddy comes home," an exasperated Burnham replied.

"Daddy's not coming home," said Junior. "They're divorced. He's banging a supermodel on the Upper East Side. It's just her and her daughter."

Junior looked at Raoul again. "We can still pull this off, right?"

"Yeah. We can do it," he said with a humorless grin. "A piece of cake, man."

6

Meg Altman was down on her knees in the garden pulling out the tangled brown weeds that the bulb package had promised would one day become tulips. It was a beautiful spring day, and she had the house completely to herself for once. She wasn't entertaining anyone. She wasn't planning to entertain anyone that evening. It was just her, doing something she wanted to do. Well, not really. Truth be told, she hated gardening. She hated kneeling down in the dirt and getting her hands dirty, even through the gloves she always insisted on wearing. What she really wanted to do was finish the mural she had started in Sarah's bedroom way back in February. But when her husband, before he left for a day of golf with his friends, gently chided her about the state of the garden and what would the neighbors think, she realized what her task for the day needed to be.

Meg was wearing a pair of old jeans and one of Stephen's Barney's dress shirts. On her hands was a pair of lambskin gardening gloves her husband had paid too much for at Restoration Hardware. They were given to her as a birthday present. A passive-aggressive hint, she felt, that her work in the yard did not measure up to that of the other wives and that it was time to try to do something about it.

Stephen always "communicated" with Meg through these little hints, never in so many words. He took a kind of pride in saying that he was not a word man—that he believed in the old adage that "actions speak louder than words." While it was irritating at times, she took it as a sign of love that he didn't want to seem hypercritical of her. He just wanted to "improve" her. It was just another aspect of her marriage that she had grown to accept and one that, in an odd way, gave her a sense of security. She always knew when she was pleasing him; it had become somewhat more difficult recently to know when—and if—she was also pleasing herself.

Just as Meg had exhumed the last of the

"tulips," the phone rang. She carefully brushed herself off and headed into the house, picking up on the fifth ring.

"Hello?"

There was no answer. Just a long pause.

"Hel*lo*?" she said again, annoyed at the silence.

"Meggie, my dear. Hello."

It was her sister-in-law, Stephen's just-barely-older-sister Virginia. Although only six years older than Meg, Virginia had always carried herself as a much older woman, like one of those grande dames that wear fur shawls in the summer and carry Pomeranians in their full-gloved arms as they sashay down Park Avenue. She had been the same way when Meg had first met her, even though Virginia was then no more than twenty-seven. Despite the affectation, however, Meg was quite fond of her sister-in-law. In fact, she adored Stephen's entire family. From the very beginning, they had accepted her into their fold and treated her as one of their own, despite Meg's less-than-adequate breeding.

"Hi, Ginny!" Meg liked to shake things up; Virginia would tolerate this nickname only from her sister-in-law. "Stephen's not home right now, he's—"

"I know, honey, I know. I'm actually calling with some terrible news—"

"Oh, God! What is it?" *Your husband is dead. He*

had a heart attack on the ninth hole. The paramedics didn't make it in time. She braced herself for the worst.

"Honey, I meant to call you earlier. I'm afraid Grandma Altman passed this morning."

Sigh. Relief. "Oh, no. Ginny, I'm so sorry. What can I do?"

"We've got it pretty much under control for now. We're at the funeral parlor." She hesitated, and her voice sounded tight and strange. "I just wanted you to know."

Jews never waited to bury their dead. Having been brought up Catholic, Meg was used to wakes and prolonged good-byes. On the whole, she preferred the Jewish tradition. She showered quickly and dressed in her ubiquitous black suit. She wasn't sure where Stephen was at the moment (Sarah was in school), but she figured that Virginia must have made arrangements to meet them there. Her mother-in-law greeted her at the funeral parlor, a perplexed look on her face. Her eyes kept darting away from Meg's.

"Mother Altman," Meg began. "I'm so very—"

"Meg, dear? What are you doing here?"

"Doing here?" Meg stared hard at her. "I'm here for the service."

"Oh, no, honey. You can't go in there. It's such a bad time. Marci's all broken up about things and—"

"Marci?" Meg continued to stare at her mother-in-law.

"Meg, it's time to go. Can't you see that you're putting us all in a very uncomfortable position here?"

"But, Mother—"

"Dammit, Meg! Can't you take a fucking hint? You're finished here. Marci's our daughter now. Marci is Sarah's mother. It's time to go."

"But I don't understand—"

"Do I have to spell it out for you? Get the fuck out of here!"

"Yeah, Ma," came Sarah's little voice from the background. "Get the fuck out. . . ."

Meg shook herself awake. She was bathed in sweat. It was a dream, of course. A very, very bad one, but only a dream. For one thing, her former mother-in-law had never in her life used a profanity stronger than "fudge." But the message was all too clear and crushing. That life was over. That family was gone. And as much as they tried to reach out to her when all the chaos went down, they, and Stephen, were as good as dead to her now.

She grabbed the bottle of warm Evian from her nightstand and took a long drink, draining half the bottle. She glanced at the floor and saw the empty wine bottle, lying on its side, reminding her that she'd have to go back to social drinking very soon or she'd never have a decent night's sleep again.

Meg popped two Advil and took another chug of water. Then she plumped her pillows and tried to go back to sleep. She didn't notice that the alarm pad just ten feet away from the bed was flashing "Disabled."

7

B urnham sat as still as he could manage on the kitchen island, elbows resting on knees, face in hands, and moving only to drum his temples with his fingers.

Junior, on the other hand, was all animation, pacing the kitchen like a leopard trapped in a cage. "Twenty minutes. That's all you'll need. You said it yourself. That's like nothing."

Burnham looked up, now shifting his hands and his weight behind him. "It's no good. She'll call the cops. They'll be here before I'm unpacked. You're going to have to find another way to get to Mexico."

"We're not giving up now, Frank."

"Maybe *you're* not. Myself, I'm all set to hit the road."

"We'll keep an eye on her," Junior said. "Raoul can totally administrate that part."

"I don't *want* Raoul to administrate that part. I don't want him to administer a fucking thing."

"Fuck you, man."

Junior turned on Raoul. "Listen, let me handle this, okay?" To Burnham he said, "Nobody gets hurt. We just get in and out of here clean. It can be done."

"Yeah, and what about us?" said Burnham. "What if she has a gun? Did you think of that?"

Junior exchanged looks with Raoul. This association made Burnham extremely uncomfortable. He sensed that there was a whole other plan going down, one he knew nothing about. He didn't trust Junior; he had known the guy was a snake going in with him. And just to prove his untrustworthiness he had brought this hood into the picture without clearing it with him. He fought the urge to check for the sign on his back that read "fall guy." He was feeling more and more uneasy and kept wondering why he was ignoring the little voice in his head that whispered over and over again: "I'm the fuck out of here."

Raoul opened his shirt to expose the dark sheen of a bulletproof vest and the answer to the question of the bulge that had caught Burnham's eye earlier: a .357 in a shoulder holster.

"What's your last name again?" Burnham asked him.

"Avila." He smirked. "You got a hearing problem, old man?"

"Don't fuck with me, Ricky Ricardo," Burnham said slowly. "I brought the expertise to this job. If we do it, we do it my way. *Comprende?*"

Raoul returned his look with a dark flash of hatred. "We'll see who does what," he muttered.

"Enough of this bickering," Junior said. "It's not productive." He tried to put Burnham at ease by pulling him aside and making him feel as though he was the main man and that without him nothing would be accomplished. He put his hand on Burnham's shoulder but the older man shrugged his hand away.

"You know we can't do this without you, man. It's still a good plan. Fuck, it's a *great* plan. It's just—you know—developed a slight twist."

"Yeah, kidnapping. Thirty years."

"We've got to go with the flow here, you understand what I'm saying? Circumstances change, we change with them, right?"

"Not if it starts not making sense."

Junior was losing patience and they were losing time. "You make a lot of promises, don't you, man? You promise me you'll do this thing, you promise your wife and kids you'll—"

"Leave them out of this."

"Hey, I'm just saying—"

"You're saying too fucking much." Burnham shot him a murderous glance.

"All right, all right. Sorry. You're right, okay? You're right. It's all fucked up. It isn't how it's supposed to be. I grant you that. But there's still these three million dollars upstairs and nobody but you and me know it's here. I want that money. But you . . . you *need* that money. So let's quit dicking around and get this over with."

"You listen to him, old man."

"Stay out of this, Raoul," Junior said. "Just shut the fuck up."

The three men sat in silence for what seemed to Junior an eternity trying to figure out how to grab the money and the videotapes, and at least one of them worried about how to accomplish this without hurting the mother and daughter fast asleep upstairs.

"No violence," Burnham said. "Either we do this clean or not at all. No amount of money is worth that."

Junior agreed; Raoul said nothing but silently regarded Burnham, his face expressionless.

And then the time to consider the options was abruptly cut short by the sound of a toilet flushing overhead.

8

Meg was pulled out of drugged but uneasy sleep once again. For a moment she thought she was back in Greenwich, then she remembered that this was her first night in a new house in the first few hours of a new life. This time there was no nightmare, no stomach queasiness due to her overindulgence; there was just the sense that something wasn't quite right. Whatever that vague something was had infiltrated her mind and forced her to come awake. She shook her head, trying to remove the cobwebs; she was pretty out of it but slowly growing more alert.

She eased gingerly out of bed, sensing that her balance wasn't all that it should be, and made her way to the bathroom, stubbing her toe on a box of books in her path. She first mistook the panic room for the bathroom, but then navigated her way to the right spot, eyes half-closed. She sat on the commode, her eyes closed, nearly returning to sleep. When she was finished she fumbled around at the back of the toilet trying to find the flusher, but it was not where she expected it to be. She squinted upward and saw the signature pull chain of Victorian plumbing and gave it a tug. Then she wandered back to the bed and landed on the mattress in a heap.

Once settled into bed, with her down comforter pulled up over her head, Meg wondered why it was getting light already as it couldn't be later than two in the morning—maybe two-thirty. She poked her head out and noticed that the lights in the panic room had been left on. *Damn. That's not where you want to go. Not in the middle of the night. Not alone.*

But with a deep sigh she got out of bed again and made her way to the panic room. She quickly shut off the lights and started to return to the bedroom. And at that moment something—a flicker of motion she caught in the corner of her eye—drew her back. It was something about the monitors. She stared, her eyes concentrated slits, as she tried to figure out what was going on. What was wrong. The feeling that something was out of place, the feeling that had awakened her, was stronger now. And then she saw it. Her hand flew to her mouth and she took an involuntary step backward. Three men dressed in dark clothing were stealing across the foyer. They were right there on the video screen. But how could that be? *How could that possibly be?* Her mind raced as she searched desperately for a rational explanation. This couldn't be happening. *They just couldn't be there. They could not be in her house.* She forced herself to think calmly. This must be an old tape—one left over from Sidney Pearlstein's collection. That had to be the answer. She moved closer to the monitors, her hand tracing the figures, and still refusing to believe that what she was seeing was real and that it was happening now.

She watched the three figures as they moved to the base of the stairs. And then one of the men walked into something. What was it? *Sarah's basketball. So they were real, and what was happening was happening right now, this very moment. In her house.* She watched with horror as the ball bounced down the stairs and fell into focus on the monitor marked "Foyer." And while she watched the ball, she was almost certain that she could hear it as well. *Outside the panic room. Away from the monitors. In her house.*

"Oh, my God. Oh, my God. . . ."

Meg bolted from the panic room and raced to get to the stairs and up to Sarah. She cursed herself the whole way. Their first night in a new house. Why wasn't Sarah sleeping in the same room with her? Why was she on another floor? What kind of a mother was she? What possessed her to put Sarah on a different floor? Why was this house so big? *Too big. And there are three men, and they're in my house.*

She knew they could hear her. In her haste all attempts at stealth were forgotten. There was the pounding of her feet, the creaking of the stairs. They could hear her and they would soon be after her. But she didn't care. Right now she had to get to her daughter and nothing else mattered.

And then she heard them.

"Top floor!" she heard a man's voice scream, a young man's voice, New York accented and nasal. "You get the little girl. I'll get the mother!"

Burnham was disturbed. He was certain that the woman knew they were in the house—she couldn't miss Junior screaming at Raoul—and that they possibly meant to hurt her and her daughter. The poor woman must be terrified. He could not help but wonder how Alison might handle this same situation. Would she be brave? Would she fold under pressure? And what about Tamika, his eleven-year-old? It sent chills through him to imagine beautiful, shy Tamika threatened by the presence of three men who had broken in with the intent of robbing the house. So when Raoul pulled his gun out of the holster before taking off after the woman, Burnham stepped toward him and raised his hand.

"No gun, man. Put it away."

Raoul flinched but held his ground. "Fuck you, man."

Junior said, "Put it away, Raoul. We're doing this the clean way. No fucking violence."

Raoul shot Burnham a dangerous look, his hooded eyes smoldering. "You better keep a sharp eye on your ass, dude. We're not done with this. I don't take fuckin' orders from no one."

"You're a big shot, Raoul," Burnham said evenly. "I can see that. I'm real impressed."

"Ca'mon, knock it off, both of you," Junior said. And to Burnham: "Stay put so they can't get out of the house, okay?"

He started up the steps two at a time, Raoul hot on his heels.

Meg staggered into Sarah's room, completely out of breath and dripping with sweat.

"Sarah, Sarah," she screamed frantically. "Sarah! *Come on, honey*. It's Mommy! Wake up!"

She grabbed the child by the shoulders, pulled her to a sitting position and shook her hard, her loose sleeping limbs flailing limply like a rag doll's. *"Wake up! You've got to wake up!"* She continued to shake Sarah, who had unfortunately inherited from her father the ability to sleep through most anything.

After a moment the child managed to utter, "Huh, wha—what is it?" Her eyes finally opened. "Hey, Ma? What time is it?" She then slumped forward against Meg's chest, continuing to sleep.

Meg was desperate. Sarah was much too big to be carried anymore even when awake—but asleep she was dead weight. Meg had to think, and think fast. She could hear footsteps on the stairs below. Whoever it was must be on the third floor now and on his way up. Time was running out. Finally, she spotted the open Evian bottle on the nightstand. She grabbed it, closed her eyes, whispered, "Baby, I'm sorry!" and doused the child with the water.

Sarah shot up in bed, swiping a hand across her face. "Hey! What'd you do that for?"

"Come on, sweetie! We've got to move. And quick! *Up! Up!*"

"What's going on?" Sarah asked her obviously deranged mother as she was being dragged out of her bed and into the hallway.

Meg pulled Sarah toward the stairs but stopped dead in her tracks when she spotted a ski-masked figure racing at them from that end of the hallway. She looked to the other side, almost expecting to see another figure appear, cornering her and her daughter, blocking any means of exit. But instead she saw the elevator.

She pulled Sarah toward it. With luck they could make their way downstairs and out of the house before they were caught. Meg repositioned her still-sleepy daughter, and dragged her by her shoulders into the elevator, and ripped the gate down.

"Mommy, what's going on? Where are we going?"

"There are people in the house."

"People?" She was slowly coming awake. "Someone's after us?"

Raoul made it to the elevator just as it slammed in his face. He and Meg, who hugged her daughter to her breast, exchanged a prey-escapes-predator stare—feral on his part, fearful on hers—as the elevator slowly descended from his view.

"In the elevator!" Raoul screamed to the others. "Both of them. Heading down!"

On the third floor, Junior sprinted to the elevator just in time to see the bare feet of mother and daughter pass on their way down to safety. He tried to jam the button to keep them trapped between the floors, but the elevator continued to move, slowly, noisily, steadily.

"Jesus *Christ*," Junior screamed in frustration, slamming his hand against the elevator panel. "Hey, Burnham," he yelled, making a megaphone of his cupped palms, "they're on their way down to you. Cut them off."

Silence.

"Burnham?"

"Yeah?"

"They're on their way down, man."

"I heard you. Let's just let them go."

"Are you fucking out of your *mind?*"

"Hurting people isn't part of the deal."

Junior said, "They get out of here, we're dead men." He flew down the stairs to intercept them.

Meg and Sarah were trapped; they had heard the young man screaming, and they knew they would be caught as they exited at either the first floor or the kitchen—the below-ground—level. So they rode the elevator up and down, trying to come up with a plan that would save them.

Suddenly Sarah turned to her mother and held her arm in tight grasp. "That room, Ma. We need to get to the room."

"What?"

"The panic room!"

Meg stared at her daughter, trying to take in the meaning of her words. "The panic room. Yes . . . *yes.*" She frantically punched the button for the third floor again and again, but the elevator continued on its downward course.

"No, Ma. Like this!" Sarah reached past her mother and hit the "stop" button. Then she pushed the button for three and the elevator slowly, creakily, began to rise. Meg's eyes filled with tears—a mixture of fear and pride. In an emergency her daughter always seemed to come through, always seemed to know the right thing to do. How the hell had the girl gotten so smart so young? And also so cool under pressure? The panic room might just save them from these killers or rapists or whatever they were.

Sarah regarded her mother with a cool expression. "Come on," she said. "You've got to cut that out, Ma. There's no time for crying—not now." She tried to smile. "Just suck it up—okay? We'll get through this."

When Junior saw the elevator change course to the up position, he yelled to Raoul, "They're heading back to you!"

He took off up the stairs, while Raoul plunged down two steps at a time from the fourth floor.

Meg and Sarah reached the third floor just seconds ahead of their pursuers and, as the elevator door banged shut behind them, they raced for the master bedroom by way of the bathroom. They scrambled from there through the bedroom and as they approached the open doorway to the panic room they crashed to the floor, tripping over all the pillows and blankets that Sarah had left in the doorway, losing valuable seconds. Junior, having thundered up the stairs, not twenty feet behind them, made the mistake of trying to enter the bedroom by the main door rather than through the bathroom. He pushed at the door, which was held closed by moving boxes. *"I can't believe this shit!"* he roared in frustration. He slammed his shoulder against the door. In the meantime, Raoul was rapidly closing in from the stairs above.

"Help me with this fucking door," Junior yelled at Raoul. They both put their weight against it and slammed with all their might. Finally it gave enough that they could squeeze through.

Meg and Sarah could feel the two men closing in behind them, but they managed to get to the panic room and lunge through the door, pulling pillows and blankets in behind them, literally steps ahead of the two men. Sarah slammed her open palm on the red button, causing the spring that held the metal door open to release. The steel barrier sprang forward out of the wall, and the last thing they saw before the door slammed shut was Junior clawing at the air after them. Just not fast enough.

"Fuck, fuck, *fuck!*" Junior punched the door outside the panic room several times, breaking the mirror that covered the door.

"Hey, that's seven years bad luck, man," Raoul said.

Junior spun on him, finding a convenient focus for his growing frustration. "Just what the fuck do you mean by that?"

"Bad luck, man. I'm serious. You can bring some evil shit down on us."

Junior just shook his head, too angry to answer.

At that moment, Burnham burst into the room. He stood silently as an enraged Junior hurled himself at the bed. He managed to lift the box spring and toss the mattress against the wall. It hit the carton that Meg had set up as a night table, upending it, sending everything flying everywhere—clock, water bottle, the photograph of Sarah. Meg's cell phone flew out of its charger and clattered to the floor, bouncing under the bed.

"They're in there," he said to Burnham, cocking his head toward the entrance to the panic room.

Burnham shook his head. "How did you let that happen, Junior? How did you manage to fuck up one more time?"

Raoul's hand instinctively moved to his belt as he eyed Burnham but he said nothing.

"What do we do now, Frank?" Junior said, drawing in a deep breath, trying for calmness. "What the hell do we *do?*"

Burnham walked over to the alarm panel on the wall, punched in a combination of several numbers, and disabled the system. He then headed out of the room again but returned in a few minutes.

"I locked the roof access," he explained. He stared at Junior. "It looks like we're in kind of a stalemate here. They're in there and can't come out. We're here and can't get in. And that's where the money is." He slammed his fist against his open palm. "We've got some big-time problems here."

Raoul was becoming increasingly bummed out by the situation. He had been released from prison not even a month ago, having served three years on a drug trafficking charge. He had no taste for prison. He would kill himself rather than serve another day. He had seen this break-in as his chance to buy some time and cool out down in the islands. Ganja, dark-skinned beauties, scraping jail time off his soul. Burnham was probably right. Junior was a fuck-up and this break-in was shit-brain-planned and they could all end up behind bars. He said to Burnham without looking at him, "Tell me somethin', hot-shot, how do we know she's not calling the cops from in there. Huh? What do you say about that?"

"Yeah. Maybe she hooked it up this afternoon," Junior put in.

"It doesn't work that way," Burnham said. "You don't just call up Verizon. She would have to have done it through MST. And they would have had to call my company. I checked the paperwork tonight before we came here. The phone in there is not connected, trust me on that."

"See, man?" Junior said to Raoul. "You worry

too much. She can't call the cops. They can't do fuck all."

"Yeah, right, we'll see," Raoul said, and pointed a finger at Burnham. "According to you, the guy who knows everything, she wasn't even supposed to be here yet."

"*He* said she wasn't going to be here, not me, man!" Burnham replied defensively, nodding his head at Junior. "This is *his* deal."

"You know what?" Junior said. "Fuck you both—she's *not* supposed to be here! What the fuck you want me to do about it? Shit happens." He shook a fist at the panic room door. "We've got to find a way to get in there."

Meg and Sarah clung to each other in the safe haven of the panic room. They were both trembling from fear and shock, but Meg was far more concerned about her daughter's trembling than her own. She knew that she was simply reacting physiologically to a bad situation, but in Sarah's case it could be a sign of stress triggering an episode. The end result could be a diabetic coma. She checked the pulse monitor that Sarah wore on her wrist and was relieved to see that she was registering normally.

Meg released her daughter and walked over to the alarm panel when it emitted a loud beeping noise. It now read "System Disabled." She continued to read the flashing red message, her mind racing. She realized that the two words spelled bad news—very bad news. If the men outside the panic room could disable the system, then they obviously had an intimate knowledge of the house and the security system. They were not here randomly, just picking any fancy apartment building to rob. This was planned. *These men knew the house.* With their knowledge they might even be able to gain access to the panic room itself. This was even worse than Meg had imagined.

She tried to put negative thoughts out of her mind for now—the paralysis that came with fear would not get them out of this. She had to think—*think.* She stared intensely at the phone located right next to the panel, as though she could see into its inner workings. She took a deep breath and lifted the handset. "Dammit," she said, scowling. "Damn you, Meg, you dummy." She had forgotten to turn this line on; one more possibility of escape had just been eliminated.

Meg moved up to the wall that connected the panic room to the master bedroom and pressed her ear up against it. "I can't hear a thing," she told Sarah. "If only I knew what they were doing, what they want." She looked at her daughter, her eyes wide. "How could this be happening to us on our first night here?"

Sarah returned her stare. "Are we going to be okay, Ma?"

"Yes," Meg said, after she took a deep breath. "We're going to be okay."

"Maybe we're going to die."

Meg shook her head emphatically. "No. We're going to get out of this." She forced herself to smile. She touched Sarah's cheek; it was cool and dry. "Things are going to work out."

Meg didn't want her daughter to worry too much, but she also knew that if push came to shove, she would need to rely on the girl's swift thinking and level-headedness. So she edited information as she perceived it (she was not at all certain they were going to get away from these men) and gave Sarah a filtered version of what she thought was going to happen. But Sarah, being Sarah, fully understood the grimness of the situation and was not afraid to ask her mother anything and to accept what was happening to them with all the grace of an adult.

"What do you think they want?" she asked.

"I don't know. Maybe they want to rob us. I just don't know."

"What do we do? There must be *something* we can do."

"Wait."

"But what if they manage to get in here?"

"They can't. They can't get in here." Meg answered her daughter with all the certainty she could muster. But she felt no such confidence. If they could disable the system, what was to prevent them from breaking in? "We're safe in here."

Sarah easily picked up on her mother's underlying fear. "I hear you, Ma. What I think is, we'd better be ready to do something when they come busting through that door. Because that's what I think is going to happen."

Knowing that she couldn't easily put one over on her daughter, Meg decided to change the subject. "Do you feel okay?"

"Yeah."

"Shaky?"

"Nope."

"Chills?"

"Don't worry about me."

But of course, Sarah's condition was all her mother could think of at this point. That and what these men intended to do. Sarah, unlike her mother, remained unfazed and even curious. She was a gutsy girl with a vivid imagination, and she looked at their situation as a problem to be solved rather than a terrible event that they had to endure passively. She crawled over to the bank of video monitors to get a better look at their captors. Meg joined her and they watched the three men argue in the living room. Then Meg noticed a panel next to the monitors with a small grilled area and a button next to it marked "All Page."

"Hey—"

Sarah nodded, and nudged her mother's arm. "Go ahead. Do it," she encouraged her.

Meg took a deep breath and picked up the intercom. "Excuse me. . . ." Her voice cracked as she spoke; she cleared it and started again. "The police are on their way. I suggest you leave before they get here."

Sarah giggled as she watched the men jump at the unexpected voice coming over the speakers installed in every room in the house. A young guy stared at the video camera, his face livid with rage. The oldest of the three guys, the black guy, turned to the others.

"She's bluffing," Burnham said. "The phone hasn't been hooked up."

"You sure?" Junior said nervously.

"Wait'll I get my hands on that bitch," Raoul said.

"Cool it," Junior said.

"Yeah," Burnham said. "You so much as touch either of them, you answer to me."

"Mister Tough Guy," Raoul hissed. "When this is over, me and you are gonna have a little meeting."

"I can hardly wait."

"I'm going to talk to them," Junior said. He walked up to the speaker and shouted into it: "We're on to your tricks, lady. You've got no phone. I'm warning you, you're just making it harder on yourself. The two of you come out now, it'll be cool. We won't hurt you."

"Christ," Burnham said, pulling Junior back by the arm. "Don't you know how a PA system works? You can shout your head off and she can't hear a thing."

"So why the fuck didn't you tell me?" He turned on Raoul. "Did you know?"

He shrugged noncommittally.

With a sigh, Burnham walked over to the camera and looked directly into the lens. Slowly he pantomimed making a phone call and wagged his finger suggesting that she could not have called the police because she has no phone. He repeated this action as he scowled into the camera.

Meg was taken aback. "How can he know about the phone?" she said to Sarah without taking her eyes off the screen. But she refused to show fear. "Take what you want and get out," she said. "We'll stay in here for an hour after you leave. I promise you that." She looked at Sarah, who smiled at her and nodded her head.

"Good thinking, Ma. And you don't sound scared."

Burnham consulted with the others, then looked up at the camera and shook his head no. Junior pushed in front of the black man and made a slitting motion across his throat with the edge of his palm. For good measure, he shook his fist at the camera.

A moment later the three men disappeared altogether. Five agonizingly slow minutes passed. Then the young guy, shorter than the others—the leader, Meg decided—came back and stood in front of the camera holding a panel of a cardboard box in his hands. On it was printed a note in big block letters: WHAT WE WANT IS IN THAT ROOM.

Sarah and Meg stared at each other; they both immediately understood the implications of that note. These men were not burglars looking for the usual prizes—jewelry and electronic devices they could easily fence. They had to be after something else—something much more sinister. After all, what was in the panic room besides various supplies and rations to stock the room in a time of emergency? Only the two of them. It was clear that these men obviously weren't after the supplies and rations. The likely conclusion was that they were rapists, kidnappers, or murderers.

"They're coming in here, aren't they, Ma?"

"No. I told you they can't get in. Remember how that man, the real estate broker, explained about the door? It's completely safe."

"We can't let them in and take our chances, can we?"

"No."

"I don't think they'd let us go."

"We can't take that chance."

Meg's anger was slowly supplanting her anxiety. As long as she could still draw a breath, there was no way anyone was going to touch her or her daughter. She pressed the button for the PA system again and boldly asked: "What do you know about this room?"

The black man spoke to the leader who wrote slowly, bent over the cardboard. Then he held up the sign: MORE THAN YOU KNOW.

"I think they're bluffing." Meg was trying to hide her fear from her daughter—and perhaps from herself. Hold on to the anger, she told herself. The anger is good. It will help you to act.

When she next spoke, her voice had assumed a firmer tone. "We're not coming out and we're not letting you in. Get out of my house," she demanded.

Sarah tugged at Meg's sleeve. "Say 'fuck,' Ma."

Meg shot her daughter an incredulous look, but obeyed. She pressed the button and uttered the word: "Fuck."

"No, Ma," Sarah groaned. Could her mother possibly be this clueless? "As in 'get the fuck' out of our *house.* . . ."

"Right. Sorry." She pressed the button again: "Get the fuck out of this house!"

A few minutes passed; the men had moved out of camera view.

"Why don't they answer?" Sarah asked. "Do you suppose maybe they just gave up?"

Meg shook her head. "I don't think so."

A moment later the three men came back with another panel from another cardboard box. The shorter man held it up. WE WILL LET YOU GO.

Meg and Sarah exchanged glances and Sarah pursed her lips and shook her head. "We're not going to trust them, right?"

Meg nodded in agreement. "Right, honey. No way."

She pushed the button and said: "Conversation's over."

The three men again moved out of camera view.

"She's not coming out?" Raoul said, bewilderment etched on his features. "What the fuck is this shit?"

"Would you if you was her?" Burnham said.

"Shut up," Junior said, "both of you. Let me think."

"I can't believe it," Raoul persisted.

"Shut up and let me think, for crissake," Junior said.

"You're gonna think," Burnham said with a tight grin. "I guess that means we'll be here all night."

"Okay, smartass, *you* think. What are we going to do? How can we get in that room?"

"What if she's already called the cops," Raoul said.

"You don't hear too good," Burnham said, "or

you don't pay attention. I already told you, she can't call out. Her phone isn't hooked up."

"She can hook it up."

"No, she can't. Trust me on that."

"But she said she called the cops."

"Well, what the hell else is she going to say? My daughter and I are completely helpless and at your mercy? You look like such nice men. Come on up and do what you want with us? She's bluffing, man. Do you think if there's any chance the cops are on their way, I'd still be standing here talking to you? She's just talking shit. She's scared. Think about it."

"Good, excellent, fine," Junior said. "We all believe you, Burnham. We all know how fuckin' brilliant you are. Now—how the hell do we get into that room?"

Burnham stared at Junior, shook his head and laughed.

Raoul took a step toward him, his hands balled into fists. "What do you find so fucking funny, hotshot? You want to share it with us?"

But Burnham shrugged. Raoul's surly attitude was no threat to him. "I've spent the last twelve years building these rooms specifically to keep out people like us. Engineering wise, every 'I' is dotted, every 'T' crossed. That room is as safe as a government vault in Fort Knox. If it wasn't, I'd be out of a job."

"Great," said Junior. "Wonderful. You sure do

have a way with words, Burnham. Now let's drop the bullshit here and cut to the chase. How the hell are we going to get into the room. There *has* to be a way."

Burnham threw out his arms in a gesture of surrender. "Junior—you refuse to listen to me. I'm going to try to tell you how it is one more time. You cannot force yourself into that room. Your grandfather—like many other rich people—he spent a fortune assuring himself he would be completely safe in an emergency. There is just no way into a panic room unless somebody lets you in. That's the whole truth. You have to begin to think differently."

Junior pushed the ski cap back on his head as he stared at Burnham.

"Yeah? Think differently how?"

"We have to make her come out."

"Why would she do that?"

"I don't know yet. But once she and the girl come out, they can't get out of this house. We keep them here and keep them quiet as long as it takes us to get the money. And I don't want any help from Joe Pesci over here. They want to hole up in this house? Fine. We'll board the place up tight as a drum. We'll make it impossible for them to leave. Then the next day, we call nine-one-one and let the cops come here and be heroes. That's the way we do it." He glanced at Raoul. "And there's gonna be no strong-arm stuff."

"But why would they come out in the first place?"

"I'm working on that."

"What's this shit about Joe Pesci?" Raoul said, glaring at Burnham.

"Shut up, Raoul," Junior said.

"**A**re you okay?" This time it was the daughter asking the mother. Sarah knew all too well about her mother's fear of small spaces, and typically, she liked to tease her about her phobias. She had seen her mother in elevators, crowded buses, dressing rooms, feeling trapped and desperate, and remembered how Meg suffered in tight-lipped silence. But teasing her now was out of the question; there was the possibility that she might freak out and Sarah couldn't let that happen. The longer they were stuck in this room, the greater the danger for her mother mentally. Sarah looked for the little signs—the eye squint, the tightening of her lips, the drawing in of her stomach, the extreme paleness. Being a sensitive and intuitive child she knew her mother was suffering and she wished there was some way she could help her.

"Ma, I'm talking to you. Are you okay?"

"Yeah," Meg replied weakly, unconvincingly.

"Try not to think small spaces." She searched her mind for some way to help her mother. "Think the sky. Think all that space up there."

"Please . . . Sarah." She screwed her eyes shut. "It's better if we don't talk about it. Really, I'll be fine."

This was not good at all. Sarah had seen her mother turn this alarmingly pale before. She knew that her mother was far from fine and that it was her turn to become the mother. It was a role reversal the two had been playing semiconsciously for years. "You can't wig out. I'm serious, Ma. You are not allowed to do that." Sarah knew that she could not survive this ordeal without her mother.

Meg understood exactly what was going on between them and was fighting desperately to be brave. "I won't," she assured her daughter.

"I mean it."

"I know. And I'll make it through, I really will." She tried to smile. "I'm trying to visualize a blue sky right now."

"Good. Put a few clouds in, too. Fluffy, white clouds are soothing."

"Clouds," Meg said dreamily. "Yes, clouds."

Sarah wasn't convinced that her mother was going to make it if they were shut up in this room for too long, but she decided to leave it alone for a while. The ten-year-old began to rummage through the stuff in the panic room and make small talk with her mother, who only responded with one-word answers. She was desperate.

"Hey, Ma, how about a game of ghosts?"

"Ghosts?"

"I know you'll beat me. You always do. But I'm getting better. Just one game?"

Meg hesitated. "I'm not sure I can concentrate on it."

"Try. I'll start with an 'a.' "

"I don't really want to."

"Just one game," Sarah said. "Okay?"

Meg released a long drawn out sigh. "Okay. One game."

"Good. It's 'a' to you."

Meg thought for a moment, then said, "Let me see. I'll add an 'n.' "

"Okay. I'll put an 'a' on that."

Meg sighed. "I don't really feel like playing."

"Come on," Sarah urged. "It's not the worst way to pass the time."

"We have 'a-n-a.' I'll add an 'r.' "

"Do I know this word?"

"Yes."

Sarah nodded. "I think it ends on me, if it's the word I'm thinking of."

"Actually there are two I can think of. And they do both end on you."

Sarah was happy to see a little color returning to her mother's cheeks.

" 'Anarchy'—that's the word, right?"

"And 'anarchist.' "

"You're still too good for me. Want to do another round?"

"No," Meg said. "But thanks. I feel a little better."

"Of course you do," Sarah said with a mock frown. "You just beat me."

She went back to watch the monitors.

"What are they doing now?" Meg asked.

"Uh-oh." Sarah leaned forward, watching intently.

"Uh-oh *what?* What's going on?"

"Well, they're in the kitchen emptying out some bags."

"Bags? Bags of what?"

"Hang on, hang on. Let's see. . . . Well, there's a bunch of tools and stuff. Looks like some long screws—"

"What do you suppose they're doing?"

"Hang on, hang on." Sarah's face was now inches from the screen. "Okay, the guy who knew we had no phone in here, he just grabbed what looks like an electric screwdriver and a bunch of screws. . . ." Sarah paused, continuing to stare.

"Now he's headed to the kitchen door." She was silent, watching.

"And?"

"And it looks like. . . . oh, shit."

"What?"

"Oh, no."

"What's happening? Tell me."

"You're not going to like this, Ma."

"What *is* it, Sarah?"

"Well, okay. It looks like he's . . . well. . . . he's screwing the kitchen doors shut." The child muttered the last part of her answer under her breath.

"I'm sorry? What is he doing?"

Louder and more clearly, but trying to remain calm, Sarah said, "I said, I think he's screwing the kitchen doors shut."

Meg whipped around to the monitors just in time to watch the black man finishing work on the two kitchen doors; when he was through he proceeded to the entryway. The guy who seemed to be the leader bolted the front door and then shoved a sofa in front of it. The skinny guy with the dreadlocks who had chased them down the hall and into the elevator was casing the entire house, screwing all the windows shut. Meg's throat was nearly closed and she could feel an ominous shifting in her chest as though one lung had collapsed. "Oh, my God, they're shutting us in," she whispered. "This can't be happening."

Meg crumpled up into a ball, cross-legged, with her arms over her head, paralyzed with fear. Sarah, though, was determined not to go down without a fight. She began scavenging through the various boxes of rations in the room, looking for anything they could use for weapons, if it came to that.

She was searching so quickly and furiously that Meg began to worry that she might possibly bring on an episode. "Take it easy," she said. "Slow down."

"Yeah, sure. This is a great time to relax, Ma." Still, Sarah did slow her pace slightly but not her intensity.

"Listen, honey, I'm serious. You know what will happen if you get too worked up."

"Huh? Sure." But she was too preoccupied to listen.

Suddenly a soft vibration resonated in the floor. They looked down, then at each other, and then down at the floor again. *Whirrrr. Whirrr.* Meg could not say out loud what she had already been too afraid to think. Was the panic room *completely* impenetrable? Or could someone possibly come through the floor if he was clever enough to figure out a way? And were these men that clever? She had already deduced that they must have understood at least the rudiments of the building's security system. If she would put her money on any of them it would be the black man. She had been studying the three men closely and she had deduced that he was quietly in charge, although the short man acted like the leader. She sensed that the black man was more methodical and less swayed by emotion than the other two. He also seemed less angry. If she had to throw her fate into the hands of one of them, she would definitely choose him.

"Do you think they're trying to come in through the floor, Ma?"

"I don't know, honey. I honestly don't know what they're doing."

Within a few minutes, the drilling had stopped and Meg breathed an anxious sigh of relief.

Just then, Sarah rushed to the far wall and rested her ear against it. "Do you hear that?"

"Hear what?"

"*Listen.* Can't you hear it? Like a kind of thudding sound?"

Straining, Meg finally heard a kind of faint, rhythmic beating. "Yes," she said excitedly, joining Sarah at the wall. They both pressed their ears against it, listening, hardly breathing. Next, very faintly, they heard a high-pitched voice—nasal, complaining. Then the thudding again.

Sarah grabbed her mother's arm. "It's got to be neighbors!" she screamed, slamming her open palm against the wall, jumping up and down.

Meg stared blankly at her daughter for a moment before finally registering that they were now living in a townhouse, which meant that, unlike in Greenwich, where often two to four acres separated houses, these houses were connected. *Of course!* There was a neighbor on the other side of the shared wall. She was amazed at her daughter's ability to think on her feet in a crisis. It was so easy to forget that she was still weeks away from eleven.

They both began shouting at the top of their lungs and banging as hard as they could through the concrete and steel envelope of the panic room, hoping to make contact with whoever was on the other side of the wall. They kept it up for five minutes, until their throats were raw, but the only response was the same light tapping and the muffled high-pitched voice from the adjoining house. No one heard their shouting and screaming. They slumped down against the wall, staring straight ahead. They felt like the castaways frantically waving a white sheet at a ship at sea and watching helplessly as it sails away over the horizon and out of sight. They felt more alone than ever, closer to defeat.

— CHAPTER —

11

Burnham followed Junior and Raoul to the kitchen, where the two men upended his bag and dumped the contents out onto the table. Every tool imaginable clattered out. Raoul grabbed a power drill and broke open a plastic box of drill bits, which spilled all over the floor. He bent down and picked up the biggest, most serious bit he could find, inserted it into the drill, and gave it a *whir*, while casting a challenging look at Burnham.

Already annoyed that they had disrespected him enough to tear through his things, Burnham was at the end of his patience. These guys were not only stupid, they had all the presence of mind of a couple of unguided missiles.

"What the hell do you think you're doing?" he said to Raoul. "Those happen to be my tools you're fucking with."

"We're coming in from below," said Junior, answering for him.

Burnham half-laughed, half-sneered at this new idiot inspiration from the mouth of this moron. If college produced men like Junior, he was glad that he'd had no part of it.

"No you're not. You're not ruining my tools for nothing."

"But we might get through," Junior protested.

"Not in a million years. Even if you can cut through the concrete, which I seriously doubt, there's three inches of steel. You won't make a dent."

Raoul pointed the power drill at Burnham like a weapon. "Let's just see, man. If we stand around with our thumbs up our ass listening to you, we get nowhere." He grinned, a kind of feral twist of his lips. "You know what I think? I think we got a *maricone* on our hands, Junior."

Junior quickly stepped in between the two men, his hands raised in a peace gesture. "Squabbling isn't gonna get this done. You've both got to cool it." He turned to Burnham. "Are you absolutely sure this won't work, Frank? If it has the slimmest chance, we've got to go for it. I sure as shit don't want to walk out of here in broad daylight."

"This is how I make my living," Burnham answered. "If some idiot with a claw hammer could break in, do you think I'd still have a job? Houdini on his best day couldn't crack that room. I don't know how to make it any clearer."

Raoul and Junior stood dumbly for a moment and actually seemed to consider his words. *Curly and Moe,* Burnham thought. *That's what I'm dealing with here. These guys are nightmares.*

"Just trust me, Junior, it ain't gonna happen. They either have to let us in or we don't get in. It's that simple."

"Well, fuck it," Raoul said. "I'm going to give it a try. I don't see no other way." He stared at Burnham. "You gonna try and stop me?"

Burnham regarded him without expression and said finally, "No, Raoul. I'm not going to do that."

"I didn't think so. Somehow I just knew you weren't gonna try that."

Raoul spent the next twenty minutes attempting to drill through the floor of the panic room. Sweating and cursing, he managed to reach the steel core between the ceiling and the safe room above, but the steel was of a strength that was resistant to the drill. He banged on the floor fruitlessly, using every colorful word in his extensive vocabulary of curse words.

Junior watched him with growing agitation. "For crissake, Raoul, give it up. Burnham's right."

"Fuck Burnham. What a pussy."

"He's right," Junior said. "You can't get in that way."

Raoul kept pounding and cursing until Junior tapped him on the leg. Raoul swiveled around, still pounding away, and took a look. Burnham approached them lugging a white five-gallon tank they had spotted earlier under the barbecue grill, and looped through the crook of his right elbow was a garden hose. Junior and Raoul watched him closely.

"You just gonna stand there?" Burnham asked. He handed the tank to Junior and removed a claw hammer from the pile of tools on the kitchen table; he then strung a couple of duffel bags over his shoulders, and hurried out of the room.

"What are you doing, Burnham? You might clue us in, man."

"Yeah, ace," Raoul said, dropping Burnham's expensive drill to the floor. "Let's not be keepin' nothin' to ourselves." With a particularly unpleasant smile, he added, "We're a team, ya know."

Burnham didn't answer but headed toward the stairs, Junior following closely behind. Raoul tried to look unimpressed, but quickly followed the other men.

Burnham went to the wall that divided the panic room from the master bedroom. He put his ear close to the wall and began to bang up and down along its length and breadth with his fist, listening intently to every sound—some sounds were thick and others thinner and slightly hollow—until he found a spot that satisfied him. Then, like a man possessed, he took the end of the claw hammer and began tearing away at the layers of sheet rock. As it fell away, the skeleton of the wall behind it revealed itself. There was a latticework of two-by-four studs, and beyond those the dull shine of the wall's metal core.

The two men watched him with total lack of comprehension. Junior said sarcastically, "Hey, Frank, do you think you could make a little more noise?"

Burnham was totally absorbed in the task, not hearing him. He continued to tear away with the hammer until he reached an air duct that ran through the wall, feeding in to the panic room through a welded hole in the steel.

"Oh, shit," Raoul said. He shook his head. He had added the propane tank plus hose plus air duct together in his mind and now knew exactly what Burnham was up to. He would never let it show, but he was actually impressed by Burnham's ingenuity. The guy was smart—a pussy but smart.

"What?" Junior whipped around and faced Raoul. He was still trying to figure out what

Burnham needed with the hose and the propane tank. It was not like they were about to have a barbecue or something. He had the uneasy feeling that Burnham in his desperation was reaching for solutions without a real plan in mind.

"Come on, Frank, what's going on? Time is flying, man, and we're nowhere."

Neither Burnham nor Raoul answered him; they were both absorbed in Burnham's movements. Raoul watched with keen interest as Burnham dropped to his knees and ripped open another tool case. He pulled out a specialized power drill and several unusual-looking bits. He selected a bit and twisted it into the drill.

"Come on—what's going on?" Junior said, a whining note creeping into his voice. "This is my job, goddamn it. I planned it. I need to know what the hell you're doing, Frank." He turned to Raoul. "Do you know what he's doing?"

"Chill, man. Just watch."

Burnham glanced up at Junior.

"You want to get in that room, right?"

"That's what we're here for."

"Do you have any bright ideas on how to get in?"

Junior slowly shook his head and shrugged.

"Then shut up and let me concentrate."

"Yeah, let him do it, man," Raoul said to Junior dismissively, for once on Burnham's side.

Burnham grabbed a pillow from the bed and

shoved it into the hole in the wall. Once it was securely in place, he buried the drill right in the middle of it. A muffled metal moan filled the air as the drill ate through the pillow and entered the air duct. Goose down feathers flew everywhere, causing a still-incredulous Junior to double over, sneezing repeatedly.

Burnham turned to Raoul, who instinctively knew what to do next. He tossed Burnham the garden hose, hanging on to the other end himself. Burnham inserted his end of the hose through the hole he had just drilled in the air duct. Pulling off a length of duct tape, he sealed the hole, making it air tight, with the hose secured in place.

While Burnham worked on his end, Raoul whipped a switchblade out of his pocket and hacked a ten-foot section off the garden hose. He stretched it out across the room and pulled it right up to the white tank. When Junior read the writing on the tank—CAUTION. FLAMMABLE—it finally came together for him. "Oh, baby!" he gushed. "Oh, *yeah*. Brilliant, Frank." He could not seem to control himself. He tried to assume the mantle of leadership once again, as if issuing a simple command would do it. "Open it," he said.

Burnham looked up at him with a scowl. "I already did."

"Well, open it up some more," Junior insisted.

Burnham shook his head. "We're just sending a message to her. She'll get the point."

"Wait a minute," Raoul said. "Let's not be dickin' around here, Burnham. Junior's right."

"You're not thinking, either of you," Burnham said quietly. "Our aim is to scare them, not kill them."

"Fuck you," Raoul said. "You've got no guts. What do you care for those two, anyway?"

Raoul practically jumped on top of Burnham and forcibly shoved him away from the tank. He cranked the valve handle to "high," and the gas gushed out of the tank with an audible whoosh.

On the other side of the wall, Meg and Sarah wondered what all the commotion with the drilling was about; their questions were answered when the smell of gas began to fill the panic room. They looked at each other and then at the vent where the gas came pouring in, wavering in the air like heat ripples. Fearfully sniffing the air, Meg jumped to her feet and glanced over to the monitors to see if she could follow the men's movements. All she could see on the "Master Bedroom" monitor, though, were the backs of three dark figures, crouched in a kind of huddle in front of what she deduced was the vent that led into the panic room.

She didn't have to actually see anything to know what they were doing. She had thrown her fair share of barbecues in her suburban life in Greenwich. She knew propane when she smelled it. The only question was, were they planning to gas her and Sarah to death—or torch them? Either thought was much too grisly to pursue to its logical end. She needed to act fast.

She rushed over to the vent and stuck her head in to see if she could make anything out on the other side. Forgetting in her excitement to hold her breath, she gulped in two large swallows of propane gas and dropped to her knees on the floor, dizzy and nauseated.

"Jesus, Ma! What's going on? Isn't that gas?"

"Sarah, get on the floor. Now!"

The younger Altman dove to the floor, awaiting her next instruction, which came like machine-gun fire from her usually reticent and mild-mannered mother. "Sarah—listen to me. Do exactly as I say. Breathe into your shirt. Try as hard as you can not to breathe without something in front of your face!" Sarah obeyed her, too dizzy and frightened to wonder if she and her mother were actually doing the right thing.

In the master bedroom, Raoul was standing over the tank like a sentry, defying either of the other two men to wrest control of the tank from him.

"Step away from the tank," Burnham said.

"Fuck you, man. Make me."

"We need to get in that room, Frank. This is

the only way. I think he's right, man. You've lost your nerve."

Burnham took a step toward Raoul. "Move away. I'm telling you for the last time."

"I'm in charge," Junior said. "Raoul's going to force them out of there. Just watch."

Raoul smiled up at Burnham insolently. "You're a wimp," he said. "A loser. You don't play the game, you don't win."

Burnham turned to Junior. "Listen to me," he said. "This is wrong, it's insane. This stuff can kill them in minutes. We get caught, this is the end for us." He grabbed Junior's shoulder. "Talk to him, man. This is fucking crazy."

Junior pulled away, not able to meet Burnham's eyes.

"Quiet," said Raoul. His ear was pressed to the wall. A smile spread across his face and he began to giggle. "It won't be long now. They're moaning in there. I can hear them moaning."

"Junior—don't do this," Burnham said, almost in a whisper. "Call your dog off."

"I can hear them coughing," Junior said, a note of wonder in his voice.

"I'm telling you, man, they're going to die in there."

"Nobody is going to die," Junior said. "Will you please for once have the balls to follow through with something? Think about it. . . . What would you do if you were in their shoes?

Stay in there and choke to death or come out? The worst that's gonna happen is, they're gonna pass out. Maybe they'll get headaches or something. They'll be fine."

"No, Junior. *You* think about it. If they pass out, how do we get in? They're probably close to passing out right now."

Junior stared at him, a puzzled look squishing his face into a frown. "You think so?"

"I fucking know so. And if they pass out, they're not going to wake up. There's too much gas in there by now. Next thing is they die. And we're out the money."

Junior turned to Raoul: "Okay—cut it back a little."

Raoul shook his head, still grinning. "You listen to that fuckhead?"

"He's right," Junior said.

"They ain't gonna pass out," Raoul sneered. "They'll throw up first."

"No. Come on, Raoul. I'm telling you, cut it back. In fact, turn the fucking thing off now. They've had enough gas. We can't get into that room if they're dead."

Raoul would not budge.

Burnham turned to Junior. "I'm not going to add murder to breaking and entering and kidnapping. Sorry, man. I'm out of here." He started to leave the bedroom.

"No, you can't do that," said Junior, sounding

frightened and uncertain for the first time. *"Raoul, turn that fucking thing off. That's an order!"* he screamed.

Raoul's shoulders slumped. Muttering under his breath, he turned a knob and got to his feet. "You're both pussies," he mumbled.

"Did you turn it all the way off like I said?"

"I turned it way down." He stared at Burnham. "You and me, man, when this is over we got some scores to settle."

"That's fine with me," Burnham said.

"Keep it down, both of you," Junior said. His ear was pressed to the wall. "I can still hear them in there. They're still okay."

In the panic room, Meg and Sarah were barely holding on to consciousness. They huddled on the floor together, coughing, and wondered how soon death would be coming. Then Sarah felt air rushing in through a vent behind her. She frantically began prying away at the vent cover, clawing away, breaking her fingernails, until somehow she managed to wrench it off. Inside the vent was a single pipe, about eight inches in diameter, that went straight through the wall and led directly to the outside of the house. Sarah took a good look through the pipe, and even though it was covered on the other end by a metal mesh sheath, she could see that the pipe went to the outside. And she could smell the beautiful smell of clean air. She called her mother over, and they both breathed greedily at the end of the pipe.

It gave them a moment's respite from the inevitable, but Meg knew that the pipe was only a temporary solution. Eventually, the room would completely fill with the gas and both she and her daughter would die. She looked up through the haze of gas in the room, and the box of provisions that Sarah had been going through caught her eye. Meg left her daughter at the vent, sucking in clean air, and scrounged through the box until she came up with a roll of duct tape. She unrolled tape from the silver wheel and used the strips to block off the vent where the propane was pouring in. Once she had the entire vent covered, though, the strips, which had congealed into a sheet of duct tape, blew right off the vent. *Dammit, Meg, dammit! Think, think. Come on, girl, concentrate.* And just then she found her solution in a box of fire starters. Sarah had been watching her mother the entire time, and when she saw Meg grab two fire starters, one in each hand, she frowned, confused. What was her mother up to?

Meg brought the fire starters over and then scrounged around the room and found several blankets wrapped in plastic bags. She tore into them and tossed them furiously over her daughter.

"Hey," Sarah started.

"Not now."

"Hey, Ma," she insisted.

But Meg was in another world. She lifted a few blankets wrapped in plastic out of the crate and read the packaging. "Good. . . ." she concluded. "This should do it."

Sarah was shocked by her mother's state of fury. She had never seen her quite like this. *"Mom!"*

Meg was so caught up she was beyond hearing her. She tossed several blankets at Sarah and demanded that she get under them immediately. She then pulled them all the way up to her daughter's disbelieving eyes. Meg was alarmed at Sarah's color: a kind of sickly whitish-green. But right now there was one thing she had to do and she had to do it fast if there was any hope of surviving. She was woozy and sick to her stomach, and she knew that she had to act before she grew any weaker. As if possessed by demons, she dropped to her knees, gulping for air, ripping more and more blankets out of the crate and piling them on top of her daughter.

"Oh, my God," Sarah said, staring at her mother with a mixture of horror and admiration. "I hope you know what you're doing."

Meg nodded at her and tried to smile. "Me too."

She flipped the crate onto its side and dragged it over to the highest vent in the room.

Then, holding her breath, she yanked the vent cover right off the wall. The duct was not quite wide enough even for her small and narrow arm to fit into, but she managed to insert the fingers of her right hand. She reached in, past a bundle of multicolored wires that ran down through the wall. She then took one of the fire starters in her hand and thrust it, sword like, through the vent opening. She looked down at her daughter, who was staring up at her, mesmerized; she squeezed the trigger. Nothing. No spark. *Dammit. It had to work.* It just had to work. She lowered her neck into her nightgown, like a bull about to charge its human target, took a short and shallow breath, and tried again. Nothing. She felt the weight of total despair. If this didn't work, what would? This was her only trump card, the card that could save them. But it wasn't working and she closed her mind to what might happen to them in the next few minutes. When she withdrew her hand, the fire starter's metal end banged up against the side of the duct.

On the other side of the wall, Burnham immediately picked up the sound and he quickly figured out what the woman was up to.

"What is it, Burnham?" Junior said anxiously.

"Quiet!" he said. He strained his ears, wanting to be absolutely sure, and when he was, he yelled frantically to Raoul. "Turn the gas off!"

"What's that sound?" Junior said, hearing the

scratch and then a muffled boom. Raoul and Burnham backed away, but Junior, with the curiosity of a small child, went right up to the wall and nearly stuck his head into the vent. Just then, a burst of flame came shooting through the vent tunnel, a streaking red comet, just missing a square hit on Junior, who jerked his body away without taking the full impact of the fire. Still, his shirt was on fire and his right arm was badly singed. He danced in circles, hopping around on one foot, fighting the pain.

"I'm coming in there, bitch!" he screamed. "I'm coming in there. I'll kill you, bitch. . . ." He flailed at his arm and ripped his shirt away from his body.

"Hey, cool it, man," said Raoul, who seemed unconcerned by Junior's ordeal. "She's gonna get what's coming to her."

"Jesus," Junior moaned. "Oh, Jesus, look at these fucking blisters on my arm."

"Second degree," Burnham said. "You're lucky." He removed a sheet from Meg's bed and handed it to Junior. "She's got stuff in the bathroom. Get some salve or lotion and spread it on your arms and chest, then cover yourself with this sheet. You're gonna be okay."

Raoul grinned at Junior. "You sure owe her one now, don'tcha, man?"

12

When the fire starter finally clicked into use, Meg ripped her arm out of the duct as quickly as she could, but still managed to pull in a tongue of blue flame that engulfed her arm. She dove under the blankets she had laid out for herself next to Sarah and quickly extinguished the flames on her arm, which luckily had done no more damage than to singe the hairs off. Almost as soon as she landed, she threw her own body on top of her daughter's, and the entire ceiling of the panic room was alight in a lake of fire that blew out the fluorescent light bulbs overhead. And then before they knew what was happening, the ceiling vents sucked the blue cloud of smoke and fire out of the room and a new element was added to the dread of the panic room: darkness. *Just like the Harrison Caves: deep total darkness. Go with it. You have to go with it. You can't let it get to you now. . . .*

Outside, Meg and Sarah could hear a man screaming and cursing, but fear of what might have become of them—how horribly burned they might be—kept Meg away from the monitors for the time being. The room had become furnace hot, and where it had seemed airless to Meg before the explosion, now she was gasping for every breath.

Her daughter, though, was hardly aware of her breathing. Never in her life had she seen her soft-spoken and passive mother rise to any occasion with such fearlessness. A child who was never at a loss for words, Sarah was suddenly rendered speechless as she stared up at her mother with eyes that showed several different emotions, from admiration to fear.

Where had this new woman come from? Was this woman really her mother? Sarah thought of all the times she had had to stick up for her—against her father, against other mothers, even against the saleswomen in the department stores. They could see her mother coming from a mile away: the easy mark; the woman you could take advantage of. Sarah remembered the time last spring when some snotty little twit of a saleswoman had tried to talk Meg into buying an overpriced dress with a small red wine stain, trying to convince her that no one would ever see it if she draped her bag "just so." In fact, the woman even tried to sell Meg an equally pricey pashmina to put on top of the dress to cover the stain. Meg was about to hand over her credit card, cowed by the saleswoman's aggressive sales pitch, when Sarah decided she could hold her tongue no longer. She approached the saleswoman as she was about to ring up Meg's purchase. "We don't want it," she said. "We're not paying that kind of money for a dress with a stain on it." She turned to her mother angrily and said, "Come on, Ma. Let's get out of here." Her mother tried to protest, but to pacify her daughter she followed her meekly out of the store. Later she admitted to Sarah that the saleswoman had humiliated her into buying the dress.

Sarah only wished she could have fought against that bitch Marci and found a way to keep her parents together. That was a battle her mother should have been able to fight for herself. But she gave in. She let that woman steam roll her. She had acted like it was her fault that Daddy had run off with that bitch. This way she had of shrinking away from life and just letting it roll over her drove her daughter crazy.

But this woman who was hugging her and checking her all over for cuts, scrapes, and burns; this woman who had just tried to torch three crooks—this woman could not possibly be her mother. And yet she was. That was the miracle. Her mother was really coming through for them when it counted the most. Sarah had never felt deeper love or respect for her.

"Are you okay, honey?"

Sarah, still in awestruck shock, said, "Yeah."

"Promise me you will never do anything like that."

"Sure, Ma."

"I might have killed somebody."

"Well, you want to know what I think? I think you were great. You did something really, really brave and you might have just saved our lives."

"There's no excuse for violence."

Sarah looked up at her mother. "Maybe sometimes there is," she said quietly.

Satisfied that her daughter was not harmed, Meg pulled away from her and rested against the opposite wall, wondering to herself just what had possessed her to use the fire starter and what the long-term consequences were likely to be. She had always tried to set an example for her daughter; to be a model of civility and graciousness. She knew that Sarah was very much in the mode of her father—high-strung and savvy and quick to take offense—and she had tried to temper those qualities in the girl by presenting an image of herself as a calm and highly rational, stable human being. Now how could Sarah ever look at her again without seeing her sending fire through that vent? How could she look at her without hearing that man screaming?

In truth, Sarah wasn't thinking about the incident. Her busy mind had moved on. It was in her nature to be active and with nothing to occupy her—no friends, no books, no music—she was starting to get bored and restless. Being a prisoner in the panic room had frightened her at first, but now it was almost more boring than frightening. She tried to think of ways to fend off the tedium. She searched the room with her eyes. There were boxes and boxes of supplies meant to keep you alive just about forever. She stared at the video display. Nothing new there. Then her glance lighted on the tube she had directed her mother to when the room was filling with poison gas. They had drawn breaths of clean air from that tube. Now that she thought about it, how had that been possible? Where had that fresh air come from? The only answer was that somehow it had come from outside—outside the house. She thought about that for a moment. The tube led out of the house—to where? What exactly was on the other side of that tube? The more she thought about it, the more she needed to know the answer.

She removed the blankets and crawled over to the tube. She pressed her face up to it, while her mother eyed her questioningly. She squinted through the tube, which was covered with mesh at its end, and in the courtyard, about twenty yards behind the brownstone, she could make out another house. She could see the backs of the brownstones on the next block. And directly across from her, she could see right into someone's bedroom, where a man lay sleeping with a book open on his chest and the light still on. *Light.* . . . That gave her an idea.

She dove back into the pile of provisions and pulled out a high-powered, halogen-bulb flashlight and loaded it with batteries. She flashed the light three times on and off on one of the walls of the panic room. She repeated this a number of times until she was satisfied with the rhythm of the message she was going to spell out.

"What are you doing, honey?"

"Wait."

Sarah went back over to her tube, shoved the flashlight in, and began to flick the light on and off. Her mother, already consumed with curiosity, crawled down to the floor and lay on her stomach next to her daughter. There was just enough room for the two of them to watch the bedroom from either side of the flashlight.

The light spilled into the man's bedroom on the wall over his bed. Sarah flashed her well-rehearsed routine: short, short, short, long, long, long, short, short, short, long, long, long.

Impressed, Meg asked her daughter: "Morse code?"

Sarah looked at her as if that was the most obvious question anyone could ever ask; she fought the urge to roll her eyes at her mother. "Yes. I'm spelling out S.O.S.," she said.

"Where did you learn that?"

"Titanic," her daughter answered.

Sarah continued to flash the code, but the man would not wake up. Finally, she managed to adjust the light so that it shone right in the sleeping man's eyes. "Come on! Come on! Wake up, you bastard!"

Meg gave her a disapproving look. *"Titanic?"*

"Yes, Ma. Why doesn't this guy wake *up*. Is he dead or something?"

Meg, worried about all the excitement her daughter had been through in the past two hours, and seeing the sheen of sweat on her face, checked her pulse monitor. The number on her wristwatch monitor had fallen to 57. That was not good. The strain was beginning to tell on her, and playing this Morse code game was definitely not helping her condition. But Meg didn't have to tell her to stop it; the sleeping man finally woke up.

"Look—he's moving," Meg shouted. "He's stretching."

"Come on, come on. . . ." Sarah prayed as she continued to flash out her message. "Pay attention, man. . . ."

"Yes, yes, yes, yes. . . ." Meg said under her breath, her eye glued to the narrow opening.

Their hopes rose as the man slowly got out of bed and, scratching his head and continuing to yawn, approached the window.

"Please, *please,*" Sarah said, continuing to flash the signal.

The man stood at the window for a moment, appearing to glance in their direction.

"Wife-beater shirt," Sarah noted.

"What's that?"

"Shirt with straps, Ma. The old-fashioned kind. Where have you been?"

She kept flashing the code and now he seemed to look directly at them. Mother and daughter held their breath, their eyes glued to him.

"Please," Sarah pleaded. *"Please. . . ."*

But the man was visibly annoyed and little else. After letting out another gigantic yawn, he reached up and closed his shade, turned out the light, and went back to bed.

Meg and Sarah stared at each other for a moment.

"I guess he doesn't know Morse code," Meg said finally. She reached out and ran a hand through Sarah's hair. "We tried. All we can do is keep trying."

Sarah was crestfallen. "We're never getting out of here, Ma."

For the first time since the ordeal began she

was near tears. She sensed the walls of the room were beginning to close in on them. "Do you think we'll ever get out?"

"I don't know."

"If we don't make it," Sarah said, struggling to control her emotions, "at least we're together."

"Yes, baby."

Mother and daughter embraced and held each other close.

13

P eople had often mistaken Junior Pearlstein for stupid, especially early on in school. But he wasn't stupid—or at least he didn't think he was—and he wasn't alone in that assessment. The school psychologist used terms like "dyslexia" and "deficient socialization skills," but never "stupid." Junior might have had great difficulty structuring a proper sentence, or spelling even the simplest words, but no one was shrewder at throwing a plan together—especially a plan that was on the wrong side of the law. He was a gifted schemer and liar. That was how he got through high school; that was how he got through college. And it was how he was now getting through life. He knew how all the elements needed to play out to work to his advantage, and he had always had a knack for positioning people in his plans—the smart guy to perform one function, the tough guy to perform another. No one was cleverer at using people. He imagined his life as a series of scale-model battlefields, with all his pawns lined up like little soldiers, and himself, the hand of God, moving them across the field of combat at his own behest.

But when Junior plotted his scheme to steal his grandfather's stash of money, and brought in two accomplices who didn't know each other—and one who didn't even know that the other one would be involved—he had made a rare mistake in judgment. He had not bargained on Burnham's sense of basic decency or on Raoul's erratic and psychotic behavior. It had never occurred to him that they would have their own ideas on how things should be done or that they would quickly take a dislike to each other. He had his purpose for each of the men; they existed solely to fulfill that purpose. Unfortunately, though, they refused to act like puppets.

He needed Burnham to help him crack the security system. Burnham had installed the panic room for his grandfather more than a year earlier. Junior had been quick to learn whatever he could about the inner workings of the security system. He had even trailed the man around to get a better sense of how it worked. But Burnham had kept to himself, at least where Junior was concerned. He knew that Burnham neither liked nor approved of him, but he put little stock in pride. It didn't matter to him what people thought of him just so long as they could serve his purpose. And, even back when the panic room was being installed, he knew that one day Burnham would serve a very important purpose in his life.

Burnham had developed a relationship with his grandfather, and Junior was quick to pick up on it. Sometimes Sidney Pearlstein would invite Burnham to stay after a day's work to have a pre-dinner cocktail, a fact that amused Junior and also sent a quiver of bitterness and envy through his system. The old man did not have the time of day for his grandson, but he loved the company of this working-class black man. Junior was aware that in his youth, his grandfather had been a staunch left-winger. He had supported the Loyalists in the Spanish Civil War and had backed the presidential campaign of Henry Wallace with huge donations of money. That explained his soft spot for Frank Burnham, in Junior's view. Guys like him always supported the underdog.

Sidney Pearlstein and Burnham would talk for hours about everything under the sun—the state of the nation, music, old movies, and questions of race. There were times when Junior tried to insinuate himself into their cocktail conversations, but his presence seemed only to create an awkwardness. When he was with them the talk became stilted, veiled, as though they didn't want to share their thoughts with him. Still, he managed to pick up information he felt would one day prove valuable. He learned about Burnham's problems at home and his serious gambling addiction. He learned about the man's deep devotion to his children. And perhaps most important of all, he picked up that because of his gambling Burnham was in serious financial straits. It was clear that Sidney Pearlstein had taken an immediate liking to the man, being the woolly-headed liberal that he was, and was lending him a helping hand financially.

Junior filed this information in his mind for future use. When the time came to make his move, he had his man. Burnham, who had installed the security system, could be bought for the right price. Men with weaknesses like his always had their price. The black man was going to help him secure what he considered his rightful inheritance. Junior was certain that he would be cut out of his grandfather's will, but at least the money hidden in the panic room would be his, minus the cuts to his two accomplices.

Raoul was another story, altogether. He had no family, aside from an alcoholic mother who had always been more of a dysfunctional room-mate than a parent to him. Growing up, Raoul wasn't your classic J.D. Sure, he got into his share of trouble, but he made a point of keeping his nose clean. Yes, he had had the usual share of run-ins with the law, but until he made the mistake of "carrying" for a syndicate in Harlem and was caught by the F.B.I. disembarking at Kennedy Airport, he had managed to avoid serious trouble. The heroin fuck-up, as he referred to it, had cost him three years in the can.

The main reason he tried to steer clear of trouble was his mother. When he was younger, he always felt that he had to look after her. She counted on him, called him her "little man," and he had spent many an evening picking her up at the neighborhood bar, punching out any asshole who was trying to lure her home, and then bringing her aspirin and tomato juice in the morning.

Raoul had actually managed to finish high school, unlike many of the guys in his neighborhood. He had done it to make his mother proud. But a couple of years after he graduated, everything changed. His mother fell for a transit worker who hung out in the same after-hours bar, and soon she stopped coming home nights. Sometimes weeks would go by before she would show her face.

Then one day, she was home for good. The bum had dumped her, and she had come back expecting her little man to take care of her again. But he was not so little anymore and a dark smoldering rage had taken residence in his heart. It was too late for her to win her son back. Raoul could never forgive her for her desertion, and while he allowed her to stay in what had become his apartment, he ignored her as much as possible.

A fire lived inside of Raoul: a fire to remove himself from a life of urban shit and decay that had surrounded him, and suffocated him, all of his life. But no one could ever have guessed that the lanky, dreadlocked punk was crazy—a car crash waiting to happen—not from the way he presented himself to the world at large. He liked to appear unfazed, on top of things—the coolest dude in the 'hood. In fact, before Junior decided to pull him into the plan, he had to do some heavy digging in the neighborhood to get the information on the guy. Junior was aware that the creep didn't like him and that Raoul resented his 2000 Mercedes and his Italian suits and his downtown life. Raoul was not a man you ever showed your back to, but he was tough and he was hungry. He had the qualifications that Junior needed.

Raoul met Junior when he was selling dope out of a bodega on 125th Street and Junior was one of his occasional customers. They had gotten on a more or less friendly basis after Junior had scored for a few months, and then one evening, Junior drove up in his 2000 Mercedes and took Raoul for a ride.

"What are your plans, man," he said. "Like, life plans. Are you just gonna peddle Mary Jane? That's a loser's life."

Raoul's eyes slid toward Junior. "What you got in mind?"

"Serious money. You interested?"

"I don't suck cocks, man. No sex stuff. Forget that."

Junior looked away from the road and gave Raoul a puzzled glance. And then he laughed out loud. "That's not my style," he said. "I'm a pussy man all the way. Anyway, I'm talking about serious cash."

"How serious?"

"We'll get to that in a minute." Junior hesitated, then added, "You served time, right?" He was guessing but he was sure he was on the mark.

"Yeah. Three fuckin' years. Never again, man."

"Tough life inside, right?"

"It sucks." He looked at Junior with barely concealed hatred. "Guys like you never make it. My advice to you is, stay the fuck out of trouble."

"I'm not looking for trouble," Junior said. "This job is safe. Let me tell you about it."

Raoul listened carefully and asked questions. He was not as stupid as Junior had thought. And, in fact, his mental alertness gave Junior pause. He didn't want the guy to be *too* smart; there were questions he did not want to have to answer. There were secrets that had to be maintained. He was interested in a strong arm, not a strong mind.

"You haven't mentioned the payoff yet," Raoul said.

"I thought I'd save that till last," Junior said, grinning. "How does a hundred thousand sound? One night's work."

Raoul regarded him, his hooded eyes probing deep. "A hundred thousand sounds real good." After a moment's silence, he added, "That must mean this is some real big haul. . . ."

Maybe too smart, Junior thought. *I'll have to keep a close eye on him.*

"Are you in?" he said.

"I need to think about it."

"No time, man. I need an answer now." This was the moment for his prepared pitch. "No offense, Raoul, but how many chances are you going to have for a quick hundred Gs? You can quit peddling dope out of some shit-ass bodega. Travel. Live a little. I'm offering you a big chance here."

He drove in silence, waiting for the answer he was certain would come.

"I'm in," Raoul said at last.

Junior had always known that information was power. He made it his business to gather information about all of his pawns so that, when necessary, he could use that information against them. But Junior had underestimated these new pawns, Burnham and Raoul. They simply refused to listen to him, and insisted on doing things their way. He sensed control being wrested from him by both men, and now he had these fucking burns on his arms and chest to deal with. They hurt like hell. He shouldn't have stuck his head near that flue. It was a stupid move, the kind of move that undermined him in their eyes. He felt his authority slipping and he didn't know how to get it back.

Once he had applied salve to his burns and stopped whimpering, Raoul pulled him aside. "We gotta talk, man," he told him. "Downstairs."

Burnham started to follow them, but Raoul shook his head.

"You stay here, man. This is private."

Burnham gave Junior a questioning glance.

"Just wait here, Frank. We'll be right back."

Raoul and Junior headed downstairs, and after a moment's hesitation Burnham decided to follow them. It was clear that Raoul was trying to close him out and he couldn't let that happen. He had come too far to back away now, and if he was taking the risk he sure as hell wasn't going to be cheated out of his take by some two-bit hood. If he and Raoul had to have it out, then so be it.

Halfway down the landing, Raoul turned to

face Junior and poked a finger in his chest. "This shit is different now," he told him. "Too many things are goin' wrong. Frankly, Junior, I hate to say this, man, but you're a fuck-up. A hundred grand ain't enough anymore, not even close. I want a full share of whatever's in there."

Junior was in no condition to fight him, mentally or physically. Every time he breathed, all he could smell was the scent of his own singed hair and flesh. He felt dizzy and was overcome by a wave of nausea. "Fine. Fine, okay? Full share—one third. You just earned yourself a million dollars, man. Your mama will be proud."

Raoul continued to jab a finger at Junior. "And you straighten out Mr. Expert's shit," he said. "I'm telling you right now. You get a handle on his jumpy ass, 'cause if you think I'm gonna let my half of the money slip away because he don't have the balls—"

"Half?" Junior stared at him, mouth open. "Did you say half? I must've misheard you."

"Half," Raoul said.

"Five seconds ago it was a third. By the time I finish this sentence, you're gonna want all of it."

"I'm telling you, that guy is a problem. And he's *your* problem, man. It wasn't my idea to bring him along."

"You're right about that, Raoul. It wasn't your idea. *None* of this was your idea. It was mine. Have you forgotten that? I'm the loving grandson who put in the fucking time with the old man. Every goddamn weekend I was here two summers ago—talking to him, dressing him. You ever had to change a colostomy bag? Do you even know what a fucking colostomy bag is? Do you have the remotest idea? I'll bet you don't. So don't give me this shit about ideas."

Raoul waved his words away with a dismissive palm. "You done?"

"No. Not yet. I haven't even fucking started. Just remember this, Raoul—*I'm* the one the old man finally told about the safe in that room and what's in that safe. *I'm* the one who found the guy who built it. And *I'm* the one who convinced him to break into it. I earned that money, and I'm not going to have you jeopardize my whole fucking plan because you have a problem relating to others. Are we clear on that?"

"Whatever."

"You get a third. Not a penny more."

"We'll see."

"We *won't* see. I've increased your take and you'd better be satisfied with it."

"I'm telling you one thing right now—if that fuck so much as touches me, I'll shoot him."

Junior had no doubt that this was the truth, and that Raoul would probably shoot him, too, if he got mad enough. But for now, he had to take a stand and show this goon that he was not afraid of him—and he was praying his voice wasn't shaking as much as he was inside.

"Any other schoolyard bullshit you need to settle?" he challenged. "Or can we get back to work."

"Don't take that tone of voice with me, asshole. I'll fuck you upside down."

"Hey, you know what, pal? You're a nickel-and-dime dope dealer. You live in a shithole in Harlem. You're a loser, man, so don't start spouting some Elmore Leonard shit you just heard, because I saw that movie, too."

Junior was proud of himself. Even though terrified of Raoul, he had taken his stand, and at least for the moment the guy had backed down. *But don't turn your back,* he told himself. *This is going to be a long night.*

— CHAPTER —

14

In the panic room, Meg and Sarah watched as the skinny guy with the dreadlocks and the guy who had been burned moved from the bedroom monitor to the stairs monitor. They seemed to be having a serious argument. Meg secretly wished she could hear them, if only to find a vulnerability that she could somehow use. If their partnership was coming undone maybe they would just give up and leave. Meg wondered why the large black guy wasn't with them. Could he be the weak link?

"Wait a minute," she told her daughter as she stared hard at the screen. She was sure she was right, but to make absolutely certain she studied the video screen again. Because what struck her was that if there were three men in the house and two were arguing on the stairs and no one was visible on the bedroom monitor, then zero were standing guard outside the panic room.

"What? What is it?"

Meg quickly realized that the intruders were getting careless. Perhaps frustration was setting in. They couldn't find a way to penetrate the room and because of that there was a growing impatience and dissension in their ranks. This was just a theory, Meg realized, but she felt it was enough to gamble on. This moment might be their only shot at contacting the outside world. It was time to act, and fast.

"Look at the screen," Meg said. Mother and daughter squeezed up close to the monitor, staring at it. "The bedroom's empty," Meg said. "Are they gone?"

"Two of them are standing on the stairs."

"And my cell phone is right by the bed. . . ."

They stared at each other. Sarah reached for her hand.

"Do it, Ma! You've got to go for it."

"But where's the third guy?" The black man was the wild card. He was somewhere off screen. *Where was he?*

"Don't wait. Come on, Ma. This is our chance."

"But where is he?"

They scanned the monitor frantically, hoping to spot him in one of the rooms or the hallways.

"I don't know."

"The bathroom maybe? There aren't any cameras in there. Where else could he be?"

"The front room. There are places where we can't see him."

"He could be anywhere, right out of camera view. Ten steps out the door and he might find me. It's a gamble."

Sarah squeezed her hand. "I know. But it looks like we're out of choices."

Meg drew in a deep breath. She had to do it, no matter the consequences. Sarah still seemed to be holding her own, but the more time they spent in that room and the more stress they endured, the riskier it would be. Her daughter's system would begin to break down, moving closer and closer to the dangerous range and a possible seizure. It was this consideration that tipped the balance for Meg. It was now or never: she had to take the risk.

"All right—I'm going for it," she told her daughter. "But listen to me. If I don't get back before they show up again, make sure you close that door."

"No."

"I'm telling you, you have to close the door. Promise me."

"I can't do that, Ma."

"Yes you can, and you will."

Sarah slowly shrugged her shoulders. "Okay," she lied. Of course she would never leave her mother outside the room at the mercy of those three men, but if she told her that, she would never leave. "Good luck, Ma." She managed to smile. "We're due for some luck, right?"

Just then, the black man approached the other men on the stairs, and he seemed very angry. Meg and Sarah had no idea what was being said, but the black man was gesticulating with closed fists and pointing at the skinny guy with the dreadlocks. The shorter man stepped between them, obviously playing the role of the moderator.

"They're all down there together, Ma. Go now!"

"Okay." Meg rose to her feet. "Here goes nothing. . . ."

She pressed the button to the panic room door and it slowly swung open.

"Go, go, go!" Sarah cried.

Meg raced across the room on tiptoe and slid to the floor next to the bed. She flattened herself to reach underneath to get the phone. As luck would have it, the phone had slid all the way to the middle of the bed. She had always wanted a low bed, no more than a foot from the floor, but now she was regretting the purchase. It was just one more in a long series of errors in judgment. They might be innocent errors, but she cursed herself for them anyway. Given her size, it would have been much easier for Sarah to reach the phone, but it was too dangerous. Meg was prepared to face the men and even to face death, but until she drew her last breath she would do everything in her power to protect her daughter.

Sweating and gasping for breath, she managed to inch closer and closer to the phone. She began flailing her legs to get better leverage, and one desperate lunge with her left leg hooked the power cord of the lamp on the night table around her ankle. The lamp crashed to the floor. She was sure that the men must have heard the noise, but there was no way she was going to leave without that phone.

A few more agonizing inches forward and she was able to dig a fingernail into the mouthpiece cover, which luckily had flipped open when the phone fell earlier in the night. And just as she nabbed it, Sarah called out, "Mom! *Hurry up!*" She had kept a careful eye on the monitor, watching the men as they reacted to the crash. They were now racing up the stairs.

"Come on, come on!" Sarah screamed.

Meg rolled out from under the bed, and made a mad dash for the panic room. She dove through the door as Sarah pressed the red "close" button. The door began to close, but

Meg's foot broke the infrared beam, causing the door to begin to open again.

"Close it!" she screamed to her daughter. Sarah hit the button again and the door slammed shut just as the three men burst into the bedroom.

Burnham paced around in a frantic circle. *That woman's smart. She's after something—something important enough to risk her life for.* He scanned the room and his eyes fell on the empty cradle of the cell phone charger. "Cell phone," he yelled out to the others. "She came in here for the cell phone."

"Shit," Junior said. "What else can go wrong?" He looked at Burnham, confused. The stupid shit was smiling. "What's with you? You wiggin' out on us?"

Burnham stood outside the panic room door, his fingertips lightly resting on it, the ghost of a smile flickering across his face. "I don't think she'll be talking on her cell phone from in there."

"Why?"

"Ever try and get a signal on a cell phone in an elevator? Imagine trying to get one through three feet of steel."

"He's right, man," Raoul said to Junior.

"Who the fuck asked you?"

Meg raised the cell phone to her ear but all she could hear was a rapid busy signal. "Oh, no," she wailed. "This can't be happening."

She frantically walked around the room, raising the phone high and low, waving it like a baton, trying to find a signal. The busy signal seemed to be cutting right into her brain. She stared at the useless piece of equipment in her hand as she felt rage and frustration build in her. She was close to throwing the phone on the floor and smashing it to pieces with one of the big hammers in the toolbox. She looked around the room, desperate to find a way out and hoping for an inspiration. Her eye caught the phone mounted on the wall next to the monitors. She continued to stare, a thought nudging her, beginning to take shape. She then looked over at the section of wall she had exposed when she had removed the ventilation grille. In the vent, alongside the duct, was the bundle of multicolored wires she had noticed earlier. That was when the idea came to her.

"Yes," she said. *"Yes!"*

"What is it?" Sarah said. "Have you come up with something?"

Meg stood at the vent and ran her hands over the wires; they were scorched but still looked intact. "I may not have hooked up this phone," she told her daughter, pointing to it as she began tugging at the wires in the wall to pull them loose. "But I hooked up the main line. We can cut in!" She jumped up and started yanking on the dead phone that hung on the wall. She finally managed to rip it free and dropped to the floor with it. She grabbed a clump of the end of the wires, pulled them through the wall, and tossed them to her daughter. "Strip them, honey," she ordered. "Expose the ends, try blue first. Blue is phones."

"Blue is phones?" Sarah said, watching her mother closely. "What do you mean, 'blue is phones'?"

"I don't know why I said that—do them all! Just do them!"

While Sarah went to work on the wires, Meg cracked open the phone and began to work on the wires nestled inside its base.

Meg was no longer concerned with whether or not the men could hear her. She was now convinced that they couldn't break into the room. She and Sarah were safe so long as they stayed in the panic room. The important thing was to get the phone to work, to be able to call out and get help.

Burnham, his face pressed up against the common wall, was no longer so sanguine. The woman was up to something and he had to admit to himself that he was clueless. Right now she was a step ahead of him. He was certain that she could not get a signal on the cell phone, so what was she up to? What was causing the scraping, scuttling noise resonating from inside the wall? He didn't like it. He sensed that she was about to cause them real trouble.

Junior started to say something and was abruptly, rudely cut off by Burnham. "Shhh!" he said. "Quiet." He continued to listen to the scraping sound, trying to figure out its logical source from an engineering perspective. Something was niggling at him, but he couldn't put his finger on it. Something was very, very wrong. There was a box at the base of the wall, unwrapped, with a new telephone in it that Meg had placed there earlier.

Junior was sick and tired of Burnham's attitude and how the bastard was always trying to step in and take charge. "What the fuck are you doing, man? Talk to me. Don't keep us in suspense."

"He's fucking out of his mind," Raoul said, shaking his head disgustedly.

Burnham pushed the box aside, revealing just what he had suspected would be there: a telephone jack. "Give me a screwdriver," he demanded and Junior, in spite of his feelings, followed the order without hesitation. He had to trust Burnham. What other choice did he have?

Burnham dropped to his knees in front of the jack and began unscrewing it as fast as possible. He felt fear building inside, but his fingers remained as deft and steady as ever. An ever-curious Junior was kneeling next to him, trying to figure out what he was up to now.

Burnham wheeled on him, the strain showing

on his face, veins throbbing in his temples. "Junior, when I said cut the phones, did you get the main line in the basement or did you just cut the cord on the phone in the kitchen?"

"I . . . ah . . ."

"You didn't cut the main line, did you?"

"Oh, Jesus," Raoul said with disgust.

"I did what you told me to do."

"I told you to cut the main line. Don't you remember?" Burnham's voice was quiet as though he was speaking to an uncomprehending child.

"That's what I thought I did."

"God, you're dumber than dirt, man," Raoul said.

Burnham simply shook his head. What was there he could possibly say? He finally managed to remove the faceplate from the jack and saw that the wires were all still there and intact. But right then, the wires began to wiggle. He reached out carefully to grab them, but just as his hand was within an inch of securing them, they zipped back into the wall. His head jerked back as though he had just encountered a rattlesnake. "What the *hell?*"

He made a mad dash out of the room, muttering to himself, and raced down the three floors to the basement.

"Nine-one-one, emergency," said the voice on the other end of the phone.

Meg couldn't believe that she and Sarah had pulled off this electronics marvel, but she had more important things to think about now. "Please listen to me, I'm at thirty-eight West Seventy-fourth and my daughter and I—"

"Please hold," came the voice at the other end before the Muzak version of Carly Simon's "You're So Vain" piped in.

"No!" Meg pounded her fist on the floor. *"No!"*

15

Marci Haynes was about ready to smother her new fiancé with a pillow. It wasn't just that he snored, *that* she could deal with. It was *how* he snored. Every rhythm pattern known to man, from chainsaw to rainstorm. And if that wasn't bad enough, he had this ridiculous, unconscious habit of grinding his teeth, then contorting his lips like a giraffe chewing on a high tree, then licking his lips three times. Always three. Never two. Never four. This cycle he repeated for hours on end once he got started, and it was exactly what he was doing right now, in the middle of the night, while Marci tried to sleep by counting the layers of dark circles forming under her eyes.

But this was her cross to bear, her price to pay. She wanted the status and the cash. She had to play her part, at least until her career took off. And she hadn't needed to work very hard to snare the most eligible non-bachelor she could find. Stephen Altman was one of the top-earning executives in pharmaceuticals, and was still on the rise. And besides, there was no such thing as a strong and stable marriage. Her mother taught her that, and from a very early age. Her mother had admitted to her once that she couldn't remember if she had ever really been in love, despite the fact that she had been married four times. She told her daughter that falling in love was a waste of energy and only served to throw a woman off focus. A woman who loved was a woman who ended up making sacrifices, giving up a part of—and in some cases, all of—herself, and to what end? No my dear, never love a man. Just choose one who will help you get to the next phase of your life and do whatever you can to snare him.

As Marci had herself learned at a very early age, any man could be enticed away from his wife and children. All it took was a little stroking, a little hero-worship, and a lot of flirtation and seduction. And mousy Meg Altman was surely no competition for her. In fact, the poor broken dear hadn't even put up a good fight. Marci got what she wanted in the blink of an eye. And now she was stuck with him. It was certainly nights like this that made her glad that Stephen was so much older than she; it was nights like this that led to fantasies of widowhood.

That in turn led to thoughts on how she could hasten the process and get to the widowhood. While she was devising her latest murder scenario, the phone rang. Naturally, the phone rested on Stephen's night table, on the opposite side of the California king size bed they shared, at her insistence. Naturally, Stephen could not hear the phone over his irritating medley of sounds, so Marci punched him in the arm.

"Stephen."

And then once again. "Stephen . . ."

And then as loud as she could. *"Stephen!"*

But there was no budging him. So she climbed over him and picked up the phone herself.

"Hello," she said, annoyed.

"Put Stephen on the phone!"

"Who is this?"

"It's Meg!"

"Do you have any idea what time it is?"

"Put him on the phone, you *bitch!*" Meg had no idea where that came from. She had never before in her life spoken to anyone that way.

Marci was as shocked as Meg. It was all the incentive she needed to wake the slumbering beast. She held the headset of the phone up over his gut and came down as hard as she could.

"Wake up, Stephen."

"Huh? What?"

"It's your ex-wife. It's three in the morning and she just called me a bitch. I am in no mood for this bullshit. *Stephen! Wake up!*"

"Huh?"

"The phone, Stephen," and she tossed the receiver at him.

"Oh. Oh. Okay."

He picked up the phone without sitting up and cradled it between the pillow and his chin.

"Hello?" he asked groggily. "What is it?"

"Stephen! You have to—"

"What? Meg? What's the matter?"

"Oh, Stephen! You have to help us! There are three men downstairs. They've broken into the house and—"

Silence.

"Meg? Hello, *Meg?* What's going on?" The dial tone returned. He listened for a moment, jiggled the dial, and then hung up the phone. He immediately tried to dial her number but got a busy signal.

"So what did she want?" Marci asked.

"I'm not sure. She sounded really strange. I think she may be in some kind of trouble." He rubbed his eyes vigorously, trying to wake up.

"And *I* think she may be using some kind of

dramatic ploy to get you over there. You have no idea how devious women can be. She's still madly in love with you. You know that, don't you?"

Stephen, half listening to Marci, climbed out of bed and stiffly made his way over to the closet, yawning and stretching. "This isn't some kind of 'nooky' call, if that's what you're thinking. She needs me. Sarah needs me. I think I'd better see what's going on. I can be there in five minutes by cab."

"First of all, it's called a 'booty' call. And second, you will do no such thing! You're staying right here."

"But what if she's in trouble, Marci. Meg sounded really stressed. I owe her."

"You owe her nothing, Stephen. You gave her all those years, and everything she ever wanted. The point is, you're mine now and I'm telling you that you should stay right here with me. She probably just had a nightmare or something. Maybe she's drunk. I mean, Ms. la-de-da would never dream of calling me a bitch sober. Bottom line, she's trying to steal you back, just trust me. And go back to sleep."

"I don't know."

"Well, I *do* know. Take that shirt off and come back to bed."

"Yeah. I guess you're right." He sat on the edge of the bed and leaned over to Marci, putting his hands on her shoulders and staring adoringly and lasciviously into her eyes. "You are so beautiful, you know that?"

There was no way he was getting any, especially after thinking he was running out to "rescue" Meg in the middle of the night. She squirmed away from him. "Don't touch me. Now get back to sleep."

Although Meg was cut off before she could tell Stephen the whole story, she hoped that he would respond. She knew that she had sounded stressful, near tears when he picked up. He would have to know that something was very, very wrong. She could see him running out of the apartment house on Fifth Avenue and hailing a cab in the dead of night. To get to them, to save them. He would do it for Sarah, if for no other reason. He loved his child more than anything in the world. She was sure of that.

"He'll do something," Meg tried to assure her daughter, but she only half believed it. Doubt twisted and churned in her stomach. She knew that she had been cut off before she could explain the whole situation to Stephen; also she knew deep in her heart that he was obsessed with Marci and was essentially through with them and that she and Sarah were on their own now. He had better things to do than to go traipsing off into the night to check in on his lunatic ex-wife and their daughter. And she could hear Marci telling him that the call was just a ploy on her part to win Stephen back.

Sometimes Sarah seemed capable of reading her mother's mind.

"He won't come," she said solemnly. "That bitch Marci will see to that."

"He'll call the police," Meg said. "He's not going to just do nothing."

"You don't know her, Ma. She won't let him. Daddy's completely under her thumb."

Meg was not about to let her daughter give up on her father, although the odds seemed stacked against his responding to her call.

"He'll know we're in trouble," she said. "He knows me well enough to know I don't make up things. He heard me. I said we need help. He's just across the park. This is why we moved close together—in case we needed each other. He'll help us."

But there was no getting anything past Sarah. "No, Ma, he won't. He might *want* to, but she won't let him. The trouble with you is, you're so nice you don't see how bad she is."

"Yes he *will*. He *will* come."

Sarah's mother had never before taken such a shrill tone of voice with her, and she dropped her head in her arms and began to shake slightly.

Stricken with guilt, thinking that now she had made her daughter cry, Meg bent down and put her arms around the girl. "Oh honey. I'm so sorry. I didn't mean to shout at you."

Sarah looked up at her mother, eyes dry, an expression on her face too weary for a ten-year-old. "I'm the one who's sorry."

"What do you mean?"

"I just am."

"But why?"

"I was trying not to tell you—"

"Tell me what?"

"I'm dizzy and hungry—"

Meg reached for her and held her close, hoping that Sarah could not see the fear on her face. She ran her hand through her hair and soothed her, and told her that everything would be all right.

Sarah had been diagnosed as a diabetic as a six-year-old after a number of fainting spells in the first grade. She had been taking insulin regularly ever since. Never once had she complained. Never once had she shown self-pity. If anything, her condition had made her stronger, more mature in her outlook. She was determined that her condition would not interfere with sports. She was a competitive and well-coordinated girl, whose special love was basketball. For years she had had a hoop above the garage in Greenwich, and she and her best friend Maureen would shoot baskets for hours. She looked forward to middle school in Manhattan a year from now and being a shooting guard on the basketball team. She put diabetes in the category of "shit happens." She was determined not to let it run—and ruin—her life.

Meg opened one of the water packets stored in a crate in the panic room and tried to get Sarah to drink. But Sarah could only nod her head. Her condition had weakened quickly, and it was all she could do to keep her head up. Meg held the water to her lips, and as it dripped into her mouth, most of it spilled down her chin. She had also begun to sweat heavily, so that any hydrating Meg was accomplishing with the water was being canceled out by the sweating. Meg checked her daughter's monitor once again: 47. It was getting worse, all the way down to the danger zone. Much lower and she could lapse into a coma. Meg smiled at her daughter, who managed to smile back. What could she do? Her back was against the wall and she had to think of some way to save them. There had to be a way.

"It's boring," Sarah said weakly. "I hate to be such a wimp."

"You're not a wimp. You're the strongest person I know."

Sarah's eyes fluttered, then closed. "I feel like I'm dreaming," she said, "but I know I'm awake."

"Come on, sweetie, stay with me, okay?" Meg cuddled her increasingly weakening child and rocked her back and forth. "Focus, Sarah. And try to take in a little water. Your reading is in the low forties, you've got to stay with me, okay? Can you hear me?"

Sarah, not one to give up without a fight, rolled her eyes at her mother. "I'm dizzy, not deaf," she half-whispered.

"Hey—my little smartass. *Ex*cellent. Did you see anything in here? Candy bars? Something sweet?"

"I, ah . . ." She was still breathing evenly, but very, very slowly. "There's still plenty of stuff we haven't been through."

"Right—let me check. I'll bet I find something." Meg opened all the crates in the room and examined them thoroughly, but there was no candy or gum to be found anywhere.

"Mom, I did it. . . ."

Meg looked at her sharply. "Did what?"

"I've been through the boxes."

"But you said you hadn't."

Sarah forced her eyes open. "I got confused— I'm sorry . . ."

Meg forced a few drops of water down her

daughter's throat. The image of Sarah having a seizure in this room with no way to help her haunted Meg, and she was determined to conjure up a chocolate bar, out of thin air if she had to. The idea of losing Sarah was too terrifying to think about. *I will not let it happen.* "You just have to calm yourself down, that's all," she said, running her hand through Sarah's hair. "Just stay calm and you'll be fine. The more you stress yourself out, the worse it gets."

"You're making me nervous," Sarah said. "You look so worried, and that makes me worry."

"I'm sorry," Meg replied. She knew that she had to maintain a better front. Somehow she had to appear upbeat. It would help Sarah to survive this ordeal if her mother could appear brave and strong.

"What if I keep dropping?" Sarah asked.

"You won't. I'll find something."

"But what if you don't?"

Meg touched her forehead. It was cold and too clammy. "I'll find a way, sweetie. You have to trust me."

"I do trust you." Her eyes suddenly opened very wide. "Am I going to die?"

"No. You are not going to die. You're going to be fine and we're going to get through this. The one thing—the important thing—is, you have to remain calm and quiet."

"Okay," Sarah said, "But what if I spazz?"

"No big thing. We've been through this before. I just jab you with the Glucagon."

Meg continued to tear away at "Meals Ready-to-Eat" packages in a mad hunt for anything with sugar. Sarah could not control her shaking as she sat huddled in the corner watching her.

"What Glucagon?" she said. "We don't have any Glucagon."

"Yes, we do. It's in the little fridge. In your room." Meg spread another blanket over her shivering daughter. She wanted to pretend that everything was under control. If it came to the point where they needed the Glucagon—and they were very close to that point now—then Meg would simply go and get it. She would find a way to leave the room, race up one flight of stairs to Sarah's room, grab the medicine, somehow avoid the three men and return to the panic room. Of course it would not be as uncomplicated a task as getting the medicine while Meg was in the middle of making dinner or painting her toenails or watching television. It would be dangerous, it would be inconvenient, but not impossible.

"In my room," Sarah said, thinking through the full implications of the risk. "I don't think so."

"What do you mean?"

"I can't let you go out there again."

"Well, I'd like to see you stop me."

Sarah stared at her mother and held back a

sob. "I'm sorry," she said. "I'm a burden. I'm really, really sorry."

"Hey, quit apologizing. You sound like Grandma."

Mention of her grandmother brought a smile to Sarah's lips. She could see the diminutive woman, her mother's mother, telling her stories and drinking amber liquid from a tall glass. She had recently started to lose her balance, the result of one-too-many Johnnie Walker Reds before dinner. Her drinking was a family secret, but one that Meg had shared with her daughter. When Grandma began apologizing it was always after the one-too-many. An image of the tiny woman wobbling and grinning, lit up on liquor, brought on giggles. "Okay, Ma," Sarah said. "I'll try not to be Granny."

— CHAPTER —

17

When Burnham finally got to the basement to disable the phone system, he yanked the pull string so hard that he burned out the light bulb. "God*damn*," he yelled. He raced out of the room to find his flashlight. He fumbled around in the bag until he pulled one out. In his panic to disable the system he hadn't realized that Raoul had followed him down the stairs and was lurking at the basement entrance. As he watched Burnham, Raoul picked up a sledgehammer among a pile of tools under the stairs and swung it back and forth, testing its heft. When Burnham found the flashlight and returned to the furnace room, which contained the wiring and phone systems for the house, Raoul quietly followed him.

Burnham ripped a metal box open, and studied the three parallel lines of circuit breakers. Then he came across another, smaller box, which was labeled: PHONES. He yanked it open and began handling the wires, deciding which he should pull out. At that moment, directly behind him, he heard a guttural, animal-like roar, and he swiveled around quickly just in time to see Raoul with a sledgehammer hoisted in the air. Burnham dove out of the way as the hammer drove into the phone box, bashing it into nothing more than a useless tangle of dangling wire.

"What the fuck are you *doing?*" Burnham said. His back was to the wall, his fists clenched.

"Making sure that cunt can't call out."

"You've destroyed the whole system."

"Who the fuck cares? I'm the only one around here with the guts to act. You and Junior, you stand around with your thumbs up your ass."

Burnham's eyes moved to the sledgehammer.

"It's a good thing I moved fast," he said. "I was right in the way of that phone box. You could have killed me with that thing."

Raoul gave him a strange look. "Yeah—you did move fast. You were smart to get out of the way."

The two men trudged back upstairs in sullen silence. They had reached the limit of their patience with each other, and Burnham wondered where it was going to end. He knew that it wasn't going to end well and he was trying to mentally prepare himself for any move Raoul might make on him.

"Well, I'd say the gas thing didn't work out too well," Raoul sneered as they reached the top of the stairs. "About the only good thing it did was burn Junior's ass."

"Using gas could have worked just fine," Burnham said. "But you had to go too far and screw it up."

"It was a shit plan to begin with."

"I haven't seen you come up with anything better."

"I'm workin' on it."

"Sure, like smashing the place up with a sledgehammer." Burnham shook his head. "You got any other good ideas like that?"

"I was just about to ask you the same thing, hotrod. What else have you dreamed up?"

They joined Junior in the master bedroom. He was suffering from his burns and growing increasingly aggravated that his two lackeys had all but stopped listening to him. He was in no mood to put up with their bickering anymore. In fact, he was thinking about throwing in the towel on the whole plan.

"Right now we're nowhere," he said. "Nothing is working. And you guys can't get along—that just makes it worse. Our one goal here—our *only* goal—is to find a way to get at that money and get the fuck out of here. Can we agree on that?"

The two men stared at him and said nothing.

Junior sighed. He hated them both. He felt that his world was going up in smoke. "Except that we're never going to get into that fucking room."

Raoul did not like the sound of that. "What are you talking about?" he asked.

"Burnham's right," Junior said. "Without their cooperation we're shit out of luck. And why would they cooperate with us? I mean we've already tried to snuff them out with gas. There's no way in hell they're going to open the door and say, 'Hi, come on in. Take what you want. We trust you.' "

"There's just gotta be a way," Raoul said fiercely. "The thing about you guys is, you're both pussies. You give up too easy."

Junior looked at the room, shook his head, pursed his lips, sighed, and shrugged his shoulders. "I've got to be honest with myself here," he told them. "I'm just not a person who needs to be involved with anything quite so harrowing or perilous at this point in my life, okay? If I don't get the money, that's just tough shit. That's show business. I'll go on to the next thing."

Burnham regarded him without expression. "Are you telling us you're giving up?" he said.

"Pretty much so—yes. I don't need this fucking aggravation."

Raoul and Burnham exchanged glances as if to say: No fucking way is he backing out of this now, but Junior continued, oblivious to the others, figuring out how he was still going to come out of the entire mess okay.

"I'll make an anonymous phone call on Monday. They'll find the floor safe. I'll inherit whatever I inherit. Unless my grandfather cut me out of the will at the last minute . . ."

Burnham only shook his head. He couldn't believe where this was leading. He had put his ass on the line. Almost got himself smashed by a sledgehammer. And now this worm was going to try and wiggle out? That was no option. He was not going to leave now without something to show for it.

But Junior kept talking, more to himself than to them. He started counting on his fingers. "Let's see . . . Stephen, Jeffrey, Catherine, David . . . plus five grandkids, sixty percent inheritance tax. Fuck—I should come away with eight or nine hundred grand in cash and keep my goddamn sanity."

When he had finished tallying up which members of his family would inherit what, he reached into his pocket and pulled out his wallet. He removed a bunch of tens and twenties, which he held out to the two men.

"Take it," he said. "Two hundred forty bucks here. Go out and get loaded. Forget this ever happened."

Raoul and Burnham, both stunned, were not about to reach out and grab Junior's pocket change—not when they were yards away from a stash that would solve their financial problems for at least the near future.

"Put your money away," Burnham said. "Don't insult us."

"Hey, man. It's all I've got."

"Save it for cab fare."

"What about you, Raoul?"

"I'm getting in that room," he said. His voice was unusually quiet, his expression deadly, his hooded eyes staring straight into Junior

"Okay, suit yourselves," Junior said as he stuffed his wallet back into his pocket. He was aware that both men were very angry, but he planned to play it cool just long enough for him to get out of there.

"Hold up a minute," Burnham said.

"What?"

"I've been thinking about what you said. About the money. Say what you just said again."

"Huh? I don't know what you mean."

Raoul, who was immediately on to Burnham's question, said, "Something ain't right here, man. Something smells rotten. Say that shit about the money again."

"What shit?" Junior said with a wide-eyed look of innocence.

"You know. What Burnham here is saying. I'm not stupid, man. I can do math. Something stinks real bad."

Burnham nodded his agreement. "I think you have a little explaining to do, Junior."

Junior was beginning to grow concerned. It was one thing for Burnham to know he was hosing them. Burnham wouldn't—or couldn't—hurt a fly. But Raoul was a different matter. He could go off and hurt you. It was only commonsense to fear Raoul, and if Raoul was beginning to catch on, he would have to be a whole lot smoother; he knew what the consequences could be if Raoul felt he was being crossed.

"Like what?" he said to Burnham. "What explaining? I have deals with both of you guys, but if we don't get the money there's zero for all of us. That's all the explaining I need to do. End of story."

"I don't think so," Raoul said. "Come on, man. Let us in on what's really going on here. It's not healthy to keep your partners in the dark." He paused, letting the words sink in. "It sure ain't going to be healthy for you."

"You're not my partners," Junior said.

Raoul exploded. "What the fuck do you think we are, your hired hands?"

"I hired you to do a job. The job hasn't been done."

Burnham said, "Let me spell it out for you, Junior. You were just doing a little thinking out loud, splitting up the money in your head. You said you'd come away with eight or nine hundred grand, right?"

Junior tried on the innocent look, but he was mentally kicking himself for having talked too much. "I was just thinking out loud. It has nothing to do with you guys."

Burnham shook his head again. He was not about to let him off the hook. "But that was after inheritance tax, that eight or nine hundred grand. Which means you'd gross like a million and a half, right?"

"Now you're a fucking tax attorney?" Junior said. "I'm out of here. Fuck this shit. I don't need this." He headed for the bedroom door, expecting Raoul to block his way, but he simply stepped aside.

Burnham, though, was not going to let him slip away so quickly. He reached for Junior's arm, stopping him at the door. "No way you're leaving—not now."

"I can leave if I feel like it." A whine had crept into Junior's voice.

Burnham turned to Raoul. "What do you think, man. Should we let him go?"

"No way."

"Don't you think he owes us an honest explanation?"

Raoul glared at Junior. "If you're holding out on us, man, I'll fucking kill you."

Burnham said, "In the bedroom, Junior. Sit down on the lady's bed. Rest your bones."

"You're going to regret this, Burnham."

Burnham's smile was tight and fleeting. "I'm not into regrets," he said. "Too late for that." He loomed over Junior, a large and dangerous presence. "So let's lay this whole thing on the table. On top of what you were going to get as an inheritance from Mr. Pearlstein, you named like eight or nine other people you'd have to split it with. Am I right so far?'

Junior said nothing.

"Is he right, man?" Raoul said. "I'm warning you for the last time. Don't fuck with us."

"Yeah," Junior said reluctantly. "That's pretty much it."

"Which means," Burnham continued, "there has to be like twelve million in that safe, give or take a couple."

"I don't know that," Junior said defensively, his face flushed.

"I think you have a pretty good idea."

"Look, man, what difference does it make? It's money you're never going to touch anyway. It's in that room and we're never getting in that room. So forget it. Let's just call it a day and go our separate ways."

Burnham regarded him for a moment. He slowly shook his head. "You don't get it," he said.

"What is there to get?"

"I want to know how much money is in there. Whether we get our hands on it or not is beside the point right now." He reached out and touched Junior's burned arm.

"Hey, man, don't do that." He flinched and pulled away.

"How much, Junior?"

"Okay, there's more than I said. There's more, okay? I wanted it to be a surprise."

Burnham nodded. Neither man could read his expression. Neither man had any notion how deep the rage was that seethed in him. He said very quietly, "You told me there was three million."

His eyes sliding away from Burnham's, Junior said, "Like I say, I was going to surprise you."

"And exactly when were you planning to *surprise* us with that minor economic detail, Junior—the extra eight million or so. Tax time? Christmas time?"

"It doesn't matter now," Junior replied weakly. "It's totally fucking moot. Why are we even having this conversation?"

"You figured you would never let us know," Burnham said. "But what were you thinking, man? What were you using for brains? There was no way on God's earth you could hope to get away with this. Come on, Junior, what the fuck were you thinking? Did you think I was gonna open that safe and then me and Raoul would just go wait downstairs while you picked out your share? What the fuck is the matter with you? Did you really have the crazy idea you could rip us off? You got us into this mess and then you were going to fuck us? Is that it? Is there something I don't get here?"

"Look, you came into this of your own free will. Don't put your shit on me. You're the one with the custody lawyers up your ass. With the gambling debts. Your eyes were round as freaking saucers when I told you about the gig. So don't play innocent with me. It didn't work out. Too bad. You've got to move on. We all do."

Junior rose from the bed and started toward the door. He looked at the two men warily. "Are either of you going to stop me? What good will it do? The money's in there." He pointed toward the panic room. "I've got nothing."

He walked slowly down the stairs with Burnham trailing close behind. Raoul also followed, fists clenched into tight balls and dug into his front pockets. He was muttering curses under his breath.

Burnham tracked Junior into the kitchen. "One way or another," he said, "I'm opening that safe. I mean it. If you leave here, you don't get anything. Not one thin dime."

"You're looking doubtful there, big guy."

Junior put his hand on the doorknob and

tried to open the door, until he remembered that they had screwed it shut. He went over to the pile of tools still strewn out on the kitchen table and grabbed an electric screwdriver. Back at the door, he tried to ignore Burnham while he coolly went at the screws, one by one.

"It belongs to me and Raoul now," Burnham said. "And we will never see you again. I mean ever. If a cop comes knocking on our doors someday, we will know you sent him and we will fucking find you."

Junior finally removed the last screw and opened the door. A blast of wind blew in. The night had grown cool and blustery. Junior turned to them before walking off into the night.

"Do what you've got to do, Burnham. I'm out of here. See you around. Later, Raoul."

He started to leave when a quiet *pffft* rang in Burnham's ear and all of a sudden Junior crumpled in the open kitchen doorway. He writhed for a moment, muttered something unintelligible and then doubled up, moaning.

Raoul held the gun at his side and stared down at Junior, who looked up pleadingly. "Liar," Raoul said in a whisper. "Your last fucking lie, man."

"Jesus, Raoul. You just shot him, man. Why the hell did you have to shoot him? *Jesus!*"

Raoul continued to stare at Junior, not hearing Burnham. "You think you're so fucking clever. How clever do you feel now, asshole?"

Burnham fought off a wave of shock and nausea. The bullet had whizzed by his head. Earlier Raoul had just missed him with a swipe of the sledgehammer. What would be his next move?

"You shot him, man. Are you crazy?"

Getting no answer, Burnham finally forced himself to look at Junior. Blood was gushing out of a silver-dollar-size hole in his head. Then he looked back at Raoul in horror.

Raoul finally seemed aware of Burnham's existence. "Fuck, man—you should see the look on your face." He laughed.

Burnham stared at the maniac in horror. He was now living inside of a nightmare. He flashed back on the night and all that had gone wrong. All the mistakes he had made. He should have left when the key to the front door didn't fit in the lock. He should have heeded that sign. And if not then, he should have left when Raoul showed up unannounced—or if not then, certainly when Raoul and Junior had walked off to conspire against him. He had known that Raoul's vibes were crazy. Why hadn't he paid attention? Was he that blinded by the money that he couldn't see the problems as they piled up? Now, not only was the person responsible for his involvement lying in a doorway with a bullet in his brain, he was left to carry through the plan with a homicidal maniac. And he could forget about leaving now. Raoul no doubt would deal with his exit the same way he had dealt with Junior's.

Burnham forced himself to look at Junior sprawled in the doorway. "I can't believe this. I fucking can't believe this." He wanted to move, to do something, to take some sort of action that would blot out this evil, but he was unable to move his legs. He felt paralyzed, rooted to the spot.

Raoul pushed passed Burnham and stood over Junior, who, no longer conscious now, was still writhing about in pain. He grabbed Junior by both ankles and dragged him back inside the kitchen, putting his head over a drain in the middle of the floor.

"Good-bye asshole," he said, looking down at the wounded man with a grin. He aimed the gun at Junior's head and fired once more. "Now at least I've got your Mercedes, man. At least I've got that. I won't leave here empty-handed."

"Why did you do it, Raoul?" Burnham said. "Why did you have to do it?"

"Hey, keep a tight asshole, old man. He was garbage."

"But to kill him?"

"He was a fucking liar," Raoul said as though that was sufficient reason to explain his actions. "Fucking liar. A jackoff. He thought he could run all over me. Drives his German car up to 125th Street a couple of times, thinks he's a real G.

Wears a fucking little ponytail like he's some groovy downtown guy. Cargo pants, a Yankee cap, wraparound shades. So fucking cool. I hate guys like him. They think they own the world."

Burnham stared at Raoul, trying to collect himself. "That first bullet," he said. "You just missed me with it."

Raoul shrugged. "You were in the way."

"And in the basement you just missed me with the sledgehammer. Was I in the way that time, too?"

Raoul grinned. "That's for you to figure out, old man."

18

Meg continued to toss through the crates, determined that she would find something for her daughter. Somehow they had to wait the men out. Dawn was only a couple of hours away and it would be dangerous for them to stay much beyond first light. She had never in her life so looked forward to a dawn. If she could find something that would at least stall Sarah's deteriorating condition, she could stay in the room until the men gave up and left. But would they give up? If she only knew what they wanted she could make an educated guess.

Sarah had revived a little in the past thirty minutes. Even though paler than ever now, she still managed to crawl over to the monitors to see what the men were up to. She stared at the screen, not sure whether what she was seeing was a scene from a horror movie or real life or a hallucination brought on by her illness.

"Oh, no!" Sarah pulled back suddenly with a sharp intake of breath.

Meg looked up quickly. She had just found a small packet of mints and was elated until she saw that they were sugarless.

"What is it?"

Sarah pointed at the screen. "Look . . ."

The skinny man with the dreadlocks had just shot the young guy with the burns as he was trying to leave the house through the kitchen door.

Sarah continued to stare, gasping for breath now.

Meg ran to her and sat beside her as they watched the man with the dreadlocks pull the wounded man back into the kitchen and shoot him again. The big black man watched but did nothing. He looked in shock. He was pulling on his ears, his mouth hanging open.

"You don't want to look at this," Meg said. She took Sarah in her arms and faced her away from the monitors. Meg didn't want to look either, but somehow she could not tear her eyes away.

Stephen Altman had not gone back to sleep. He had lain awake for half an hour, creating the worst possible scenarios in his mind. Finally, over

Marci's bitter objections, he dressed, put on his topcoat and hailed a cab on Fifth Avenue. In five minutes he arrived at the house. When he tried to enter through the front door with a key that Sarah had given him, he figured she had just gotten the keys confused and given him the wrong one. So he walked around to the back. What he had hoped to find were Meg and Sarah in the kitchen eating ice cream or upstairs giggling about the noise they had heard and how silly they were to think it was an intruder. He would come in and share the laugh with them for a while, then tuck Sarah into bed and head back home. But all the time he knew that picture was wrong, that it was wishful thinking. Meg had seen three men. She had said so on the phone before they were cut off. He tried to shrug off the scene when he was leaving the apartment—Marci screaming at him, threatening to pack up and leave, calling him a coward and half a man. But he couldn't think about that now. That was for later; right now he had to get inside the house.

He took a deep breath and entered the kitchen just in time to witness a skinny guy with dreadlocks and a husky black man screaming at each other. For a moment they weren't even aware of his presence.

Then he spotted the dead body. "What the hell," he muttered under his breath, involuntarily taking a step backward.

His heart was pounding and his mouth went dry. Three men, just as she had said . . . One of them dead or dying . . . Of course Meg had told the truth. How had he even allowed himself to think that everything was okay and that they were safe? Why had he let Marci sway him even for an instant? *She doesn't give a fuck about my daughter* . . .

Before he could even decide how he was supposed to react, Raoul was on him like a cat. He punched him in the face, knocking his glasses off and sending him in a heap to the floor. At that moment, Burnham, sensing he had his chance to escape, started to sidle toward the still-open door. But Raoul was watching him every step of the way; he trained the gun on him. "Forget it, Burnham," he said. "No way you're leaving here without me, man." He gestured at the door with his gun. "Shut it, lock it, and get away from it."

"You don't need me," Burnham said. "If you can get in the room, the money's yours. All of it."

"Forget it," Raoul said. "You're the expert tool man. You're gonna stay and finish what you started."

Stephen watched the two of them from the floor. The man with the gun had spoken and the black man was in no position to argue. That was valuable information. The men might be accomplices but they were also enemies. Somehow there might be a way to use that, to use the wedge between them and drive it in deeper.

"Where are my wife and daughter?" Stephen said. "What have you done with them? If it's money you want, I can give you money. Just name the price. I just want my wife and daughter."

Raoul walked up and stood over him. "Shut the fuck up, four eyes. I'll deal with you later." He kicked him hard in the side, causing him to curl up into a ball. "You want more? Just keep talking. I'll give you more."

Meg watched the monitor with horror. When Raoul hit Stephen and knocked his glasses off and then Stephen slumped to the floor, she let out an involuntary wail, "Oh, my God, no! Don't hurt him! Please don't hurt him!" Her outcry caused Sarah to try to squirm out of her arms to see what was happening on the screen. Even though Meg was in shock she held her in a tight grip and Sarah was too weak by now to struggle out of her arms. Stephen had actually come, he was downstairs, the monster with the dreadlocks had knocked him to the floor. The man who had wrecked her and Sarah's lives was writhing on the floor in pain and she could no longer feel hatred or disgust but only overwhelming fear and sadness that he was hurt and she could not help him. He had come. He was here to save them. Tears were streaming down her face as she watched the dreadful man with the dreadlocks kick him repeatedly.

Her maternal instinct gave her the strength to restrain her squirming child.

"Ma, I want to look. What's going on?"

Finally Meg could no longer bear to watch the brutality. It filled her with rage and impotence and she had to move herself and Sarah away from the monitors. She suddenly knew something about herself that she had never even suspected. She was capable of murder. If she had a gun and the opportunity, she would kill the man with the dreadlocks.

Helplessly watching Raoul beat on the man, Burnham began adding more years to his own jail sentence. Life plus a hundred years sounded about right. Burglary, kidnapping, murder. Yes—murder. How was he ever going to prove that he had nothing to do with killing Junior? It was Raoul's word against his. Black man's word against a white man's. And even if that woman and her kid were watching, and understood what they were seeing, why would they want to defend his sorry ass? To them, he was just one of three men who had broken into their home bent on ruining their lives. But then he stopped thinking about himself when another horror washed over him. This man was the daughter's father and she was up there in the panic room watching him being beaten to a pulp.

"Come on, Raoul," he said, trying to sound

calm and reasonable, "enough. There's no point in torturing the guy. That's not going to get us the money."

Raoul, who was bent over Stephen, turned to stare at Burnham. Slowly he stood and moved toward the black man, his gun extended.

"You have something to say to me?"

"Leave him alone, man. What's killing him gonna get us?"

"Are you giving me an order, old man?"

"I'm only saying—"

Raoul pressed the barrel of the gun up against Burnham's eye socket, hard. The gun was still warm from the shots he had fired into Junior. Burnham could smell oil and metal, and, though he knew he might be imagining it, burning flesh.

"Who's the big guy now?" Raoul said. "Junior thought he was a big guy. He was wrong. He was a dead guy. I know you think I'm just a clown, an asshole, a fuck-up. Right?"

"No, I don't think that."

"Oh, yes you do, hotshot. But you're wrong. You know who the clown is? You know who's the fuck-up asshole here?"

Burnham felt the pressure of the gun in his eye in the back of his head. "Me. I am."

"What are you? Say it." He pressed the gun even harder. "*Say* it, Burnham."

"I'm the clown. The fuck-up. The asshole."

Raoul's lean face broke into a smile. "I'm glad we understand each other."

"Hey, man, the gun is burning me. It's burning my skin."

"I have the gun. The man with the gun is boss."

"Yes. I understand that."

"Well, don't forget. Any more shit from you and I won't be so understanding."

"I won't forget."

After one last jab at Burnham's sore and bloodshot eye, Raoul removed the gun from his face and pointed it at the intruder. He was curled up on his side, moaning.

"Find out who he is."

Burnham bent down to the floor and searched the man's pockets for a wallet. When he finally found it, he riffled through and took out the driver's license. He squinted, holding the card at arm's length. He needed reading glasses but refused to wear them. "Stephen Altman," he read.

Burnham glanced at one of the cartons waiting to be unpacked on the kitchen floor. The words ALTMAN KITCHEN were scrawled in black magic marker on the top and side of the box.

"Looks like Daddy's come home to play the hero," Burnham said to Raoul. "That must've been the call she was making before we cut her off."

Raoul went down on one knee, his face inches from Stephen's.

"Okay, pal, let's have ourselves a little talk."

Stephen lifted his head off the floor for an instant, only long enough to nod weakly. "What do you want," he said faintly. "I'll give you anything you want."

"Did your wife call you?" Raoul said.

Stephen managed to mumble, ". . . Yes . . . Cut off . . . I . . ."

"Speak up," Raoul demanded.

". . . Emergency . . . She said . . . emergency." Stephen screwed his eyes tight shut and groaned.

Raoul stared at Stephen and shook him by the shoulders.

"Where do you live?"

"Here in Manhattan."

"Where? Park Avenue? I'll bet you live on Park Avenue."

"Fifth Avenue. Right across the park."

"I should have guessed it. You're rich, right? Another rich Jewish guy."

"I can give you what you want," Stephen answered. "Just tell me what you want."

"Did you call anyone after she called you?"

Stephen shook his head "no."

Raoul picked him up by the hair and banged his head on the floor. "Did you call the fucking cops, asshole?"

This time, Stephen mustered up the strength to shake his head more convincingly.

"I think he's telling the truth," Burnham said.

Raoul whipped around and turned the gun on Burnham. "Did I ask your opinion?"

"No."

"Then shut the fuck up." He paused and stared at Stephen, who continued to moan as he drew each breath. He gave a satisfied nod. "Yeah, he's telling the truth. When I do this—when I wave a gun in some guy's face—people don't lie to me. The gun's better than a truth serum."

Burnham said nothing, which annoyed Raoul. He pointed the gun at him again. "Don't you agree?"

"Yes, I agree."

Raoul fastened his hooded eyes on him, regarding him thoughtfully. "It's time you earned your money."

"What do you want?"

"What the fuck do you *think* I want? Get us into that room."

"I can't," Burnham said.

"Sure you can, old man. You're full of ideas. You just need to squeeze one out. One measly little idea."

"I'm telling you I can't. The room is totally foolproof."

"Well, you ain't no fool, are you?"

"No."

"I didn't think so. You're going to think up something, hotshot." His eyes burned into Burnham. "Aren't you . . ."

Burnham sighed. "There is no way."

"You've got till the count of three. Then you'll end up like him." He nodded over at Junior's body. "Do you want to end up like him?"

"No."

"Okay—I'm glad to hear that." Raoul clicked back the safety. "One. I'm starting to squeeze the trigger, old man."

Burnham tried to call his bluff. "This is just stupid. . . . I'm telling you there's no way in there unless she lets us in—"

But Raoul was not bluffing. "Two. Squeezing a little harder now."

Burnham stared at the gun, mesmerized. "I don't know what to tell you—"

"Three. Here we go—"

"Okay! Okay! Okay!"

Raoul slowly lowered the gun. "A smart choice," he said. "You got an idea?"

"Yes," Burnham said. "I know what you can do."

Meg and Sarah sat in the panic room, Sarah still locked in Meg's embrace. Meg could see the screen but Sarah's head was buried in her lap. She was so weak that she kept drowsing off every few minutes. Meg watched in horror, unable to take her eyes off the screen. At least the awful man with the dreadlocks had stopped hitting and kicking Stephen. She had thought for a moment that he was going to kill the other one, the black guy. He held a pistol to his head but then he lowered it. She didn't know whether she was relieved by his not killing the black man or not. If he killed him, there would be one less man to deal with. But she knew by his actions that the black man was not the dangerous one. If only he could wrest the gun from the guy with the dreadlocks and kill him. She realized that in only a few short hours, after a lifetime of nonviolence, she had become obsessed with murder.

She watched as the three men left the kitchen. The black man was practically carrying Stephen, who was too weak to stand on his feet. She followed them on the monitors through the foyer, up two flights of stairs, and into the master bedroom. She stared, unblinking, not wanting to miss anything. Suddenly Stephen's face appeared on the bedroom monitor. It was his face all right, there was no mistaking his kind and yet serious expression. But Meg was confused. Why on earth was he smiling? What could he possibly be smiling about? Also, his features looked too perfect, too untouched by the violence he had just experienced in the kitchen. Her puzzlement caused her to loosen the tight grip she had on Sarah. Once free, Sarah, half-awake, turned slowly to see what was happening and yelled out in shock: "Daddy!"

Just as suddenly as it had appeared, Stephen's face was ripped away from the camera, and Meg realized that what they had just seen was Stephen's driver's license ID photograph. She was praying for Sarah's sake that they would not show Stephen in his present condition, and yet somehow she knew that they would. The next thing they saw was the big black guy standing directly in front of the camera, while the skinny one with the dreadlocks held Stephen up in the background. After staring at the camera for a few seconds, an evil grin on his face, the man threw Stephen to the floor and kneed him on the way down.

"Hey. Take it easy, man," Burnham said, but his plea fell on deaf ears. Raoul only became more violent, picking Stephen up again by the collar and belt, and bashing him against the metal door of the panic room. The sound of the impact of Stephen hitting the door caused Sarah to cry out.

Burnham looked straight into the camera and mouthed the words, *"Open. The. Door. This. Will. Only. Get Worse."*

As Raoul kicked Stephen again, this time in the ribs, Sarah sobbed and turned away, crushing her face against Meg's chest.

Burnham moved back from the camera. He was afraid of Raoul's craziness, afraid of the gun, but he had had enough of this senseless brutality.

"Knock it off, for crissake," he said. "Do you want to kill him?"

"Maybe. And maybe you, too, Burnham, if you get in my shit."

"Be cool, man," Burnham said, still trying to reason with him. "You just have to make it look good. She'll cave in."

"Are you trying to tell me what to do, hotshot? Haven't you learned your lesson yet? You fuck with me and you'll regret it."

Meg could not hear Burnham, but the strained look on his face and the way his eyeballs popped when he made his request a second time convinced her that he was very serious and very concerned.

He stared straight at her and said, *"Open. The. Door. Please. His. Life. Is. At. Risk . . ."*

Meg glanced at the green button that would release the door and thought for a moment that she should open it. Otherwise, they might kill Stephen. They had already killed one of their own. What difference would the death of this middle-aged rich man, a man they didn't even know, make to them? She could not be responsible for any harm that might come to Stephen. She would never be able to live with herself. And yet something held her back. What if she opened the door? What was their leverage then? What would stop them from killing all three of them? She was certain that Stephen was their bargaining chip, the only one there was. They were not going to kill him, not as long as the panic room door remained closed. If they killed him, they had gained nothing.

Stephen, confused and badly beaten, screamed out, "Don't do it Meg! Don't open the d—" He was stopped by a vicious kick to his midsection. Raoul followed that with a kick to the side of Stephen's face. He was overcome with an uncontrollable rage now, snarling like an animal. He drove a fist into Stephen's stomach, doubling him over. Then he raised his shoe and sent another kick into the crippled man. "She opens the door, man," he screamed. "Otherwise you're dead. And your wife and kid are dead, too. This way, you live. What the fuck is wrong with you? If I don't get in that room, I'm going to kill you—you got no fucking choice!" As he screamed, he continued to kick the man.

Burnham knew that he had to act. He used his considerable bulk to push Raoul away from Stephen.

"What's he supposed to do, man? That's his kid in there."

Raoul stared at Burnham, a hint of surprise in his expression.

"You just don't learn, do you, old man. I'll settle with you later." He turned back to Stephen, but Burnham grabbed his arm. The rage was finally welling up in him now, and he knew himself well enough to know that if his rage reached the boiling point he would care less about saving his own life than ending Raoul's. "Stop, for crissake, you're killing the poor bastard." He held Raoul's arms behind his back in a tight vise. "His kid's in there watching this. I can't let you do it." If he couldn't stop the beating, he could at least protect the little girl from having to witness it. While he wrestled with Raoul, trying to keep him away from Stephen, he managed to throw his coat over the camera to black out the action from the panic room.

The incessant kicking, the brutality, was driving Meg insane, but she could not risk her life and Sarah's by opening the door. If she had to decide who was more important, the two of them or Stephen, there was no choice. She knew deep in her heart that she still loved her ex-husband, but he had left her and his daughter for another woman. If it was only the black guy, she might be willing to risk letting him in to take whatever he was after, but she would never open the door to the other one.

Meg and Sarah clung to each other, trying to avert their eyes, but it was impossible to look away. Meg felt a moment of sudden warmth, of not being quite so alone, when the black man ripped off his own jacket, ran over to the camera with it, and tossed it over the camera to cover it up. The scene played out on a dark screen now.

She could hear through the wall some muffled screaming and what sounded like furniture being tossed around.

As she listened, holding Sarah close, she wondered how and why this man had decided to team up with the others. He seemed so different from them. What was there in his life that had driven him to this? But the moment of wondering was over in a flash and the feeling of gratitude that he had covered the camera to spare them the violence in the bedroom quickly turned to anger and resentment. The counter on Sarah's wrist began to beep furiously. Meg checked the counter and realized in horror that it now read 30. She mustn't ever forget that he was one of them. He might be better, but he was still one of them, and she held him just as responsible as the others for Sarah's condition.

She held her daughter at arm's length for a moment, studying her face; her color was now a deathly gray, with an ominous tinge of yellow, and her eyes were rolled back in her head. Meg kept her eye on the counter as it inched down to 28. Then the beeping again went from fast to one continuous beep.

"Oh, God!" she uttered. "Please, Sarah. Please, baby. Just hold on. You've got to hold on . . ."

There was no more time for the waiting game. Meg needed to act fast. Her daughter's life could be measured in a matter of minutes.

Her body had gone stiff and was beginning to jerk. She screamed as her tiny lungs began to compress and the air was forced out of them. Her jaw clamped shut and her fingers curled into claws. She began to twitch and convulse, and managed to buck right out of Meg's arms and onto the floor. Helpless and in total despair, Meg know that she had to clear an area where her daughter could flail about without hurting herself. The convulsions finally subsided, and the counter on Sarah's wrist was still beeping. But it would happen again, and soon, if Meg didn't do something. The next time Sarah might not pull out of it.

Sarah, eyes closed, whispered to her mother, "I'm sorry. I'm really sorry. I'm no help at all."

"Just rest, sweetheart. This will be over soon. I promise you."

"I love you," Sarah said in a whisper.

"I love you, too," Meg said.

"I'm sleepy," Sarah said and her eyes fluttered and then closed.

Meg's eye went to the monitors again. The bedroom monitor was still covered by the black man's jacket, but the monitor for the stairs showed him carrying the guy in the dreadlocks down the stairs. He was draped limply over the man's shoulders and he was wearing his ski mask. She guessed that all the noise and screaming she heard before Sarah's episode was the big guy fighting it out with Stephen's torturer. Maybe she could forgive him, if she ever got the chance. Maybe he wasn't so bad after all.

It was time to take action. Meg looked down at Sarah drowsing fitfully in the corner. She could not live much longer without her medicine. She had to get to Sarah's room, no matter what lay in wait for her. It was life and death now, and if Sarah died she would have no reason to go on living.

She stood at the door and drew in a deep breath. She had been terrified locked in this room and now she was equally terrified to be leaving it. But she had no choice. She had to go. She took one last look at her daughter, put her fingers to her lips and threw her a kiss. She then pressed the "open" button for the panic room and sneaked out the door as quietly as possible. She looked over at the bed and saw a figure lying face down covered in a familiar brown topcoat. "Stephen! Oh, my God—" she called out. She nearly went to help him, but there was no time. Sarah came first. She had to have her medicine; that was the only thing in the world that mattered now. Stephen would have to wait.

Meg left the master bedroom through the bathroom, as light on her feet as a cat. She padded down to the other end of the hallway and hurried up the landing toward the top floor.

She raced into Sarah's bedroom and tore open the door of the mini-fridge beside Sarah's bed. Among the many small bottles was one labeled "Glucagon," which she grabbed along with a black leather pouch that was sitting on top of the fridge, then headed out the door.

Downstairs, on the second floor, Burnham glanced up at the ceiling when he heard footsteps. Not heavy, angry, man's footsteps, but the delicate, light footsteps of a woman in bare feet trying not to be heard. He set Stephen's unconscious body in a chair in the solarium and ripped off his mask. He was not happy about the deception, but how could you argue with the business end of a gun? The woman had no way of knowing that while the screen was covered by Burnham's coat, Raoul had exchanged clothing with the husband. Raoul was now in her bedroom, covered in her husband's topcoat, pretending to be unconscious. Lying in wait for her. It was too bad, but then it all had turned out bad. Getting his hands on the money was no longer the main thing. He just wanted to get into the panic room, remove the videotapes that could incriminate him, and get out of the house.

In the bedroom, Raoul felt the woman's breath as she bent over him and said "Stephen! Oh, my God—" He then heard her quickly leave the room and steal upstairs. He sat up. The door to the panic room was wide open. He got off the bed, grinning. It was all coming together; it was going to work after all.

Burnham made his way upstairs in time to meet Raoul by the open panic room door. Burnham no longer feared for his life. Now that the door was open, Raoul could not lay a hand on him because he was the man's ticket to the money. Once he cracked the safe, he realized that he would be in great danger. He would no longer be of use to the man. Burnham had no strategy to handle that, but he hoped that he would find some way to get out of the house alive and carry with him at least some of the money. He was aware that the next hour would be the most crucial one in his life.

"Let's hit it, man," Raoul said. "No time to waste."

He stormed the panic room with Burnham directly behind him. They both ignored the little girl huddled in the corner, comatose, eyes closed. Burnham went straight for the monitors and punched the "eject" buttons on the VCR panel underneath. He punched them again, more firmly this time, but nothing came out. He tried a third time and then stuck his finger into the slots to try and manually eject the tapes. But there was nothing inside. *There never were any tapes.* Burnham felt sick to his stomach as he realized that he could have left long ago, and no one would ever have known that he'd been in the house.

In the meantime, Meg came flying back downstairs with the medicine. She approached the door to the master bedroom to look in on Stephen. She would quickly give Sarah the medicine, and, if the coast was still clear, she would sneak back and help Stephen.

But the bed was empty. He wasn't there.

She looked around wildly, then she turned toward the panic room door, and standing in front of her, leering at her, was the man with the dreadlocks. *He was wearing Stephen's topcoat. He had been the man on the bed.*

"Well, well, I finally get a chance to meet the lady of the house. You're some pain in the ass, you know what I mean?"

She held the medicine in front of her like a shield. "I have to give this to my daughter. She's dying. You have to let me give this to her."

"You're a whole lot of trouble, lady." He spoke with a light Hispanic accent and his tone was surprisingly soft, almost feminine. But his next sentence sent chills up her spine. "We've got your daughter in the panic room. Whether she gets the medicine is up to you." His dark hooded eyes were frightening. After a pause, he added, "Ca'mon." He took her arm in a rough grasp. "Let's get this over with."

"You can do whatever you want with me," Meg said. "Just leave my daughter alone."

At the entrance to the panic room she saw her daughter curled up in the corner where she'd left her and the big guy was standing by the monitors. He slid his eyes toward her, acknowledged her with a nod; that was all. She was about to move into the room and administer the medicine to Sarah when she was grabbed from behind. There was no time to think. Only to react. Meg dropped the medicine bag as she grappled with the man with the dreadlocks. She tried to claw him with her fingernails, but he was much too strong for her and threw her across the room. With a strength of will she did not know she possessed, she lunged right back into him, slamming him into the outer panel door to the panic room. He tightened his grip on her, but she was thin and wiry, and easily squirmed out of his grasp. Showering curses on her, he shoved her hard and she fell next to the medicine bag, which she immediately batted across the threshold and into the panic room.

The man leaped toward the panic room and the medicine bag, but Meg was determined that this maniac not get near her daughter. With a deafening screech, she jumped at him again, this time managing to grab a fistful of the topcoat and she pulled on it from behind him. He twisted and contorted his body to throw her off and managed finally to tear himself out of the coat sleeves. The momentum of the tug-of-war landed Meg on the floor, holding the ripped coat in her hand, and carried him into the panic room. He grabbed onto the doorframe to break his fall, just as the black man, watching him closely, pressed the button to close the door to the panic room. In an instant the door slammed shut and the man with the dreadlocks screamed as the spring-loaded panic room door shut on his fingers, crushing them.

19

M eg watched the panic room door slam shut. Her daughter was inside with those two men and the bag with her medication, and she was on the outside. She fought not to cry. Tears were a luxury now; she was beyond tears. She felt that she had somehow betrayed Sarah, felt that she was the worst mother who had ever lived—worse even than Medea. Sarah was trapped in that room with two men who meant her only harm and the medication that could save her life was also in the room. She felt as though she had pretty much signed, sealed, and delivered her daughter's death warrant.

But at least the evil one, the man with the dreadlocks, was suffering. She could hear his high-pitched screams. He had stumbled as the door was closing and he must have been caught by the weight of the steel door. She stood there, fighting for calm. Now it was she who was desperate to get into the panic room. There had to be a way. She had to think—*think*.

Burnham stood at the video console staring at Raoul, watching him suffer. He made no move to help him.

"My fucking fingers!" Raoul wailed. *"Goddammit*, man, help me. . . ."

Burnham was staring at his maimed right hand, part of which was jammed in the door. "Where's your gun?" he asked.

"Open the fucking door!" Raoul screamed.

Burnham pushed him up against the control panel, accidentally activating the intercom system. His face inches from Raoul's he said, "Where is your gun? What happened to it?"

"Out there!" Raoul shouted. "Open the door. Come on, man. I can't stand the pain."

Burnham regarded him with disgust. He was totally psychotic, and, worse, he was stupid. "She's got the gun," he said. "You let her get the gun. Why did you have to mess with her anyway? You've fucked us now, man. You've really fucked us good."

Raoul was writhing in pain.

"Please—for crissake, Burnham—open the door."

Burnham shook his head. He stared unblinkingly at Raoul, watching him suffer. He now had the upper hand and was not about to relinquish it.

"My hand is killing me," Raoul said, beginning to whimper. "I can't stand the pain."

"You don't seem to understand," Burnham said, making no move to help him. "She has the gun, asshole. She has the fucking *gun*. We're screwed, man."

Meg could suddenly hear the two men.

"Where is your gun? What happened to it?"

"Out there. Open the door. Come on, man. I can't stand the pain."

"She's got the gun. You let her get the gun. Why did you have to mess with her anyway? You've fucked us now, man. You've really fucked us good."

Meg turned and dropped to her knees. The gun was lying under the topcoat she had ripped from the man during their struggle. She promptly snatched it up.

She held the gun straight in front of her and approached the panic room door. She held it in both hands, with her finger trembling on the trigger. Meg had never felt such rage. She was ready to shoot the minute the door was opened. There was no doubt in her mind that she would shoot. She stood there and listened to their voices coming through the speaker.

"The door—Jesus, please, Burnham, please open the door. I can't stand it, man. The pain is awful."

"Be quiet. She can hear you through the door."

"Who gives a shit, man? I'm suffering. Oh God, just open the door. You want the money? You can have it, I don't care anymore. Just open the door."

"She'll shoot us. Don't you get it, you stupid shit? Thanks to you, she's got the gun and don't think for a minute she won't use it."

"I don't give a fuck. She can shoot me. Just open the door!"

She stood at the panic room door, her hand steadying. She wondered about the black man. Was he deliberately torturing his accomplice? Half an hour ago—what seemed like a lifetime ago—she had begun to see him as a decent guy, decent for a crook. In little ways he had tried to make the experience as painless as possible for her and her daughter. But then he had switched the clothing and tricked her into getting separated from her daughter. So he was no good. He was just as bad as the other guy. She would have no compunction about killing either of them, if it came to that. She would blow them both to fucking hell.

"I'm going to try talking to her."

"First open the door, man. Please!"

"Later. Right now we've got to get things clear with her."

Silence. Meg pressed her ear against the door, waiting.

"Oh, shit!"

The black man's voice.

"What is it?"

"The goddamn speaker was on. One of us must've hit against it. She's heard everything."

Another silence. Then the black man's voice: "We know you've got the gun. Can you hear me?"

Meg took a deep breath. "I can hear you."

"Put the gun down, and get away from the door."

"My daughter needs an injection."

Silence.

"I have to give it to her right now."

"Drop the gun."

"Open the door. I have to give her her medication."

"We can't do that. I open the door and you'll shoot us."

"Then you give her the shot. The medicine is in the black bag."

Burnham grabbed the bag and opened it. He turned to Sarah, still huddled in the corner like a crumpled doll.

"You need this?" he said.

She nodded a weak yes.

"Can you do it yourself?"

A weak no as her eyes fluttered closed.

Burnham studied her. She was so small, so pale. He thought of his daughter, about the same age, and tried to blot the image out of his mind.

"Tell me the truth—what's going to happen if you don't get it?"

Sarah swallowed and licked her cracking lips. She could hardly speak, but she managed to force out two words: "Coma. Die."

Both her parents, her mother outside the door and her father regaining consciousness in the solarium, could hear their child's words. Both listened in terror.

Meg, beside herself with fear, began to kick the door as hard as she could. Every time she made impact with the door, fresh pain would shoot up Raoul's arm from his damaged hand. Meg was determined to get inside. She would kick the door down if she had to. She would do anything to get to her daughter and make sure she got that shot.

"Stop kicking the door, bitch!" Raoul cried out. "Fuck! Burnham, *you've got to open the fucking door!*"

Burnham understood what Meg was going through. He tried to imagine what Alison would be like in her shoes—what *he* would be like. He didn't like the feeling and tried to shut it out of his mind. He could not let this child die. He knew he had to compromise.

"Listen to me," he said. "Put the gun on the floor where I can see it and go downstairs—all the way downstairs. Then I'll give the kid her shot."

Meg ran to the top of the stairs, the gun still in her hand. She started down.

The deep voice boomed out of the loud-speaker. "I said leave the gun."

Meg turned and waved the gun at the camera. "Fuck you!" she screamed, and flew down the stairs.

Burnham, sensing that the woman wouldn't shoot them if they didn't hurt the little girl, pressed the "open" button for the panic room door, and Raoul pulled his hand out. Burnham tossed Raoul a surgical glove he had found among the overturned crates. Raoul groaned as he tried to insert his fingers. Three of them had been smashed. He sagged to the floor, cradling the hand in agony.

Burnham picked up the bottle of Glucagon and turned toward Sarah. Raoul followed his movements, his hooded eyes smoldering.

"What are you doin', man? We have no time for this shit. She's gonna call the cops."

"Are you going to open the safe?"

Raoul just looked at him.

"I didn't think so. Now shut up and let me get this over with."

As Burnham crossed the room and crouched on his knees in front of the child, Raoul made eye contact with Sarah, who was staring at him.

"Don't you look at me," he said.

She quickly looked away and into the eyes of the dark burly stranger. He smiled. "All I know about this is what I see on *E.R.* You'll have to talk me through it, okay?"

Sarah tried to form words but she was too weak to manage more than a nod.

"Okay, no talking," Burnham said. "No problem. TV doesn't lie, right? Those *E.R.* folks are on the ball."

Burnham ripped the Velcro on the pouch and rolled it open on the floor.

He glanced at her and he couldn't help the feeling of protectiveness that overcame him. He couldn't control the father in him. When you look at a child in need, you don't ask questions, you just do what needs to be done.

"Hey," he said gently. "Nod or something, will you? Let me know you're still with us."

Sarah obliged with the tiniest inclination of her head.

"Attagirl," he said.

He needed her to talk him through the procedure, but he knew this was out of the question.

He pointed to various implements in the pouch to find out what he needed in order to give her the shot. By this point in her weakened state all she could do was blink when he touched the right implement.

He filled the syringe with Glucagon, making small talk with the girl because if she was anything like his daughter, shots were absolutely terrifying.

"Some place you got here. You're mom's pretty rich, huh?"

"My dad's rich," Sarah replied in a hoarse whisper. "My mother's just mad."

For some reason, that brought a smile to Burnham's face. "Yeah. Been there. Divorce is hard." He studied her pale face and noticed the dark rings under her eyes. "How old are you?"

"Ten."

"You seem older."

"I'm almost eleven."

Burnham held up the syringe and asked the child what he was supposed to do next. Sarah reached down and weakly pulled up her T-shirt.

"Stomach?" he asked.

She nodded, and then with all the effort she could muster, she pinched some of her skin together to make a roll. Burnham reached in to help. "Like this?"

Sarah nodded. Burnham then started to lower

the needle, but Sarah's eyes widened and she pushed it away in fear.

"Tap it. You have to tap it," she muttered faintly.

"Oh yeah, right. Sorry. Yeah." *E.R.* had not gone into this much detail. Burnham tapped the needle to clear the air bubbles (he remembered seeing that on TV), squirted out a few drops, and looked at her for approval. She seemed calmer now. He hoped it was because he was doing the right thing and not that she was too weak to correct his mistakes.

"Wish I could bring my kids to a nice house like this," he said as he administered the shot. "I just wish I could *see* them. Sometimes you can't make things right. You want to, but all kinds of problems keep cropping up."

The little girl looked up at him and he could tell that she understood him completely. She seemed so mature for her age, so wise.

"It wasn't supposed to be like this, you know. I had it all worked out. We were supposed to just get in and out of here, one, two, three. You never would've even known we were here." The shot finished, Burnham gently pulled Sarah's shirt back down.

"Feel better?" he asked her.

"Yeah, Burnham."

How did she know who he was? He was genuinely puzzled for a moment until he looked down and saw his name clearly emblazoned on his coveralls. He shook his head. *What kind of an idiot wears a nametag to a robbery?*

He looked at Sarah again. "Like I said, it wasn't supposed to be like this." He hesitated, then added, "I'm sorry."

Raoul had been watching the procedure with increasing impatience. He held his good hand under his mangled hand and glared at Burnham. "You had your fun, doc? That was a waste of fucking time."

Burnham returned his glare. "You wouldn't have given her the medicine, right, Raoul?"

"Shit no. Why should I?"

"I feel sorry for you, man."

"Fuck you," Raoul said. "You're just a bleeding heart old guy. A loser."

Burnham clicked on the intercom: "Your daughter is okay," he said, his deep voice reverberating throughout the house. "This'll be over soon. We have to finish what we came to do and then we'll leave."

Raoul had had enough of the father dearest, goody-goody routine. It was time to talk sense to the man.

"What happens when we get the money, Burnham?"

"What do you mean, 'what happens?' Like I said, we leave."

"But what about them, man? They've seen

us." He stared at Sarah, who quickly looked away. "This kid has practically memorized my face."

"That's your problem," Burnham replied.

"No, I don't think so. It's our problem, man. You're here with me. You're on the hook for it. Buy one, same price for the rest. You know how this has got to end."

"You'd better stay the fuck away from me," Burnham said. "You're scum. And stay the fuck away from this kid. I mean it. You may think I'm old but I can kill you with my bare hands. Without your gun you're just another punk."

Raoul stared at his wounded hand and said nothing.

Using his fingers as a rule, Burnham measured six lengths in from the wall of the panic room, then dug his fingernails into the weave of the carpet, looking for a seam. When he found one, he grabbed hold of it on one edge, and ran his other hand along the seam until he found a spot where the seam appeared to turn a corner. At that point, he pulled the carpet back with both hands, revealing the smooth metal door of a floor safe. He unsnapped his satchel and up-ended it to reveal a wide array of safe-cracking tools.

Raoul continued to stare at his hand with morbid fascination. Someone was going to have to pay for his pain. The woman, the girl, the husband—they would all buy it. And then there was Burnham. *Good-bye Burnham, you smug no-good asshole. You got the glory but the money is mine.* He looked up and caught the girl staring at him again. "Stop looking at me." *You little rich bitch. You and your mama and your daddy all gonna get yours and all the money in the world ain't gonna save you.*

20

M eg headed straight for the solarium, where on the monitors in the panic room she had watched the black man drop Stephen off. Stephen had been savagely beaten, his right eye was closed, there was an ugly red gash on his cheek and his shoulder was twisted into an ugly, unnatural position. As angry as she'd been at him over the past several months, she couldn't bear to see him this way. She knelt beside him and stroked his head.

"Can you move?" she asked.

"Not much. I think my kneecap is broken. Also my arm—my right arm. And my collar-bone—I think he broke that."

"Can you raise your arm?"

He tried and the effort brought tears to his eyes. He lay back and gritted his teeth against the pain.

When she stood he saw the gun in her left hand. His eyes widened. "Don't do anything stupid, Meg," he pleaded.

"They're going to kill us," she said.

"No. Do everything they ask." He winced. "It'll be better that way."

"They're going to kill Sarah. The guy with the dreadlocks—the one who beat you up—he's crazy. He's already killed one man. He's a maniac. I have to stop him."

Just then, a deafening sound rang through the house.

Her eyes darted to the front door and then back to Stephen.

"That would be the police," he explained.

She stared at him. "Oh, God! No. You called the police?"

"You're damn right I did. I was scared for you. What was I supposed to do?"

Of course he was right. That was what she had hoped he would do when she called him. But now that those animals had Sarah, everything had changed.

The doorbell rang again and she knew there was no way the men holding Sarah hostage could have missed it. She reached up and removed the shade from the lamp on the table next to

Stephen. She placed the lamp on his lap along with the gun and whispered to him, "Don't say a word." He nodded, dazed, confused. She combed a hand through her hair and headed for the door. On her way, she grabbed a ski parka from the hall closet to throw over her night-gown.

She picked up the electric screwdriver she had carried in from the kitchen and calmly began to take the screws out of the door. "Just a minute." As the last screw fell to the floor, she pulled the door partially open and stuck her head out under the chain. "Yes?"

"Everything okay?" one of the men in blue asked.

"Huh?" she said, feigning sleepiness.

"Are you okay, ma'am?" the second one asked.

"What are you guys doing here?" She yawned. "What time is it?"

"About four o'clock."

"Four? Four in the morning? I don't under-stand why you're here."

"We got a call."

"Someone called you?"

"Can we come in?"

"What do you want?"

"We'd like to come in."

"No, you can't come in."

"Are you okay?"

"I'm fine."

"Can we come in?"

"Stop asking me that. Who called you?"

"You don't look so good."

"You wake me out of a sound sleep at four in the morning and then tell me how I look? You don't look so hot yourself"—she peered at his nametag—"Lopez. I'm freezing here. Thanks for checking in. Can I go back to bed now?"

"You said there are three of them. They were breaking in."

"Huh?"

"Your husband says you asked for help. That you said 'there are three of them . . .' That was right before you got cut off."

"Oh . . . that phone call . . ."

"Yeah."

"Well, ah, it's a little embarrassing."

"And somebody behind your courtyard called about a loud television, or a loudspeaker or something."

"Oh, sorry. Must have been the TV. It's off now."

Speaking very softly, the one called Lopez asked, "Ma'am, if there's something you want to say to us that maybe you can't say right now . . . maybe you just want to give us a signal. You know, blink a few times or something like that."

She paused.

"That's something you could do. Safely."

She glanced from one to the other, then burst

out laughing. "Oh, you guys are good. You mean, like, if somebody was in the house or something? That's great! They really train you guys, don't they?"

The one named Lopez gave her a thoughtful look. "We're trained to look for trouble. Are you in trouble?"

"Everything is fine. Really. Cross my heart—"

"May I ask what the rest of that sentence was going to be?"

"Huh?"

"The sentence about the three of them breaking in. What was the rest of it?"

"Okay, look. As I said, this is embarrassing. My husband and I just broke up. It's my first night in the new house and I was feeling a little lonely and drunk. What I planned to tell him was—if you really must know—I planned to say, 'There are three things I'll do for you if you come over right now and get in bed with me.'"

The one who was not called Lopez laughed out loud.

"But thank God I came to my senses before I said all that and hung up instead, so nobody would ever know what I was thinking. Unless, of course, two policemen showed up in the middle of the night to interrogate me about it."

"Should we go now, Rick? Or do you want her to tell us which three things?"

*   *   *

Meg closed the front door by leaning on it with her back. She stepped into the foyer, where she watched the patrol car pull away from the house. She looked up at the nearest camera as if to say, "See, I got rid of them," but then, as if out of nowhere, she heard a metallic, piercing sound from somewhere upstairs. From the panic room, she thought . . . *If they're hurting my baby* . . .

She flew up to the solarium to find that Stephen was now sitting up, grimacing with pain but alert. She reached behind him, unbuckled his belt and removed it. He wondered what she was up to, but he was much too weak to argue with her. She took the gun, placed it in the palm of his hand, and wrapped the belt around it, tying it tight to his wrist. "Lift it," she commanded. Stephen obeyed, lifting his hand about six inches, but the pain was so unbearable that he was shaking badly. He choked back bile.

"What are you doing, Meg?"

She shook her head. "No time." She could see he was skeptical when he looked up at her. "You'll see."

She knew that her daughter's life was at stake and every second was precious now. "*Lift the gun!*" she screamed in his face. He obeyed, fighting back tears of pain, and she secured his arm to the chair so that he was sitting now with the gun pointed directly ahead.

She quickly made her way throughout the

house, grabbing anything she thought would be useful. She sifted through the various tools on the kitchen table but couldn't find what she needed. She moved on to one of the kitchen drawers to grab a skeleton key that she remembered was located there. But there was something else that she needed—something that would truly make a statement. And then it caught her eye: the sledgehammer was propped against the wall next to the stairs leading to the basement.

She picked it up and slung it over her shoulder, amazed at how heavy it was and yet how easily she had managed to lift it. She wriggled out of the parka she was wearing and set off to do some real damage.

She eyed the video camera in the kitchen— her first target. She lifted the sledgehammer and brought it down on the camera with all her strength, smashing it to bits. She then moved from room to room, smashing every camera she could find and feeling stronger and stronger with every act of destruction.

— CHAPTER —

21

S arah watched them intently. Burnham and
the awful man were too busy to notice that
the TV monitors in the panic room were
starting to go to static, one by one. She could
hardly believe her eyes when she saw what was
happening throughout the house. The shadow
of her mother was moving from room to room,
and whenever her shadow appeared in a room,
the screen would go blank. She couldn't believe
that her mother was swinging a sledgehammer,
smashing camera after camera with it. Sarah was
awed at this gentle woman, her mother, who had
suddenly morphed into a woman possessed. *Way
to go, Ma . . .*

She prayed that the two men would stay busy

and forget about the video camera. A few minutes earlier when the doorbell rang and the two policemen arrived she had thought it was all over. The men had followed her mother's every move and Burnham had told the awful man that her mother would handle the situation and the awful man had argued with him, but he was more concerned with his mangled hand and then the cops had gone away and Burnham had gone back to prying up a piece of the floor. They were looking for a safe and she hoped they would find it fast and then leave. The awful man, with his dark angry eyes, freaked her out. He kept looking at her and then telling her not to look at him. He was really jumpy and in awful pain. If Burnham wasn't in the room she was sure he would kill her.

Every time he looked up his eyes would go to her, and he would scowl at her for looking at him. It had become a weird sort of game. She kept looking at him even though it made him angry because it was a way of keeping his attention away from the monitors and her mother. But then she screwed up. When he raised his hooded eyes and stared at her, she was watching one of the monitors.

His eyes followed hers. "What the *fuck!*" he muttered as he watched the image of a tiny woman in a blue nightgown raise a sledgehammer and slam it down on the camera, causing the screen to go immediately to static. *"Where the fuck is she?"* He stared at the monitor, open-mouthed. Meg finally arrived at the last camera, the one that had, until now, been obscured by Burnham's jacket. The awful man put his face right up to the monitor, just in time to see the jacket yanked off the camera and her mother's face twisted into a ferocious scowl as she brought the sledgehammer down. Blackness.

"Hey, Burnham, she's destroyed all the cameras. *We* should've thought of that. Now we got no idea what's going on out there."

Burnham, busy at the safe, did not answer. Sarah covered her ears against the screaming drill as it pierced the metal. When the drill stopped, Raoul rose to his feet with a groan and limped over to observe his progress. As he watched, the safe clicked open. He stared inside, then turned to stare at Burnham.

"It's empty, man. The fucking thing's empty!"

"These safes often have false bottoms," Burnham explained, not seeming at all fazed. He pried up the bottom plate, and inside was a thick manila envelope. He removed it, turned it around slowly, examining it.

"Ca'mon, man, open it," Raoul said eagerly.

Burnham slit the seal carefully with a knife blade and stared at the contents. "Bearer bonds," he said. "Million dollar denominations." He began to count. "Three, four, five . . . eleven,

twelve . . . sixteen, seventeen . . . twenty-one . . .
twenty-two . . ." He stopped, staring at the
money. He slowly shook his head and smiled.

"What?" demanded Raoul.

"Twenty-two bonds," Burnham said calmly.
"Twenty-two million dollars."

"Get the fuck *out* of here." Raoul was stunned
and he stared at Burnham slack-jawed.

"Twenty-two million," Burnham said. He
stuffed the envelope into his jacket.

"That lying little shit!" Raoul shook his head,
ground his teeth. "He deserved to die." In his excitement he had failed to notice that Burnham
had pocketed the envelope.

Burnham rose to his feet and dusted off his
trousers.

"Time to go," he said. He turned and bent
down to Sarah's level, putting his hands on her
shoulders. "You're gonna be okay. I promise."
Sarah nodded. She didn't know why, but she
trusted this man. If he said that she was going to
be okay, she was ready to believe him.

Burnham opened the panic room door. He
stepped out first, eyes darting left and right as he
entered the empty room. Raoul was close behind
him, with Sarah sandwiched in between. When
the three of them entered the bedroom, the
house was completely dark. Raoul flicked the
light switch to the "on" position but nothing happened. As they walked farther into the room,

there was a crunching noise under Burnham's boot. Broken glass. "Shit," he said. Not only had the woman pulverized all the cameras in the house, she had actually smashed out the light bulbs, too. She was dangerous. Dangerous and clever. She was hiding out somewhere in the house with Raoul's gun and the sledgehammer and they had no idea where. Sarah was their only ticket to safety, although he hated to think of her that way.

When Sarah heard the crunching under Burnham's feet, she stopped dead in her tracks. Raoul tried to push her along but she refused to budge. "There's glass," she said, pointing down to her tiny bare feet.

"So what?" Raoul said roughly.

"I don't want to get cut. It's all over the floor."

Raoul sighed and shook his head. *Fucking kid.* He bent down in front of her, offering his back. "Come on. Up you go." Sarah was not happy riding piggyback on the back of this awful man, but she knew she had no choice. When she was up on his shoulders, he said, "Hold on, dammit," and she did. Much tighter than she ever thought she could.

They moved out of the bedroom and into the hallway, which was brighter because of the moonlight filtering through the skylight. Even though Raoul felt he was safe with the girl riding on his back, he still insisted that Burnham go first.

"I need the vest, then," Burnham said. Raoul had had the foresight to bring a bulletproof vest on the job.

"No."

"If I'm going first, give me the vest."

"No way, man. I brought it, I wear it."

There was no time to argue. They walked through the hallway, past the elevator, and headed down the stairs to the second level. Sarah thought she heard something—a soft sound from above. Was it her mother? She turned slightly to look up, but could see nothing. Feeling her turn, Raoul also turned but saw nothing.

As they made their way into the foyer, a bright light flashed on, blinding them. In the middle of the foyer, slumped in a chair, Stephen was pointing a gun directly at them and the bright light of the lamp shone in their faces. Burnham let out a yell when he saw the man. He had left him half-dead in the solarium not more than an hour before. How could he be sitting up holding a gun?

"Daddy!" Sarah screamed out. Raoul took a step back, flipping Sarah around from his back to his front as a kind of shield.

"Wait! Wait! Don't do that. Don't!" Burnham said, in desperation.

Sarah strained forward, saying. "Don't shoot him, Daddy!"

"We're finished, okay?" Burnham said to the man. "We just want to leave. We're going out the back door. You'll never see us again. Come on, Raoul."

Burnham edged toward the patio doors, with Raoul following close behind. He was still holding Sarah, who had begun to struggle in his arms.

"Put her down," Stephen demanded. But Raoul kept walking backward, holding tight to the child.

"Put her down," Burnham yelled at Raoul. *"Put her down!"*

"Fuck you, man," Raoul yelled back at him. "She's my protection."

From the corner of her eye Sarah saw her mother stealing up from behind, clutching the sledgehammer in both hands. Sarah held her breath. The two men were not aware of her.

Once Meg had moved close enough to reach Raoul, she made a karate chop gesture to her daughter. Sarah twisted around and slammed both her hands into the man's midsection. Surprised, he released her and she fell to the ground. She immediately sprang to her feet and started to move away, but Raoul grabbed her and then whipped around just as the sledgehammer came down straight for his head. "What the *fuck. . . ."* There was no time to even duck; Raoul received a blow to the side of his face severe enough to send him over the railing, pulling Sarah with him.

Sarah grabbed for the railing on her way over, and dangled there until her mother dropped the sledgehammer and pulled her up by the wrists. Mother and daughter looked down to the next level, where Raoul lay in a contorted heap, twisting and moaning. Meg scooped her daughter up in her arms and crushed her to her chest.

"Are you okay?"

"Yes."

"Did they hurt you?"

"No."

"Did anybody touch you?"

"No."

Burnham, realizing that he was no longer the center of attention, made his move. He quickly bolted out the French doors and into the night. Meg and Sarah stood at the railing and looked down at the kitchen floor. To their horror, Raoul had managed to rise from a puddle of blood and drag his mangled body to the stairs. He slowly, painfully started to climb them. *Thump. Drag. Thump. Drag. Thump . . .*

Meg put Sarah down and reached again for the sledgehammer. Raoul emerged at the top of the stairs, swaying like a wounded beast: bloody, bruised, dangerous. He edged toward Meg and Sarah.

Stephen summoned his remaining strength and pointed the gun in Raoul's direction. He fired two shots, screaming in pain as the gun's recoil twisted his broken collarbone. Both shots missed, and Stephen's shoulders sagged. There was nothing more he could do.

On the patio and about to climb the fence, Burnham heard the shots and Stephen's screams. He stopped, in spite of himself, one leg up on the fence. He was in the clear. He was free. There was no evidence of his having been in the house. No videotapes. No one to have to share the money with. He was set for life. He would win his wife back. He would regain the respect of his kids. His life was just about to begin. All he had to do was put his other leg over the fence, jump down on the other side and keep on running. Running to a better life. Running to the future.

Raoul lunged toward Stephen and the gun at the same moment that Meg dove for him, wielding the sledgehammer. But this time he was ready for her. He ducked under her blow and grabbed her by the ankles, flipping her over his head onto the marble floor; she landed hard on her shoulders and head, with the wind knocked out of her.

Stephen, his eyes full of tears from the pain, fired the gun again, just missing Meg.

"Son of a *bitch*," Raoul screamed as he pushed Stephen off the chair, sending the gun flying out of his hand. He struggled to reach it, but it had slid out of his reach. Raoul limped over to Meg, sitting on the floor dazed, grabbed her by the hair with his good hand and dragged her across the floor to where the sledgehammer had landed. His plan was to choke her to death, then bash her brains out with the sledgehammer. Then he would shoot the other two.

Sarah crawled across the floor to her medicine bag. Out of habit she had brought it with her from the panic room. Meg and her doctors had drummed into her that she should never be without her medicine. She ripped the bag open, grabbed three hypodermic needles, and leaped up onto Raoul's back, jabbing the needles into his neck.

He shouted in pain, grabbing for the needles. With his elbow, he batted Sarah away. She tumbled against the brick façade of the fireplace, cowering and screaming.

With guttural growls, more animal than human, he reached for the sledgehammer, picked it up, and raised it over Meg. She rolled onto her side, barely avoiding the blow. At that moment she saw the black man come crashing into the room. He stooped to pick up the gun under Stephen's chair and inched toward Raoul, who never knew he was there.

Burnham and Meg exchanged glances for an instant and then he fired into the side of Raoul's head. Raoul was dead before he hit the floor.

Meg staggered over to her daughter, who was screaming, her hands to her temples, and scooped her up in her arms. Burnham bent down to Meg and Sarah and gently set the gun in front of them. "I told him," he whispered, not for a second taking his eyes from Meg's.

Just then, the house filled with flashing red lights and the sound of screaming sirens. Without another word, Burnham zipped up his jacket over the bonds, which in the melee had torn loose from the envelope, and raced out of the house.

He ran through the backyard, the bearer bonds falling out of his jacket with every step. In the backyard, he was trapped by three police officers, hands clenching bonds raised overhead. He threw his head back and released them into the wind, into the night. Gone forever.

The police rushed into the house, where Meg and Sarah were locked in an embrace, staring at the gun. Stephen finally managed to drag himself to a sitting position. "Daddy!" Sarah cried, struggling to release herself from her mother.

Meg hugged her daughter and then let her go. "It's okay," she said.

Sarah threw her arms around her crippled father, holding him tight.

"You came, Daddy," she said. "I always knew you would come. I knew you'd never let us down."

Stephen held his daughter, rocking her back and forth, saying her name over and over again.

He looked over at his ex-wife, curled up with her knees at her chest, her arms folded over them and chin resting on her arms. She was watching them. He was watching her. Meg didn't seem so small or insignificant to him anymore. She seemed more like the shape of the only world he had ever really known.

EPILOGUE

A few days later, after the house had been thoroughly inspected and cleaned, the detectives stopped coming around all the time. The general air of chaos had settled. Many weeks after that Meg Altman sat with her daughter Sarah in Central Park, as they read through apartment listings, enjoying the peace of an unseasonably sunny and warm late autumn day. Sarah held the pen and she was marking down the promising listings.

"Two bedroom with den or third bedroom, Seventies east," Sarah recited, reading from the newspaper spread on their laps.

"Daddy's on that side of the park," Meg said. "I think we're better off on the West Side, don't you?"

"What difference does it make?"

"A little distance."

Sarah studied her. "You mean for you."

"Yes, for me, sweetie. Do you mind?"

"I don't mind." She grinned. "There's one advantage to having divorced parents."

"Oh, really? And what could that possibly be?"

"You get a lot more presents. Guilt pays dividends."

Meg laughed in spite of herself. "You are the limit."

Sarah returned to the paper. "Okay, what about this one? This sounds cool. Sixty-first and Central Park West. Bank foreclosure, must sell. Luxury doorman building. Health club, concierge, executive services. No pets. No sublets—"

"—no thank you," her mother said, shaking her head emphatically. A sublet sounded just perfect to her. Something not too permanent. The last thing Meg wanted was to be trapped in another apartment that would take them months to unload. And besides, a guard dog didn't seem like such a bad idea anymore. A Rottweiler. A big and menacing beast to protect them. It had taken her thirty-six years of living, but Meg had finally lost her innocence.

Sarah went back to her research, twirling the back of her hair with one finger while she scrolled down the page with pen in hand to the next listing.

"What's WEA mean?"

"West End Avenue."

"Okay—that's west then. Just what you want— right, Ma? How about this one? Eighty-first and West End Avenue. Three bedrooms plus den or fourth bedroom, spacious living room, family room plus office and/or maid's quarters, cathedral windows look out over—"

"Who needs all that space?" Meg interrupted.

"Ma, cut it out now. You're driving me nuts!"

Meg shot her daughter an incredulous look, to which Sarah rolled her eyes and stuck out her tongue and giggled.

"Okay, lady," she said in her grown-up Katharine Hepburn drawl. "Here's my best offer. After this, you're on your own. West Eighty-third Street. Two bedroom, doorman building. Park block. Partial views. Bright and cheery flat, high ceilings, wood floors." She looked up at her mother with a bright grin. "Now don't tell me *that* doesn't sound cool."

"Well, it does sound promising."

"Well, hurray! Now we're getting somewhere!"

Meg watched her daughter intently, wondering how deeply the whole experience had affected her, including the divorce. Would she ever trust men in her life? Would she make bad decisions? Would she marry a man who would leave her one day with a small daughter and a broken heart? Would she heal?

She marveled at her daughter's ability to snap back. Because after all that had happened she still seemed like the old Sarah—strong, funny, wise and irreverent. In an odd way, Meg had always looked up to her daughter and wanted to be as strong as she. And then she realized that she was.

"So when do we go see this fabulous apartment *that we're both going to want?*" Sarah said, nudging her mother.

Meg folded the newspaper neatly and put it in her purse. "Well, let's call the agent and take a look right now. There's no time like the present, is there?"

With casual simultaneity, all fissionable material on the planet had been exploded with an efficiency ranging from eight to eighteen percent conversion. Every missile and bomber base; every bomb in flight; every nuclear power station and every refinery where the stocks exceeded a couple of kilograms had mushroomed into fire. It was a day and a half before the survivors knew it wasn't war.

During that time something became clear ... modern industrial society was like a watch. To drop a single pinch of sand into the works was to ruin it. And this was no pinch of sand—it was a truckload.

There was a time during which the world churned like an overset beehive ... It was in this period that the alien cities were built.

AGE
OF
MIRACLES

John Brunner

DAW BOOKS, INC.
DONALD A. WOLLHEIM, PUBLISHER

1633 Broadway, New York, NY 10019

First DAW Printing, March 1985

1 2 3 4 5 6 7 8 9

PRINTED IN U.S.A.

1

Like needles thrust into a wax doll, images stabbed him.

During the summer there was plenty to eat. The fox avoided the place where his world was being invaded: the clanking mysteries, the smoky smells, the bellowing bipeds. Summer ended. For a while there was mud. Rain soaked his coat and sharpened the edge of the wind. By frost there was a hard place and a succession of stinking roars and flashes. The fox turned aside, slinking back into the long grass and the bushes. The grass became dry and yellow, the bushes stood out bare as an engraving against the sky.

Snow brought scarcity.

The fox grew resigned to the new thing in his world. It was not a change he understood, but no more could he control it. Printing his traces in the snow, breaking through the thin frozen crust although lack of food was lightening him daily, he came to the borderline and paused—not for reflection, but because a complex balance of instinctual drives was seesawing between *hunger here* and *unknown there*. A roar began. Automatically the fox ran forward. It was his last action but one.

Afterwards, when they had cleared away the wreckage and the bodies—including the fox's—men came with guns and searched the area. His vixen and his last litter of cubs were shot. On the new road cars went cautiously as winter spread the concrete with a glaze of ice.

He moaned in darkness. Wet, clammy, unpleasant, something slimy on his face, his chest, the front of his legs. Lying in dirt he battled ghosts.

The man—something familiar about him—in a place lit by candles, windowless, the door locked and barred against intruders ... Working, but pausing every few seconds to look around him nervously.

We know very little about them. A sardonic curl of the lip, here. We know beyond a doubt that they can set off fissionables at an indefinite distance because we learned that the hard way. (No, it wasn't funny.)

Another nervous glance, and back to work. Knowledge is the first weapon. People generally say we're fighting in the dark, but you can't call it fighting when you don't know what your enemy is or even whether he regards you as his enemy. (Was that a noise? A footfall? Nothing to be seen ... of course.)

After a petrified pause, the conclusion that it was a trick of over-active imagination. Something found now, something to claim all attention and generate pulse-pounding excitement. Could it possibly——?

He lay alone in darkness, soaked with thin wet mud, and writhed as violently as if the blow had been physical in this instant of time.

*   *   *

Blasphemy! The howl came, the blow followed, then the laughs of triumph. (Shalt not suffer a witch to live.) Seek to probe the secrets of what is hidden not in knowledge but in faith! Blasphemer!

Spittle on his face. Like maddened animals all around. A snag-toothed mouth grown to enormous size, stretching from horizon to horizon and speaking the dogmas. If you would enter the holy city among the shining angels go in humility not arrogance blasphemer and upstart!

After that, boots: kicking again and again.

He tried to crawl away, and his eyes opened. For a little he could not see and thought he must be blind. Then he rolled over, the mud plopping; its sour taste was in his mouth. Man the crown of creation (irony) lying in dirt like a hog in its wallow.

Anger burst out and bloomed in him like a fireball, lighting the landscape of his mind with a beautiful and deadly brilliance. Who put him here in the dirt? Who threw him down in a ditch like a dead cat?

He did.

The man began to pick himself up, clawing at the sides of the trench for a purchase. He felt the horrible clay fill the space between his nails and his fingertips, foul as faeces. His limbs were like wooden rods, uncontrollable. He was about three-quarters dead, but his mind was alive with hate.

Dark—night—dark—night . . .

Over the lip of the ditch he saw lights and thought of lights he had seen before. He desired to go towards them. Clawing, scrabbling, thrusting, he tried to force himself up and out. Failed, and fell back. Like a man handcuffed in a cell awaiting the torturers' return, he railed against the slippery clay, his weak body, his powerlessness. White-hot, the hate crumbled his humanity as lava can crumble a peasant's hut on the slopes of Etna.

Inhuman, he found neither time nor space so impassable a barrier as the sides of this deep trench.

When the figure appeared in the restaurant, everything stopped. Only for one moment was a man's high-pitched voice raised into the appalling silence, closing a bargain with a woman for the night. And then nothing. The remembered sound of chattering and music hung in the air like dust.

His mere presence was a slap in the face. To look at him was to realize what he was, and recall that all humanity had been disgustingly insulted. Not the masquer of the Red Death, not Naaman white with leprosy, could have chilled the company as this man did. Ripped, his clothes hung from him like the bannering rags on a scarecrow made of poles. Dirty brown mud glistened wet on his face, chest and legs. He left smeared footprints as he lurched across the restaurant's floor.

Seconds passed. There were a few half-hearted screams, but it was clear from the focused intensity of the man's burning glare, from the straight-line course he was following, that he was concentrated on one individual among those present. For what? Vengeance? You could not be sure. In this Age of Miracles, you could not be sure of anything.

He's after someone, Den Radcliffe thought. It seemed a vaguely silly idea, like the delusive insights of a dream full of surreal absurdities. *Me. He's coming directly towards me.*

The tick-tock of heartbeats told him that time was passing; so did the foot-dragging approach of the stranger. Nothing else did. As though sunk in a block of transparent plastic he sat rigid beside his companions at the table. The width of the table, at least, was between himself and the intruder.

The distance narrowed to twelve paces, ten, eight. Suddenly the girl on his left—he knew her only as Maura—screamed and leapt to her feet, and others imitated her. The spell broke. Den Radcliffe could move, do something to drive away this horror, break it, smash it, this obscenity walking like a man!

He snatched up what his hand encountered on the table: a heavy glass pitcher full of water. He hurled it, and it struck the man's shoulder, making him check his stride for a second while its contents slopped some of the mud from his cheek.

A bottle, caught around the neck for a club. On his feet now, Den Radcliffe felt all his nerves sing back to life, stinging as a limb stings when circulation returns after tourniquet-like cramp. Bottle raised, liquor spouting from its neck and flowing down his sleeve, he waited in the vain hope of help. The man spoke. His nauseous screeching voice filled the room like air rushing into a punctured vacuum. 'Damn you!' he howled. 'Damn you damn you *damn* you! You did this to me, you bastard!'

Superstition, against his will, shattered the self-control which Radcliffe had already weakened with drink. He swung the bottle and let it go. It broke on the man's forehead, gashing the skin, scattering with a tinkle across the floor. Then there was the long-repressed panic. Chairs crashed over, tablecloths were dragged unheeded by scrambling fighting crazy-milling men and women, shedding cutlery and plates ringing and breaking. The waiters went with the rest; so did the musicians from the band, using their instruments as clubs. A hundred people were rushing the yard-wide exit door before the manager turned on the ceiling panic sprays and oblivion came sifting down like snow.

Still the ghastly figure stood facing Radcliffe. He hurled things at it like wooden balls at a cockshy—bottles, glasses, what his hands chanced on. The table-knives would not throw; their handles were too heavy. A plate caught the air and swung aside, like a badly-aimed discus.

He heard the hissing of the panic sprays, and terror seized him. For all he knew, the *other* confronting him might not breathe, might not draw in air and be immobilized by the anaesthetic. He snatched his own last lungful before the gas came down, hooked his hands under the table's edge and lifted it with insane violence from the floor. As it came up, he somehow got another purchase on its underside so that he leaned forward into it and turned it, brought it slamming down on the impassive, hate-auraed figure, and fell forward, triumph colouring his slide into unconsciousness. After him tumbled and clattered his past and his hopes for the future.

2

'The history of the last years of the twentieth century,' Waldron said under his breath, 'is going to be the story of how nothing happened.'

'What was that?' Across the desk Canfield—suspicious, touchy—stiffened, sure he was being snidely insulted.

'Nothing,' Waldron said. 'Go on.' *That is*, he added without even moving his lips, *if anyone bothers to write history again.*

Canfield was still glaring at him, his dark face full of hostility. Abruptly, unable to bear that scowl any longer, Waldron snapped, 'Go on, damn it! You came to give a report, so spit it out.'

Canfield grunted and turned back the leaves of his notebook. He said, 'I took a crew down to the City of Angels as soon as the call came. It was a shambles, but the manager had turned on the panic sprays. According to him, the weirdo just appeared, on the dais inside the entrance by the checkroom, and walked straight across the room towards one particular table. He watched it happening from a sealed armour-glass compartment on the——'

'I know the City of Angels,' interrupted Waldron.

11

And, as he saw self-righteous disapproval gather in Canfield's mind, added, 'I go there all the time! When I can afford to, anyhow.' He made no attempt to interpret Canfield's reaction in words, but the latter pursed his lips hard for several seconds, as though forcibly blocking off a sharp retort, before he continued.

'Of course, it's ridiculous to say that the weirdo just *appeared*. I brought in the doorman and the bouncer, naturally, and questioned them on the way—they missed most of the gas because they were right next to the exit. Either they're lying or they panicked and don't want to admit it.'

Leaning back in his chair and closing his eyes, Waldron said, 'What state was this weirdo in when you picked him out from under the table?'

His train of thought broken, Canfield hesitated. 'Filthy,' he said at last. 'Smeared with wet mud, ragged, bruised—but some of that was due to things being thrown at him, I guess.'

'A man in that state wouldn't be let into the City of Angels through the main entrance,' Waldron said. 'I'm not asking you to speculate. Just tell me what you found when you arrived.'

Canfield shut his notebook and rose to his feet, his mouth working, his Adam's apple bobbing on his stringy neck. He said, 'What the hell are you trying to do—make me angry enough to give you an excuse for throwing me off the force?'

'Shut up and sit down,' Waldron said. 'Or if you don't want to go on give me your notebook and I'll pick the details out of it myself.'

Canfield took another few heartbeats to boil over. Then he threw the notebook on the desk in front of his chief—it made a noise like an open-handed slap—and strode out, slamming the door. The ill-fitting windows rattled in their frames; the pencils on the desk rattled against each other.

It seemed suddenly very dark in the room, although the high swinging light-bulb was new and free of dust. Waldron sat a while without moving, looking at the black cover of the notebook.

The story of how nothing happened . . .

That was what was going to break James Arnott Waldron: the hysterical pretence that it was still the same old world. One day he was going to scream at some idiot like Canfield and say, 'How the hell dare you claim that you are Man, the lord of creation? You're a rat, you're an insect, you're a dirty little crawling louse scavenging after the angels—a dung-beetle butting at your ball of muck and fooling yourself that you're trundling the sun!'

Why do I hang on here? What's the point? Why don't I simply quit?

His eyes drifted from the oblong of the notebook to the oblong of a map on the wall—not the city map, the hemisphere map. That bore hand-made additions and amendments; you couldn't buy a commercial or even a government-issue map which showed the world as it really was. Consequently he was not altogether certain his was accurate. But it was as truthful as he could make it. Not from masochism, as Canfield and so many other of his colleagues seemed to think. From honesty.

Why can't they understand it's necessary?

The pock-mark gaps in the neat mesh of human symbols—the devastated areas, the fallout zones, into which the lines of highways and railroads led like footsteps over precipices—*had* to be included on the printed map; it would be beyond anybody's powers of self-deception to pretend that Omaha, for instance, still existed. (Though of course you didn't have to keep stating aloud that the city had gone.) But the heavy black border isolating a tongue-shaped area in the centre of North America, the other similar border surrounding a kidney-shaped zone in Western Brazil, and the patches of silver foil like distorted pentagrams which indicated the alien cities—those, Waldron had applied himself the day after he grew tired of the popular fiction that governments in Washington and Ottawa still held sway over the whole of their former territories.

'One day,' Waldron declared to the uncaring air, 'I'll wire up a bell and some flashing lights and stick a sign under the map saying DON'T KID YOURSELF. And fix it so it comes on when the door is opened.' But he knew he wouldn't go that far. It was all very well to insist that people must face the facts; it would take more than words, whether written or spoken, to bring the result about.

He was as scared as anybody else. He was as ready to hide from reality as anybody else. All he had as margin was a kind of shame. He could easily lose it. Maintaining its original force was straining his nerves. Otherwise he wouldn't have snapped at Canfield.

He drove himself to pick up the notebook at last and flip through its pages, seeing the familiar shorthand it was filled with, as clear and as easy to read once you had the context as ordinary print.

Is that symptomatic? So many of us now seem to need to do small things perfectly, as though we're resigned to giving up the big things . . . for good and all.

He hoped not. He thought of his own laborious attempts to perfect Beethoven's Opus 111, first without a wrong note or shaky time-value, then without a flaw of expression. He didn't want to write that off as mere compulsiveness.

All right! The symbols danced on the page. He froze them by an effort of will. At the City of Angels—the name was a gesture of timid defiance, of course, on a par with a boy thumbing his nose at an adult whose back is turned—there had been this extraordinary intrusion. Words like 'extraordinary' were losing their force. Lately you didn't even hear people say as they had used, 'The Age of Miracles is not past'. Now they said, with a wry shrug, 'A of M!'—and that was its own explanation.

Canfield had arrived and found people jammed, physically jammed, in the exit doorway, and sprawled all over the low dais leading to it, dropped where the panic sprays had caught them. And crushed under a table, the weirdo. And on top of the table was the man the manager believed to have been the target of the weirdo's interest. And on the floor nearby two girls and a man who had completed this particular party.

The man lying on the upturned table was called Dennis Radcliffe.

Waldron frowned. The name rang a distant bell. But he couldn't place it immediately. He wasted no time trying to puzzle it out—he could have the records checked easily enough. The manager said Radcliffe had gone wild and started to hurl things: bottles, knives, crockery. But he hadn't seen what happened after that because of the rush for the exit and the need to turn on his gas-sprays.

So Canfield had closed the place, of course and taken all the 140 names of clients and waiters and other staff by a slow process of searching pockets and purses for identity papers, and had brought here the people most directly involved: the manager, the bouncer and the door-keeper he suspected of lying, Radcliffe and the rest of his party, the weirdo himself, and half a dozen people picked at random to give corroborative evidence. A thorough job. Now it was 3.10 a.m. and Waldron felt his vitality at such a low ebb he hated the prospect of sifting through the data Canfield had meticulously assembled. But it was going to have to be done.

Where the hell do you start on a thing like this?

He shut the notebook and thumbed switches on his desk intercom in the hope that it might have started working again by itself. It hadn't, and no one would be in to fix it before nine. He repressed the urge to throw it at the wall and got out of his chair.

The basement, white-tiled and forbidding, always put him in mind of a public lavatory. There was something of the same stench about it, too, when the cells were full. Under harsh lights some of those arrested tonight moaned in their sleep; others, thinking even trying to sleep was futile, sat on hard benches and stared at nothing, eyes rimmed red with weariness. The people from the City of Angels were still unconscious for the most part, and lay like morgue-delivered corpses on the benches and floors in the end three cells.

At Waldron's appearance the men at the desk facing the cells glanced up. There were Rodriguez, the duty sergeant, Dr Morello, one of the regular police surgeons, and Canfield, who glowered and bared his teeth.

Controlling his movements deliberately, Waldron descended the last few steps and held out the notebook. 'I'm sorry I snapped at you, Canfield,' he said. 'Tired, I guess.' He planted an elbow on the corner of the desk. Canfield accepted the notebook and said nothing.

'Well, doc?' Waldron went on, his voice brittle. 'What brings you here—the City of Angels affair, is it?'

Morello, whose eyelids were puffy and whose hair was uncombed, was writing out a report with the stylo chained to the desk in front of Rodriguez, and the chain was hampering. After favouring it with a muttered curse, he said, 'Sure, they dragged me out to look at this weirdo. Could have waited until morning. Any fool could have seen he was dead.'

'Did you say "any fool"?' Canfield inquired in a tone as light as a caress. And when the doctor didn't respond, he went on, 'I did what the regulations say! If you don't like being woken at 2 a.m., you don't have to have a police card. Want us to revoke it?'

Morello grimaced. 'What the hell difference does it make if I get my patients from the police or pick 'em up off the street?' he said sourly. 'Same colour blood, same broken bones whichever way.' Completing the last line of his scribbled report, he signed with a flourish and pushed the paper towards Rodriguez.

'Anybody got a cigarette?' he added. 'I forgot mine.'

'Here.' Waldron proffered a pack. 'I didn't realize the weirdo was dead, by the way.'

'He wasn't when we brought him here,' Canfield supplied. 'He died about ten minutes before I came to see you. I'd have told you if I'd had the chance.'

Ignoring the gibe, Waldron turned to Morello. 'So what killed him? The things Radcliffe threw? The table falling on him?'

The doctor shrugged, 'Contributory, maybe.' He drew on his cigarette, closing his eyes momentarily as though to drown consciousness in the smoke. 'But I doubt if you have a murder charge. Cerebral haemorrhage, far as I can tell. A whole slew of ruptured blood-vessels. His eyes are like cherries. My guess when they open up the skull at the autopsy, his brain will look like it's been stirred with an eggbeater.' He uttered the similes with gloomy relish.

Uncomfortable, Waldron noticed that a woman in the cell directly opposite the desk was listening, her mouth slack, her eyes wide, and that now she was shuddering and licking her lips like a spectator at a *grand guignol* show. He decided not to look at her again.

'Okay,' he said. 'Who was he? Anything known?'

'No papers on him,' Canfield said. 'Nothing. Wearing rags. Looked like he'd been through hell.'

'No tattoo marks or anything like that, either.' Morello spoke through a yawn. 'Body covered in contusions a day or two old, plus fresh ones probably due to what was thrown at him. No major scars.'

'Take his prints, then,' Waldron said. 'Have him cosmeticized and get some as-in-life pictures. Any hope of photographing the retinal patterns, doc?'

'Take the retinas out at the autopsy,' Morello said. 'His eyes are too messy to do a proper job through the corneas. I told you: they're like cherries.'

'A lot of trouble,' Rodriguez grumbled. 'For a weirdo!'

Waldron didn't comment.

'Shouldn't be too much sweat.' Morello yawned again, more widely. 'Got one unusual thing about him, mirror-image layout. Heart on the wrong side, large lobe of the liver on the wrong side, all the way down the line. Shouldn't be surprised if he's one of a pair of identical twins.'

'Ah-hah!' Waldron said. 'Got that, Chico?'

'It's in the report,' Rodriguez grunted.

'So that's finish for me,' Morello said. He picked up his bag from beside the desk. 'Don't bother me too early in the morning. He's in freeze, he won't rot before the afternoon. And I'm short on sleep.'

When his footsteps had died away on the echoing staircase, Waldron beckoned Canfield and walked over to the cells where the unconscious people from the City of Angels were lying.

'Which is Radcliffe?' he asked.

'That's him.' Canfield pointed out a dark-haired man in very expensive clothes. Even in his drugged stupor

his rather swarthy face wore a look of remembered
terror. Waldron spoke to avoid thinking about the reason for that expression.

'We know something about him, don't we? I'm sure
I've heard the name before.'

'Could be, but not because we ever booked him here.
He's the famous Den Radcliffe. Not a nice guy. Free
trader, spends most of his time over with Governor
Grady. They told us from the West Coast he'd been
seen out of Grady's territory. Maybe you spotted the
name on the teletype.'

Not a nice guy! Hell of a mealy-mouthed way to put it!
And anyway, what right did a Canfield have to dismiss
such a man as his inferior? More gutsy than a Canfield,
at least: not content to lie down in the shelter of the
universal cheap pretences . . .

'Should we start with him?' Canfield proposed—eager,
perhaps, to shift this living reminder of the plight of
the world from under the roof they presently shared.
Waldron had intended to leave Radcliffe until later
anyway; hearing Canfield's tone, he felt the decision
gilded with a veneer of malicious pleasure.

'No, I'll start with the manager and his staff, and the
people you picked up for corrobs. I'll have Radcliffe
and the party who were with him after I've got the
general picture from the ones who weren't directly
involved.'

For a moment he thought Canfield was going to raise
objections. But he merely shrugged and called Rodriguez
to open the first cell.

3

     Appeared out of thin air. Looked around and spotted Radcliffe. Walked straight towards him—no, more kind of *plodded*, like he had weights tied to his ankles. Said something. Things were thrown. Panic, and oblivion. No, never saw him before. No idea who he might have been. Anyway, how to tell when his face was plastered with mud?

By the time he had picked through a dozen substantially identical stories, Waldron was regretting his petty desire to extend Canfield like a man on the rack. When Radcliffe was finally shown into the office he studied him with unconcealed curiosity. Radcliffe returned it with interest, his gaze lingering a long while on the hand-altered map pinned to the wall before he obeyed Waldron's invitation to come and sit down.

'You're Dennis W. Radcliffe, that right?' Waldron said.

'Right.' Radcliffe crossed his legs. 'Mind if I smoke?'

'Go ahead.' Waldron turned the pedestal mike on the desk a little more towards the other's mouth. 'This interview is being—'

' . . . Recorded and may subsequently be used in

evidence,' Radcliffe interrupted wearily. 'I've been through this sort of drill before.'

'Have you had the full treatment?' Waldron countered. 'The man you threw the table at is dead.'

For a moment a wary flicker showed in Radcliffe's face. It vanished, and he was shrugging. 'So? The panic sprays were on. Between inhalation and unconsciousness there's a period when a man isn't necessarily responsible for his actions.'

Neat. Waldron took a cigarette for himself, wondering what set a Radcliffe so far apart from a Canfield.

'Are you making a charge?' Radcliffe added.

'Not yet. Do you wish legal representation?'

'Why should I, before you make a charge?'

'Yes or no, please!'

'Not yet—and I quote.' Radcliffe grinned without mirth.

Waldron let it go at that. 'Particulars, then. Age, birthplace, current address, permanent domicile, profession.'

'Born Minneapolis. Age forty.' Waldron had imagined him five years younger. 'Hotel White Condor, suite 215. And I'm a free trader with a permanent domicile just outside Gradyville, but I don't believe you recognize the existence of such a place.'

Defiance flavoured the last words. Waldron extended his hand. 'Documents?'

'They impounded them downstairs.'

Waldron cursed inwardly. But Rodriguez must have done that to save time in compiling the written report; he couldn't complain.

'Right, let's go straight to the point. What's your version of this affair?'

It dovetailed exactly with the other accounts he had heard, but included one significant addition.

'He spoke to me,' Radcliffe said. 'He sounded crazy-mad. He said something like, "Damn you, you did this to me!" I concluded he was insane and obviously dangerous.'

'Are you qualified to pass judgement on people's sanity?'

'I deal with a wide and varied cross-section of the public in my profession,' Radcliffe answered, without the bat of an eye.

'Go on.'

'He made a move towards me which after his *seemingly* insane verbal attack I interpreted as hostile. To forestall an actual assault I threw a water-jug at him.'

A pause. 'Is that all?' Waldron pressed.

'When he kept coming, I threw something else—I forget what, because it was about then that the panic sprays came on. I made to raise the table as a barrier between us, I recall that, but I lost consciousness while doing so. I woke up on being revived in the cell downstairs.'

Waldron probed further, but Radcliffe was too cagy to qualify what he had said. He switched the line of his approach.

'Who was this man? Had you seen him before?'

'Not to my knowledge. Of course, he was a weirdo, so—'

'What makes you so sure?'

'Jesus! I'll lay a bet that people in the restaurant who'd never before been within a hundred miles of one pegged him as soon as they laid eyes on him. And me, I've seen plenty.'

Waldron hesitated. He said, 'You describe yourself as a free trader. Define the term.'

Oddly ill at ease for a moment, Radcliffe said, 'I buy and sell—uh—rare artefacts.'

'In the vicinity of the so-called alien city?'

Radcliffe lifted his chin half an inch. 'Yes.'

'That's where you've seen so many weirdos?'

'Of course.' Radcliffe had apparently expected the questioning to turn overtly hostile; recognizing he was wrong, he sounded puzzled. 'That's why I say I hadn't seen this character before to my knowledge. I didn't recognize him, I don't know his name or anything about him, but conceivably he may have seen me— uh . . .'

'On Grady's Ground?' Waldron suggested softly. His superiors wouldn't like that in the official record, but the hell with them. 'What were you supposed to have done to him?'

'Heaven knows.'

'You don't recall offending a weirdo lately, maybe?'

'I wouldn't even know how to go about it. They kind of lose touch with the world everyone else lives in, you know. Most of them are harmless, but some aren't. So I keep my distance from them.'

'I see. So you'd never consciously met the guy, you don't know and won't guess what grudge he had against you, he made a crazy-sounding verbal attack on you which you thought was about to turn physical, and you were trying to drive him back when the panic sprays went on and you fell on him with the table. That correct?'

'That's the size of it.'

Waldron studied the other for a few seconds, then gave a noncommittal grunt. 'How about the other people at your table? Who were they?'

'The man's called Terry Hyson. A business contact of mine. I don't know anything about the girls except the blonde is called Sue and the brunette is called Maura. Terry provided them for the evening. I guess he had them from a supply agency.'

'They charge?'

'Two-fifty.' Radcliffe shrugged.

They would, of course. Someone like Radcliffe wasn't apt to get it any other way outside his home ground. As though Grady's dirt, rather than his own guts, were the significant thing. Abruptly Waldron found himself feeling angry on Radcliffe's behalf. He said, 'Okay, I guess that's enough. If we want you again we'll trace you through Hyson or at your hotel. When do you plan to leave the city?'

'Not before the weekend, as things stand.' If Radcliffe was surprised the interview had been so easy, he didn't show it.

'Fine. You can go.' Waldron moved pencils randomly on his desk.

But Radcliffe didn't make to leave at once. His gaze roamed the office, coming to rest on the hemisphere map, at which he jerked a thumb.

'You haven't got it quite right.'

'What do you mean?'

'This.' Radcliffe rose and approached the map, laying his finger on the western edge of the black tongue-shaped outline defining Grady's Ground. 'Goes forty-fifty miles farther west here.'

'Thanks for the information,' Waldron muttered.

'You been out that way?' Radcliffe cocked his head.

'No.'

'You should.' He gave a crooked smile. 'Some time when you get sick of making phoney gestures in this smelly little room, come out and see me. I'm not hard to track down.'

How the hell did he know? For a short eternity Waldron saw nothing but Radcliffe's eyes, and then he heard himself say, 'I guess—yes, maybe I will. Maybe I will.'

When the door closed, Waldron found he was sweating. His teeth were going to chatter if he didn't set his jaw hard. He looked towards the window. Dawn was breaking over the city.

He was kidding himself, worse than the Canfields of the world. Radcliffe had seen right through him in a few minutes. Sticking a map on the wall and thinking that was as far as honesty need go . . .

The door opened and the first girl came in. She was very pretty, with sleek dark hair braided to the back of her head with gold wire, but she looked peaked with cold. Not surprisingly. She wore a synsilk nightsuit of dark red tassels on net covering her left arm and breast, her belly and buttocks, and her right leg. *Two-fifty,* Waldron thought. *At that price I guess she can afford to shiver.*

'Sit down,' he said. 'Name?'

'Maura Knight.' She dropped into the chair. 'Got a cigarette?'

'No. Particulars?'

When she gave her profession as 'secretary', he pounced. 'So what are you charging Radcliffe—overtime?'

'Sure, overtime!' she snapped. 'If you know girls who don't charge, they're probably rich!'

Waldron framed a retort, then sighed and changed his mind. It wasn't her fault that nowadays sex seemed to be bought and sold more often than given, as though along with its old ambitions the human race had abandoned any conception of love in the bright awful shadow of Earth's invaders.

He asked for her version of events, and she recited it in dull fatigued tones. Once again it tallied exactly, up to the point at which the weirdo spoke. And then a little life seemed to enter her; she sat forward on the chair, looking past him into memory, and her voice rose from its former colourless level to a pitch almost to be called passionate.

'He said something like, "You did this to me, you damned bastard!" I looked at Den—I mean Radcliffe. I've never *seen* such a murderous look! He picked up this heavy jug and threw it, and that wasn't enough. The weirdo hadn't done anything and he still didn't do anything. He just kept glaring, his face full of hate. And Radcliffe threw a bottle, and it smashed on his head!' She closed her eyes and sank back. Staring at her, Waldron saw her swallow as though fighting the need to vomit.

'I tell you, I saw him smash the bottle on the guy's head. And then he threw anything else he could find, like a lunatic trying to ruin a doll. Plates, knives, anything. As though he'd gone completely berserk.'

Waldron didn't say anything. But he wondered why she hated Radcliffe so, on such short acquaintance.

'He was trying to throw the whole damned *table* when the gas came on! Listen, why did he want to do that?' She opened her eyes again, this time wide with incredulity. 'Sure, this weirdo looked revolting, but—but . . . Oh, I don't know much about these things, but I always thought a weirdo gets that way because he doesn't just sit around like everybody else letting himself be treated like vermin by the—the whatever they are. He's someone who's tried to do something, even if he has wound up crazy. I think he was telling the truth. I think he wanted to get his own back because Radcliffe had done something terrible to him. Cheated him, maybe. How do the free traders get their stuff, anyway? Do they really scavenge for it, or do they leave the dirty work to other people and kick them out if they take one risk too many and lose their minds?'

'Shut up,' Waldron said coldly. He was taken aback, not only to hear her uttering comments on this level, but also to find that he half-wanted her to continue.

Even to talk about defiance was better than ignoring reality altogether.

'You met Radcliffe for the first time last evening, didn't you?' he demanded.

She gave a sullen nod.

'Then you'd better think twice before jumping to slanderous conclusions, hadn't you?'

She was ice-calm suddenly. 'Weren't you just trying to insinuate me into your records as a professional prostitute? After an even shorter acquaintance!'

He was in acute danger of losing his temper, Waldron realized, and over people he didn't give a damn about at that. He told her to go. Shivering, she moved towards the door. Just before going out, she gave him a glance sharp with contempt.

She has no right . . . But the thought would not complete.

When he had spoken to Hyson and the other girl, Susan Vey, he felt physically and emotionally drained. He could risk napping for the rest of his tour if Canfield had nothing more for him—but to find out whether that was so, he would have to go down to the basement again. *Damn* that intercom.

As he turned the corner of the stairway and came in sight of the cells, the fact that some of the prisoners had broken out of their apathy and were staring towards the desk told him something must be wrong. He hurried down the next half-dozen steps and could then see for himself: Canfield and Rodriguez were each grasping Radcliffe by one arm, while facing him, her cheeks very white, her lower lip puffy and a trickle of blood creeping out of the corner of her mouth, Maura Knight still held up her hands defensively as though to ward him off.

4

Waldron felt as though the world was throwing events at his head the way Radcliffe had bombarded the weirdo (*had* it been like a madman smashing a doll?) and it was making him giddy. It seemed when he spoke that plates of hard dry skin were flaking around his mouth.

'What the hell is going on?' he demanded.

Canfield and Rodriguez let Radcliffe go. The trader took a step back and shrugged his coat into place around his shoulders, his expression stony as a statue's. Canfield jerked a thumb at him.

'I imagine Radcliffe is going back in the cage,' he said. 'I never saw a man hit a woman like that before. Did he break any teeth?' he added to Maura.

She shook her head numbly. Feeling the blood on her chin, she wiped at it with the back of her hand.

'What for?' Waldron said, addressing Radcliffe.

'She didn't expect to find me waiting for her,' Radcliffe snarled. 'Thought she could slip out of here and sneak off home. But I want value for the two-fifty I gave her!'

'You can have the money!' the girl cried. 'You——'

'I want what I paid for! Come across, or I'll help myself. It's up to you!'

'Be quiet!' Canfield rapped. 'I don't know what the hell you do on Grady's Ground, and I don't care. But what you're going to do here is head back into a cell the moment she says the word.'

'Listen, you wooden-headed angel-chaser!' Radcliffe began, balling a fist.

'Hold it!' Waldron barked. 'You! What's your name? You, Maura! Want to charge him with assault?'

'No, I don't want to have to see him again, even in court. He can take his dirty money. Now I have some idea how he gets it I'd rather be rid of it before I catch——'

'Chico!' Waldron exclaimed, and Rodriguez clamped down on Radcliffe's arm before it could deliver a second punch. 'Take your money, Radcliffe. Count yourself lucky she doesn't want her pound of flesh. Free traders aren't any too popular around here.'

The anger drained from Radcliffe all at once. He relaxed, eyes on Waldron. 'I guess you're right,' he admitted. 'You take the money off her, then. If I go any closer I'm apt to forget my good manners.'

Where the hell could she be carrying money in that outfit, anyway? Oh: the gold-braided hair on the back of her head was a chignon. She lifted it off, produced the bills; Canfield returned them to Radcliffe.

'Now—out,' he grunted. 'And remember what the lieutenant said. You're *damned* lucky.'

'Aren't you going to give me a head start over him?' Maura said. 'You heard him say he didn't want the money, he'd rather take what he paid for.'

Radcliffe grinned. Waldron caught the expression as it came and went, but couldn't be sure whether it was wry or—what to call it? Vicious? He passed his hand across his face.

'Send her home in a squad car, God damn it!' he ordered. 'Anything for the sake of peace and quiet!'

In the main lobby he paused, looking out through the doors at the early-morning street. A cleansing cart was crawling by, its huge vacuum mouths slurping up their diet of litter, its hind end giving back a flood of detergent and water like urine. His mind seemed to switch off, and minutes passed without his realizing. Then there came a tap on his shoulder.

'I appreciate what you did for me there, lieutenant,' Radcliffe said. 'Back home, I guess I'm in the habit of doing as I see fit and to hell with the consequences. It isn't often that someone can talk me around as neatly as you just did. I'll settle matters some other way, or if I can't, what the hell? Either way, I promise it won't concern you.'

He drew back half a pace and looked Waldron over with a searching stare.

'Don't forget what I said, will you? I'm accustomed to making snap judgements, you know—I have to, because all the time people are wandering on to the Ground, and I have to decide usually on the basis of a five-minute chat whether it's worth hiring them or letting them go to somebody else. And I've made my mind up about you. I have a security problem. You could handle it the way I want. Give me the chance to return the favour—come out where things actually happen. You said you very well might.'

Had he really said so? The memory of his own words came back to Waldron from infinitely long ago. He gave a listless nod.

'Great. Take your time to think it over, of course. But my guess is that you've already had your bellyful of this playacting. See you shortly!'

With a smile and a wave Radcliffe headed for the exit, while Waldron returned to his office.

Like a lunatic trying to smash a doll . . .?

He had thought of laying his head on the desk and trying to doze away the last hour of his shift, but that was out of the question, for he could hear the sounds of the building coming to daytime life: office-cleaning machines going up and down the service racks between floors, coffee-and-rolls trolleys rattling down the corridors for the overnight staff. One more mortal hour before he could leave. Of course, this had been a good night in one sense—no shootings, no arson, no gang-rumbles or major riots . . .

How were things in the old days?

The coffee trolley stopped at his door and hooted. He collected his ration. Sipping it, puffing at the latest of too many cigarettes tonight, he stared at the map. Radcliffe had claimed that Grady's western boundary reached forty or fifty miles farther out. If he made the change, nobody would notice. Or—well, they might, but they'd think of it as a gibe, not an attempt to face the truth. *De jure,* they would say, the U.S.A. is still the U.S.A., Canada is still Canada. *De facto,* of course—but that's not exactly our fault, is it?

Where would we have got to by now if the aliens hadn't come?

He remembered the beginning with fearful vividness. No one had known what was really happening, of course—they'd taken it for a mere crisis in human affairs. Internal, so to say. (Almost funny, that. Like a cerebral haemorrhage. It occurred to him that the reason why Morello had been so pleased with his comparison of the weirdo's eyes to cherries was that a kind of dark cherry was called a Morello.)

With casual simultaneity, all fissionable material on the planet had been exploded with an efficiency ranging from eight to eighteen percent conversion. Every missile and bomber base; every bomb in flight; every nuclear power station and every refinery where the stocks exceeded a couple of kilograms had mushroomed into fire. It was a day and a half before the survivors knew it wasn't war. With the exception of those who would have started such a war. They knew. But for that day and a half they withheld their knowledge out of panic.

During that time something became clear which previously governments and general staffs had preferred to play down, since they still existed in a fantasy world where concepts like 'victory' and 'conquest' were meaningful. Modern industrial society was like a watch. To drop a single pinch of sand into the works was to ruin it. And this was no pinch of sand—it was a truckload. The anti-missile missiles, ranked in sets of forty per million population, naturally did the most damage; each had a warhead designed to knock down an enemy rocket on a seven-mile near miss. The bombers and I.C.B.M.'s were in comparatively isolated districts, or aboard submarines far out to sea, while the Minutemen and other city-wreckers wasted their blast on their underground silos.

It wasn't the explosions, or the gigantic fires—worst on the West Coast, where they swept thousands of square miles at the end of a dry summer—or even the fallout which caused the disruption of North America. It was the people who fled from the fires, abandoning their homes and their jobs; it was the plagues which ran through refugee camps when city-dwellers drank bad water; it was the National Guardsmen and hastily sworn-in armed deputies who fought pitched battles to turn back swarms of metropolitan fugitives made mindless by terror when they reached the outskirts of smaller towns. In Europe things were infinitely worse, because the giant opposed armies went into battle like machines turned on by the nuclear explosions, and ravaged both Germanies, most of Czechoslovakia and parts of other countries before it was possible to switch them off.

There was a time—according to what event one chose to mark its ending, one said it lasted weeks or months—during which the planet churned like an overset beehive, and nobody seemed able to think far enough ahead to restore any organization. It was in this period that the alien cities were built.

One said: 'alien city'. And was no wiser.

Bewildered governments brought their immediate problems under control, arranged emergency food supplies, drafted doctors to the rash of refugee camps, charted the fallout zones, and learned with relief and dismay that the calamity was as world-wide as the distribution of fissionables. It was in Israel and India, Chile and China. (Inevitably, though, the countries where weapons had been readied suffered worst.)

Also they learned that in the north middle west of the U.S.A. almost touching the Canadian border, in western Brazil, in Russia a short distance east of the Urals, in Australia's Nullarbor Plain, and in the Antarctic, there were . . . strangenesses. From the air they were seen as distorted five-pointed stars, glowing translucent, vaster than any city yet seeming to be single buildings—if they were buildings. There was energy in them; the radio bands crackled with static, electrical storms gathered around them, and occasionally a shattering noise was heard, though such phenomena dwindled and eventually ceased. Within the boundaries of these places—misty, sometimes nearly opaque and sometimes glass-clear, constantly radiating unpredictable patterns of colour—could be discerned shining entities. Question mark.

People thought: invasion. And within a few more

weeks moved against the intruders. It was still impossible to assemble more than two or three kilograms of fissionable material anywhere; that was tried and proved. But they sent armies with conventional bombs and rockets, and thought in terms of siege, and were repulsed with madness.

What it was due to—poison gas, telepathic bombardment, mass hypnotism, a virus—no one knew. But the armies dispatched against the shining cities reached a certain point which might not even be in sight of their target, and then mutinied and turned back. They raved across the countryside wrecking, looting, burning—fire gave them especial pleasure and they would stand watching a haystack blaze until it was almost all ash, then pour gasoline on it to enjoy another few minutes of flame. Overhead, planes released their bombs anywhere but on the alien cities, then sought a funeral pyre in a human city or, most favoured, an oilfield.

It became impossible to pretend to the continuance of national government anywhere near the alien-controlled areas. You couldn't tell whether the army battalion which came to invest your town was under orders from Washington—or Moscow, come to that, for the terror reigned everywhere—to protect you, or was waiting with lunatic glee for night to fall so that your home might be set ablaze with maximum spectacle.

Little by little things settled towards a semblance of normality. No further assaults were made on the alien cities. It was in their vicinity that chaos lasted longest. Realizing that no government would dare send in troops to re-establish authority for fear of adding to the toll of those rendered insane, a few men saw their chance, and snatched at it. In Russia, the man who emerged as ruler of the no-man's-land was called Buishenko; in Australia it was Villiers-Hart; in Brazil, Neveira; and in North America the self-styled 'Governor' Grady.

These had fought other, less astute rivals to seize the reins of effective power in the lull between the extremity of the crisis and the present. It did not seem to matter if humans squabbled among themselves in plain sight of the alien cities; the madness only struck if they actually contemplated an attack.

Like speculative builders erecting apartments on the San Andreas fault, like peasants farming the slopes of a volcano, others joined them and accepted their arbitrary rule. They were lured by greed.

For there were what Radcliffe had called 'rare artefacts' —the garbage, perhaps, of the non-human beings who had descended on Earth. They hinted at fantastic new principles, undiscovered laws of nature, energy-states which were neither matter nor radiation. Instantly, commercial and governmental interests set to squabbling and bargaining for them. In the States all that was found was nominally Federal property, but the decree was a nullity. So, trading like vermin on the refuse of a higher species, Grady and his counterparts enjoyed a tenuous security.

But it took guts, didn't it, to perch there on the volcano's lip, trying to snatch meagre clues to the nature of the invaders? Most of humanity, ran a phrase which seemed apposite to Waldron, was writhing like a snake with a broken back. The free traders were at least the equal of rats . . . also a species preying on the leavings of a higher one.

His aimless musing was interrupted. The door opened to reveal Canfield, extremely weary. He said, 'About the weirdo . . .' And waved a sheet of teletype paper.

'Yes?' Waldron stirred. 'Have you identified him?'

'Not exactly. But you remember what Morello said—he might be one of a pair of identical twins, seeing his body is laid out mirror-fashion. So when Washington said they didn't have his prints on file, I said to try reversing them.'

'Ah, hell!' Waldron said with incipient scorn. 'Not even twins have identical prints, you know that.'

Canfield bristled. 'Haven't you put me down enough for one night, even yet?' he snapped. 'Not that I give a shit anyhow. I *found* his twin.'

'*What?*'

'See for yourself.' Canfield dropped the paper on the desk. 'A guy called Corey Bennett. Works for the Federal Scientific Service. The match-up of the prints is *exact.*'

A cold shiver invaded Waldron's spine. 'But it's impossible,' he said faintly.

'A of M!' Canfield grunted, and marched out.

5

'Are you *sure* it isn't a trap?' Jespersen said again.

Orlando Potter glanced around. All lights were out on the bridge of the jet-driven Coast Guard launch, bar the shaded lamp over the navigation table, but the northern summer sky was bright enough to show faces. Not for the first time he regretted bringing along the rangy Swedish-born physicist as 'scientific adviser'—hell, what use was human science where the aliens were concerned? Irritation embrittling his voice, he said, 'I've *told* you! We know beyond a shadow of doubt they're desperate. Isn't that proved by what they did for Congreve?'

Not turning his head, continuing to stare across the smooth shield of the sea, Congreve gave a cynical grunt. 'I sometimes think you've stopped regarding Russians as human, doctor! They're as capable of being frightened as you and I. And believe me, they *are* frightened.'

Improbably out of place in this stark, almost warlike setting—blonde hair hanging loose, make-up impeccable, her only concession to the task in hand being her choice of a jerkin-and-pants suit in dark suede rather than one of her regular bright and revealing costumes—Greta Delarue tossed in one of the innocent-seeming questions that often made it impossible even for Potter to tell which way her mind was running ... and she had been his mistress for six months now.

'Obviously, Mike. But which are they more scared of: the aliens, or Buishenko?'

Congreve didn't reply immediately. During the pause Potter found himself studying the spy for the latest of many, many times, struggling to discern from some outward clue whether his loyalty had been undermined.

Congreve was still in Russian clothes: the green zip-fronted jacket, the black pants with elasticized cuffs and baggy calves reminiscent of Cossack breeches which had been fashionable at the latest period when there were still fashions to engage the attention of Russia's prosperous new class. His Moscow-styled hair was growing out of its intended neatness, but since his return he had hardly had time for such minor problems as getting it trimmed.

By their tens of thousands, Potter thought, *men in such clothes are falling under Buishenko's sway. He's gobbling up Russia like a new Khan of the Golden Horde. Did any of his agents get to Congreve? And if so—how?*

'I wish,' Congreve said finally, 'people could be cured of this contempt for spies! I'm a damned good spy, and proud of it. I've been in and out of the Soviet Union for more than eight years, and they still weren't sure I was a foreigner even when they decided to make their approach. They took a gamble. I spent a full week checking before I came into the open. And they sent me out through Austria by one of their own routes, on a government pass with 10,000 roubles and the message. In my judgement they're equally scared of both the aliens and Buishenko because you can't separate them. If it hadn't been for the aliens he could never have achieved power. You haven't seen what he's doing to Russia. I have!'

Abandoning his contemplation of the sea at last, he turned. 'That's not like Grady's Ground, for God's sake—it's not just a kind of make-believe Gold Rush enclave! It's a cancer of barbarism, and it's spreading like a forest fire!'

'I only wish'—Potter heard his own voice with vague surprise—'that we knew exactly what we're supposed to be waiting for.'

'It could be any of half a dozen things.' Greta shrugged. 'My guess is an alien device in operating condition. If I'm right, it would be worth much greater risks than those we're actually taking.'

Jespersen snorted. He was a tall man, and anxiety had wasted him until his skin hung loose on his bones. His hair, which had been light brown before the coming of the aliens, had turned to silver and started to fall away almost by the handful. 'Going by what they told Congreve, we can't be certain of anything. A lot of gibberish and doubletalk, that's what I call it.'

'Here we go again,' muttered Congreve. 'I was hoping that scientists might be a bit less hidebound than politicians, or my own people, but it seems I was wrong . . . No, Dr Jespersen, it wasn't gibberish! It made perfectly good sense. They've managed to get their hands on something which Buishenko will stop at nothing to get back. They can't keep it in the Soviet Union because the country is just tumbling around their ears. They can't take it out westwards because Central Europe is impassable on land and anyhow Buishenko controls half their surviving anti-aircraft guns and missiles and any plane they tried to put into the sky would probably be shot down. There is no point in taking it out northwards; that's a dead end, and it would probably be stuck in Finland until Buishenko marched in there, too. But they did think they could get it out through Vladivostok and if I could arrange safe custody for it on delivery they'd make the attempt.' His voice was tinged with weariness. Potter wondered how often he had already recited this story—under hypnosis, under drugs, his mind being probed to its roots in search of any hint of treason.

The radio mounted over the navigation table came to life, and the naval commander sitting there answered without taking his eyes from the radar screen.

'Harlequin, Harlequin—pawn to rook four!'

'Columbine,' a distant voice said. 'Queen to queen one, check.'

'They're coming!' Potter said under his breath, and moved to peer over the commander's shoulder. At the helm the captain—also naval, not a Coastguard officer—demanded to know whether they had a fix yet.

The commander shut off the radio briefly to say he had a blip at the extreme limit of range, but nothing definite, and relayed similar information in verbal code to the headquarters ship referred to as Columbine. It was a curious makeshift fleet they had mounted to carry out this operation: after the world-wide destruction of fissionables, the Navy was left without its aircraft carriers, without its cruisers and destroyers, without its nuclear submarines . . . 'Columbine' had been a lowly pre-atomic sub-chaser, cocooned and due for the scrap-yard.

An eternal pause followed, during which all their eyes focused achingly on the commander's face, eerily lit by the shaded yellow lamp above, the green glow of the radar below.

'Harlequin,' he said finally. 'Discovered check—very neat. King's knight to queen five.'

'If anybody's listening,' Jespersen grumbled, 'they'll

be damned sure we're not just playing chess to pass the time!'

'The moves are legal!' Congreve snapped. 'It may not be a good game, but it is a game! Damn it, I spent two weeks working up the code, didn't I?'

Jespersen scowled but fortunately forebore to answer.

'What the hell . . .?' the commander said, half to himself. 'Either there's something wrong with the radar, or—no, it's really there!'

'What?' the captain snapped.

'I don't know. Not quite what we were expecting, that's definite. The range is closing on every sweep, and the speed . . .' The commander checked a printed list pasted beside the radar screen. 'Christ. It says sixty-five knots. Are you sure we're expecting a watergoing vessel, Mr Congreve?'

'That's what I was told,' Congreve answered. 'I guess they might have managed to get their hands on a plane after all, but at the time they were quite definite. In any case that's too slow for a plane, isn't it?'

'A helicopter, wave-hopping to keep below following radar?' Greta offered.

'Possible,' the commander conceded. 'But could we have silence now, please?'

He resumed his coded contact with the headquarters ship.

Pointlessly, Potter, Greta and Jespersen formed up in a line to stare in the direction from which the Russian craft was approaching, though they well knew nothing was to be seen as yet.

'How soon will it be close enough for us to spot it?' Jespersen muttered, fingering a pair of binoculars on a strap around his chicken-thin neck.

'Depends what size it is, doesn't it?' Congreve answered mockingly, and the tall Swede flushed.

The voice from Columbine muttered, 'Uh—now what

the . . .? Oh yeah. Castle king side, check and double-check on the next move. With the queen's knight. Better watch it.'

'What's that supposed to mean?' Jespersen growled.

'They're being followed,' Potter said. 'Right, Congreve?'

The spy nodded, gazing anxiously up into the twilit sky.

Their own vessel's 'counter-move' Potter failed to catch. That didn't matter, though, for the next statement from headquarters was about pawn taking pawn, and from somewhere astern a string of half a dozen glowing objects crossed the zenith like shooting stars in reverse. Tension grew. Then——

'Got them!' Greta said with uncharacteristic excitement. Something had shone red on the horizon and faded instantly.

'What was it, could you tell?' Potter asked the commander in a hushed voice.

'Air pursuit,' the officer answered equally quietly. 'I don't know why the shots came from astern, though. We're supposed to have a couple of conventional-missile ships ahead of us."

'Guard your queen!' Columbine said sharply, and in the same moment Jespersen, binoculars raised, let out a muffled exclamation.

Even without glasses Potter could not only see the thing rushing towards them, but recognize that there was something peculiar about its design as soon as its movement attracted his eye. 'What is it?' he exclaimed.

'I think it's a *Red Whale*,' Congreve said.

Potter struggled to make sense of an incongruous lopsided form half in, half out of the water. 'What's a *Red Whale*, for God's sake?'

'Hydro-aerofoil,' Greta said unexpectedly. 'Four turbines, two underwater foils, two wings. Experimental. Meant for high-speed transit in the China Sea. If it's only doing sixty-five knots it's loafing. Its design speed is 110.'

'Shut up!' the captain ordered, and Potter realized they must have missed some vital exchange with Columbine, for the whine of the engines had sharpened noticeably.

The commander gave a nod, and the captain's hand shot to the power control. He barked at his passengers. 'Hold on to something! Here we go!'

They all grabbed at the metal rails which ringed the bridge, and in the same second the pursuit launch took off: bump-bump-slap on three consecutive waves and then up on its foils and dead steady, like a limousine on a concrete road. The plume of the jets stretched astern for a hundred yards.

'Something wrong?' Potter demanded.

'Very,' the captain confirmed. 'There's a 'copter up there with infra-red cameras and an electron-multiplier. Pilot reports one wing shot off the Russian—ah—vessel, one engine stopped to balance the drag, and a nose-down attitude. Must have been hit before we took out the plane that was chasing her.'

'I can see the damage!' Jespersen burst out. 'How is it still afloat?'

Potter seized a spare pair of binoculars from an overhead rack he had only just noticed. Jespersen was right. Not only was one wing of the awkward craft missing; there was a hole in the hull, and water was slapping up towards it.

The radio emitted an abrupt blast of frantic Russian. Congreve was translating before he was asked.

'They're in great danger—at this speed the hydro-foils hit a critical resonance and make the hull shiver—if they reduce speed they'll drop and water will come through the hole—if they go faster they'll tip over because of the missing wing! They must ditch as soon as possible! If we can come close and pick them out of the water flash a light three times.'

Instantly the captain hit the main deck-lights switch. The whole of the boat stood out in sudden glaring whiteness.

'Look!' Greta whispered.

The monstrous, misshapen Russian vessel had swung broadside in a terrific swirl of spray. Something detached from it: a jettisoned hatch, leaving a bright oblong on the hull. A figure tumbled out. Another. Another. Like toys."

'But why on the turn like?' the captain said to no one in particular. And then : 'oh, of course. Centrifugal force—toss them clear of the wake.'

'Whoever's at the helm knows his business,' the commander said soberly.

The captain dropped the launch back to slow ahead and the uneven rocking of the waves. A searchlight from her bow swept the water and picked up three bobbing heads in quick succession.

The *Red Whale* completed a 180° turn and slammed back on its original track. One more doll-like figure dived out—and a heartbeat later the craft dipped, dug its nose in, and shattered to pieces with a grinding roar.

'Made it!' Potter cried, beside himself with uncontrollable excitement.

'The hell you say,' Greta snapped. Potter gave her a blank stare. She repeated: 'The hell you say! Whatever they were bringing, they didn't push it through the escape hatch, did they? I only saw men going into the water, not taking anything with them—which means the reason for all our trouble is at the bottom of the Pacific!'

6

In the excitement of watching the brilliant manoeuvre carried out by the Russian helmsman, Potter had completely forgotten about the consignment they were expecting; he had been concentrating on the figures pitching out of the emergency door. And for the next several minutes too much was happening to permit quiet thought. He comforted himself with the idea that perhaps the precious object—whatever it was— might be very small, pocket-sized . . . though that hardly matched the scale of the alien cities or the mysterious entities which had been glimpsed within them.

All four of the survivors' life-jackets had inflated properly, and although one of them appeared to be unconscious and they were widely scattered, there was no need for excessive haste. Potter stood by on the afterdeck while muscular sailors operated a retrieval device : a cross between a grapnel and a lasso designed to catch a floating body in a padded ring.

First to be rescued was a grossly fat man whose lifejacket would barely fasten over his chest. He was coughing helplessly from a lungful of water, and had still not recovered from his convulsions when the second followed: a pale man with a spade-shaped brown beard salted with grey.

This one was in sufficiently good shape to stand unaided as he reached the deck, and even to bow his thanks to the sailor who had hauled him up. Congreve addressed him in Russian and at once had both his hands clasped fervently.

'What's he saying?' Potter whispered.

'His name's Alexei Zworykin. Medical doctor. Says he was never so glad in his life as when he saw us flash our lights.'

'What's his reason for coming along?'

'I haven't asked that yet.' Congreve resumed his questioning.

Number three to be fished up was the unconscious one. The instant he came into view at the gunwale, limp as a dead fish, Zworykin forgot everything and dashed forward with an oath. Dropping to his knees, he checked the newcomer's pulse and rolled back his eyelids. He uttered an impatient order to Congreve.

'We must get him below at once,' the ex-spy relayed. 'He has a very frail constitution.'

'I can believe that,' Potter agreed. The white impassive faced showing above the collar of the life-jacket was somehow—wrong. Deformed. The features were in a false relationship: forehead too low, eyes too far apart, mouth slack and idiotic.

'He's diabetic,' Congreve said. 'Also has a skin disease and something else—a medical term—I can't remember the English for.'

'Well, if he's here presumably he's important,' Potter grunted. 'Get them below and see the doctor's given whatever he needs.'

He turned to see how the fat man was, and found Greta and Jespersen in halting conversation with him, their Russian badly accented and full of struggling pauses. Even so, Potter—who had not even a nodding acquaintance with the language—felt envious.

'Who is he?' he inquired.

He had meant the question for Greta, but it was Jespersen who replied, with thinly veiled contempt. 'Don't you recognize him? Pavel Abramovitch, their Minister of Science!'

Of course! Potter damned himself for not identifying the man, but somehow, even after what Congreve had reported, he hadn't expected anyone of this eminence to be with the party. Abramovitch was no chair-polishing career politician, either—he had already been an Academician of the U.S.S.R. with a noteworthy research record when one of the periodical Kremlin reshuffles brought him into the Supreme Soviet.

He was about to request a formal introduction, when there came an exclamation from behind, and he swung around.

Number four of the survivors was climbing aboard without the aid of rescue apparatus. Sleek black hair running-wet framed a square Slavic face; on sallow skin red lips showed like an open wound. A woman? Well—unmistakably!

In excellent English she said, 'Thank you very much. I was hoping we could get all the way under our own power, which was why we asked for a jet-propelled boat to meet us and ride into port together. But it was hard to evade the attacks because seawater is not my usual habitation!' She bestowed a sunny smile on everyone in view.

There was a moment of enduring astonishment. Potter ended it by moving forward, hand outstretched.

'Ah—I'm Orlando Potter,' he said. 'Theoretically I'm in charge. I'm deputy chairman of the Congressional Committee on Emergency Countermeasures, if that means anything to you.'

'It would be like our commission on . . .' The girl snapped her fingers. 'Oh, I don't know the English for that! I'm Natasha Nikolaevna.'

Her self-possession impressed Potter tremendously. He said, 'You were the—the pilot of the ship?'

'I was steering, yes.' A wry grimace. 'But it was not what I am used to, you understand. I am a cosmonaut.'

A cosmonaut! That word brought a rush of agonizing nostalgia to Potter: so many aborted dreams . . . Before he had framed a suitable comment, Greta came tapping him on the shoulder.

'Orlando, you must come and talk to Abramovitch. He has something important to say, but he won't tell anybody below government level.' There was a hint of irritation in her voice. Potter made to excuse himself to the Russian girl and comply, but she shot an urgent question at him.

'How is Pitirim? Is he all right?'

'Do you mean the sick boy?' Potter found the words came automatically; on reflection the unconscious survivor had seemed very young, perhaps in his 'teens. 'He's below with the doctor, being well looked after.'

'I'm so glad,' the girl exclaimed. 'Any of the rest of us could have been lost, but I was afraid for Pitirim.'

Why? What could make a mere boy—an apparent mental defective, at that—more important than the Minister for Science? But Potter had no chance to ask, for the captain called from the bridge.

'Mr Potter, take everyone below, will you? We're getting under way, and even if we can't hit 110 knots there'll be a slight breeze here on deck.'

A slight breeze, Potter repeated to himself. The pursuit launch was slicing the night at about forty-five knots now, and the wind-noise and the yammer of the turbines permeated the entire hull, making conversation in the cramped quarters amidships a matter of slow well-articulated shouting.

Congreve came to join them, and reported that Zworykin was wearing a comprehensive medical kit strapped around his body in a waterproof covering and didn't want anyone else to interfere while he attended to the unconscious Pitirim. He sat down next to Abramovitch; the fat man was at a worse disadvantage than the others when trying to talk above the noise, because his fit of coughing had left him hoarse. But anything he wanted to say would have to be relayed anyhow by Congreve or Natasha, and they were either side of him.

Potter caught Natasha's eye. 'Please explain to Mr Abramovitch who I am. And please tell him, too, that Dr Jespersen is Associate Professor of Physics at the University of British Columbia and Miss Delarue is a senior executive of our Federal Scientific Service, so he can speak freely to all of us.'

Natasha complied. Waiting for her to translate the reply, Potter found himself glancing at Greta. There was an unexpectedly sour expression on her lovely face. It couldn't possibly be jealousy, could it? Yes, it could. For on reflection he realized it had made its appearance as they were coming below, when the captain had called from the bridge to compliment Natasha on her skilled handling of the *Red Whale*. He knew very well it was not to Greta's taste to have other women around who excelled her in anything, be it looks or ability.

She must be quite a girl, this cosmonaut . . . I wonder how she feels about the aliens, whether she finds it possible to hate them. How many years of ambition, how much tough training, went to waste because of them? It will be long before another spaceship leaves this ravaged planet.

But he himself had long ago realized, to his surprise, that he did not hate the aliens because he could not.

They were too foreign to his understanding. One might as well hate a bacterium, or a storm-cloud.

'He finds it difficult to talk,' Natasha said now, turning back to Potter. 'His throat hurts. So please put your questions to me, and I will only translate them to him if I cannot answer. Is this okay by you?'

Imperfections were beginning to show in her generally astonishing English; that faintly archaic phrase was one. Nonetheless her accent was superb. Potter shaped his first query and was forestalled by Greta in a voice as bitter as aloes.

'Is there any point? You saved nothing from the wreck except yourselves.'

'Please?' Natasha countered, eyes widening in puzzlement.

Potter scowled Greta into silence. Plainly she was still concerned that no alien device had been salvaged from the sunken boat, but there was nothing in the Russians' demeanour to suggest that they considered their venture a failure. On the contrary, they seemed in very good spirits.

'Miss—ah—Miss Nikolaevna,' he said, 'we ought to start with the full background to the story, you know. What Mr Congreve was told didn't make it at all clear.'

She checked rapidly with Abramovitch; on his confirmatory nod she leaned back and crossed her legs.

'Very well! First, you know what it is like in Russia now—there is Buishenko who has risen like a mad dog to the top of a pile of mad dogs, and his saboteurs and criminals are breaking up the organization of our state and fighting over the pieces. It is like a jungle! First there was only the part around the—the alien city, I think you call it in English. We are discouraged to call it that. Officially the name is "energetic phenomenon". But I myself am sure there are thinking creatures inside, much advanced over us.

'Well, it spread like a plague, you see. But we could not understand why Buishenko gained so much support. We have done much for our people, and believed them mainly loyal. It is in some way a superstition, but there is great love of Mother Russia. Of course he began with the remnants of the maddened leaderless armies we had sent against the—the aliens. Many thousands of them survived but had no organization until he enrolled them. Also many people joined him through fear, or for bribes, or to save their skins from his terrorist forces. But this could not be the whole of the story. There were still gapes, do you follow me? Ah—gapes . . .?'

'Gaps,' Potter supplied.

'Thank you, yes. So we spied, and we sent commando forces into his territory, and we interrogated those we captured in battle against him, and it came out. Our government had done its best against the aliens, and they spat on our petty achievements. Buishenko had done what we could not manage, so in face of the terrible strange threat people turned willingly to him.'

She paused impressively, looking from face to face.

'What our captives said was this: Buishenko had found a way to enter and leave the alien city at will, and had obtained many strange marvellous objects as proof.'

'You mean'—Potter heard his voice shaking—'he didn't go out of his mind?' In memory, scores of movie films showing those who had tried to enter the city in North America and been rendered instantly insane. The weirdos.

'In our country too we have many who went crazy trying it,' Natasha agreed. 'Still, this really did seem to be how Buishenko could accrete—no: augment his support. We presume, naturally, he must have come on the secret by chance. Perhaps he located some alien-made thing which can protect him. Perhaps some scientist is working for him and has made a new discovery. At all costs we must find out. So we make plans to spy in his headquarters. That was formerly an emergency army base, underground in the Urals, intended for use in nuclear war. We have all the maps and can fix the alarms and boobytraps. But if we manage to steal this thing of his, what can we do with it? Soon no part of Russia—'

'We've heard all that!' Greta broke in. 'So what became of it? Is it at the bottom of the ocean?'

Natasha was incredulous for a moment. Then she threw back her head and pealed with laughter. 'No, no! Our guess was wrong! It was not a machine that was so useful to Buishenko. It was a person. And though eight of our men were killed, we brought him safely away— Pitirim!'

There were long seconds of silence while they thought about the pasty-faced, slack-jawed, sickly boy. At last Jespersen said faintly, 'Him? But what can he do?'

'Go into the alien city and return, bringing things with him,' Natasha said patiently. 'Which until now he has handed always to Buishenko. That man is a wild animal caring for no one but himself. I think, I hope, we are caring for everybody on Earth. Is it not better for Pitirim to give us what he can gather?'

7

Crooning to himself, clutching his prize tightly in both dirty hands, Ichabod scurried crabwise along the dusty path, now and then chuckling and shaking back straw-fair hair from his bulging forehead. He paid no attention to the people coming and going around the shacks of scrap timber, plastic or salvaged bricks mortared with clay which he passed, and correspondingly they ignored him. Everyone knew Ichabod—a little touched in the head, but harmless, unlike some of the other kids.

The path wound randomly. He followed it as automatically as a trained rat in a maze. At one corner he stopped to relieve himself against a post, not letting go of what he held, and his crooning took on the words he had heard every Sunday and sometimes weekdays as well, since he first learned to talk:

'Praise the Lord for He has sent
Angels from the firmament!'

(He knew exactly what the firmament was. It was a big town up near the stars. You couldn't go to it—though

some people had impiously tried to—but you didn't
have to. Not now.)

> 'Sinners He will likewise throw
> To the raging fires below!'

(He knew what that would be like, too. His father had
shown him by dropping his pet frog into the stove.)

Hardly waiting for the last drop to fall, he went on
his way. When he came close to his home, though, he
progressed more cautiously. It was one thing to have
got hold of something which had belonged to the angels;
it was another to keep it secret. If luck was with him, he
might be able to slip indoors and hide it in his bed. He
had to make it himself, so that was a good place to hide
things . . .

No. He couldn't sneak in. Peeking around the corner
of the fence, he could see—and hear—his parents in
the frame of the downstairs window. They were arguing as usual. Ichabod accepted such arguments as a
fact of life. He would just have to wait until one or both
of them went out.

Squatting against the fence, he wondered if he dared
risk another glance at his treasure. Nobody was in
sight. He opened his hands and gazed down with wonder and fascination. Surely this must be beryl, or
chrysoprase, or one of the marvellous coloured stones
people said were used to build the palace of heaven!
Even between his hands it glowed red, green, blue,
while if it was held up to the light it was dazzling!

'Hello, son. What have you got there?'

Gasping, Ichabod snatched the stone down between
his legs, overcome by a wave of terror. He had been so
absorbed he hadn't noticed the cat-footed approach of
the man who had spoken. It wasn't anyone he knew,
but a stranger—and he had been told that 'stranger'

almost beyond doubt also meant 'sinner'. He tried to huddle himself up so small that he would vanish from sight.

The man—he was medium-tall, but to Ichabod's frightened vision he seemed a giant—dropped to his haunches and leaned forward cajolingly. 'Show me what you got, son. It's pretty, isn't it?'

'You leave me alone!' Ichabod commanded fiercely.

The man rocked back, feeling in the pocket of his neat, unmended jacket. 'Show me, son. I might like to buy it off you. You ever had this much money, son?' He shook a dozen jingling coins in his outstretched hand.

'No! No! No!' Ichabod yelled, jumping to his feet and dashing up the noisy planking of the steps before the house. The door swung open as he charged towards it, and he slammed full tilt into his mother's apron-front. Behind her he saw his father coming more slowly, his dark face set in a threatening frown which Ichabod for once found welcome.

'Make him go away!' he shouted.

His parents exchanged glances; then his father strode over to the stranger, who had risen to his feet and stood calmly on the path.

'A'right, mister—what've you been doing to my kid?'

'Nothing.' The stranger smiled. Ichabod didn't trust people who smiled like that—just with their mouths. 'My name's Corey Bennett. I do a little trading in rare artefacts. Do you have any idea what that thing your boy is holding might be worth in the right quarter?'

'What thing?' His mother glanced accusingly at Ichabod and shot out her arm. He tried desperately to cling to his treasure, but fingers like steel claws pried apart his grip and revealed the gorgeous polychrome glitter of the relic of angels.

'Ichabod!' she snapped. 'Where did you steal this?'

'I found it!' Ichabod wailed. 'It's mine—give it here!' He stretched after it; a smart cuff above the ear was his reward, and he turned aside, blubbering, while his mother held him by the shoulder to stop him running off. After a thoughtful examination of the flowing colours, she spoke up.

'Excuse my being uncivil, friend. I'm Martha Sims and this is my man Greg. You know what this thing is?'

'I reckon I may do, if I can take a closer look.'

'Here then.' She held it out. Bennett got up on the step and took it from her, studying it closely.

'Now wait a second!' Sims said. 'That from the city?'

'Looks like,' Bennett agreed.

'That's holy, then!' Sims stepped forward. 'Martha, are you going to sell a holy thing to a sinner? It rightly belongs like all of its kind to—'

'You'd do well to talk less and work more, Greg Sims!' his wife broke in. 'Can you eat it? Can you keep warm at night with it?'

'You sell that, you might as well sell your soul!' Sims raised his hand. 'Bring the money-changers back to the temple, would you? I'll beat sense into you first!'

'Lay a finger on me and I'll lay a pole on you—I've done it before! At most I'll tithe it, but that's all, you hear?'

Bennett's shrewd dark eyes lifted for an instant from the gem, or whatever it was, and flickered over the faces of the couple. He gave a discreet cough and held the object out as though to return it.

'If it means something special to you, I wouldn't cause dissension,' he said. 'And the boy does seem to set store by it.' He was pleased to see the light of cupidity gleam now in Sims's eyes as well as his wife's.

'Got no business setting store by anything in this world,' Sims growled. 'Lay up your treasure in heaven— hear me, you little sinner?' He shook a fist towards his son, who cringed away. 'Maybe the lesson he'll learn if it's taken—a lesson against avarice—maybe it'll outweigh the stain of passing it to an unbeliever.'

'Who said I was?' Bennett objected. He made a quick pass with his hands; he had learned many such since arriving here and found them useful. 'In my view this is what the relics are for. Don't we draw from them the funds which enable us to survive, an island of faith in a sea of unbelief? Doesn't the apostle say, "To the pure all things are pure"? Money isn't evil in itself. Only lusting for it is.'

Sims drew puzzled brows together. 'Whose teaching do you follow, then?'

'Should it be anyone's but Brother Mark?' Bennett didn't wait for further comment, but rolled the gem around his palm; it was shaped like a long thin egg. 'I don't know that this thing is *more* than pretty, though . . . Well, someone should buy it gladly for a jewel. For the sake of feeding and clothing honest folk I'll take the chance. A hundred dollars.'

He could see his pointed remark about lust for money had sunk deep in the minds of the Sims couple and was festering. Without making himself look dishonest, Sims couldn't argue the price up; his wife was only too well aware that if she tried to haggle her husband's piety might re-assert itself and prevent any agreement. Ichabod had settled to a dull moaning.

While they were still hesitating, Bennett made it $120 and closed the deal.

A genuine free trader—the notorious Den Radcliffe, for instance, or any of Grady's own buying staff—secure in the knowledge of a minimum thousand percent profit, might have paid twice as much and then had to bribe a Federal agent as well before he could dispose of it as jewellery.

Corey Bennett *was* a Federal agent. And jewellery was the last purpose he had in mind for his prize.

He was almost light-headed with excitement as he picked his way out of the shanty-town towards the highway. It was the second such settlement on this site. Refugees fleeing aimlessly from explosions at S.A.C. bases south of here had established the first, but it had been burned almost at once by maddened troops after an abortive attack on the alien city. Some of the present inhabitants had lived through that, and—having nowhere else to go—had doggedly rebuilt. A much greater number were rootless wanderers, attracted to Grady's Ground because the rule of its self-appointed 'Governor' offered safety from Federal law and a chance to get rich quick which had eluded them elsewhere. Another third or thereabouts were like the Sims family and had been lured by the widespread belief that the shining city was the home of angels sent to Earth to scourge sinners. Bennett had learned to prove this latter view from the Book of Revelation. Practically anything, he had decided, could be proved from the same source.

Grady's Ground was in no sense an attractive place to live. The cities which had escaped destruction by maddened soldiers were overcrowded and dilapidated, while the shanty-towns were still worse, and Bennett was relieved to be back on the highway where he had left his car. But his heart sank when he saw a patrolman in one of the local peacock-gaudy uniforms standing beside the vehicle.

There was nothing for it but to walk up with an innocent expression. He did so, mopping his brow because the sun was strong today, while the dark glasses shielding the patrolman's eyes from the glare fixed him with the impassivity of a basilisk.

'Documents,' the man said, one elbow on the car's

roof, the other hand outstretched. Bennett produced them.

'Free trader,' was the neutral comment. 'Okay, what have you picked up today?'

In a split second Bennett made his decision. He was a comparative newcomer here, but already he had had a good number of 'rare artefacts' through his hands—or sacred relics, according to your point of view. He had dutifully paid on each the levy exacted by Grady's tax-collectors, who were more like a protection gang, in fact, though one had to admit that some of their take did get channelled into public services. It was unlikely that a lowly patrolman would risk offending him; his record suggested that one of these days he would bring off a really profitable coup.

So he dipped in his heavy pocket and displayed only a handful of the coins he carried because so many people around here had become disillusioned with paper money . . . not, luckily, including the Sims family.

'In that overgrown garbage pile?' he said. 'Hell, those people won't trust anybody they haven't known for years. I thought I was coming to be pretty well respected, so I went and asked around, but clams aren't in the same class with them when it comes to keeping their mouths shut.'

It was at least half true, and Bennett could see the patrolman's mind turning over. Imperceptibly he tensed, because if the man decided on a search he would have to risk jumping him. He had been hunting ever since his arrival for what he had obtained from Ichabod.

'Okay,' the patrolman decided, and handed back the documents. 'Better luck next time. Show your face around more, is my advice. Make friends with one of their nutty religious groups. I could live the rest of my life on the stuff locked up in one of their tumbledown churches.'

'Let me sell it on commission and you'll be able to afford two lifetimes instead of one,' Bennett suggested, smiling. The patrolman cracked a faint grin in response and stood back.

It cost Bennett all his self-control not to touch the pocket where he had put the precious object, to reassure himself it was still there. But he managed it, and when he was well down the road found he had been holding his breath since starting the car.

Almost, he had recognized the thing when he saw it in the crippled boy's hand. The shape had seemed familiar, but the shining colours were so extraordinary he had thought he was confronted with some entirely new type of artefact.

This, though, was what he had been seeking. He had seen six or eight similar, all broken, all dull and colourless. This one was intact. He formed the words to himself: *in working order!* (Did that have a meaning? Did the aliens' products *do* anything, in the ordinary human sense?)

If that patrolman had guessed what I'm really up to . . . !

Piece by painfully gathered piece, the first complete alien 'machine' to fall into man's possession was being assembled here under the very nose of Grady, to whom what he carried would be only a gewgaw for sale to some fat rich woman in Dallas or New York. The machine had cost two lives already, to Bennett's certain knowledge: once when a man tried to rob the store of a local church for a part rumoured to match what he was looking for, once when Grady's patrols caught a man trying to smuggle something away for study at U.C.L.A. Now, though, it was within sight of completion.

'And it's here in my pocket, the missing bit!' he whispered, trying to make the idea come real. 'What's it doing? It's processing energy, that's for sure. What kind of energy? How much? How? Will I be able to tell without breaking it open and ruining it?'

And the worst question of all, of course, was this: what would the finished device do—this mysterious apparatus that he, third in line of succession, seemed fated to perfect? Like a three-dimensional jigsaw puzzle, it had been compiled from many sources. Suppose, after such effort, after such loss of life, it was something a human mind could never comprehend?

'Or something useless and pointless,' he said to the air. 'Like a bust of rich old Uncle Joe. But what the hell? We'll see. One of these days, we'll see.'

He had been saying that to himself ever since the aliens arrived. It was becoming more and more difficult to believe.

8

It was as though humanity had fled in two directions through time from the catastrophe accompanying the appearance of the aliens. Or that was how it struck Orlando Potter, anyway. Some small part had exploded towards the future, in the sense that many national boundaries had collapsed; here he was in Victoria, after all, on the southern tip of Vancouver Island, and nobody was raising objections because an American official was requisitioning Canadian facilities and had had his temporary office tied in by phone and teleprinter to the surviving nuclei of government in the United States. Of course, rules, regulations and traditions had already taken a severe beating when the Canadian Parliament was transferred here in the immediate post-disaster period.

Curious, this preference for an island. A survival of British-oriented thinking, perhaps. Or possibly it was rather less subtle. Maybe they had simply foreseen the risk that the chaos now reigning on Grady's Ground might spread, wildfire fashion, and decided that Vancouver Island would be easier to hold against a wave of barbarism than a site on the mainland.

Because by far the majority of the human race had exploded towards the past, not the future. Remembering the civil wars in miniature that had been fought so bloodily south of here, especially in California, when panic-crazed city folk clashed with small-town vigilantes determined to keep what they had, Potter felt his mouth twist as though he had bitten a putrescent fruit.

That was a scattering backward through time, surely. To the days of closed peasant communities, suspicious of any stranger; worse, to the days of feudalism—for what after all was Grady but a feudal lord of the manor, governing his followers as absolutely as a mediaeval baron his serfs? So now, rat-like, men squabbled and quarrelled among the ruins of their once-proud civilization, and here and there a few of them toiled to assemble the broken pieces in a new form.

Can we coexist with the aliens? The question was an eternal one. *Can we simply draw back from where they have set their cities, and be our own masters everywhere else? After all, natural forces have barred us from parts of our planet in the past: deserts, icecaps, trackless forest . . .*

Probably not. Potter wished achingly that the solution could be so simple, but he knew it would never happen. There were two insuperable obstacles: first, it was impossible to predict whether the aliens intended to spread further across the surface of the globe; second, it was not in keeping with the monkey-curious nature of man to ignore a mystery of this order.

He stared through the window of his temporary office, high in a recently-built tower block. From it he could see the sea. The water was calm, and the summer sky was clear and blue. He would have preferred it storm-dark, to match his mood.

He was stuck here because of Pitirim. The original plan had been to fly him onward after their landing at Victoria, the nearest usable seaport; the whole of the

far north-west of the U.S.A. was a fallout zone following the immense explosions at the I.C.B.M. sites there,
and anti-missile missiles had created comparable havoc
around all the conurbations farther south.

But Zworykin had forbidden them to take the sick
boy any farther for the time being. The American and
Canadian physicians and psychologists who had been
flown to join him, under the leadership of the famous
Dr Louis Porpentine, concurred with his judgement.
Life was being adequately, though precariously, maintained in his feeble body. His equally feeble mind,
though, had suffered trauma upon trauma, what with
being kidnapped from Buishenko's base under the Urals,
and shot at by pursuit planes, and at last unceremoni-
ously dumped in the Pacific. He was now terrified of
his own shadow, literally, and it would be a long while
before he could stand any further strain—even longer,
perhaps, before he could be persuaded to co-operate
with strangers the way he had obeyed Buishenko.

So: a temporary headquarters for 'Operation Pantomime', as some idiot had code-named it—hence the use
of terms like Harlequin and Columbine during the
rendezvous at sea. It was his responsibility. He had
pressed for its approval by the Committee on Emergency Countermeasures, and to go back without tangi-
ble proof either of success or of unavoidable failure
was a prospect he dared not consider. His confidence
was badly enough undermined already. So was the
trust the rest of the committee reposed in him.

There were few surplus resources left here after the
importation of Canada's emergency parliament. However, the facilities were tolerable. The standard of hospital care was as good as could still be found on the
continent, and that was the chief consideration. There
were the top four floors of this building, in near-new
condition; moreover the previous occupant had been

an insurance company—insurance was a bad line to be in during the post-disaster period—and had left behind a computer of very respectable capacity. The Canadian government had automatically requisitioned it, but they hadn't yet put it into service and were only moderately unwilling to let it go again. There were teleprinters and telephones, enough to go around, so Potter ought to feel he'd been very lucky.

In actual fact . . .

His head was beginning to ache from long staring at the bright sky. With an effort he brought his mind back to the tasks in hand and took up the topmost of many sheets of paper from the in-tray at his left. For a long moment he failed to make sense of it, and thought this was because his vision was swimming with after-images of the sunlit window. Then words penetrated—something about a policy on the life of a ship's captain—and he realized he was looking at the wrong side of it. Even in this country, formerly one of the greatest paper-producers in the world, it had become necessary to use both sides of the sheet. Some of the forests had burned for six weeks. Turning the document over, he discovered the usual brief daily bulletin from the doctors attending Pitirim. It could have been summed up in three words: 'Hardly any progress.'

Heaven's name, how long is all this going to take? He thrust the paper blindly at the filing basket and took up the next report.

He was only halfway down the first of its ten paragraphs when he stiffened and began to read with absolute concentration—so total, indeed, that it was a shock when he came to the end and on glancing up discovered Greta facing him. He had not heard the door open. She was scowling.

'Yes?' he said—more abruptly than he had intended,

for his mind was still preoccupied with the implications of what he had just read.

'I think we're being made fools of,' Greta said. 'Got a cigarette?'

'Oh—yes.' Potter pushed an almost empty pack across the desk, and a book of matches. As she helped herself, he went on, 'What was the point of that crack?'

'I said we're being made fools of,' she repeated, dropping into a chair. 'I don't believe for one moment that this idiot child they're fussing over is more than simply an idiot. I agree Buishenko may very well have stumbled across some way of getting in and out of the alien city, but I think he tricked those feather-brained Russians, and we've been deceived in our turn. After all the trouble we're being put to we shall be no better off than we were before.'

There was a long silence after that passionate outburst. She must have been brooding over this for days, Potter told himself, perhaps even rehearsing the words in her mind; it was her usual habit to keep quiet about something which worried her until it boiled over absolutely without warning.

'So that's what you think,' he said neutrally. 'Okay, then I'll tell you what I think, though I'm afraid you're not going to like it. *I* think you're crazy-jealous of Natasha, and you'd dismiss out of hand anything she was involved in, whatever it was.'

'What?' Greta nearly jolted to her feet.

'That's what I'm driven to believe,' Potter said. 'Of course, if I'd known you in the days before all this' —waving a hand to encompass the world—'I'd have a better standard of comparison but—'

She cut in, pale-cheeked. 'I've had as much as I can stand of your parlour psychology, Orlando! What the hell do you think you're doing, having an affair with me or carrying out a social survey? "Standard of comparison" be damned! You're talking to me—me! And you just insulted me and you can damned well apologize.'

'No, I can't,' Potter said after a second's hesitation. 'If I can't wake you up to what you're doing, the result will be disastrous. Hear me out—*please*. I was very impressed when you were first assigned to my staff. Why not? A young woman looking like a fashion model in spite of the mess the world is in, who turns out to have her bachelor's in science and says she decided to join the Scientific Service when she was fourteen—remarkable! Out on the boat that night when we made the rendezvous with the Russians I remember feeling very envious because along with all the rest it turned out you could string a few words of Russian together, while the best I can do is order a meal in Spanish. And then, the moment Natasha came aboard, you started to show another side of your character altogether.'

She had become like ice now. He chipped at the frozen façade.

'Anything you can do . . . Isn't that about the size of it? She's a trained space-pilot; she's a first-rate engineer; she speaks marvellous English even though she's never been in an English-speaking country before. She overshadows you, and you took an instant dislike to her. Ever since you've been taking it out on me, on Abramovitch, on anybody who comes handy, and now you've decided to take it out on Pitirim as well.'

'Give me one shred of proof,' she said between her teeth, 'and I'll write out what I said and eat the paper. Until you do, I'll go right on saying we've been made fools of, and you're behaving like the worst fool of all.'

'Ever heard of weirdos?'

The question, as he had meant, surprised her. An answer struggled on the tip of her tongue with a continuation of her tirade, and emerged first.

'Hell, of course I have! What about them?'

'Define the term as you understand it.'

'What is there to understand? You can't understand them. Supposedly they're people who tried to get into an alien city or spent too long trying to figure out an alien artefact and—well, something happened to them and they wound up filthy, hostile to ordinary people, and generally schizoid.'

'Pitirim?'

Potter let the name hang on the air like a wisp of smoke. Greta did not stir to disturb it for long seconds. At last she leaned to tap her cigarette-ash into a tray on the desk. With infinite weariness she said, 'Okay, you win. Know what I was going on to say?'

He shook his head.

'I was going to talk some more about your parlour psychology. The way you manipulate people to serve your ends. But—oh, damn you. You're good at it. I never thought you'd pull it on me, but you just did, and it worked. Yes, yes, it can be argued that Pitirim didn't have enough of a mind to be driven crazy . . . Oh, aren't you the clever son-of-a-bitch, though? You're power-hungry—'

'No more than most people,' Potter snapped. 'If it hadn't been for the aliens, do you think I'd be deputy chairman of a congressional committee? The hell I would. I never wanted to be a Big Boss. I'd have had to pay too high a price.'

'Maybe the talent came naturally, but you have it. You can make people feel weak and—and naked. You know how to lean on them, and when you feel like doing it you don't even pretend to be nice about it.'

'Think weakness is a virtue?' Potter said harshly. 'Do you? Garbage, it's a luxury! One we can't afford any more. We could get along when there was no competition bar other human beings, also with weaknesses like our own. But the aliens aren't people. If we're even going to survive in face of the challenge they present, we're going to know ourselves more intimately than ever before. We're going to have to criticize ourselves ruthlessly. We've got to give up making mistakes!'

Her only answer was a grimace. She stubbed her cigarette as though wishing she could crush him equally easily.

'But,' he resumed, 'as it happens none of this is of immediate consequence. Here, read this report, and then go pack your bags.'

Hand poised to take the paper he was offering, she checked. 'So you have decided to move me over!' She flared. 'God, you're the most egotistical bastard I ever met! Nothing short of a space-pilot is good enough for you, is that it?'

Potter gave a weary sigh. 'No. No, in fact in spite of there never having been much affection between us I shall miss you and hope you get back soon. I don't imagine you'll believe me, but I've never spent as long as ten minutes alone with Natasha and as far as I know she's shown no interest in me or any other man here. But we have to get someone reliable to Grady's Ground, right away. Since you complained when you came in about wasting time here on a fool's errand, I thought you'd welcome the assignment.'

She had scanned the paper while he was talking. Now she said, not looking up, 'I see. You're sending me there alone because there's a fair chance I may not come back. I'll no longer be a nuisance to you.'

'Not alone,' Potter said patiently. 'Not if you can persuade one key man to co-operate. He can provide you with a flawless cover. Well?'

She pondered for a moment. Finally, sighing, she handed back the paper. 'Very well. This place is getting on my nerves. And so are you. It wouldn't be a bad idea for us to separate for a while.'

'But the assignment!' Potter said. 'Did you actually read all this?'

'Yes.'

'Doesn't it—well, doesn't it sound . . .?' He groped in the air as though in search of a word, and ended lamely: 'Doesn't it sound exciting?'

'I don't think I know what that means any longer,' Greta said, rising and turning to the door.

9

It was abominably hot tonight. Restless, Waldron paced his apartment. For a while he tried to settle to his piano, but he felt oppressed and could not concentrate; all the channels of the TV were spewing forth infantile rubbish, repeats and old movies from the days before the aliens, and when he thumbed through his records not one tempted him to set it on the player.

He stopped before the small table under the main window and for perhaps the thousandth time picked up what lay alone on the varnished wood. What *was* this damned thing? A stubby rod, eight and a quarter inches long, of something which was not glass but had cracked irregularly, glass-fashion, down the centreline, with spiny quasi-crystals embedded in its clear substance. From each apex of the crystal-like forms threads thinner than hairs wound out towards the surface—not in any formal pattern, but with a symmetry like that of a living organism.

A bit of garbage, tossed aside by a higher race. He had bought it nearly a year ago; it had cost him 800 bucks, and that was the lowest price paid at the auction sale he'd attended. Most of the other bidders had been speculators, as usual frantically seeking something from which a fortune might be made on resale to the government or to one of the corporations which still had research labs in operation. He had only wanted an object—any object—made by the aliens, as a barb for his mind.

Now, as occasionally before, the useless thing sparked his memory. Of course: he was neglecting the most important of his self-imposed tasks, the keeping of a journal which he had begun when he realized there was bitter truth in his habitual gibe about no one bothering to write history any more.

He picked up his recorder and carried it to his most comfortable chair. He poured a drink, then sat down and thumbed the control knob to recording position. He gave the date, hesitated, and suddenly uttered words he had not thought over.

'I have a mental picture of Washington. A pillar of smoke by day and a pillar of fog by night. A solid week now since Bennett walked into the City of Angels and died after Radcliffe's attack on him. Within hours of our reporting his suspected identity they'd descended on us. I wasn't there because I'd had the night shift and was home trying to sleep. When I got back they'd sucked his body into the Washington fog and given strict orders not to mention the name Bennett to anyone. And a day later I received a call from somebody who wouldn't give his name, just a departmental reference—I traced it to the Secret Service—who commended me for not arresting Radcliffe and making it harder to hush this affair up.

'He didn't say "hush it up". But that was what he meant. Lord, I wish those underground bunkers in Washington hadn't been so efficient! The fires and the fallout might have cleaned house for us, and given new people with fresh ideas a chance to tackle our problems.

Instead of which, we're stuck with pretty much the same old gang of hidebound bureaucrats and party wheeler-dealers, whose ideas fossilized in the Stone Age of the seventies. What's going to become of us with *them* still in charge?

'They must know that Bennett didn't walk in the front door of the City of Angels. That's been sworn to, over and over, and anyhow he wouldn't have been let in, looking such a mess—would he? So how did he get where they first spotted him? Did he materialize out of thin air? Did he jump clear from Grady's Ground, where Radcliffe said there are so many weirdos? Hell, it ought to have been the biggest news since—since the aliens landed!

'But I guess there's a protocol laid down. I guess it's "not expedient" to investigate too closely. I guess it's all being smothered under labels saying "Top Secret". Maybe not even his brother has been told he's dead. If he has a brother!'

He stopped abruptly. This was the point past which, ever since the chilling moment when Canfield brought him the news about the reversed identical prints, he had not dared to push his thinking.

A of M! The Age of Miracles is not past!

Into his moment of blankness the sound of the door buzzer broke like a saw-blade. His hand flew to switch off the recorder. Who the hell could that be? He didn't want to be interrupted. Let the caller wear out his patience and go away. But the caller had more patience than he'd expected. After the third buzz he leaned on the button and waited. Waldron jumped up with an oath and stormed to the door.

The sight of an elegantly-dressed woman through the spy-hole in the door brought an automatic assumption to his mind. Opening on a security chain, he said harshly, 'I'm not interested! And watch who you pick on—there are still laws against prostitution and I'm in a position to enforce them!'

He made to slam the door.

'Lieutenant Waldron!' the woman snapped. She had coloured a little, but betrayed no other reaction.

That shook him. If she knew his name and rank, clearly she was not just working her way around the bachelor apartments in search of a client for the night. Wondering, he unchained the door and swung it wide.

'I want to talk to you,' the woman said. 'About the death of Corey Bennett.'

The words seemed to rest on the surface of his mind for a moment, as stones might rest on thin ice before breaking it. He looked her up and down. She was slender, almost as tall as he was; her face was rather thin, and jade-dust makeup lent her complexion a luminous pallor. Her fair hair was shoulder-long, gathered by a comb to the left so that it emphasized the delicate moulding of her skull. She wore a dark-green bolero over rust-red leotards patterned with silver. The ice cracked and the stones sank. He heard himself say, '*Corey* Bennett?'

The woman nodded, her expression sober. 'I somehow expected that to surprise you. Here, you'll want to see my I.D.'

She zipped open a change-pocket on the hem of her bolero and proffered a small yellow card bearing her photograph. It identified her as Greta Helen Delarue, BSC, Office of the Federal Scientific Service, Washington D.C.

Waldron grunted. 'Come to commend me for keeping my mouth shut?' he suggested sourly as he gave back the card. 'Okay, come on in.'

He waved her to the chair he had been using, picked up his drink, and sat on the edge of a table facing her. There was a brief silence. Eventually he had to make an impatient gesture. 'So talk to me! You said you wanted to.'

She was gazing at his alien artefact. 'From the way you said "*Corey* Bennett?" I imagine you've already worked out a lot of what I thought I'd have to explain.'

'I'm not allowed to talk about it to anybody,' Waldron snapped. 'But I sure as hell have been thinking about it. I don't believe in identical twins with mirror-image prints.'

'Correct. Corey Bennett was an only child. By the time our experts got at the body, organic death was well advanced—I must say your police surgeon isn't a paragon of efficiency, and that didn't help either—but we established his identity beyond doubt. And wound up with a far worse headache than before.'

'Trying to figure out what turned him around?' Waldron said. 'Well, what did happen to him?'

'I'll come to that in a moment. As soon as we—'

'*What happened to him?*' Waldron slammed his glass down on the table, and it rang into shivering fragments. He stared at the mess stupidly for as long as it took the pieces to stop rocking.

'I'm sorry,' he muttered. 'I'll get the disposall.'

'Leave it, please! Why don't you sit down properly? I appreciate the strain you must have been under, but it'll make things a lot clearer if I can come to the point in my own way.'

'Then get to it, instead of dancing all around it!' Waldron flung the words over his shoulder as he unhooked the disposall from its bracket and ran the nozzle over the wet table.

'Corey Bennett has been with the field branch of the Scientific Service since June last year,' Greta said. 'Four months ago he was assigned to a purchasing mission on what I gather you insist be called by the slang name of Grady's Ground. At present he is making good progress;

his last report came in the small hours of yesterday morning.'

'What?' The disposall thumped to the floor; Waldron kicked the power-switch before it could ingest the carpet, and spun to face her.

'I've been checking up on you, Mr Waldron. Apparently you like to complain that nothing is being done about the—well, the aliens. I promise you, a great deal is being done. We simply dare not publicize the fact, though. For one thing, we'd face instant opposition from the relidges, and even though they're cranks there are a lot of them, too many for us to want to stir them up. For another, we're fairly certain that the aliens can read hostile intentions from a human mind. There's no other reasonable explanation for the way our armies were driven mad when they tried to attack their cities. The aliens could probably sterilize the planet if we annoyed them sufficiently, just as we could exterminate rats and mice if we sank all our efforts into the job. The most flattering assessment of their and our relative intelligence puts us no higher than rats.

'Still, we do what we can and right now we have a problem which demands immediate and intensive investigation, but we have an incredibly small number of people to call on. Our resources are stretched so tight you can hear them twang.

'It goes like this. Corey Bennett is dead. His body is in one of our labs, being taken to very small pieces like a delicate machine. And Cory Bennett is at the same time probably engaged in the course of action which will lead to his death.'

The following silence soughed through the room like a cold wind. In memory, Waldron heard something which Maura Knight had said concerning weirdos. He moved to a chair, sweating.

'You mean he jumped through time as well as space to get to the City of Angels?' he said incredulously.

'It's the only halfway rational explanation we've hit on. Can you improve on it?'

Waldron shook his head.

'Can't you—well, warn him he's in danger?'

'Do you think we dare?' Greta countered. 'For all we can tell, the warning might trigger the event. On the other hand, if we do nothing, we know that sooner or later ... Oh, the poor bastard is a condemned man either way. All we can do is draw some profit from the situation. For the first time ever we're in a position to observe an alien process. It must be alien. And ... Well, this is not supposed to be made known, but it's something you deserve to be told. Bennett's assignment was to try and complete an alien device which two predecessors had made progress with. According to his latest report, he thinks he now has all the parts, and he's going to assemble it and see what if anything it can do.'

Waldron whistled. 'Is it that which—which *twists* him?'

'That's what we're hoping to find out. Our theoreticians have suggested that he might have made a trip in Möbius space. Think of a hollow tube of triangular cross-section. Rotate one end through 120° and close it up into a ring. That would do it. Among the few things we know about the aliens is the fact that they're capable of intense local distortions of the continuum.'

'Why are you telling me this? What does it have to do with me?'

'As much as you want it to.'

'What do you charge for straight answers?' he snapped.

'I'm sorry. What first drew our attention to you, of course, was your fortunate decision not to arrest Radcliffe on a homicide count. I doubt if you did that for the right reasons, but it was a stroke of luck for us.

That, plus the fact that apparently he attacked the girl he'd hired for the night and came close to being booked for assault on her, only you talked him round, left him with a debt to honour some time. Out on Grady's Ground, they tell me, they have the omertà bit in full form. And after the conclusion of your formal interview with him, we found something else on the tape—not very well recorded, but decipherable. He actually invited you to go out and join him on his home patch. Talking to his associate Hyson the following day, he specifically mentioned the offer again.'

She raised her head and looked him square in the eyes. 'When you answered, your tone suggested that you found the proposition attractive.'

Waldron felt perspiration creeping down his back. 'That was then!' he barked. 'I was angry at myself for something. I guess . . .' He hesitated. 'I guess I'd invested Radcliffe, as a free trader, with a spurious artificial glamour. But I promise there's no risk of my throwing up my job and heading for Grady's Ground, even if he would like to hire me to run his security force.'

'Very well, then.' Greta started to her feet. 'I'd hoped you might feel otherwise, but if I must I'll go on my own.'

'Wait.' Waldron felt a stab of puzzlement. 'I—uh—I seem to have missed something, don't I?'

She approached the table by the window, letting her hand fall to the stubby cylinder which was not of glass. Shrugging, she said, 'I've been assigned to watch Bennett do the things that will lead to his—his arrival in the past. In my profession we aren't content to say "A of M!" and forget about it. But on Grady's Ground it's difficult for an unattached woman to act independently. It occurred to us that if you were sincere in your complaints about the general apathy, you might be willing to exploit your contact with Radcliffe and provide me with a cover. It would make it a hell of a sight easier to get on the Ground, you know. They're fierce with strangers, and Radcliffe's safe-conduct would make all the difference.'

There was a roaring in Waldron's ears. He felt as though the room were afloat on a rough sea. His stomach churned and his palms were wet.

Dear God! whispered some far-distant part of his mind. *It wasn't enough to talk about it. Something has to be done, sooner or later. And now I've got to be the one to do it. I didn't mean to get trapped but I am trapped—I was never so frightened in my life and I don't want to say yes but if I don't how shall I ever be able to face myself again?*

His voice, however, was perfectly calm as he spoke. 'Sit down again. Have a drink. I wish you'd mentioned this when you first came in. It would have saved a lot of time.'

10

After Floodwood neither of them spoke for twenty hot miles; they sat, sweating and apathetic, while U.S. 2 went reeling under the wheels like an endless humming tape. Waldron had stopped at a drugstore in Duluth and bought a cheap pair of sunglasses, but they didn't completely screen the glare from the road and wrinkling up his eyes made his forehead ache.

He had written to say he was arriving. But the U.S. mails did not recognize the existence of Grady's Ground, and there was no way to be sure the letter had reached Radcliffe. At all events there had been no answer. Still, they dared not wait for ever.

The country, for some distance past, had begun to look neglected, like a room used but undusted for months. When there were people to be seen, they went timidly in patched shabby clothing. In every small town after Floodwood there were ruins burned by the mad armies—charred beams poking up from mounds of rubble, dark stains washed down by rain on the surviving walls, seedlings sprouting atop the mess. But for the fact that the worst potholes in the road had been recently levelled with stonechips and asphalt, Waldron would have taken it for granted that Minnesota had been abandoned by anyone with more ambition than to live as a grubby peasant.

A tilted sign stood by the road, its painted face chipped by bullets and cancerous rust eating at the metal: DANGER FALLOUT ZONE. From the anti-missile missiles around the Lakes, presumably; the wind would have carried a lot of the dust this way. But the count would have gone to 'safe' long ago.

The people had fled from the fallout zone, of course—not officially evacuated, just panicking away. Where had they ended up? Shot on the Canadian border, maybe, or killed by disease, or trapped by despair in some refugee camp to the south. Whatever had become of them, they hadn't returned. This area not only *looked* empty, which would have been commonplace to a visitor from the crowded East; it *was* empty, and felt like an aboriginal wilderness.

Beside him Greta reached to the switch of the radio, and a sentimental pre-catastrophe ballad with a backing of lush strings oozed on the air. Waldron uttered a wordless objection: *do we have to endure this garbage?*

'It's in character,' Greta said. 'We'll have to pass a border check somewhere soon.'

'Already?' Waldron betrayed his astonishment.

She gave a twisted smile. 'I thought you were the man with a map of Grady's Ground on his office wall.'

'Stop needling me!' Waldron ordered savagely. Now the journey was nearing its end, all his half-formed fears were clamoring in the back of his mind again. *I thought my talk would never have to become action . . .* He spoke aloud to silence the mental uproar.

'I was told that Grady controls North Dakota, part of South Dakota and Montana, a wedge of Manitoba, and only a narrow strip of Minnesota. Hell, we're not through Grand Rapids yet!'

'Not Grady's border post. Ours.'

'What?'

'You never heard of such a thing. I know.' She spoke with exaggerated weariness. 'Christ, Jim, do you imagine the government wants to admit we've had to set up border posts on our own territory? They masquerade as forward defence posts, cordoning off the area dominated by the aliens. But they're border posts in fact if not in name, and it's no good claiming otherwise.'

Waldron was at a loss for a moment. The sickly singing galled him. He said abruptly, 'If you must play the radio to bolster your rôle, at least pick another station!'

The record ended. An unctuous voice said something about Lampo Products being better than.

'Can't,' Greta said. 'It's Grady's. Has a monopoly. Sabotaged every station for almost 200 miles and trucked in all the gear he could to use for his own. Now it's the most powerful west of Chicago.'

'Grady's? But . . . You mean he gets advertising?'

'Why not? There are a hell of a lot of people anxious to sell things to the richest community in North America.'

'The richest?' Waldron felt like an idiot, parroting the succession of questions. He snapped his mouth shut, half-afraid of it hanging slack and foolish. Another pre-catastrophe record began, this time a pounding rock number.

'Jim, haven't you boned up on what you've let yourself in for?' Greta demanded. 'I assumed you knew what it's like on Grady's Ground.'

'I never had any intention of going there,' Waldron sighed. 'So what point would there have been in boning up? And least of all I never expected to go there to watch a man doomed to die and not tell him anything!'

'If only I'd realized,' she muttered. 'Better hurry with

the questions. We can't have you pumping me for information once we're on the Ground. Somebody might start wondering how it is I know so much more than you do.'

Waldron looked at her sidelong. No, she didn't give the impression of being a well-informed person. Not any more. He couldn't determine what else the Federal disguise experts had done besides coarsening the line of her mouth and rinsing her hair in some chemical to make it look bleached even though it was naturally fair. But the effect was unmistakable. Any man would assume that here was a selfish, pampered woman, losing her looks and afraid of it, but too spoiled not to be excessively fond of martinis, cigarettes and late nights.

She was supposed to be his mistress. It didn't say much for his taste or his sex-appeal, in Waldron's view, but it was pointless to argue. This was the commonest type of woman now moving into the Ground—usually with a couple of failed marriages behind her—and so Greta Delarue had been transformed into Greta Smith, slut.

Putting up with her is going to be the worst part of the job . . .

Aloud he said, 'To start with, I want to know why you expect the border check so soon.'

'There's a no-man's-land. The border posts are on the line where the maddened troops were first affected. Some of them got closer before turning back, but none were initially affected further away. For a long while that was as far as they dared go. When they eventually tried to push ahead again, Grady was there and sinking roots. He likes having a big moat around his territory. It means he can run down smugglers without Federal interference. He uses helicopters and Dobermanns.'

Trying to recall the geography of the area, Waldron said, 'Whose is Bemidji, then?'

'Nobody's. Or it would be if it was still there. It was razed during the madness. I've seen aerial photos. Nothing but rubble.'

The announcer cut short the record and read another commercial. Greta turned down the volume. 'Jim, what kind of analogies do you have in mind for the situation on Grady's Ground? Or don't you have any?'

He was going to take a long time to get accustomed to her using his first name so—so *maritally*. He shrugged. 'I thought I had some ideas. You seem to be torpedoing them all.'

'This is gold-rush territory. Grady has a monopoly on this continent of what's potentially the most valuable commodity in history, and he's sewed everything up tight. He runs the Ground on police-state lines, except that the major crimes aren't political—they're financial. Smuggling, for instance; failure to tithe alien artefacts, or pay a redemption fee in lieu. And so on. Everything is taxed, on top of being hideously expensive, and Grady is the chief tax-collector. Of course he does maintain the public services—the utilities which escaped the catastrophe, internal mail-distribution, drainage and garbage clearance, the bare necessities. But do you know how much money he has to do it with?'

Waldron shook his head.

'The Revenue people calculate that the income from selling alien artefacts last year must have topped one and a half billion dollars.'

She took a cigarette from her pocket and pressed the dash lighter home. 'Grady, his staff, the top free traders, and a few others who've made themselves indispensible to the Governor, altogether about a thousand, are dripping money all over the Ground and hardly know what to spend it on. Like those oil-rich sheikhs used to out in the Persian Gulf. Gold-rush territory!'

The lighter popped out and she applied it to her cigarette.

'You'd think they'd try and close him out,' Waldron said sourly. 'Given that all alien artefacts are supposed to be Federal property.'

'How? By sending in another army and having it run wild all over the countryside the way the rest did? Lord knows how the aliens discriminate between an organized body of men and the riff-raff they tolerate on their very doorstep, but they manage it somehow. We have 130 million people left to cope with. Grady's going to have to stew until we've put our own house in order.'

And there it was: the border.

The road had been widened by the addition on either side of a large flat concrete pan. Concrete blockhouses with machine-gun slits commanded the approaches and both pans, and barbed wire encircled the whole area, leaving only a gap on the road wide enough for a single vehicle and closed by heavy timber gates. In either direction stretched a line of watch-towers with searchlights and radar on top. An army helicopter was parked alongside the nearest blockhouse. Also there were six trucks: two of them heavily armoured, the others—each with a trailer in tow—being two flatbacks and two tankers. They were painted dull grey.

'That's a bit of luck,' Greta said softly, turning up the radio a little. 'An ingoing convoy.'

'So I gather. Why a convoy?' Waldron took his foot off the accelerator and let the car coast towards the gates.

'The no-man's-land is rugged and full of lakes; a lot of hijackers work it, so the wealthiest residents on the Ground bring in their household supplies under escort. And goods for other people too, of course—at a price.'

A voice boomed from a megaphone, ordering them to halt. As soon as the car stopped, a sergeant and two privates, all with slung carbines, appeared to open up for them and waved them towards a clear spot on the nearer pan. The sergeant approached with a bored expression.

'Read this and signify that you understand it,' he told Waldron, proffering a much-stained printed form pasted on a card. Waldron scanned it: now entering a zone defined as an emergency zone by Federal Emergency Regulation number so-and-so, act of proceeding beyond this point implies recognition that the Government of the United States cannot be held responsible for—et cetera. *A polite way of saying you're going abroad,* Waldron translated.

He returned the card. The sergeant beckoned the nearer private, who took out a notebook and scribbled down the licence number of the car before coming to ask their names.

'Okay, wait there,' he said. 'May take a while.'

Greta put on a sour expression. 'We have to sit out here scorching to death? What for?'

The private gave her a grin full of stained teeth. 'For all I know, lady, you and your pal murdered grandma and pawned the family jewels, hm? Or maybe it's a hot car and I don't mean from the sun.' He grinned again and went into the blockhouse. The sergeant had walked over to the tail truck of the convoy and was talking to a man leaning down from the armour-glass window of the cab. The remaining private stood staring at Greta with his gun levelled and his jaws chomping rhythmically on a wad of gum.

Waldron's hand went to his pocket and began mechanically to stroke his alien artefact, which he had picked up just before setting out. *As an amulet? Have we become that irrational?*

Time passed. From the blockhouse emerged two men in sweat-damp overalls, guns belted at their waists; one of them was stuffing a packet of papers into a satchel. They must have been going through some form of clearance procedure, Waldron decided. The first to catch sight of Greta nudged his companion and rounded his lips in a mocking whistle. They both advanced on the car.

'Waiting got you down, sugar?' the first man said, bending to the passenger's window. 'Why don't you ditch this creep and ride along with us? We're pulling out right now.'

'Yeah,' the other supplied. 'You stick with this guy, you could be here all day. I bet they're going through every wanted file they got looking for his ugly mug—hey, Rick?'

Chuckling, Rick glanced at Waldron for the first time. A startled expression crossed his face. He said, 'Just a moment, Bill. Mister, is—is your name Waldron by any chance?'

Waldron stiffened. 'Yes, it is. How the hell did you know?'

'Jesus!' Rick straightened. 'Bill, get in there and tell that assheaded soldier to quit messing around and clear this car to ride in with the convoy. This here is our new security chief. The boss said he'd be arriving soon!'

Waldron and Greta exchanged looks of astonishment. In an agony of apology, Rick mumbled excuses for not having recognized them, and Waldron dismissed them with half his mind while the other half wondered why in the world Radcliffe had not replied to his letter, given that he had obviously received it.

Well, it wouldn't be long before he had a chance to ask in person. Here was Bill coming back, and the private looking horribly embarrassed, and the sergeant bawling him out, and one way and another it was clear that around here Den Radcliffe swung rather more weight than the Army and the Federal Government put together.

11

Den Radcliffe sat under an awning on the upper-level balcony of his house. He had had it built for him by an architect who was almost pathetically grateful. Since the catastrophe he had designed nothing but emergency prefabricated apartments to be stacked on top of one another like drawers in a chest. Radcliffe's assignment was so perfect an opportunity to pretend that the world was back to normal, he would probably have accepted it without pay.

There were eighty-eight rooms. There was a private lake. There were fortifications on nearby hilltops. There was an underground generating plant which could be switched from diesel to windmill or watermill drive if need be, diesel fuel being imported and expensive. The building was the modern counterpart of a medieval baron's castle, capable of withstanding siege . . . if not nuclear attack.

But one didn't have to worry about that any more.

Gradyville was just out of sight behind a row of hills. So was the alien city. When there was low cloud, the light from the latter could be seen reflected in the sky.

That was the one thing Radcliffe regretted about the site he had chosen for his home.

A phone buzzer sounded. He said to the air, 'Get that!' While it was being got he went on wondering whether he should go down to the lake for a swim or merely call for another beer.

He was feeling very pleased with himself. He put over on Grady the slickest piece of trickery anyone had ever managed against the big greedy slob. He had come back from his recent trip around the States to be greeted by his apologetic staff with bad news. The greater part of a convoy of goods he had dispatched from California had been hijacked in no-man's-land. The total value of the lost consignment was about $100,000, on which he would have stood to pay Grady fifty percent import duty.

He had stormed and reprimanded left and right; he had fired his security chief—Waldron's letter had arrived during his absence, and offered a providential bonus for the scheme; in sum he had generated an impenetrable smokescreen. Behind it he had quietly sold off the goods under Grady's very nose, making a handsome profit *and* escaping the duty. The hijackers had been a team of his own men—not his estate staff, but members of his private army about which Grady knew only that it existed.

Radcliffe had built up that army by slow, cautious degrees. It came in handy for operations like mock robberies, but that was not its real purpose. Ultimately it was destined to oust Grady and install Den Radcliffe as his successor.

He chuckled, picturing the look on Grady's face when he learned he was about to be deposed.

'It's Rick Chandler,' the girl who had taken the phone-call reported. 'The convoy is just leaving the Ball Club post now. They're bringing in the new security chief, too.'

Radcliffe gave a satisfied nod. On this convoy, of course, he would meekly have to pay the duty, but to have sneaked even one load through without . . .

'What was that?' His head snapped around. The girl, dark-haired quite naked, stood in the opening of the double glass doors leading on to the balcony, clutching the phone. He liked to have naked girls around him. 'Did you say the new security chief?'

'Mr—uh . . .' A frown creased the girl's tanned forehead; she found remembering things rather difficult. 'I guess he did say what the name was, but I forgot it again.' Her voice was flat, characterless, like a machine's.

'Give me the phone!' Radcliffe barked.

Frightened, the girl came running, almost tripping over the extension cord. Radcliffe cursed her for a clumsy idiot, and she dropped the instrument at his side and fled.

'Rick!' he exclaimed. 'Is it right that you have Waldron with you?'

'Sure we do. I—uh—I guess I have to admit I didn't recognize him straight off, but you showed that picture and I thought he looked kind of familiar, so I up and asked him, and it's him okay. I've seen his ID. He's the one.'

'When you get here, bring him straight to see me,' Radcliffe ordered.

'Yessir. And his girl friend too?'

'He's not alone?'

'No, he has this blonde along. Dye-and-paint job and not so young as she once was.'

'Hmm!' Radcliffe pondered. 'Get one of your men to take over his car, then, and have Waldron and the woman ride with you in the lead truck. Talk to him, get acquainted. I want your opinion of him, and some of the other men's, before I definitely hire him. The starch doesn't wash out of a cop that easily, you know. If he's not the type you can get along with, I'll have to look for someone else.'

'Okay, Mr Radcliffe,' Rick said. And added after a pause: 'It's good thinking, sir. I know some of the guys aren't too happy about the idea. But me, I trust your judgement and I'll do my best to talk 'em around.'

Radcliffe set the phone down, very thoughtful. Waldron's letter had seemed like pennies from heaven when he found he could tie it to the pattern of deception he'd woven to bolster the mock hijacking. Over the past few days, however, he'd been having second thoughts, which was why he had not written back extending a formal invitation, and he had been winding up to telling his men that there had been a change of plan.

Still, here he was, and it might turn out for the best in the end. He called philosophically for another beer and went on musing.

It was phrased as a polite request; nonetheless it was an order, and Waldron complied, letting Bill take over his car while he and Greta accompanied Rick to the armoured monster heading the seven-vehicle string. He was curious to know what the armour was protecting apart from the occupants, and when he saw crates of liquor and exotic foods he was mildly amused ... and more so when he heard the tankers contained gin.

It was convenient to have this post of authority readymade for him. He could reasonably inquire about details of Radcliffe's organization which no ordinary stranger would be told. Moreover if they had driven in alone they might have run foul of hijackers or had to bribe Grady's patrols even for directions to get where they were going.

There were comfortable padded seats in the back of the cab, plenty large enough for Rick, Greta and himself. He passed cigarettes, learning as he did so that the driver was called Tony.

'I—uh—I heard about you from Mr Radcliffe,' Rick ventured. 'You did him a good turn when he was in the East, that right?'

'More sort of prevented him doing himself a bad one,' Waldron answered dryly. 'Say, how did you come to recognize me, anyhow?'

'Oh, Mr Radcliffe showed us your letter, and he had this photo of you from somewhere. Don't know if you sent it—did you?'

Waldron shook his head, impressed with Radcliffe's efficiency but a trifle disturbed also.

'Pretty good likeness, too,' Rick went on. 'Of course I should have looked at you before I—What is it, Tony?' In response to a muttered exclamation from the driver.

'Only a weirdo,' Tony answered. 'Thought for a moment it was someone else.'

'A weirdo? Where?' Greta had spoken little since leaving the border post; now she craned around like a tourist.

'Over there.' Rick pointed through the side-window of the cab. 'Like a scarecrow—see him?'

Some thirty yards off the road, on a hillside thick with weeds, a man was standing stiff as a post, his clothes ragged, his face turned ecstatically to the sun and his eyes wide.

'What's he doing that for?' Greta whispered. 'Looking at the sun like that, he'll go blind!'

'Maybe that's what he wants,' Rick said contemptuously. 'How can you figure what goes on in a weirdo's head? Nutty as a candybar, him. Tony, why are you so nervous?'

'I thought for a moment he might not be a real weirdo,' Tony muttered. 'That's how the boss lost that big load the other day, right? Guy spotted the convoy by pretending to be a weirdo, gave the signal for the hijackers.'

'Mr Radcliffe had something hijacked?' Waldron probed.

'Afraid so,' Rick confirmed, and told the story. He, naturally, accepted that the robbery had been genuine; Radcliffe had carefully restricted the number in the know.

'Is that going to be one of my jobs here?' Waldron said. 'Preventing hijackings, I mean?'

Rick nodded. 'The guy before you didn't do so well,' he said. 'That's why the job came vacant.' He hesitated. 'I suppose I ought to say,' he concluded, 'that it'll be vacant again if it happens twice.'

'Oh, I didn't come all this way to turn around and go straight home,' Waldron answered with a confidence he did not feel. Out here, away from the familiar surroundings and the pretended normality of New York, he felt naked and terribly vulnerable. But he must put a good face on things at all costs.

A few miles farther on, Tony began to whistle under his breath. Glancing up, Waldron realized why. They had traversed the no-man's-land. While the U.S. government might prefer to call its border posts anything but, Grady had no such scruples. Ahead was a squat concrete building on whose roof an enormous garish red-and-white sign announced GRADY'S GROUND! complete with exclamation point.

'Two miles to Gradyboro,' Rick said contentedly. 'Then just another twenty or so to Gradyville, and a mile and a half beyond and there we are.' He peered past Tony's shoulder. 'Who's coming out for us—can you see?'

'Mother Hubbard,' Tony grunted.

"Ah, shit. Just our luck."

Guards in musical-comedy uniforms barred the roadway; at their head was a bulky woman with grey hair cut man-short who alone among the dozen or so carried no gun. Tony wound down the window beside him and leaned out.

'Evening, Captain Hubbard!'

The woman didn't return the greeting. Her face was as sour as a green apple. 'What you got this trip?' she demanded. 'Where you been?'

'General purchasing mission. Over around the Lakes.'

'Ah-huh. Want to pay up now or have everything listed and sealed?'

'Better seal it, I guess. It'll be quicker. We have an important passenger along.' Rick gestured for Waldron to show himself, and Tony presented him. 'Ex-Lieutenant Jim Waldron of the New York police, our new security chief.'

'Started well, hasn't he?' Captain Hubbard grunted.

'What?'

'Kept the hijackers off you this trip, I mean.' She turned away, signalling to her subordinates, who promptly and efficiently began to inspect the contents of all the trucks.

'I wasn't expecting this,' Greta ventured. 'It all looks so—well, so *official*.'

Rick gave a proud-father smile. 'We're no messy barbarian mudhole here,' he said. 'They tell me this is the richest community in North America—did you hear that?'

A fragment of history was chasing around Waldron's

skull. Abruptly he caught up with it. 'Katanga,' he murmured.

'What?' Rick said, on the verge of leaving the cab.

'Nothing.' But Waldron saw that Greta had reacted to the word and was nodding.

It took only half an hour or so to list and seal their cargo, and then they rolled again. Darkness was gathering as they reached Gradyboro, and huge neons were lighting the façades of the few intact buildings, advertising in about equal proportions gambling and girls. There were no streetlamps, but their absence didn't matter. On several streetcorners they saw groups of people waving banners and handing out tracts to passers-by.

'Relidges,' Rick explained in answer to a question from Greta. 'Cranks who think there are angels in the alien city. We put up with them. They do our dirty work for us. Not bright enough to do more than haul garbage, most of 'em.'

It was fully dark by the time they reached Gradyville, equally bright, a gap-toothed city where ruined buildings had been cleared and the rubble levelled to accommodate tents and trailer-homes which had moved into the vacant sites. By then Waldron was so tired, he found he could not remember the original names of these towns which Grady had re-named after himself. There was also a Gradywood farther on.

'That's the governor's place,' Rick said, gesturing at a distant floodlit edifice with fountains playing before its portico. 'Big—but wait till you see ours. Grady just took that one over and dolled it up. Mr Radcliffe had his built special.'

The convoy, headlights ablaze, rounded the shore of a darkling lake, and there it was: Radcliffe's mansion, a sprawl of armour-glass and reinforced concrete faced with colourful tiles, with pools and flowerbeds and a horde of scurrying servants who closed in on the trucks,

and a scatter of lesser buildings all around, some looking like defence posts, others like barracks or family
accommodation.

'I'm to take you straight to Mr Radcliffe,' Rick said,
helping Waldron and Greta down from the cab. 'And
when he says straight, he means it. Sorry. I guess if you
need to go to the can we could spare that much time,
but that's the limit.'

So, barely having had time to glance around, they
were escorted into the house, along a corridor with one
glass wall fronting the lake, through a door and into a
room dominated by a vast dining-table at the left end
of which sat Radcliffe in an immaculate white suit,
contemplating the remains of what must have been a
gourmet's dinner. But at the other end of the table . . .
Waldron's heart lurched in his chest.

'Ah, Mr Waldron!' Radcliffe said silkily. 'I see you
recognize my companion. Well, I told you I'd get what
I paid for, didn't I? One way or another!'

He gestured for Rick to leave the room. Waldron
didn't notice his departure. His eyes were riveted on
the woman—not on her body, though she was completely naked, but on her face. It was a vacant face
now, almost devoid of intelligence, but there was no
mistaking the identity of Maura Knight.

12

A long and terrible silence followed, as empty of time as of sound. Waldron had no idea whether it lasted seconds or minutes. Eventually Radcliffe stirred.

'Thank you, Maura. You may leave us now. Have someone come with drinks for Mr Waldron and his friend.'

Obedient as a trained dog, Maura rose from her chair. As she passed Waldron on the way to the door, her eyes scanned his face, and briefly a gleam of recognition shone in them; then she was gone, and he was reacting with a fit of almost physical nausea.

'Sit down,' Radcliffe invited, waving at chairs on his right. 'Ah . . . I didn't have to introduce you to my girl friend, but I don't believe I've met yours.' He cocked a sardonic eyebrow.

Mechanically Waldron shaped words. 'Greta—Greta Smith. We—uh—we decided to travel together. I hope you don't mind.'

'Mind? Hell, no. Sensible of you. Half the women on the Ground are whores and the rest are so damned ugly you wouldn't want to look at them twice. Apart from those who are in service with free traders, I mean.

We can get the best in that area, too. Heh-heh!' He chuckled thickly, and Waldron realized abruptly he was drunk. He carried his liquor well, but the tell-tale signs were perceptible in his voice and his flushed face. 'Come on, sit down—how often do I have to tell you?'

They complied. Radcliffe leaned both elbows on the table and stared fixedly at Waldron.

'Well! What made your mind up for you, then? I'd more or less decided you were too fond of your roots to do more than talk about coming here. It was kind of a surprise when I got your letter.'

Waldron had to lick his lips. The shock of finding Maura here had reminded him with painful vividness of the night of their first meeting, and though he could only guess what Radcliffe had done to get what he had paid for he could be damned sure it wasn't pleasant. 'I got tired of making phoney gestures in a smelly office, like you said I would. I wanted to see if it's true that out here things actually happen.'

'Has meeting Maura again changed your mind back where it was?'

Waldron hid his hands under the table so that he could drive the nails into the palms unobserved. He said, 'I didn't think she was likely to speak another civil word to you. What did you do?'

'None of your business,' Radcliffe said, and laughed. It was a horrible laugh, half drunken, half mocking. 'Are you shocked, Waldron? If so there's no point in your staying here. Except maybe you could gang up with a bunch of relidges. We don't live by the book here, you know. We don't waste our time filling out forms and inventing petty regulations. I guess it'll take you a while to get used to that. Maybe you'll never make it. Some people don't.'

A liveried manservant tapped at the door and brought bottles and glasses on a trolley. Radcliffe held out his own glass with an imperious gesture and before serving the guests the man half-filled it with straight whisky.

'Coming in with Rick's convoy,' Radcliffe went on, 'you must have got better acquainted with Grady's Ground than most newcomers manage right away. What do you think of it? Is it like you expected?'

'I wasn't sure what to expect,' Waldron parried. He wanted very much to look at Greta, maybe draw her into the conversation, but he dared not. Her role was exclusively that of a sexual convenience he'd brought along; as much attention as possible must be diverted from her if she was to have any hope of carrying out her mission.

'The hell with that,' Radcliffe said. 'I'll tell you what you were expecting, shall I? I've seen enough strangers react like you. You expected a kind of Wild West show, a patch of anarchy, an every-man-for-himself sort of scene. Balls! We have the civilized amenities. We have flush toilets. We keep our roads mended. We pay taxes, for Chrissake.' He chortled as though at a private joke. The sound turned into a burp. 'We have patrolmen— like regular police except a lot of people who came here thought that was a dirty word. We run this like a modern country, with radio, TV, phones, everything. What's more they work. Yes, that's what it looks like: a modern country. But do you know what it *is*?'

He was leaning so far forward now his chest was almost touching the polished tabletop, and his voice was gruff with the intensity of sudden emotion. Greta, alarmed, fumbled for Waldron's fingers under the table.

'I said do you know what this place is? It's a rat-hole! It's not a country or a community or an empire or what the hell label they last stuck on it! It's a nest of *god damned rats*.' He spaced the words with emphatic care.

'Know something, Waldron? Last time I saw you I was out of the hole. I was on human territory. I was kidding myself I was still a man, rational, intelligent, master of our own planet. And when they radioed me you'd shown up, I got to thinking. I been drinking with it. You noticed.' He drained his glass and threw it tinkling to the floor.

'That kid Maura . . . A rat! Hear me? That's all any of us are—rats, and worth no more than rats. You think I oughtn't to have changed her mind to get what I paid for? You think she didn't deserve it? You do, damn you! I can see it in your eyes!'. Radcliffe slapped the table with his open palm and leapt to his feet so violently he overset his chair.

'Hell, then! I'll have to prove I'm right! I won't have you sitting there thinking you're really a man!'

He stormed to the door and bellowed at the top of his voice for Rick Chandler. Waldron, not moving, remembered that infinitely long ago he had sat in his office and compared free traders like Radcliffe to the same animals: rats, preying on the work of a higher species.

The two identical cars which were waiting at the door when Radcliffe harshly ordered them out of the house were familiar to Waldron only from pictures: silent, luxurious Mercedes limousines with recirculating Freon-vapour engines listed at a basic price of $40,000 and supplied before the advent of the aliens to heads of state and royalty-in-exile exclusively. Rick, looking very tired and struggling to hide his ill temper, was at the wheel of the one into which they followed Radcliffe; the driver of the second was accompanied by four armed bodyguards, two black and two white.

'Take 'em up and show 'em the aliens!' Radcliffe barked, and slumped against the cushions.

Greta gave a whimper of alarm. Waldron wondered how much of it was genuine, how much feigned. He himself was very frightened. The dark night seemed full of unspeakable menace, and Radcliffe, drunk and depressed, was in a dangerous mood. But there was nothing he could do except keep quiet in the hope of not making his new employer still more angry.

The road they took led past two shanty-towns where there were no lights but kerosene lamps, dim in unglassed windows, and another small town almost as shabby, almost as dismal, emitting a stench of sewage that percolated the car's air-conditioning.

'Rats!' Radcliffe repeated, sniffing and jerking his thumb at the car's window.

Waldron tried to orient himself, but failed. He had covered up the roads and names on this part of his map with the lopsided five-pointed star of silver foil he'd pasted to it. He had made it far larger than scale, thinking otherwise it would not show up well enough. And indeed its glow must cover a huge area; the highest hill ahead was peaked with a roseate aura.

Moving towards him as though for protection, Greta asked diffidently, 'How—how much farther?'

'We can get a clear sight from the next rise,' Rick answered. Radcliffe snapped at him.

'Don't stop there! Keep right on going until I tell you!'

Rick gulped audibly, and then nothing more was said for long minutes.

They could see it.

Monstrous beyond conceiving, as though the cities of London and Tokyo and New York had been piled together and turned into a translucent, mist-veiled, iridescent unity. The natural features of the landscape had been ignored; somewhere under the shining mass there had been lakes and hills, roads and small towns, woods and fields—and they *were not*, stamped flat like lumps in muddy dirt. Stabbing hundreds of feet into the night, shafts of luminescence rose: a myriad gems thinned to the substance of a higher cosmic plane. Lights sharp as stars flashed and faded, and the colours rioted—tonight, the commonest was rose-pink, but ever and again blues, greens, pure flame-yellow and white of a clarity to terrify an onlooker crossed the background and dissolved.

Opal and chalcedony, jade and chrysolite, jacynth and amber, ruby and emerald, everything which mankind had ever meant by the word 'jewel' was epitomized in this majestic, awful creation: sixty-six miles from tip to farthest tip of its deformed pentangular outline. Waldron's mouth was dry. He wanted to shrink away from his eyes, cut the nerves conveying knowledge of such a reality to his brain. Not only the sheer integrated size of the alien city—for from this point one could see a mere fraction of it—but the implication that its builders must be not simply more powerful, not simply more advanced than man, but utterly and inconceivably different, made him cringe and whimper silently: *I dared imagine we could act against them? I was a stupid arrogant fool.*

'We live off their garbage,' Radcliffe said in a thin voice. 'How do they think of us? The way we think of flies and maggots . . .? Rick, stop the car.'

Face beaded with sweat, the driver obeyed. The lights of the second car bloomed briefly in the rear-view mirror as it swung out and came to a halt alongside.

'How—how is it obtained?' Waldron forced out. 'I mean the garbage.'

'Oh, it turns up all over the countryside for about fifty miles in any direction,' Radcliffe sighed. 'As though they throw it away at random when they have no further use for it. I . . .' He hesitated, uncharacteristically, as though the awe-inspiring vision before them had sobered him. 'I keep a bit which killed a kid,' he concluded. 'Came slamming in through the window of his room. Cracked his skull.'

'You—uh—you keep a watch on the place?' Waldron hazarded. 'Try and spot the stuff as it comes out?'

'Oh, sure, we tried that. Or rather Grady did. Can't be done. You can't see it being tossed out, you can't photograph it, you can't pick it up on radar . . . I guess it kind of skips the first bit of its trip.'

Greta's hand closed painfully on Waldron's arm. He knew why she had reacted so violently. Corey Bennett, too, had 'skipped'.

Or rather: he's going to.

'So we gave up,' Radcliffe said. 'Only people now who keep watch on the city are relidges. Some of them out there tonight, in fact. Hear them singing?'

Until this moment Waldron hadn't noticed the sound; when his attention was drawn to it, he found he could hear it clearly, slow and solemn and rather sweet.

'Show 'em, Rick,' Radcliffe ordered. Rick switched on a powerful spotlight attached to the side of the car's windshield and swivelled it around. Its beam sworded across a small group of ragged men and women, a few hundred yards distant on a bare hillside, staring with adoration at the alien city.

'You saw some like that back in Gradyboro, remember?' Rick said to Waldron and Greta. 'They come out here one or two nights a week and sing hymns through to dawn. Bring their kids and all. In the rain, too. Even in the snow I've seen 'em.'

For the first time Waldron felt less than contemptuous of the fanatics who had jumped to the conclusion the aliens were visitors from heaven. Certainly they must be closer to the angels than mankind . . .

'Rick, douse that light!' Radcliffe had glanced to his left; now he was peering down the dark hillside. There, a dry gully was shielded from the otherwise all-pervading luminance of the city, and something like a firefly was moving across it, flickering irregularly a few feet from the ground.

'Someone carrying a flashlight?' Rick suggested.

'Flashlight hell!' All the drunkenness and maudlin depression had vanished from Radcliffe's tone. 'Look, it's changing colour all the time. Call the other car. I want whoever it is surrounded—quick!' He flung open the door.

Rick uttered brief commands to a radiophone under the dash, and the guards leapt from the second car and spread down the hill towards the darting polychrome gleam.

'What is it?' Greta asked.

'Could just be that someone's found a live relic,' Rick grunted. He fumbled out a cigarette and lit it without taking his eyes from the half-seen men fanning out around the spark of light. It had stopped moving, as though its bearer had realized he'd been spotted and was about to turn tail.

'A live relic?' Waldron echoed.

'Mm-hm. Turned on, or whatever. In working order, I guess you'd say. I've seen a few, but they pretty rare. The boss got thirty thousand for a big one last summer. He won't let this one slip through his fingers, that's for sure.'

13

Ichabod's first horrified thought as the moving shapes closed on him out of darkness was that his impiety in coveting the pretty relics of the angels had worn out their patience, and avengers were coming to punish him for his sins. Then a flashlight beam sprang up, and he realized those approaching were merely men. Not that that was any great comfort. They would certainly take his prize away from him. Like that nasty Mr Bennett!

Silent tears coursing down his cheeks, he stood with his treasure englobed in both hands, its brilliant multi-coloured splendour leaking out between his fingers. If he had thought of stuffing it inside his shirt . . . But it was too late now.

He cast a frantic glance towards the spot, higher on the hill, where his parents sang lustily with their friends under the fervent exhortation of Brother Mark, and wished he could turn back time and once more find himself on the fringe of the group, cancel his decision to sneak off and search for another beautiful heavenly jewel to replace the one his parents had sold.

'Why, he's only a kid,' one of the silhouetted men said to another.

'And crippled with it,' confirmed the second man. 'Hey, is the boss around? Didn't I see him get out of the front car?'

'I'm here!' an authoritative voice called from slightly higher up the hill, and the speaker came scrambling and grunting to Ichabod's side. 'Get it away from him, Gabe.'

Reflexively Ichabod tucked his hands, and the thing he held, between his legs and doubled up, yelling. It was no good. Strong fingers pried loose his grip and held up the coruscating ball.

There were low whistles, and by the ball's light faces could be seen reflecting awe. 'That's a beauty!' one of the men said in an impressed tone. 'Never saw one that bright before.'

'Give it here,' Radcliffe said, and it was placed in his palm. It was about three inches in diameter, slightly warm, slightly slippery from Ichabod's perspiring clutch; that apart, it was ordinary to the touch, being about as smooth as window-glass. Its appearance, though, was not at all ordinary. Within its translucent depths moved colours as rich and varied as those of the city itself. Radcliffe's earlier despondent mood had faded the moment he saw this object in the distance; now he felt it return, but tinged this time with gentle envy of beings who could create such lovely things.

'Why should they want to chuck away something like that?' Gabe asked rhetorically.

'By mistake?' offered another of the guards.

'You really think *they* can make mistakes?' Gabe countered, and that question went unanswered.

Radcliffe turned to the soundlessly weeping Ichabod with an ingratiating smile. 'Where did you find this, son?' he cajoled. 'Right near here, was it?'

'None of your business!' Ichabod retorted.

'Oh, come now, son,' Radcliffe reproved. 'Sure, it was very smart of you to find it, but finding it doesn't make it yours, you know. Didn't your mother ever tell you that when you find something you have to give it back to—?'

'Boss!' Sharply from Gabe. 'Trouble's coming!'

Radcliffe swung around. The relidges had ceased their singing and a group of half a dozen had detached themselves and were heading this way in the wake of a tall man with a full black beard, wearing a black robe with a big silver cross hung around his neck on a thong.

'Gabe, go back to the car and ask Rick for all the cash he has on him,' Radcliffe instructed. 'For a relic like this they'll probably stand out for at least a thousand.'

'Boss, I have a thousand right in my pocket,' Gabe grunted. 'But don't you know who that is leading them? That's Brother Mark. You could offer him a million and he'd only curse you for a wicked sinner.'

'So that's the famous Brother Mark, is it? How do you know? I've never seen him, or even a picture of him.'

'Right. He says photos are graven images and forbidden. But my kid sister is in his church.' Gabe spat sidelong by way of comment on his sister's views.

They waited. The relidges advanced at a steady pace, not hesitating or hurrying even when they came close enough to see that Radcliffe's men carried guns. Ichabod let out a wordless yell when they were ten paces off, and hobbled at maximum speed to throw his arms around the man third from the front.

'What the hell——? I mean, what are you doing here?' the man gasped. 'Brother Mark! It's my boy Ichabod!'

Brother Mark took no notice. He marched straight up to Radcliffe and held out his hand.

'Give it to me,' he said. 'It's holy.'

Radcliffe studied him. He was an impressive figure: very tall, high-browed, with deep-set dark eyes. But Radcliffe was seldom daunted by appearances.

He let his gaze flicker towards Ichabod's father, and spoke in a deliberately loud voice. 'I was just about to offer the kid a thousand dollars for it.'

At that even Ichabod forgot to cry for several seconds, while his father—one hand on the boy's shoulder in a melodramatically protective pose—gave an audible gasp.

Brother Mark took a pace back, horrified. 'You'd buy and sell a relic of the angels?' he thundered. 'Who are you—apart from being an ignorant blasphemer, which is obvious?'

'I'm Den Radcliffe. Maybe you've seen my place back towards Gradyville. It's not easy to overlook. About twenty times bigger than that hovel you miscall a church.'

At hearing his sect's headquarters dismissed as a hovel, Brother Mark was nettled. He tried not to show it, but it was plain from the sanctimonious tone of his answer.

'What need do we have of splendid churches when the very hosts of heaven have built a temple for us?'

'I never saw you or your followers going in there for Sunday service,' Radcliffe gibed.

'We shall enter in due time, when we are cleansed of our earthly pollution,' Brother Mark snapped. 'You of course will go to hell—though you could gain grace by handing over that relic. Its proper place is in my church. You defile it even by looking at it, let alone touching it!'

Radcliffe tossed the ball casually into the air and caught it again. He shook his head. 'I'm not going to part with it. I'm licensed by Governor Grady to be in possession of things like this, and you're not. I'll pay a fair price, but I won't let it go.'

'But it's mine!' wailed Ichabod, leaving his father's side. 'It's not fair! It's mine, and I won't let you take it away! They took the other one and—and they didn't even give me any of the money!'

His father rushed after him and clamped a hand over the boy's mouth, fractionally too late. Brother Mark had heard the betraying words.

'Greg Sims!' he rasped. 'Has your boy found a relic before?'

Sims moved his feet in the dirt like an embarrassed child. He said, looking at the ground, 'Well—uh . . .'

'Yes or no?' Brother Mark blasted.

'Well . . . Well—yes.'

'A bright and shining relic of the angels?'

Sims nodded miserably. 'But it wasn't my idea—it was Martha's.' The flood of self-justification came with a rush. 'I said give it to the church but Martha said no, tithe it if you like but we must have food and new clothes . . . I did pay the tithe on it, I swear! Paid the whole twelve dollars!'

'Who bought it off you—this unclean sinner here?'

'No, it was a man called Corey Bennett. He made the sign you taught us and said he follows you.'

'No disciple of mine would sell a holy relic for dirty, disgusting *money*!' roared Brother Mark. He flung out his arm, like an angel ordering Adam and Eve to quit Eden. 'Go!'

Shocked murmurs were heard from the other relidges; they drew aside as from lepers. Sims, clutching his son's hand, tried to argue, but Brother Mark would have none of that.

'I said go!' he repeated. 'And take the boy with you! He must be a vessel of evil, or he'd have brought what he found direct to me!'

Catching Gabe's eye, Radcliffe nodded towards Sims. Gabe understood, and as the father and son trudged dejectedly away he followed them. At a discreet distance he invited them to halt, and they complied and stood waiting. So far, so good. Anybody, child or adult, who could find two live relics was worth investigation.

'Now do you give that sacred object over?' boomed Brother Mark. 'Or must I call on angels to visit you with all the plagues of Egypt?'

'Call the angels as much as you like,' Radcliffe answered. 'I'm going to buy this off the Sims family. If you're going to throw them out of the church, they'll need funds to keep them, I guess. You don't come into it at all.'

'Then I curse you!' Brother Mark shouted, and his fingers curled over like claws. But Radcliffe, his expression bored, merely tossed the gleaming ball high in the air again—higher than before, higher in fact than he had intended.

Much higher.

The shock was fearful. He looked at where the ball ought to be. It wasn't. And it had not come down. Only a stain of radiance in the air suggested that it had ever existed.

Vanished!

'I . . .' whispered Brother Mark his eyes bulging, 'I curse—'

'Oh my God!' cried one of Radcliffe's men, and turned and ran.

Radcliffe stood frozen for long moments. He was recalled to awareness of the relidges' hasty departure by a fist pummelling at his arm. It was Ichabod, hysterical with fury. Radcliffe tried to brush him aside, but he persisted.

'Give it back!' he wailed. 'It's mine, it's mine! I want it back!'

'Ichabod, you dirty little sinner!' his father bellowed, stumbling after him through the darkness.

'Leave him be, Mr—Mr Sims, isn't it?' Radcliffe recovered his self-possession with an effort. 'I want to talk to you. I gather your son found one of these relics before.'

'Uh . . . Yes, sir, he did.'

'A hundred and twenty dollars and you didn't give me a cent!' moaned Ichabod. Sims cuffed him into silence.

'Was the other one like tonight's?' Radcliffe continued.

'More like a long thin egg, I guess you'd say.'

'No, I mean did it shine with its own light?'

'Oh, sure. Like the ones they have in the church.'

Radcliffe swallowed hard and tried to slow the pounding of his heart. The disappearance of the shining ball had shaken him, but he was getting over it. After all, just because no live relic had been reported as vanishing before didn't mean there was anything frightening about it. It could well be that the aliens had tossed it out—he remembered Gabe's question—because they knew it was near the end of its useful life, due to go pop like a perished balloon.

Yes, that argument made excellent sense. And the crucial fact remained: Ichabod had found two live relics.

Also Corey Bennett had secured the other one for a mere 120 bucks, when its price on resale would certainly be in the tens of thousands and if it were a particularly fine example even higher. One of Grady's had reputedly fetched a quarter of a million. That wounded Radcliffe in his professional pride. Bennett was new on the Ground; they hadn't even met each other yet.

'Mr Sims, I want you to come and see me in the morning,' he said. 'Bring your son with you. Gabe! Give Mr Sims a hundred, will you? It's—ah—compensation. And another ten for the kid. He deserves his share.'

He cut short Sims's garbled thanks and strode up the

hill towards his car, repressing an irrational desire to glance over his shoulder at every other step for fear an alien was coming after him to reclaim the property filched by this inferior species.

Rick had the use of a pair of binoculars kept in the car, but Waldron and Greta had had only a poor view of what was passing between Radcliffe and the relidges. While the gleaming ball was lighting the scene they could see fairly distinctly, but after it vanished there were only dim shadows.

'Clever!' Rick said admiringly when the ball disappeared right in front of Brother Mark. 'The boss is always pulling new tricks!'

On that basis they expected Radcliffe to be jubilant when he rejoined them. On the contrary; his face was dour and he refused to utter another word until they returned to the house. Then he merely said, 'Rick, get somebody to show them to their room. Good night.'

And that was that.

14

During the last half-minute before 10 a.m., the official starting-time for the conference, Potter looked down the long table and reflected on the paradoxical nature of the gathering. To satisfy those who were still concerned with legalistic niceties, he had had to constitute this group into a sub-committee of the Congressional Committee on Emergency Countermeasures, with unlimited discretion to co-opt.

But was there ever anything so absurd? We're meeting on foreign soil. We include a Soviet cabinet minister, not to mention a woman cosmonaut and a doctor, also Russian; we have three Canadians, an American psychologist, a professor of physics born in Sweden . . .

Who, he realized abruptly, wasn't here. As the wall-clock's minute-hand closed on the hour-mark he said, 'Where's Jespersen?'

A saturnine man named Clarkson, one of the Canadian observers, glanced up in faint surprise. 'Haven't you heard? His plane was overdue at Calgary. They've mounted a search for it.'

'What? What took him to Calgary?'

'He heard a rumour about a live artefact being offered for sale there and flew down to check on it. But he never arrived.'

That's a cheerful note to start the day's proceedings on!

'Excuse me.' Natasha leaned forward. At these meetings she carried on a running translation service for Abramovitch, and frequently had to have post-catastrophe terms explained to her. Potter had not previously realized how many there were. 'He heard about a—what?'

'A live artefact. An alien object showing signs of activity, radiating or vibrating or something like that.'

. 'Thank you. By the way, Mr Potter, I should also say that Dr Zworykin apologizes to be a little late. Pitirim has shown hopeful signs today.'

The others brightened, as though they had been dispensed a careful ration of optimism, like a mental vitamin pill.

'Good,' Potter said. 'But I'll call the meeting to order without waiting for him. Before we get down to regular business, I understand Mr Congreve has something to say. Mike, go ahead, but keep it short, please.'

Congreve rubbed his chin. 'Well, it wouldn't be easy to make it long, because there's damned little to it bar a sneaking suspicion. What I just heard may reinforce it a bit, but . . . Okay, for what it's worth. As you know, Academician Abramovitch is in contact with sympathetic members of the rump administration in the Soviet Union, and at considerable risk to themselves they've managed to relay some messages to us by short wave. I've been analyzing them, and they're very suggestive.

'There's been a noticeable slacking-off in Buishenko's advance. The government forces have held two cities which they'd formerly scheduled for—ah—tactical evacuation this week. Last night's messages were even hinting at counter-moves to regain lost territory. All this

implies that losing Pitirim did indeed undermine
Buishenko's grip on his followers. But . . .!

'Since Buishenko set up his H.Q. in what was designed as an emergency Kremlin during a nuclear war,
it's possible for the government to monitor his transmissions. He's using known cipher-modes and scramble-
patterns. Some of the intercepted traffic recently has
been . . . well, enlightening.

'First off: there was to have been a blitz-style raid
with air support on the government's temporary capital
in the Samarkand region. It's been called off. My assessment is that Buishenko started by assuming Pitirim was
in government hands, but has received information
showing that he was wrong.'

Potter's imagination filled with a picture of the situation in Russia as described by Natasha and Congreve:
the whole monstrous sprawling nation torn to shreds
by Buishenko's Tartar-like hordes, communications
broken, government reduced to impotence by the sheer
distances involved . . . In comparison it made him feel
that North America was the size of a suburban lawn.

'Two: we know that the air pursuit which followed
the *Red Whale* cannot have been Buishenko's. He has
nothing far enough east with adequate speed or range
to have made the interception. In any case why should
he have imagined that the vessel had anything to do
with him? We've been assuming that some local loyalist
air force commander mistook what was going on for—
oh—regular smuggling, or something like that.

'But putting that together with the cancellation of his
planned raid on the temporary capital, another and
very disturbing possibility emerges. We suspect that a
reactionary faction on the government side got wind of
Abramovitch's plan to take Pitirim out of the country
and determined to stop it at all costs.'

Potter sighed, thinking: *let not thy right hand know . . .*

Yes, it was a safe bet that plenty of the surviving high
officials in Russia would judge Abramovitch's scheme
by an obsolete yardstick and treat it as simple treason.
Old habits were dying very hard in this new age of the
world.

'Are you saying they would give the information to
Buishenko?' Natasha demanded. 'Surely they would
never do that! Besides Pitirim could have been taken
anywhere! Buishenko cannot search the entire planet
Earth for him!'

'Well, there's another and even more alarming point—'
Congreve said, but he was interrupted as the door
slammed open and Zworykin came in, his face a battle-
ground between fatigue and jubilation. Directly behind
followed Louis Porpentine, head of the American medical team working in co-operation with him.

Abramovitch hurled an eager question at him and
received as answer a snapped, *'Khorosho!'* That much,
Potter didn't need translated but the rest of the exchange was incomprehensible. He looked appealingly
at Congreve. Before the spy could interpret however,
Porpentine dropped exhaustedly into Jespersen's vacant chair and announced, 'Finally we managed to get
him talking!'

'And are we right?' Potter demanded.

'I guess so.' The psychologist yawned cavernously.
'Excuse me—they called me out at 5 a.m. You'll have to
get the details from Alexei, because I don't speak word
one of the kid's language, but what it boils down to is
this.'

While Zworykin explained the news to his compatriots,
the non-Russian-speakers craned excitedly towards
Porpentine.

Young Pitirim *has* been into the alien city not just
once but several times. What's more, he enjoys doing it,
and the reason he's given for not co-operating before is

that we took him away from Buishenko who allowed him to go in and out of the alien city as often as he wanted.'

There was a stunned silence, except for a murmur of Russian from Natasha.

Potter said at last, 'But how? Without going crazy I mean. And he isn't *that* crazy, is he?'

'God knows.' A lock of hair had fallen into Porpentine's eyes; he shook it aside irritably. 'As you know, Mr Potter—though maybe some people here don't—I've spent over a year evaluating interactions between us and the aliens. I've sifted through literally hundreds of rumours about people who've managed to get into the alien city over here and return alive. I've arranged for Federal agents to enter Grady's Ground and check out the most promising of the stories. But when they tried to pin them down with names and dates they invariably wound up with a reference to some hopelessly schizoid weirdo or else, if they fell in with a religious maniac, they were told about some mythical new saint who's now more than likely ascended to heaven in a fiery chariot. I guess there must be stories like that in Russia, too'—with a glance at Natasha.

'What? Oh! Oh yes, many of them. At the beginning we took them seriously enough to ask for volunteers who would enter the alien city and sabotage it. But . . .' She lapsed briefly into her own language to ask Abramovitch a question, and resumed. 'Yes, it is as I thought. Not one attempt was successful. Either the man vanished, or else later he was found dirty, ragged and insane.'

Abramovitch spoke up, and she translated. 'We shall not know whether Pitirim can do as he says until we have taken him to the alien city here.'

'That won't be so easy,' Potter sighed. 'It's quite true that we can occasionally inject an agent into Grady's

Ground, as Dr Porpentine mentioned—in fact Greta Delarue is there right now.'

Along the table a few cocked eyebrows, a murmur which quickly stilled.

'But the difficulty is that even though Grady may not be a ruthless tyrant like Buishenko he does exert tight control over his territory. A native American can be eased across his border with a good cover-story and preferably a skill that's in short supply there. But what cover you could invent for a mentally-retarded and very sickly Russian teenager, I've no idea. Obviously, sooner or later we shall have to find an answer because otherwise there's no point in having Pitirim over here. But I must stress that it's going to be a very tough problem.'

He hesitated. 'Dr Porpentine, are you certain Pitirim is telling the truth? Couldn't his boast be—well, a fantasy?'

'I doubt it. As you say, he's extremely backward, and his I.Q. is probably under eighty, so it's unlikely he could elaborate such a well-detailed fantasy. But there's no hurry to devise this cover for him, you know. If we take him away from here too soon, we might very well drive him back to his former apathy. I'd say it'll be at least a month before we dare even take him out of the hospital for a walk. On top of which, as you know, he's physically unwell. Buishenko's medical services must be worse than rudimentary.'

'But you're going to have to move him,' Congreve said.

'What?' Porpentine blinked at him.

The spy leaned forward. 'I said you're going to have to move him. For the good and sufficient reason that in a very short time Buishenko is going to know where he is.'

There was a blank pause. Natasha said eventually, 'Mike, I simply don't believe that even the reactionary faction on our side would pass the information to him. Or are you saying that he has agents among them?'

'Neither.' Congreve bit his lip, then seemed to reach a sudden decision, and addressed potter. 'Mr Chairman, I was going to withhold this until I'd discussed it with you privately, but I've changed my mind. I hadn't heard before that Dr Jespersen was supposed to be flying to Calgary in search of a live artefact.'

'What do you mean, "supposed"?' Clarkson countered. 'I saw him take off with my own eyes.'

'Yes, he flies his own plane, doesn't he?'

'Why not? The R.C.A.F. is as short of pilots as your own air force, you know.'

'I'll tell you why not. Because the search party isn't going to find any wreckage on his line of flight. You see, Dr Jespersen has always claimed that he was born in Norrköping, Sweden. But he wasn't.'

Potter felt the world tilt to a crazy lopsided angle.

'Things are still functioning fairly normally in Scandinavia,' Congreve pursued. 'So I arranged to have some checks carried out. I'm now ninety percent certain that Dr Jespersen is one of our Russian friends' most remarkable achievements. I think he's a hypnospy!'

He glanced around, sharp-eyed. 'Anybody here need that term explained? Yes? Well, it simply means that he's had a complete artificial personality constructed for him under deep hypnosis. Suitable subjects are very rare—I believe we only know of about forty cases altogether. They hoped I might make one, but it turned out that although I'm a good hypnotic subject I'm not quite good enough.'

'But what does all this have to do with moving Pitirim?' Porpentine demanded.

'Yes, with the state the world's in now it might seem irrelevant, but for one thing. Among the secrets the Russian government—ah—failed to hide from me while

I was working over there was the location of the report-in point for returning hypnospies. It now lies deep inside Buishenko's territory. I've no idea how Jespersen proposes to get there, of course. His plane has nothing like the range to fly direct. He may very well be shot down, or killed when trying to leave government-held territory. But I can say this with confidence! Nothing short of death will stop him from returning to his base, and the only factor I can think of that might have caused him to go home and report in person is the presence of a Russian cabinet minister here, explicable—according to the principles he was indoctrinated with—solely in terms of defection. And where Abramovitch is, Pitirim can presumably be found also.'

15

Waldron awoke to discover with some surprise that he was lying with his arms tight around Greta. They were supposed to be lovers, so the fact that the guest-room to which Radcliffe had dispatched their baggage was furnished with a double bed had had to be accepted, but it had been Waldron's impression that the pose was to remain a pose. Yet here they were as cosily entangled as newly-weds.

Then he remembered why. For fear the room was bugged—a precaution you might expect a successful free trader to take in the dog-eat-dog society of Grady's Ground—they had cuddled up to whisper their comments on the awe-inspiring spectacle of the alien city. So far, quite clear. But when tiredness overtook them, they had separated, surely . . . And clung to one another again when dreams assailed them. That was it. Waldron felt a prickle of sweat spring out on his forehead.

Because fearful images crowded his sleeping mind— entities as bright and pure as sunbeams, cold as crystal, implacable as fate itself—he had sought comfort, child-fashion, in the warm presence of another body.

Reflexively he hugged her, not from affection but from gratitude that he had not had to be alone. Asleep, without the daytime makeup designed to suit her rôle as a greedy ageing slut, she was more than just attractive; she was beautiful. He had not realized that before. Awake, she maintained a cool aloofness that shifted occasionally into affected superiority, and he had subconsciously edited her appearance to match her manner, thinking of her as hard-faced and emotionless.

Part of that illusion had been dispelled by what she had said last night. The alien city had shaken her as much as it had him. No amount of pictures or descriptions could have prepared a human mind for that astounding reality.

Now her eyes flickered open, and she looked vaguely surprised, but made no move to push away from his embrace. She said only, 'You had a bad night, didn't you? Nightmare?'

'Yes. And you?'

'Yes. About the aliens.' She rubbed her eyes as though afraid of slipping back into sleep. 'Jim, are we crazy? I don't mean you and me. I mean the whole human race. Even to think of opposing creatures like them . . .!'

'I don't know,' Waldron muttered, and rolled towards the side of the bed. 'What I do know is that if we quit, Radcliffe will have been proved right. We'll just be rats and not men any longer.'

'Why was he so bitter about it last night? It had something to do with that girl at dinner with him, didn't it? I meant to ask, but last night I couldn't think of anything but the alien city.'

Waldron, face dark, told the story of Maura Knight. Greta shivered!

'Oh, my God. I assumed she was just a beautiful mental defective. Some men like their women to be stupid. You mean he made her that way.'

'Obviously. Though I haven't the least idea how.'

'Oh . . . Well, it could have been dociline, I guess.'

'What's that?' Waldron glanced up from the case, open at the foot of the bed, from which he was extracting clothes to hang in the closets.

'A drug that a chemist at Pfizer came up with about ten years back. Never publicized. They were evaluating it at Fort Detrick for a while. The Russians were also said to have it. Ten ccs is equivalent to several months' intensive brainwashing.' She shuddered. 'I never saw anybody who'd been given it, but from the reports I read I got the mental picture of somebody like that girl—*drained*.'

Waldron recalled with shocking violence that last night they had worried about the possibility of eavesdroppers. He slapped his hand over his mouth in a gesture for silence, and dismay spread swiftly across Greta's pale face. Not saying another word, she rose and headed for the bathroom.

If there were spy-mikes, those responsible for monitoring them hadn't yet passed on their findings to Radcliffe. Though it was late when they emerged from their room, already past 10 a.m., they were taken to him sitting at the same table as last night, a half-eaten dish of pancakes before him, a servant silently keeping his coffee-cup filled, a cigarette spiralling smoke up from its perch on a portable radio, which wasn't playing!

He greeted the visitors with a curt nod, but said nothing until they were provided with coffee and food. Then he took a last drag on his cigarette and as he stubbed it addressed Waldron.

'Well, *rat*?'

'Yes,' Waldron said. 'It made me feel that small.'

'Good.' Radcliffe took another cigarette and the servant standing by was quick to light it. 'I wish someone would drag Governor Grady out some night and rub his nose in the same sight. I hear it's more than a year since he last set eyes on the alien city. Too long. I go out and refresh my memory every month or so.' He gave a bitter laugh. 'You know, I read once that when they gave a general a triumph in Ancient Rome, they had this slave standing beside him in his chariot to whisper in his ear all the time, "Remember that you're only a man!" ' He emptied his coffee-cup with a nervous gulp and waved away the servant's offer of more.

'But it's better to be like a rat than a mouse, isn't it? Rats have sharp teeth! Rats carry plague. They aren't creatures you can quietly ignore because they're too insignificant to bother about. How do you feel about it? The same way I do?'

Waldron gave a cautious nod.

'Yes . . .' Radcliffe tapped ash off his cigarette. 'You know, when I first saw that map on the wall of your office I thought Christ, here's a rat-type in this swarm of worthless mice. Then I thought again, and decided that if you were content to waste your life in that kind of job now there are aliens on Earth, you must be a mouse at heart after all. And mouse-types make me want to throw up. We have them here on the Ground too, you know. Those relidges! What happens to us if they win out? Why we'll spend the rest of eternity singing jolly hymns to a god who doesn't give a damn about us even if he's up there, and praising angels who are no more angels than I am!' He snorted loudly.

'Grady's not a rat-type, you know. I don't know what you'd call him! Spider, maybe? He runs this Ground pretty damned well, I give him that. But he hasn't been out for over a year to call on the characters he ought to thank for putting him where he is. Instead he sits in the middle of his web listening to the threads of it twang, and sucking the weakest of us dry. But the hell with him, too. He's not concerned about the future. Say, is your breakfast okay?'

Greta nodded, mouth full, and Waldron said, 'This is the best food I've had in months. Best coffee too.'

Radcliffe gave a sardonic chuckle. 'That's what comes of spending the kind of money I have. I do spend it. What the hell would be the point of saving it. Tomorrow the aliens might perfectly well decide they've had enough of us and wipe us out altogether. That's what's wrong with what you were trying to do, you know. What happens if the government pulls things together, maybe manages to regain control of the Ground? Will we be any better off? Hell, no. We'll be tailing along behind people who'd rather pretend the aliens don't exist—fooling ourselves on the grandest possible scale!'

Another servant had silently entered and was waiting by the door for permission to speak. Radcliffe ignored him.

'What we need is guts. That's all. The guts to stand and face that great shining monstrosity and say, "Damn you! Whatever you are, damn you! We have as much right in this universe as you, and a lot more right to this planet! So we're going to kick you back where you belong, and you'll never dare mess with us again!" Agreed?'

'Yes, but . . .' Waldron hesitated.

'But what?!'

'I was going to say I'm not sure we're capable of living up to a promise like that. There's something so completely un-Earthly about the alien city, as though they're not only ahead of us, but started from somewhere different anyway.'

'So what?' Radcliffe grunted. 'Men don't have wings, but show me a bird that can go supersonic! Yes?'—to the patiently waiting servant.

'There's a man called Greg Sims to see you, sir, and a kid with him. Says you told them to call here this morning.'

'I was wondering when they'd get here. Put them in the audience room and I'll be with them in a moment.' Radcliffe pushed back his chair. 'As for you, Waldron, I'll tell you how I want you to spend today. Wander about the Ground. Watch the mice at play. Take in one of these nutty relidge meetings. Say hello to the gamblers and the whores and the rest of them. Ask all the questions you can, get 'em out of the way. Because tomorrow I'm going to put you to work, and from then on I want you to concentrate. Is that clear?'

'Absolutely,' Waldron said, and rose politely as Radcliffe strode away. From the corner of his eye he saw that Greta was having difficulty in concealing her delight. They could hardly have wished for a better break.

At Radcliffe's entry Sims jumped to his feet from the chair on whose edge he had been perching. Carefully drilled, Ichabod copied his example.

'Mr Radcliffe, sir! I'd have been here earlier, but we had trouble last night. I got into this argument with my wife, and then Brother Mark sent a cursing party to sing outside the house and stop us sleeping, and there was this fight with someone from over the way who was being kept awake too, and—'

'Shut up,' Radcliffe said, and dropped into a soft leather-cushioned chair. 'What's your boy's name?'

'Ichabod, sir,' Sims answered, and added apologetically, 'My wife's choice, not mine. Says it means "the glory is departed". I never could see that because according to Brother Mark the glory has come to us now and—'

'Sims, if you always talk like this I'm surprised Mark didn't throw you out of his church long ago. Will you *shut up?*'

Appalled, Sims subsided back to his chair. Ichabod, however, remained standing, his eyes fixed on Radcliffe's face and eloquent of his resentment.

'Good morning, Ichabod,' Radcliffe said levelly.

The boy turned down the corners of his mouth. 'I hate you,' he said. 'I wouldna come if pa hadn't beat me first. You took my ball. I found it! It was mine!'

'Ichabod!' Sims exclaimed. 'You mustn't talk to Mr Radcliffe like that!'

'Sims, if you open your mouth once more I'll throw you out of the room, is that clear?' Radcliffe snapped. And to Ichabod in a coaxing tone: 'Now listen, son. What did your pa say when you had the pretty thing before, the first one?'

Ichabod scowled. 'Said it wasn't right I should have it 'cause I'm not supposed to want anything except grace. He kept on saying that even after he took it away and sold it to the man.'

Sims squirmed, but the force of Radcliffe's threat kept his mouth shut.

Something is going to have to be done about Corey Bennett. But Radcliffe kept that to himself. Aloud he said, 'So where did you get the first one, son?'

'It come from the holy city,' Ichabod said.

'Well, of course it did. But where did you find it? Just lying on the ground?'

Ichabod rubbed his hand on his leg and didn't answer, his eyes roving all over the room.

A little more gentle probing satisfied Radcliffe that like a good many of the unschooled kids from the shanty-towns hereabouts his sense both of past time and of geographical location was poorly developed; moreover, his bulging forehead suggested he must be retarded. He switched his line of inquiry.

'Well, how about the ball you found last night? How did you come by that?'

Ichabod was more forthcoming about this. Half by deduction, half by guesswork, Radcliffe prompted him along a chronological sequence of events that looked highly promising. He learned, in some detail, Ichabod's opinion of all-night hymn-singing sessions, while Sims sat squirming but not daring to interrupt.

Eventually, Ichabod admitted, he'd become so bored that he had simply sneaked away.

'And your parents didn't notice?' Radcliffe inquired.

'Them? Of course not!'

'So what did you do when you sneaked away?'

'Went and got the ball, what else?'

Radcliffe started. It wasn't possible that Ichabod . . . Or *was* it? Memory threw fragments at him: Brother Mark saying that his disciples would enter the heavenly city when they were cleansed of pollution, a look on Ichabod's face which had not been simple rage. He drew a deep breath.

'Now let's get this straight, son. You mean you went into the holy city and just picked it up?'

'Well—well, I guess they must have an awful lot of this stuff because they throw so much of it away, so I thought they wouldn't mind if I . . .' Ichabod's voice trailed away as he stood torn between pride in his own daring and the anticipated wrath of his father.

Which erupted. No threats could have silenced Sims in face of such blasphemy. 'Why, you lying little devil!' he roared, drawing back his fist for a fierce blow to the boy's head! 'I'll teach you to mock at holy things!'

Radcliffe jumped from his chair and caught the up-raised arm a fraction before the punch landed. He kicked Sims's feet from under him and the man found himself dumped foolishly on his backside. By that time alert servants, hearing the outcry, had rushed into the room.

'Sims, I warned you,' Radcliffe said, breathing hard.

And to the servants: 'Take him away. But leave the kid.'

'What?' Sims struggled to his feet, bewildered.

'The kid stays,' Radcliffe said, and noted Ichabod's reaction. Sudden wild hope had flared in his dull eyes.

'But you can't take a man's son away from him!' Sims exploded.

'It's him I'm interested in, not you. Ichabod, what do you think?' And, seeing that Sims was on the verge of another outburst: 'Hold your tongue!'

Ichabod hesitated for a long moment, then gathered his courage. 'Mister, I always wanted to beat pa the way he beats me all the time! And you knocked him down and—and he deserved it. All the time he beats me and sometimes he kicks me, specially when he's drunk. And ma's no better. Worse maybe, 'cause she takes a broomhandle to me. Uh—you won't beat me all the time, will you?'

'I will not. That's a promise.'

'Then I want to stay right here,' Ichabod said firmly.

'When I get my hands on you, you sinful little—' Sims began. Radcliffe cut him short.

'But you won't. There may not be a Society for Prevention of Cruelty to Children on the Ground, Mr Sims, but from what the kid says I'm doing him a service. Of course, it's true that he'll be doing me one . . .' He paused. 'There should be a fee for that, don't you think? Shall we say a hundred dollars a month?'

'Two hundred!'

'One hundred, take it or leave it. Well? Fine!'

And that's a bargain, Radcliffe thought, *considering he looks like a lever to topple Grady for good and all!*

16

'What shall we do first?' Waldron murmured to Greta, and her answer was prompt.

'Go see Bennett—what else?'

He checked in mid-stride; they were walking down the same long corridor with one glass wall which had been the first part of the house they saw last night. 'Isn't that risky? We don't want to draw Radcliffe's attention to him.'

'We know for certain that one way or another a connection has been or will be made between Radcliffe and Bennett. Remember he headed straight for Radcliffe when he turned up at the City of Angels. And it's more likely to be "will be" than "has been". Unless they've got acquainted since Bennett last filed a report, at this moment in time the two of them haven't met.'

Hearing the paradoxical reality of the situation summed up so bluntly made the blood rush and thunder in Waldron's ears. It almost drowned out the rest of Greta's argument.

'On the other hand we don't know from what point Bennett gets—gets displaced. For all we know he may already be involved in the actions which lead up to that.

We can't miss the chance of contacting him at once just because Radcliffe might start wondering if I'm not the person I pretend to be.'

Unanswerable logic. Waldron shrugged and came to a halt at the end of the corridor. 'Where do you imagine they put the car? And do they have proper gasoline distribution here on the Ground?'

'No, but the free traders are never short of it. Grady writes contracts like a South American dictator with most of the big corporations. Look, there's somebody we can ask about the car.' Greta pushed open a swinging door and called to a passing servant.

It took them nearly an hour's search to locate the address Greta had for Bennett; they had to give the impression of chancing on it, for fear that if they asked directions the news might filter back to Radcliffe. It was the only one of a group of four five-storey apartment buildings to have survived the passage of the mad armies. The sight of it, fresh with paint and all its glass sparkling, was incongruous by contrast with the other three so similar and so close, but windowless and with smoke-stains licking up their walls.

'You're sure that's it?' Waldron said in low tones as he braked the car.

'Certain. Look, someone's coming to meet us. You'd better talk to him.'

Waldron nodded, feeling by reflex for the alien artefact he had again slipped into his pocket when he dressed today. Lucky charm or not, he did find its presence comforting, a memento of his old home and his old life.

From the main entrance of the building a tall black man in tan coveralls with an embroidered name on the chest was emerging. He wore a Sam Browne-style belt with a holstered .45. As he came closer Waldron saw that the embroidered name was BENNETT.

'Is—uh—is Mr Bennett at home?' he called out, rolling down his window.

'Could be,' the man agreed warily. 'Depends who's asking, doesn't it?'

'Would you give him this? I think he'll see us when he's read it.' Waldron handed over an envelope; it contained a note scribbled by Greta which consisted of three Scientific Service cipher groups.

The man took the note and went indoors again. Waiting, Waldron glanced up the face of the building and saw that at three of the high windows men were peering watchfully down.

'I guess they don't care too much for strangers here,' he said.

'I know what you mean,' Greta answered in a whisper. 'I feel on edge. As though murder might be done at any moment.'

Neither of them spoke again until the same man returned and curtly invited them to come inside.

They found Bennett in the penthouse, among fine pictures and luxurious furniture: a man of middle height, well dressed, with sandy hair receding and watery blue eyes. The horrible thought crossed Waldron's mind: *so that's what colour they were before they became like Morello's cherries!*

They had come to call on a dead man, and they dared not warn him of the death sentence. He was unspeakably glad that Greta, not he, had to do the talking.

The moment the door closed behind the man who had escorted them, Bennett exploded.

'So you're Greta Delarue, are you? They told me to expect you. But what the hell are you doing here? I'm in a tricky enough position without gratuitous outside interference!'

Not waiting for a reply, he waved them irritably to chairs and sat down himself. 'Who's the impatient son-of-a-bitch behind all this?' he went on. 'Orlando Potter? He's the meddlesome type, I know that only too well. I said I'd need a full year to consolidate myself. I said it was probably over-eagerness that screwed up the last two agents you sent in. Here I am standing in dead men's shoes, damn it! And I've only been here about four and a half months, and here you come, charging in like a herd of buffalo and more than likely leaving a trial a mile wide that anybody with the brains of a mosquito could follow! Am I right about Potter?'

'Yes,' Greta said in a tight voice, sitting very straight on the edge of her chair, her hands white-knuckled in her lap.

'I was sure of it. That slick-tongued bastard with his Committee on Emergency Countermeasures and all that garbage . . . Listen, I may not have been on the Ground very long, but I've been around long enough to realize one thing. All these so-called "countermeasures" are makebelieve. Fairytales designed to help people kid themselves that we can put the world back together and carry right on as though the aliens don't exist.' He gave a scornful snort. 'Hell, it may very well be possible, I admit that. There they sit and ignore us except when we try and attack them, and even then—well, do they actually pay attention to us, or do they simply hang up a few extra flystrips?'

Bennett must have been boiling up to this for a long time, Waldron decided. He exchanged glances with Greta, who moved one eyebrow to signal that they should let him talk himself out before trying to argue.

Leaning back in his chair, he glanced around the room while Bennett concluded his tirade. According to his sketchy briefing, Bennett had come here in the guise of a former insurance salesman. Insurance, notoriously, had foundered in the aftermath of the aliens' arrival. He was in fact a physicist with a good research record, and there were few such people left because so many universities and large laboratories had been in urban fallout zones. His orders were to apply for a free trader's licence—Grady issued the licences—and buy in all the artefacts he could, using government funds, to try and complete the only alien device ever to fall into human hands whose function seemed in the least comprehensible . . . or, if not its function, at any rate the pattern in which its parts ought to be arranged.

He'd done well. Moreover he had displayed considerable talent for his adopted rôle. He controlled this building, he had a staff of over twenty, and—as was clear from the lavish appointments of this penthouse—he enjoyed a very comfortable existence after a remarkably short time.

'We'd get somewhere if we only kept our priorities straight!' he was declaring. 'I've said this again and again in my reports. We're wasting our scientific resources by deploying them so thinly. You know, some of the stuff I've seen imported to the Ground recently makes me *sick*. Thirty-nine-inch colour TV sets! Fruit machines and one-armed bandits! My God, Grady bought himself a chess-playing computer the other day! That sort of thing takes precious skills away from the only job we ought to be doing—studying the aliens!'

He jumped to his feet and began to pace back and forth. 'Here I am working by myself, not even allowed to know how many other Federal agents we've got here, and all around me I see people trading in things that could offer us invaluable data. I don't mind so much about the corporation scientists. I'm friendly with quite a few of them, in fact. I know what they buy up does find its way back to labs with decent facilities, even though their bosses hope to make a fortune before they pass on what they learn. Nonetheless, the situation's ridiculous. They passed that bill saying alien artefacts were Federal property, and no one takes a blind bit of notice, so we may very possibly have the separate parts of a workable device sitting in three different labs this very minute . . . But what makes me want to puke all over the floor is seeing ignorant bastards like Grady and Radcliffe and the rest just grabbing what they can and selling for all the market will stand. Listen, the other day I salvaged something I hadn't expected to find in less than a year's hunting. I say salvaged, because if Grady got hold of it he'd sell it for jewellery! But it's a working artefact, damn it, and—'

He broke off. 'I don't have any business saying that,' he corrected himself morosely. 'We don't even know whether what the aliens build can be said to *work* in any human sense.'

'But according to your reports,' Greta said, 'you think you're on the verge of confirming that they do.'

Bennett hesitated. At length, with a nod, he resumed his chair.

'I think and hope I may be. You see, ever since I arrived here I've been trying to force myself into a different frame of reference. I've been after an intuitive understanding of our relationship with the aliens. A mathematician would probably be better equipped for the job than a physicist like me, but . . . Well, a few weeks ago I had a dream about something I haven't thought of since I was a kid. My family had a weekend place in the mountains, and they built a new freeway that ran right past the end of our land. And the first winter the road was in use, there was a fatal smash on an icy downgrade. They found a fox tangled up in the wreckage. So they went out and shot his mate and cubs.

The more I think about that dream, the more I come to believe my subconscious is telling me something very important. I think these so-called "cities" are nothing of the kind. I think they're interstellar transport nexi.'

Greta whistled. 'It could fit,' she said, staring into nowhere. 'I've seen reports that mention intense gravitational disturbances—intense by comparison with the regular shift due to tides, for instance, though still only detectable with sensitive instruments.'

'I wish to God they'd send me reports like that,' Bennett said savagely. 'Your precious Mr Potter is ready enough to interfere with my work, but he does damned little to help it along. Ever since I hit on this hypothesis I've been asking for data about the colour-patterns in the cities, because if I'm right there ought to be recurrent cycles and maybe synchronicity between various points on Earth. But I can't get an answer.'

'That's not altogether surprising,' Greta countered. 'I mean, the fact that we can get this close to the city here is pure accident. In Russia, Buishenko would shoot down any government scientist who tried to tackle the job. So would Neveira in Brazil, and there's dense jungle in the way there too, while in Australia—'

'I know, I know. Waterless desert!' Bennett sighed. 'And in Antarctica there's literally nobody at all. Oh, well: maybe when we've convinced people that there is a chance of comprehending what the aliens do, we'll get some action. And with luck it won't be long before that happens.'

Waldron tensed. So did Greta, who said, 'Something to do with the live artefact you just mentioned?'

'Exactly. Down in my basement strong-room—it is a strong-room, and of course everyone assumes that's all it is, when in fact it's a pretty fair lab, apart from my having to work in there by candlelight because it might attract attention if I drew power for lamps as well as the instruments I have . . . Well, right in there I have—'

A buzzer sounded. Automatically Waldron and Greta looked around for a phone. It proved to be concealed in the chair where Bennett was sitting. He spoke to its back.

'What is it?'

'Anne Street lookout here, Mr Bennett. Two big limousines coming this way. Mercedes like the ones Den Radcliffe owns . . . Yes, they're his okay. I just got a clear sight of them.'

Bennett started. 'Radcliffe! What the hell can he want? Unless—Oh, no!' He jumped to his feet.

'What's wrong?' Waldron demanded.

'If Radcliffe's heard about that live artefact I bought . . . It was too precious to report to Grady, you see, so I didn't pay the duty on it. It would have wrecked my pose if they'd started wondering why I didn't resell it for jewellery. I hope to God that's not what brings him here. There are some swine on the Ground—like Grady himself—but Radcliffe is a self-styled rat, and he's determined to topple Grady regardless of who gets trodden on. You've heard about him, I guess?'

Waldron and Greta exchanged glances. 'We—we know him,' Greta said. 'It was because he decided to hire Jim that I got the cover I'm using.'

'You're working for him?' All the colour drained from Bennett's face. 'Then get out—fast! Before he comes in sight of the building and recognizes you or your car! Christ, I knew this was a mess when you said Potter was behind it, and now I have Radcliffe on my back because of you!'

'We made sure we weren't followed!' Waldron flared. 'And we checked the car for bugs!'

'Stuff your excuses! Move, both of you! Get lost—and don't come back, or I swear I'll have my sentries gun you down!'

17

'Could they have spotted us?' Waldron whispered. Consciously he knew it was absurd to keep his voice down, but it seemed natural.

Twisting around to peer through the rear window, Greta said, 'I don't think so, but I can't be sure.'

'We'd better get well clear anyhow,' Waldron said, and swung the car around a sharp corner with a screech of tyre-rubber. 'How the hell could he have tracked us to Bennett's?'

'Maybe he didn't. I'm sure there isn't a tracer on this car, and it's a common make and a common colour. More likely Bennett was right the first time.'

'Yes, what was all that about evading tax on the live artefact?'

'Grady imposes a levy on all the free traders he licenses. He insists on all finds being declared. If something extra-special turns up, he tries to buy it in himself so he can cream off the profit, and if the owner refuses he has to pay for the privilege of keeping it—*what the hell?*'

Waldron had jammed on the brakes halfway around another corner, and the car had skidded on a patch of gravel. Across their path, broadside on, was a large black patrol car. Beside it stood four men, all armed, in Grady's gaudy uniforms, who waited silently while Waldron brought his own vehicle back under control and halted it, then moved forward in puppet-like unison.

The most heavily-braided of the four bent to Waldron's window with an insincere smile. 'Morning!' he said. 'I'm Captain Bayers. You're new on the Ground, aren't you? I don't recall seeing you before. Identification, please, and if you'll take my advice you won't argue.'

Sweating, Waldron fumbled out his papers. Greta did the same. Bayers examined them carefully.

'I see,' he said at length. 'Hired by Den Radcliffe and came in yesterday. Okay, get out. Leave the car here. You can pick it up afterwards if it hasn't been commandeered. The governor wants a word with you. And you'd better come along as well, Miss Smith.'

For a moment neither of them moved. Then, suggestively, Bayers dropped his hand to his gun.

'No, I don't want to come in and talk to Mr Bennett,' Den Radcliffe said to the black man who had warily accosted him. 'I want him to come down here. All I want is to show him something.'

The man made to voice an objection, changed his mind, and went back into the lobby of the building where he could be seen talking to a wall-mounted phone. Radcliffe lit a cigarette and glanced at Ichabod, next to Rick in the front seat. The kid had been washed and clothed and Radcliffe's personal physician had applied ointment to a skin condition he was suffering from— like most of the shanty-town children—and shot him full of vitamins and a broad-spectrum antibiotic. He had been troublesome at first, especially at the sight of the hypodermic, but on this drive he had sat as quiet as could be wished, fascinated by the size and comfort of the car.

The black man returned. 'Mr Bennett says—' he began, but Radcliffe snapped at him.

'Hell, if he's scared to show his face let him just peek out of an upstairs window! I guess he owns a pair of binoculars, doesn't he? Rick, open the near door and let Ichabod out for a moment. That'll do.'

Rick complied. Uncertain, Ichabod lowered his feet to the ground and stood blinking in the sunlight, one hand on the car's door-handle as though afraid they might drive off and abandon him. Radcliffe scrutinized the face of the building for any sign of Bennett—and there he was, visible behind an upper window. At any rate the sandy receding hair answered to the description.

'That your boss?' he asked the black man, pointing.

'That's Mr Bennett, yes.'

'He'll go on being Mr Bennett,' Radcliffe said, and curled his lip. 'But he won't be your boss much longer.'

He ordered Rick to help Ichabod back in the car, and subsided with a grunt of satisfaction into the soft upholstery. He had been concerned about Corey Bennett as a possible rival for some while; the newcomer was making too much of a mark far too quickly. The sight of Ichabod, from whom he had bought a live relic which he then failed to declare—Radcliffe had verified that thanks to a spy in Grady's financial records office— could be relied on to make him thoroughly rattled. It would not be surprising if he now quietly decamped. Alternatively he might beg Radcliffe not to tell Grady of his transgression. Either way, he would never pose a threat again.

It was all working out very neatly.

Camouflaged guard-posts protecting the approaches to the Governor's Mansion shot challenges at the car over its radiophone. Bayers replied crisply and the driver did not slow down.

Last night Waldron and Greta had seen the house from a distance. Certainly it was palatial; otherwise it had appeared ordinary enough, an extravagant exercise in mock-classical idiom probably dating back to the early years of the century. As they drew closer, however, they realized it had been turned into a fortress, its façade reinforced with concrete false-walls, its roof screened with armour-plate, its windows eyelidded by heavy steel shutters poised to drop down on a moment's notice. The grounds were densely planted with hedges and shrubberies, but gaps revealed tantalizing glimpses of the private army Grady maintained—men drilling by squads on a gravelled pathway, the crew of an armoured car servicing their guns, six or seven tracked troop-carriers in a tidy line.

At one point the driver swerved sharply to the left, then to the right again, for no apparent reason. Noticing his passengers' surprise, Bayers chuckled.

'Mined, just here,' he said. 'In case you were wondering. The governor doesn't much care for—ah—uninvited callers.'

And he added after a pause, 'Don't worry, though. We have them set so they won't go off simply by being trodden on. Mr Grady likes to take a stroll around the place now and then, you see. And he's a lot heavier than you or me.'

Waldron feigned amusement, though in fact he was too tense to think of anything except the central question: what could Grady want with them?

Before the portico of the house, other cars were parked: one snow-white Rolls-Royce, another patrol-car similar to this, and a red convertible. As they rolled to a halt, a man in impeccable clothes emerged from the house, escorted by an armed guard, and got into the red car. So did the guard, who seemed to be issuing directions. Waldron wondered how many visitors had been accidentally blown up thanks to someone's carelessness.

Bayers and his men led them to the door, handed them over to the resident guards, and turned away, Bayers giving a mocking wave by way of farewell.

The hallway was like a Hollywood reconstruction of a Byzantine palace, marred by piles of loot along the walls. It was clearly loot, even at first glance: pictures wrapped in sacking, rough wooden crates leaking excelsior, furniture draped with plastic sheets. Armed men were everywhere, suspicious, hard-eyed.

Their new escort spoke with a thin man in a black suit. They waited while he vanished and reappeared, beckoning, then followed him down a long corridor towards the back of the house. Greta's hand found Waldron's and clutched it tightly.

Double doors were opened by yet more guards; the doors were of beautiful natural oak, with handles and fingerplates of gold. And here, at a desk bigger than the legendary Pershing desk, framed by a vast window beyond which sun lay bright on long lawns and immaculate flowerbeds . . .

'Governor Grady!' their escort rasped, and threw up a perfectly drilled salute.

Perhaps it was Bennett's description of the governor as a swine which had caused him to expect a gross man, Waldron reasoned. He wasn't gross. He was big, but well-proportioned: six foot three or four tall, with smooth black hair combed over a widening bald patch, a heavy Teddy Roosevelt moustache, red cheeks, sharp dark eyes. He wore a shirt the colour of ground cinnamon; a cream jacket and a black cravat were tossed on one corner of the immense desk, half-concealing a bank of phones and intercoms.

Notoriously he was a self-indulgent man. In front of him was a tray of bottles and glasses, along with a case of eight-inch cigars and a stack of colourfully-wrapped goodies: chocolates, liqueur chocolates and candies. But he did not exude the aura of a decadent feudal lordling. He looked precisely like a man capable of carving out a private empire while most of humanity was on the run like so many frightened rabbits.

He was not alone; there were two pretty girl secretaries sitting on chairs against the wall, one with a notebook and the other with a recorder, while at another much smaller desk a blond man in grey was studying the new arrivals unblinkingly. After a moment he produced a camera and took two quick pictures. But Grady's presence reduced these others to less than life-size.

'Mr Waldron and Miss Smith,' the escort said. Grady gave a nod.

'Get them chairs. They may prove co-operative, and I believe in giving people the benefit of the doubt.'

Chairs were promptly provided. Mechanically Waldron and Greta sat down.

'Right,' Grady said, leaning back and waving one of his cigars absently in the air, a gesture which brought the nearer of the girls hurrying to light it. 'I guess you're wondering'—puff—'what I brought you here for, hm?' Puff, and a mutter of thanks. 'So I'll go straight to the point. I don't have time to waste, you know. I have the Ground to run with an estimated population of nearly a million, and I *run* it, believe me—keep my finger on its pulse night and day. Or I wouldn't be here. So tell me: what's cooking between Corey Bennett and that bugger Radcliffe?'

There was silence. Waldron's mouth was absolutely dry.

'Ah, come on!' Grady barked. 'I know you're new on Radcliffe's payroll, I know you left Bennett's half an hour ago, I know Radcliff went there but left again directly because you'd already gone ... On my Ground I'm like God, you know. Not a sparrow falls but I get to hear *Well?*'

Once more, silence.

'This is your last chance,' Grady said eventually. 'You don't know me yet, do you? You're too new here. Think you can keep secrets from me? Then listen. This morning comes in the boss relidge, the screwball who goes by the name of Brother Mark, to fink on some of his own flock—a guy called Sims, Greg Sims, and his wife Martha. Report is, they have a kid name of Ichabod who found a live relic and sold it to Corey Bennett. Bennett's a free trader. I license free traders on conditions, including that they declare what they find. Bennett didn't declare any live relic. Also I hear that last night the same kid found another one and Radcliffe tried to take it off him. Were you there?' he interrupted himself, catching some betraying reaction on Greta's face. 'Thought you might have been. It'd take some special reason like inducting important new staff to keep Radcliffe away from his bedmates at that time of night!' He chuckled coarsely.

'Now today you go down to see Bennett, and you're the first birds to tangle in the net I'm putting around him. The second would have been Den Radcliffe and his men—except I thought, why the hell put Radcliffe's back up? He's a conceited bugger, thinks I don't know he dreams of the day when he'll be here instead of me. Let him dream; he'll fall over his own feet in the end. Also he hasn't declared any live relic lately, either, and particularly not the one he took off the kid last night. Brother Mark says the angels came and took it back, but he'd say that anyway. No, my guess is that Radcliffe and Bennett are trying to screw me, and I don't propose to let 'em.'

He leaned in fake-confidential fashion on the desk. 'I don't blame you for being taken in by Radcliffe's lies, you know. I'd be the first to admit that he runs an impressive operation. But if he snowed you with stories about how he's going to move me over, he was conning you the way he cons himself. He's the one due to go crash—and soon, too. So if you don't want to be dragged down with him . . .'

Waldron took a deep breath. 'Mr Grady, we only arrived yesterday, you know. Mr Radcliffe hasn't even briefed me on my duties yet. I can say one thing, though: he didn't pick up any live relic last night. It did vanish. I guess it—well, maybe it sort of burst.'

'That's a good one,' Grady said. 'Tell me another. Tell me for instance why you just went to pay a social call on Bennett, hm?'

The words hung on the air as though engraved in fire, and no sound followed them. Waldron glanced past Grady's shoulder, and froze rock-still, and knew without looking that Greta and the secretaries and the guards and the fairhaired man were staring at the window too. As though moving in deep mud, slowly and with infinite effort, Grady also turned his head.

Coming up the long sweep of lawn, not on the ground but—above? No, somehow *around* it, around any ordinary direction of travel. What? *Something*. Something hurtfully bright to the eyes. Something moving within itself without relation to its forward progress. Something as alien and as terrible as the monstrous city they had gone to see last night . . .

18

Sweating, Bennett twisted the combination on the door of the strong-room which occupied more than two-thirds of the basement of his home. He knew the door to the stairs was shut and bolted, and he had welded steel bars across the elevator shaft himself. Nonetheless he kept looking over his shoulder expecting to find that he was being watched.

There was only one explanation for the charade Radcliffe had mounted. He knew about the live relic Ichabod had found, and proposed to betray its existence to Grady.

Damn fool that I was, to lie and hide it! But what else could I have done? Grady would have wanted to know when I sold it and to whom, and if I'd delayed he'd have started wondering why and if I'd faked a sale he'd probably have investigated the buyer because there aren't many people who can afford a live relic . . .

The door of the strong-room creaked as it opened. The hinges needed oiling. The hell with them. He struck a light for his candles. Crazy nuisance having to use them, but if he were to run a thicker cable than would be called for by a single lamp into what was

147

supposedly no more than a store for money and valuables, someone might start asking inconvenient questions. Loyalties were fragile here on Grady's Ground; every servant seemed to dream of being a master, and he had had to let himself be regarded as a miser whose favourite pastime was gloating over his possessions rather than risk sharing the secret of his laboratory with anybody.

And there it was: the climax of his achievement.

When it came to studying the aliens' artefacts, conventional methods were virtually useless. They could be weighed, measured, examined through optical microscopes . . . but try for X-ray diffraction patterns and their internal structure would prove opaque; test them with reagents and even under fluorine the surface would be stubbornly unaffected; bombard them with neutrons and there would be no disturbance of the flow, as though the particles had encountered a perfect vacuum . . .

As though they're not at all! What then? Energy somehow stabilized into a non-entropic condition? Words! What could creatures capable of such marvels have had to fear from mankind's petty stocks of H- and A-bombs? Maybe the equivalent of the static electricity generated by people wearing synthetic fibres, guilty of screwing up the micro-circuitry of computers!

So the only possible course was to piece random items together, with infinite patience: choose from hundreds, even thousands, of broken and inoperative odds and ends those which looked as though they might fit.

Like these . . .

It began with a sort of bowl, a foot across, having on its upper surface two indentations following the tautochronic curve, one larger, one smaller. The larger held a half-egg form with three more irregular objects on

top; the smaller held the thin near-ovoid he had acquired from Ichabod. It was—well, it was somehow
complete, not in a technical sense (for he still had no
inkling of what if anything it was *for*) but in an aesthetic
one. He recalled how his hands had shaken when he
set the live artefact in place, thinking that the whole
assembly would perhaps vibrate or glow or—or *something*.
It had not done so, and he was gloomily being forced
to the conclusion that the three irregular objects should
in fact have been one, combined or fused. But how
could they be repaired, if indeed they were broken?
One could not weld, or glue, or braze this impossible
substance . . .

No time to stand around brooding, he told himself.
He had to get this prize of his off Grady's Ground, and
not later than tonight. It should be in a proper government lab. All the aliens' scrap and rubbish should go to
a proper lab! He needed a crate. What could he pack
the stuff into?

On the verge of turning to peer under a bench for
suitable containers—he was sure he had some lying
around—he checked, startled. Was something happening to the . . . device?

He stared. Yes! From the small glowing ovoid, the
pattern of light was now *oozing*—permeating the bowl-
like base, spreading into the larger ovoid, infecting the
three objects piled above!

'Oh my God!' Bennett whispered.

For the process was not stopping when it reached the
limits of the alien substance. It was spreading still
further—staining the very air with radiance and taking
on the shape of something as incomprehensible, as
majestic and as fearful as the place from which its
scattered parts had come. He gasped . . . and the inhalation drew with it some of the stained and coloured
air.

There was a sensation like a blow delivered to—not his physical brain, but—his abstract mind, and he collapsed on the floor without another sound.

When he woke, it was to total darkness and total silence! He cried out, and only echoes answered. Clumsily and timidly he rose to his feet; by touch he found his way to the stairs and up them to the door which was still locked and bolted. All he wanted was to get back to light and fresh air. He did not pause to grope along the bench where he had assembled the artefact and check whether it was still there.

All the lights in the building were out. No one came in response to his moans. The floor of the lobby was littered with broken glass and his shoes crunched at every step. Beyond the doors light beckoned; the neon signs were still ablaze in Gradyville! He moved towards them like an insect courting a lamp.

'There! That's him!' a voice shouted from the shadows outside, and a flashlight beam stabbed him in the eyes. Men came rushing, while he screamed and flailed his arms in vain, and dragged him feet first down his own front steps to spit on him, and beat him, and kick him, the blasphemer who had profaned a holy relic and brought the wrath of the angelic hosts on Gradyville.

When they had finished, they threw him in a ditch half-full of wet mud.

The intercom on Potter's desk buzzed. He had been gnawing at nails already bitten to the quick and staring at the black rectangle of the window, punctuated only by stars. They had ordered a blackout for tonight, preparing for the worst.

More than likely someone wants to know why I haven't drawn the curtains to hide the glow of my cigarette . . .

'What is it?'

'Air Marshal Fyffe and his aide are here, sir.'

'Send them right in,' Potter said, and rose to draw the curtains and switch on the lights; one could hardly receive the acting Chief of Continental Defence in a starlit office.

One glance at the face of the elderly man who entered told him that the news was bad.

'Buishenko's taken Vladivostok!' he exclaimed.

The Air Marshal nodded. 'Worse than that. Better let Farnsworth give you the details—he heard them direct.'

The younger man, in R.C.A.F. squadron leader's uniform, who had come in with Fyffe passed his brown leather gloves from hand to hand nervously as he spoke. 'Well, sir, it's pretty difficult to get a coherent picture. Apparently there have been massive defections on the government side and their forces are completely disorganized, so Mr Abramovitch's contacts haven't been getting through at the agreed times. We have jamming on their regular wavelength, which suggests—'

'For heaven's sake, man!' Fyffe rapped. 'Stop maundering and come to the point!'

Farnsworth reddened. 'Sorry, sir. I was just trying to make it clear that we're only getting scraps of data. But we do know Buishenko took Vladivostok five or six hours ago against negligible resistance, which means he'll have suffered very few casualties, whereas we hoped he might have to lick his wounds for a bit. And, just to cap the rest, our naval forces standing by off the coast have been attacked with a new weapon.'

The words took time to register. Potter felt as though liquid air had been poured into his skull, freezing his mental processes. 'Something he got from the aliens?' he whispered at last.

'Presumably,' Fyffe grunted. 'At first, from the description I was given, I thought it must be something conventional like the "flaming onions" the Germans used for metropolitan defence in World War II. But we've had a few television pictures now, and they're definitely not ordinary missiles that he's using. They're large, diffuse, glowing balls that last anything up to a quarter of an hour. They seem to pop out of nowhere. They get sucked into a plane's jet intake, or drift down a ship's ventilator, and explode.'

'Our reports indicate that the entire air defence system around Vladivostok was taken out with these things,' Farnsworth amplified. 'After that Buishenko moved up in division strength, following a feint towards a point on the coast farther north, and surrounded the city and its port. Then he dropped paratroops. But nothing like as many as we know he can call on. I'm afraid he must be reserving the rest for us.'

'Invasion?' Potter spat out the word as though it had burned his tongue.

'We've got to be prepared for one,' Fyffe confirmed. In the same moment the intercom buzzed. Potter snapped the switch.

'What the hell do you want? I'm busy!'

'Message for the Air Marshal, sir. We have a Cardinal on radar at 65,000 feet.' The voice sounded vaguely puzzled. 'I'm told just to say that, and he'll understand.'

'Thank you,' Potter said, and to Fyffe: 'The Cardinal—isn't that their ultra-high altitude spy plane?'

Fyffe nodded.

'Can we shoot it down?'

'No, we can't.' Fyffe's shoulders hunched as though they bore the cares of the entire world. 'We have nothing on the whole western seaboard that could reach 65,000 feet and intercept.'

'I presume this means that your Mr Congreve was right about Dr Jespersen,' Farnsworth said. 'It can't be simple coincidence that Buishenko has concentrated all his efforts for the past week on moving eastwards.'

'No, he's obviously following a lead. And if Pitirim was responsible for him getting hold of a weapon based on alien principles, no wonder he's desperate to get the boy back!' Potter rubbed his weary eyes. 'So we'd better move him out of here, right away. Air Marshal?'

'I've laid on a plane,' Fyffe said. 'It's on ten-minute standby. Dr Porpentine thinks the strain will drive him back to the state he was in when he arrived, you know, but Dr Zworykin thinks he'll be all right provided he and the girl—what's her name?—Natasha go with him and keep on reassuring him in Russian.' He hesitated. 'We haven't been told which flight-plan to issue yet, though.'

'We'll go straight to Grady's Ground,' Potter said. 'Away from an alien city, he's an idiot and nothing more. If it's true that Buishenko has a brand-new weapon, I don't think anybody can doubt that we've got to make use of his talent, too.'

'But it'll be courting disaster if one of the free traders hears about him,' Farnsworth objected. 'I'm told they run private armies and sometimes they fight regular battles. If Pitirim really is such a prize—'

'Courting disaster,' Potter cut in, 'is what the human race has been doing for centuries. Should we choose to be different? Besides, what you said is only part of the picture. Grady runs his empire with a tight leash. Some of our own agents settled there, doing research and keeping us posted, and they all say life is much quieter than it was a couple of years ago. What's more, if Buishenko does invade, Grady will have a refugee movement on his hands, and I think we can hole out with—'

The intercom buzzed again. 'For the Air Marshal, sir! Forward naval units report radar contact with massive wave of aircraft, speed height and direction consistent with airborne—*invasion?*'

'Where are they now?' Fyffe barked.

'E.T.A. given as plus four hours fifteen minutes.'

'Four hours!' Fyffe looked at Potter. 'You'd better hurry, then, if you want to be on Grady's Ground by then. The best of luck, anyway. They call this the Age of Miracles, don't they? I hope one turns up. Because otherwise . . .' He turned over a gnarled hand as though spilling a little heap of sand.

'What the hell can they be shifting those troops in?' Farnsworth muttered, half to himself. 'Surely he can't be building his own planes yet!'

Potter thumbed the intercom again. 'Call the hospital, tell Dr Zworykin to get Pitirim to the airport for immediate evacuation. Say I'll meet them there. And have my car at the front door in two minutes.'

'Yes, sir. Uh—where are you going, sir? In case I'm asked.'

'Grady's Ground,' Potter said, for the hell of it. 'As things stand, we're a damned sight safer dealing with the aliens than with our own lunatic species!'

19

Waldron groaned. The act of drawing breath for the groan hurt acutely, because all the muscles of his chest and belly were terribly bruised. But the pain was welcome as evidence that he was still alive.

He opened his eyes and saw only darkness. Something heavy, he realized, was pressing down on his legs, and at once he felt panic in two successive stages: first, thinking of being weighed down under rubble or a beam, deadfall-fashion; second, because the thing on his legs moved slightly and conjured up inconceivable horrors.

There were noises in the gloomy night. Distantly, he heard explosions—perhaps gunfire. Closer, there were scrabbling sounds, crunching sounds, scraping sounds. With slow effortful patience he identified them, shaping words with his stiff lips to make sure he understood himself: *Feet moving in gravel or suchlike, a door being forced wide, someone stubbing his toe . . .*

Abruptly there was light, so brilliant it stung his eyes, and a booming exclamation.

'So he is dead! I couldn't believe it!'

Who's dead? I'm not! I'm NOT! Waldron found his

voice, deep in a throat as dry as a dustbowl, and uttered a meaningless croak.

'What was that?' another man said sharply, and then the first speaker.

'It's Waldron! What the hell's he doing here? Look, behind that pile of furniture. And his girl friend, too.'

I know those voices . . . Oh, yes. Rick Chandler. And the other's Tony, who drove the truck.

'Get them out,' Rick ordered. 'Maybe they can tell us what's been going on.'

Did he say girl friend . . .? Oh! Oh, of course! This heavy and moving thing across my legs. a human body. Yes. Greta. I—I somehow remember her as a soft weight . . .

Figures half-seen in the clash between total darkness and tremendous glare—they had brought a searchlight that required two men to carry it, one for the powerpack and one for the reflector—moved and grasped and helped to stand. Waldron found himself on his feet, one arm around dizzily-swaying Greta, whose face still showed the imbecilic emptiness of shock.

'The boss has been asking after you two,' Rick said. 'Grady's mansion was the last place we expected you to turn up. Don't try any tricks—I'm warning you. He'll want a lot of explaining done, you know.'

'Who's—who's dead?' Waldron forced out. 'Is it Grady?'

'See for yourself,' Rick grunted, and gestured for the man with the light to turn his beam.

Where Grady had sat commandingly at his enormous desk, there was a hole in the floor. Bright shards of glass from the shattered windows overlay everything with a spangling of diamond-dust. Half in, half out of the hole Grady lay, his skull cracked like a boiled egg.

'What killed him?' Greta whimpered, clinging to Waldron as to a life-raft of sanity in an ocean of madness.

'You're asking me?' Rick countered sardonically. 'But you were here when it happened!'

'Rick!' Tony said. He had gone closer to the body, but not to look at it—to peer down between the dangling legs into a pit which had been revealed below. 'Rick, what do you suppose this was, under the floor?'

'Get the guy we caught in the driveway,' Rick said. 'He was one of Grady's top security men, so he may know.'

There was a coming and going, and then from the direction of the double doors a man was thrust forward limping, his hands lashed behind him, his gaudy uniform dirty and a smear of blood drying on his forehead. Waldron recognized the patrol captain who had escorted them here—when? Yesterday, earlier today? He had no idea how much time had passed.

What's the name? Bay-something . . . Bayers!

'There's a big hole under the floor there,' Rick was saying. 'What was it? It didn't get there by accident.' And when Bayers didn't answer at once, he added, 'Spit it out! You can see your boss is dead, so make things easy for yourself, why not?'

Bayers seemed to wilt. He said in a thin voice, 'That was the governor's vault. He kept his best purchases in it. Mostly live artefacts, I believe.'

'Live artefacts,' Rick repeated slowly. 'Yes, that figures—as much as anything does!' He rounded on Waldron. 'Say, what the hell were you doing here?!'

'Ask Bayers,' Waldron sighed. 'He stopped us as we were driving around and told us to leave the car and come here because Grady wanted to talk to us.'

'Is that true?' Rick demanded, and Bayers gave a resigned nod.

'I see. So what actually happened? Did you see it?'

Waldron hunted through a dazing mental fog, and images began to emerge. There had been the—the shining thing, moving towards the house . . . 'I think,' he said at last, 'one of the aliens came to get his property back.'

He had expected Rick to react with surprise, but instead he countered, 'You mean like when the chief threw up that shiny ball last night and it vanished. It fits, I guess.'

'And the churches too,' Tony grunted. Greta was shaking dreadfully; reflexively stroking her head to soothe her, Waldron looked a question, and Rick amplified.

'All hell's been let loose since you've been unconscious. The relidges are up in arms because they say their churches have been looted—you know they had a lot of live relics, and they've all been taken. Then there was this deal where Corey Bennett bought one off the Sims kid, and something happened at his place like what's happened here. We found it empty, all the lights out, the staff run off in panic, nobody around but a bunch of relidges chanting a—an exorcism, I guess. Grady's staff ran off, too. Or tried to.' With a sour grin at Bayers.

'Dirty bastards,' Bayers said. 'No call for them to hand the Ground to Radcliffe on a platter!'

'But that's what's happened, isn't it?' Rick said. Bayers's answer was to spit sidelong into the wreckage of Grady's desk.

'Right, let's get home,' Rick said after a pause. 'Can you walk okay, Waldron? No, you look shaky. Someone give him an arm, someone help Miss Smith too. Move it now—the boss is going to be very interested in what they have to say.'

'Orlando! *Orlando!*'
The words jolted Potter out of the half-sleep into which he had finally managed to subside despite the

maddening drone of the lumbering 'copter's engines. They had decided on a 'copter for the evacuation because it was uncertain what night-landing facilities existed on Grady's Ground. The governor was known to maintain a small private airfleet, but it consisted mainly of helicopters used for chasing smugglers across no-man's-land and a couple of executive jets reserved for him and his personal staff. Servicing and fuelling modern airliners or military planes was probably beyond even his astonishing private resources, so he had not kept up his one available commercial airport, and their landing might have to be made on a highway or rough ground.

'What the hell—?' Potter grumbled, then realized that it was Congreve bending over him; they had included him in the party because they wanted to have as many Russian-speakers around Pitirim as possible. He tensed. 'Is something wrong?'

In a single quick glance he surveyed the interior of the cabin. Nothing was obviously amiss. Forward, the Canadian pilot Fyffe had assigned them—a young man named Stoller—with Natasha next to him as co-pilot; Pitirim stretched out in a semi-coma, watched over by Zworykin; nearby Porpentine was dozing, his head against the shoulder of Abramovitch who was also sleeping. Apparently normal.

'I'm afraid there may be,' Congreve whispered. 'Come over here to the radio. I'll show you.'

Taking great care not to trip over Porpentine's outsprawled legs, Potter scrambled awkwardly to his feet and accompanied Congreve to the navigator's table, over which their radio was fixed.

'Listen,' Congreve invited, handing him a pair of earphones. 'That's Grady's station.'

Nothing was audible but a strong hum. 'Are you sure?' Potter demanded.

'As sure as I can be. We have a directional antenna. The ground-location checks. So does the frequency. So does the power output. But Grady's supposed to operate a round-the-clock commercial sound service, and since I first picked up the signal I've heard nothing but the carrier.'

Potter fought weariness to the back of his mind. 'Uh—have you checked the other wavebands? Could the dial be miscalibrated?'

'I've done everything I can think of,' Congreve broke in. He twisted the tuning knob with angry fingers. 'Here—here's Federal Mid-West out of Chicago, which ought to be harder to catch than Grady's station right now. Here's Federal Far-West out of Spokane. I've had all three Canadian services—hell, I've had the Mexican Government broadcast out of Baja California, clear as a bell! But Grady's, which ought to be loud enough to shake the ship, is—' He snapped his fingers.

'How far are we from the Ground now?' Potter demanded.

'That's the hell of it. We're practically in sight of the alien city. Up ahead there's a faint glow through low cloud which might be a reflection from it, I guess. I never saw it before. You ever seen it?'

'Once,' Potter said curtly. 'After the first of our troops mutinied and turned back—the night they burned Bemidji, in fact. I was sent out to survey the situation, and I saw it then. From the air.' He hesitated. 'I never wanted to see it again, to be frank.'

Natasha called out suddenly. 'Yes, that must be it! Mike, I can see it clearly now! Can you still not raise Grady's station?'

'No!' Congreve said. And to Potter: 'So what can we do?'

'Set course to skirt the alien city to the south. Keep a good distance. See if you can find any transmission at all—police band, hire-car service, anything. If you still draw a blank, we'll just have to announce ourselves.'

Congreve stared. 'Are you sure that's wise?'

'What else can we do, God damn it?' Potter snapped. 'Grady's proud of his radio and TV service. Things must have blown up in his face if they're off the air. I don't want to put down blind, late at night, into heaven knows what—rioting, maybe!'

'Yes, but—'

'Mr Potter!' Stoller, leaning excitedly forward, was pointing through the nose window. 'Down there—flashes on the ground. Looks like rifle-fire. And there's a burning building, too.'

'Sure it's not a reflection from the alien city?'

'No, that's away to port. I'm setting a course to the south—I overheard what you just said. My guess is that we're practically over Gradyville.'

Potter hesitated fractionally, then barked at Congreve. 'Mike, put out a call. Try the old North Dakota State Police frequency—we know Grady uses that. Identify us as a Federal-authorized flight and ask for a landing site.'

'But—!'

'Do as I say!' Potter wiped his face; sweat had sprung on it and he was itching.

Reluctant, Congreve obeyed. For several minutes there was nothing to hear. Ahead, the burning building grew clearer, and at last they flew over it, jouncing in the uprush of hot air. On the streets which the flames illuminated, figures no larger than ants were scurrying about.

'This is worse than I ever expected,' Stoller muttered.

'Look! Look!' Natasha had been peering into the darkness with binoculars; now she was pointing to starboard. 'It's another helicopter, closing on us fast!'

'Mike, call them!' Potter cried.

'I'm trying, I'm trying!' Congreve retorted. And in the same second a voice burst from the radio, harsh and authoritative.

'Federal 'copter! Federal 'copter! Land at once!'

Potter snatched at the mike. 'Hello! Hello! This is the Federal 'copter. We wish to land at a safe site and be conducted to Governor Grady. We can't land blind in the middle of a riot, or whatever is going on. Over!'

There was no reply for endless seconds. And then, with the horrifying inconsequentiality of nightmare, a yammering string of flashes lit the dark shape of the other 'copter and a line of holes sowed itself along the wall of the cabin and the last slug of nine tore open the chest of Pitirim.

20

It was still hard for Den Radcliffe to believe, but it appeared to be true: no one else on the Ground had made preparations against the chance that Grady might drop dead or be assassinated, and consequently the rulership of this territory was falling into his hands like a ripe fruit off a shaken branch.

He sat alone at the custom-built electronic desk he had had installed in an underground sanctum beneath his house. From this one console, he could not only sweep the neighbourhood with hidden TV cameras and maintain radio communication with any of his forces, but also direct the fire of his outlying fortifications, erect barricades, raise and lower steel shutters over all the windows, and in the last resort detonate any or all of over a thousand mines.

But he wasn't going to need his armaments. Not by present accounts, anyhow.

It had been an incredibly confusing day, but sense was finally emerging from the chaos of it all. The information Rick Chandler had radioed in from his car, outside the governor's mansion, had completed another section of the overall picture, and doubtless when they arrived Waldron and his woman would fill in the smaller details.

Meantime he had the chance to savour the taste of power. Pushing a stud on the side of the desk, he said, 'Bring me some cigars and a jug of Martinis, and make it fast!'

Then he leaned back with a feeling of work well done.

First had come garbled news of something amiss at Grady's place—the staff panicking, the private army scattering, forgetful even of their weapons, carrying only some crazy tale about aliens attacking the house. That had been enough to spur Radcliffe into action. His own personal army was both less numerous and less conspicuous than Grady's, but his men were still chortling over the smooth way the governor had been cheated when that consignment of valuable goods was 'hijacked'. Two or three score people had shared the profit on that swindle, beside himself, and when he alerted them they were ready to trust his judgement implicitly.

Then followed the uprising among the relidges, sparked by another similar report, this time to the effect that angels had invaded Brother Mark's church and another or possibly several others, and driven out the worshippers with flaming swords. One rumour claimed that Brother Mark was dead, but so far that had not been confirmed.

Those of Grady's forces—chiefly car-patrolmen—who had not yet heard what had happened to him, because nobody at the mansion had dared announce the news over the radio, found themselves inundated by mobs of frantic relidges. That tied them down very conveniently.

By early afternoon a good deal of street-fighting was in progress; there had also been much looting and a little arson. The relidges had attempted to storm the

radio and TV stations and inform the unbelievers that
the wrath of the heavenly hosts was about to descend
on Gradyville, and since late afternoon there had been
no transmissions on either sound or vision. The defenders had held out until sundown, but either they had
been too busy to go near a microphone, or—more
likely—they were afraid to do so, just in case Grady
proved to be alive after all. If he were, his vengeance
on anybody who had broadcast a report of his death
would certainly be terrible.

Well, by this time they had been disabused of that
idea. Radcliffe's forces were in possession, and waiting
for a land-line to be patched in over which he planned
to announce his accession to the governorship later
tonight, when things had quietened down. He had midnight in mind, since it felt like an aptly symbolic time.

The relidges had also carried out a series of sporadic
attacks on the governor's mansion, but had been re-
pelled by a handful of desperate or disbelieving 'heroes'
and after a good few had been killed had wandered off
in disgust. Also around nightfall, Rick and his men had
moved in and disarmed the defenders, who were well
aware by then that Grady was in fact dead.

Other relidges, with the plain intention of visiting
Brother Mark's curse of last night on its designated
victim—since the angels seemed to have got hold of the
wrong end of the stick—had marched on Radcliffe's
own home. But they had easily been beaten off. It was
from wounded survivors that he had obtained a great
part of his information about the day's events.

Still other relidges had made for Corey Bennett's
place, and there they had not met with such a hot
reception. Radcliffe regarded Bennett as the most likely
among the smaller free traders to keep his head and
try to profit by the crisis; after what had happened this
morning, moreover, his wits would very probably be at

their sharpest. But when a party of his men warily approached Bennett's home after dark, they found the building empty, and a gang of relidges chanting hymns on the sidewalk nearby, smug in their belief that proper vengeance had been wrought on its former owner.

And not one of the other free traders seemed to have reacted positively to the challenge. Radcliffe chuckled aloud—and then grew grave. It was as though a voice had whispered in his ear the phrase he had quoted to Waldron: 'Remember you're only a man!'

Yes, I must drive out and look at the alien city as soon as it's safe for me to leave here. If we've finally provoked the aliens into paying attention to us, I may not enjoy my inheritance for long . . .

Angrily he tried to stifle the thought. He wanted to relish his success at least for a few hours. When a knock came at the door he welcomed it, shouting loudly, 'Come in!'

And here, bringing a box of cigars and a jug and glass and bowl of olives on a tray, unclothed as he had ordered her to remain unless told otherwise . . . Maura Knight.

Wordlessly she set the tray down at his side, and stood back, looking hopeful. Of—? Praise, possibly. Or even punishment. Just so long as he paid her attention. That was her sole reward for living now.

He stared at her, and as though a maggot were gnawing at his brain he felt his triumph turn bitter and putrid. He recalled how he had told Waldron that he was going to get what he'd paid for, one way or another. And he'd done that. She would never refuse him anything for the rest of her life.

Yet he felt cheated. Awareness of that fact had begun to claw its way up from his subconscious yesterday, when he learned that Waldron was on the Ground; that was why he had drunk so much last evening. The same disappointment was undermining his pleasure at winning control of Gradyville.

What drives me? The same need people outside feel, to pretend they are masters of something, or of someone, when compared to the aliens we're mere vermin? But I'm different from them. I'm better. I admit that I'm a rat . . .

It wasn't enough. He couldn't convince himself. The sour thoughts flowed on:

I didn't win this woman. The drug won her for me. I didn't win Gradyville. The aliens gave it to me. What the hell have I ever done that I can be proud of?

Abruptly he realized that someone was peeking in through the door, which Maura had left ajar, and he glanced around. The intruder was Ichabod, looking shy—as ever—but determined.

'Mister, can Maura come back now, please?' he ventured. 'I—I'm kind of scared after all that shooting, and there's nobody else for me to talk to. I guess I'm lonely without my folks.'

What became of the Sims couple in today's riots? Did they get shot down, or wouldn't the relidges have anything to do with them? Maybe they were attacked by their former friends! They'd have been an easy target . . .

Emboldened, fascinated by the contents of the room, Ichabod had advanced across the threshold. With a quick glance at Radcliffe, as though seeking his permission for even such a trivial action, Maura held her hand out for him to grasp.

'You like Maura, don't you?' Radcliffe said gruffly, more to still his dismal train of thought than because he cared about the answer. Ichabod blushed tremendously and gazed at the floor.

'Y-yes,' he said in a near-whisper. 'I—uh—I always wanted to see a pretty lady without any clothes on . . . I did try once. I went around the back of Mrs Harrison's house and looked in the window, but Mr Harrison caught me and beat me, and then he took me off home and my pa beat me too!' He giggled loudly. 'But she shows *anybody*, and I don't feel I'm a dirty little sinner for liking it!'

Radcliffe felt a blast of laughter charging up his throat. He slapped the smooth metal of his desk and whooped and gasped and hooted and almost slid off his chair, while tears poured down his cheeks and the others, at first timidly and then with gusto, joined in.

When he could, he said, 'Oh, Ichabod, that's the medicine I needed! God, I don't know when I last laughed like that—*years* ago! Yes, have your Maura back by all means. Have her all to yourself for as long as you like. That is'—with sudden total calmness—'if she doesn't mind.'

'No, Mr Radcliffe,' the dull voice said. 'I don't mind.'

And, still holding the boy's limp hand, she led him out.

A moment after the door closed, the radiophone in the desk buzzed, and he recalled himself to business.

'What is it?'

'Mr Radcliffe, a 'copter's approaching Gradyville from the west. It looks like a Canadian machine, but someone's calling on our regular patrol frequency claiming that it's a Federal-authorized flight and demanding to be taken to Governor Grady.'

'Hah! They're due for a disappointment, then, aren't they? Where are you?'

'About a mile from them, sir. This is Keene, in the Sikorsky. I've been on survey duty. Base just contacted me and said to go look the intruder over.'

'Well, order them to land at once. Are you armed?'

'Just a sub-machinegun, sir. I mean that we have shells for. We had to use up most of our ammo on a relidge riot. I guess a couple of shots will show we mean business.' And a little more faintly: 'Chuck, you heard that, did you? I'll close the range.'

'Just a moment,' Radcliffe grunted. A light was flashing on the desk now, indicating that someone was approaching the outer defence perimeter. He spoke to an internal phone.

'Who's coming in?' he demanded.

'Rick Chandler's party, sir,' a voice crackled. 'Bringing Waldron and the girl.'

'Fine! Put 'em in the long room. I'll be with them in a minute.'

'Yes, sir.'

Radcliffe turned back to the radio. 'Keene! I'll leave this to your initiative. Shoot through their rotor-sweep, or something. But get them down! After what's happened today I don't want any aircraft bumbling around close to the alien city—it might get mistaken for a bomber!'

Alarm clear in his voice, Keene signed off.

Rapidly, Radcliffe checked with all his outstations in succession, and received reassuring reports from each. The Ground was under his control beyond a doubt.

I wish it didn't taste like ashes . . .

He set the desk on automatic, and rose. As he made to leave the room, though, the radio buzzed again, and he hesitated. A grey cloud of doom blurred his mind, as though he had already heard the message and it was of a nature to destroy his still-fresh victory. But he accepted the call anyway.

'Yes?'

And instead of Keene's voice, it was a stranger he heard, a man almost crying, with other noises blending in: engines droning, a woman shouting, three of four other men cursing. But the man near to tears was shrieking within inches of the microphone, and what Radcliffe heard was this.

'Bastard, bastard, *bastard!* You've killed him, do you hear? You've killed the only person in the world who can walk into an alien city and come out again! You've *killed Pitirim,* you son of a bitch! Murderer! Traitor! *Mur-der-er!*'

21

It dawned only gradually on Waldron that something was badly wrong with Radcliffe. Shock from the fearful experience he had undergone accounted for part of his slow-wittedness; in addition, while he was being interrogated he was also being checked by Radcliffe's personal physician, whose fingers stabbed with painful precision at his injuries before the verdict was pronounced: no broken ribs. He and Greta had been amazingly lucky. Whatever force the alien had used to enter the vault under Grady's office, it had been violent enough to shatter the walls and bring the ceiling down.

And, of course, to smash Grady's skull.

Finally, however, he did realize that Radcliffe was showing none of the signs of satisfaction one would have expected. Why not? A stroke of fate had made him undisputed master of the Ground. It might take a while to consolidate his holdings, persuade the other free traders to recognize his authority and cool down the most fanatical of the relidges . . . but he had such a long start over his competitors that his ultimate victory was beyond doubt.

Yet here he was, betraying no hint of jubilation—looking, indeed, downcast and apprehensive.

Can it be that he's afraid the aliens will snatch his new power from him before he's had time to enjoy it?

It seemed like the only reasonable explanation. Naturally, however, Waldron did not dare broach the matter directly, and before he had the chance to lead up to it by a roundabout route, there came an interruption which put all such matters out of his head.

One of the many nameless servants entered, bringing an extension phone, and whispered to Radcliffe. Seizing the phone, Radcliffe said, 'Yes, Gabe? What's going on?'

Waldron strained his ears in the hope of catching Gabe's distant words, but it was no good; the doctor was putting away his instruments and making too much noise. Still, enough could be deduced from what Radcliffe himself was saying.

'Where did they come from? . . . I see. Is it going to be difficult getting them away from there? . . . Damn the relidges! Run 'em down if you have to! . . . I know, I know, but I want them all brought here right away! . . . Are any of the others hurt? . . . Orlando Potter? Who's he? . . . Is he now? Do any of the others claim to be anything special?'

At mention of Potter's name, Greta had tensed and given a stifled exclamation. This did not go unnoticed by Radcliffe, whose eyes flickered to her face and remained there until he finished talking to Gabe.

'The Russian *what*? . . . What the hell have you found, a bunch of megalomaniacs with delusions of grandeur? . . . Yes, yes, okay. Just get them to the house and I'll make up my own mind. And don't let anybody slow you down, is that clear?'

He slammed the phone back into the hands of the

waiting man-servant and addressed Greta. 'The name Orlando Potter seems to mean something to you!'

Greta licked her lips and sought advice with wide and frightened eyes from Waldron, who had none to give. At last she said in a resigned tone, 'Yes, you're right. He's—uh—he's on the Congressional Countermeasures Committee.'

Radcliffe pursed his lips. 'Interesting! I mean it's interesting that you should know that. I didn't think many people paid attention to the Countermeasures Committee. It's a farcical idea, planning countermeasures against the aliens, isn't it?'

He stroked his chin, looking thoughtfully from her to Waldron and back.

'I suspect we've only had half the truth out of you two,' he went on. 'For instance, you said you were in Grady's office because Bayers picked you up while you were driving around the city. You didn't mention that you'd stopped to pay a call on Bennett. Why not?'

Waldron and Greta exchanged glances. They had had no chance to consult on details of their story . . . but it would have been useless anyway, since Bayers was in a position to punch holes in any lie they used to cover up their visit to Bennett.

'Out with it!' Radcliffe snapped. He leapt to his feet and took two long paces to confront Greta. Shooting out his hand with finger and thumb forked, he pressed cruelly under her chin and forced her to turn her face upward. 'How do you know Orlando Potter, to begin with?'

She jerked her head free and shrank back in her chair to elude a renewal of the grip. 'All right, I'll talk!' she blurted. 'I know about him because I'm an executive of the Federal Scientific Service. He's my chief.'

Radcliffe let his hand fall to his side. 'So that's it,' he said softly. 'I take it Smith is not your real name.'

Sullenly she shook her head. 'I'm Greta Delarue.'

'Did you know about this, or did she fool you?' Radcliffe demanded of Waldron.

'I knew,' Waldron sighed.

'Hah! So why the interest in Bennett? Let me guess. You wanted to move Grady over, and you thought he'd be more tractable than I would, is that it?'

'Hell, no,' Greta muttered.

'There's no point in sticking to a lie, you know!' Radcliffe barked. 'Bennett's probably dead. He's missing for sure. I've had my men combing the city for him, and they haven't found a trace anywhere.'

Waldron jolted on his chair. *Of course not!* he thought. *He's gone looking for you at the City of Angels! What more likely departure point into time than the day when the aliens take a hand in the affairs of Gradyville?*

He turned to Greta, wishing he could come straight out with the idea that had just struck him. She seemed to mistake his expression for advice to make a clean breast of everything. Shrugging, she told Radcliffe, 'No, he's one of my colleagues. A physicist, buying in artefacts not for resale but for study.'

Radcliffe spun on his heel and resumed his chair. When he next spoke, his manner and tone had completely changed.

'I thought those bastards in Washington had turned their backs on the aliens and were concentrating exclusively on their own patch of dirt. Do you mean it isn't true?'

'Of course it isn't. But—Christ, with a hundred and thirty million demoralized, hysterical fools cluttering up the continent, how much manpower do you think we have to spare for work here?'

Radcliffe pondered for long seconds. Eventually he said, 'There's one thing I don't get. I've been priding myself on knowing everything about the Ground. I never had the least suspicion that Bennett was a Federal agent. So if his cover was good enough to fool me, why didn't you go straight to work for him? Why all this pantomime about being Waldron's mistress?'

Greta let go the final devastating blast. 'Because at all costs he mustn't be allowed to find out that he has *already* walked into the City of Angels and accused you of—'

She broke off. In utter amazement Waldron saw Radcliffe's face turn white as milk; his eyes closed, he slumped sideways in his chair.

He had fainted.

To Potter, the events following Pitirim's death were as inchoate as a nightmare. Everything looked, sounded, felt *flat*, the way he had once heard someone describe the experience of a nervous breakdown. There was no emotional depth to his perception of the gaping wound in the boy's chest, of tears coursing down Zworykin's face, or Congreve's hysterical cries flung at the radio. It was as though the fabric of time had been ripped and clumsily darned: things were happening, but they were jumbled out of rational sequence.

He struggled to wrestle his memories into the order in which he knew intellectually they must have occurred. The descent came first, of course, a tangle of noise and blood and stinking kerosene from a punctured fuel-tank. They landed on a highway, with no lights nearby. The other 'copter followed and armed men rushed to surround them and order them out. Over frenzied yelling he had heard Natasha blistering their captors' ears with a medley of archaic, literary insults.

After that, vehicles came roaring up: two huge armoured trucks, their headlights like the eyes of dragons. One of the men who arrived with them was called Gabe, who took efficient charge, silencing the commotion and putting crisp direct questions. He relayed the information back to his base by radiophone from the leading truck. At the edge of consciousness Potter picked up scraps of news: Grady was dead, Radcliffe was taking over the Ground, the rioting they had seen from the air was due to the relidges, the aliens had intervened, or people were saying they had . . . It was too much. All he could think of was the mystical trust he had had in Pitirim, to whom he had never even spoken.

Packed like cattle in the leading truck, they were then carried off for display to Radcliffe. Meantime, what else might not be going on in the world? Potter wondered whether Buishenko's hordes were drifting from the sky like snowflakes, wielding the new weapon he had heard about; whether the aliens were discussing the day's events, after their fashion, debating the need to make another smashing onslaught against the local vermin . . . It was intolerable to think about such possibilities. He let his mind fold inward, passively enduring what the world might offer.

It was not until they had been hustled out of the truck and herded down a long bright corridor into a room where Radcliffe waited for them, that anything struck through his armour of apathy. Then he came back to the present with lightning speed.

Greta!

She looked at him wanly, according him a mere nod for greeting. Beside her was the man Waldron, her associate for this assignment, recognized from a photograph. Both were in torn dusty clothing, and scratches and bruises on their hands and faces had been smeared with yellow salve. They were clearly on the verge of exhaustion.

So, too, was the man presiding over this encounter, Radcliffe himself, whom Potter also recognized from pictures he had seen. But what kind of a person was he? Cast from the same mould as Grady—self-indulgent, unscrupulous, careless of the future? Presumably. That was the likeliest type to rise to the top in this environment.

'I guess you must be Orlando Potter,' Radcliffe said slowly. He did not rise on their entrance. 'And Mr Abramovitch, and Mr Congreve and Miss Nikolaevna and . . .?'

'Flight Lieutenant Stoller,' the pilot said in a dull voice.

'I see. Sit down; there should be enough chairs. Gabe, what did you do with the boy's body?'

'Brought it on the second truck,' Gabe answered.

'Have it put in cold storage. I don't know if there's anyone on the Ground who could learn anything from it, but we'll make sure it's preserved just in case. They can take it to Washington later if they like.'

He glanced at the newcomers, sitting down as they had been told: rendered compliant by weariness, or shock, or despair, or sane unwillingness to offend this unknown tyrant.

'Mr Potter,' he said—not looking directly at him, but slightly to one side, as though ashamed of something— 'I've been talking to Miss Delarue and I've learned a lot I didn't know before. In particular I've been told that the weirdo who attacked me at the City of Angels was, in fact, Corey Bennett.' He moistened his lips. 'I had his place searched, floor to roof, earlier on. No sign of him. But a few minutes ago some of my men called in to say they ran across some relidges who were boasting about how they set on him, threw him in a ditch and left him for dead. He isn't in the ditch now. I reckon he's *gone*.'

Silence; except for loud breathing from fat Abramovitch.

'You're wondering, I suppose, what kind of man you have to deal with,' Radcliffe resumed, and gave a bitter chuckle. 'You know something? So am I. I've been used to calling Grady a swine and myself a rat, and there's a grain of truth in that. But today I've discovered I don't know how to be a *good* rat! Rats carry plague! Rats gnaw power-cables! Rats jam machinery and foul granaries and—and hell, they kill kids! I want to do that much to the aliens, at least, and I don't know how. I want somebody to teach me!'

Potter conquered his astonishment and tracked down his voice in the recesses of his dry throat. He said, 'God damn it, we might have been able to, but—'

'But the boy you brought from Russia has been killed,' Radcliffe broke in. 'Greta told me about him. I wish . . .' He hesitated. 'But you can't turn back the clock, can you? So the hell with it; I'll say this straight out. You're wrong—the Russian kid wasn't the only person in the world who could walk into an alien city and come back again. Right here in this house I have a boy called Ichabod who last evening did just that and what's more brought out a live artefact. You can have him, and all the facilities you need. What I haven't got already, I'll send for. You can make better use of him than I could in a thousand years.'

22

Potter had slept very badly. Last night's events had made him feel as though he had undergone a displacement like Corey Bennett's and been twisted through an alien dimension. *(How? How? But it's pointless to puzzle over that for the time being. One day perhaps we'll find out. Now all we can do is accept it as one of the facts of life—'A of M!' and make the best of it.)*

Moreover the first thing he had heard on waking was a radio news bulletin, which—after insisting that Grady was definitely dead and Radcliffe had taken over—repeated an account of Buishenko's airborne attack on Vancouver Island picked up from the Federal Far-West station at Spokane. It sounded as though he had managed to establish a beach-head within a matter of a few hours.

The son of a bitch . . . I wonder if he'd give up and go away if we delivered Pitirim's corpse to him . . . No, not a hope. He's neither a swine or a rat. He's the mad dog type. It would only make him even more furious.

But Radcliffe had invited them all to breakfast with him, explaining that for the rest of the day he would be tied up with urgent administrative problems, and since the food and coffee were both excellent Potter was growing marginally more cheerful.

As servants deftly and silently cleared away plates and cups, Potter spoke up. 'Mr Radcliffe!'

Instantly there seemed to be a shift of focus, as though—once more—some dimensional distortion had occurred and what had been the head of the table was now its foot.

'Mr Radcliffe, I gather there are at least a few scientists on the Ground sent here by commercial corporations. I don't doubt you can fulfil your promise to provide all the facilities we need, but what we're shortest of is manpower. Do you think it's worth involving people like that in our discussions?'

Oh, this automatic formality . . .! But it's comforting. It props up the illusion that we live in a human-controlled world.

'No', Radcliffe said flatly. 'Scientists can be as greedy as anyone else, and those who've come here for the big corporations are out to make a fortune if they can. I don't believe there's a single one who's genuinely interested in mastering the aliens' techniques for the sake of it. I could be wrong, of course; after all Bennett's cover fooled me, and I guess other people may be keeping up a front. But I doubt it. What about your own committee?'

Potter hesitated. Reaching a sudden and unexpected decision, he said, 'Frankly, they're worse than useless. Let's face it—the people with enterprise and guts were mostly blown to bits when the aliens fired off our nukes, and what we have left is second-rate talent dragged from backwater jobs to hold the line. The idea that we might still be able to make progress hasn't penetrated to them yet; if they can stop us from degenerating into chaos, they're satisfied.'

'Didn't even the news about Bennett shake them out

of their rut?' Radcliffe demanded. He glanced around the table. 'Everybody's been filled in about that now, right?'

'Yes, I think so,' Greta said. 'I told Natasha last night, and I presume she passed it on to Mr Abramovitch.'

'We still have not been told one thing,' Natasha said. 'It occurred to us at once. What was the immediate cause of Bennett's death?'

'Our police surgeon'—from Waldron—'said it was cerebral haemorrhage.' He shuddered. 'You should have seen his eyes. They were all red.'

Natasha translated for Abramovitch, and relayed his reply. 'Yes, that corresponds with what we have found when examining the brains of what you call "weirdos". Naturally we have studied very few, since we cannot approach in Russia the vicinity of our alien city.' She paused. Abramovitch spoke again.

'Yes. It is that name, "alien city". Do we believe them literally to be cities?'

'Bennett had a theory about that,' Greta said, and summarized his hypothesis about transport nexi. That provoked excited nods from Abramovitch. 'But,' she concluded, 'he complained that no one would supply the data he needed to confirm the idea.'

Potter sighed. 'I know only too well. I saw the furious memos he kept sending, telling us to analyze the colour-sequences showing at the other locations. He never seemed to register the fact that ours is the only—ah—city which we can get at. As a first step I did try and persuade my committee to fly a plane over the one in the Antarctic and shoot some film at a pre-arranged time while Bennett was doing the same here, but they outvoted me on the grounds that they couldn't spare an aircrew ... What does Mr Abramovitch think of Bennett's idea, by the way?'

Natasha translated. 'It fits very well. Particularly it

fits the reversing of Bennett's body. Clearly an interstellar transport system limited by the speed of light would offer few or no advantages over physical dispatch of spaceships, but given Bennett's appearance in New York at a time when he was known to be still in Gradyville we have evidence to assume the system operates in directions varying from our normal time-axis.'

'It fits something else, too,' Greta said. 'Whatever the alien artefacts are made of, it isn't matter in any form we recognize. Suppose they aren't matter at all, but—well, coagulations of energy somehow . . .'

'Slowed down?' Potter suggested.

'I guess that's what I mean.' Greta put a hand to her forehead, as though dizzy. 'I can almost see it, but I can't put it into words.'

'Does this tell us anything about the aliens themselves?' Congreve demanded. 'Are they made of coagulated energy too—whatever that is?'

'Not necessarily.' Natasha exchanged several sentences with Abramovitch, while all the others bar Congreve waited impatiently. 'It is possible,' she continued at last, 'that they are not unlike ourselves. Consider: they have chosen *this* planet for their base, with its atmosphere and gravity, when others are available, particularly Mars. We may have seen only manifestations of automatic processes which to us are inconceivably advanced but which to the aliens may be as commonplace as—' a glance at Radcliffe '—mousetraps!'

'It would explain something else, too,' Radcliffe said unexpectedly. 'The fact that Bennett could . . . Well, unintentionally make use of one of their processes.'

'Right,' Potter said with a nod. 'Given that he was reconstructing one of their devices. Hmm! Maybe it also explains why weirdos go crazy. Suppose their time-sense becomes deranged—suppose, for instance, they start remembering things that haven't happened yet?'

Apologetically he added, 'It's just a suggestion. I haven't worked out the implications.'

'One thing we aren't short of on the Ground is weirdos,' Radcliffe said. 'Any time you want a few for study, give the word and I'll send you dozens of 'em.'

'On the other hand,' Waldron ventured, 'this flatly contradicts the fact that Pitirim and Ichabod have been in and out without being harmed. If the aliens really are fundamentally like us, or at any rate more like us than we've been assuming, why don't their processes affect everybody equally?'

Reluctant nods conceded the validity of his point.

'And another thing,' he continued, emboldened. 'Isn't it true that some people have wandered into the alien city and never been heard of again?'

Potter glanced at Porpentine—who had so far said nothing, like Zworykin, as though Pitirim's death had temporarily abolished their interest in the world—and recalled his reference to 'mythical saints who by now have gone to heaven in a fiery chariot'. He started.

'Lord, yes! I wonder whether they . . .'

He didn't need to complete the sentence. It was obvious that the same idea had occurred to everyone. Congreve chuckled and looked at Radcliffe.

'Say, last night you were listing some of the things rats do to humans. You left out one important item. They get on ships, don't they?'

A grim sort of joke, Potter thought. He said, 'You know, the more I consider this, the more I like it. The time aspect in particular. Isn't it true that our concept of time is a highly specialized one? It's not universal, by any means, even among human cultures. Maybe the aliens' attitude to time is different—so different that most people are shaken to the foundations of their minds if they risk entering an alien city. Excuse me; I think we're stuck with the name. A child, though, and especially one whose mental functions are disturbed anyway, might not . . . Well, might not care!'

' "Except ye become as little children",' Congreve murmured. 'The relidges would love to hear you say that, I imagine.'

'There's only one way to find out,' Radcliffe said. 'We shall have to take Ichabod out there and conduct a test.' He hesitated. 'I—uh—I guess I ought to say I'm obliged to all of you, by the way. I never had a bunch of people sit down with me and talk rationally about the aliens before. It makes them look a lot less frightening. I think we've been running scared without any need. I look forward to making a lot of progress very quickly.'

'It's not that simple,' Potter said greyly. 'We're in an island of temporary calm right now. But what's going to happen when Buishenko's forces move inland? The Canadians will do their damnedest to stop them, of course, and we're bound to send all the reinforcements we can spare to help. But our defences on the West Coast are practically back to the musket stage, and Buishenko has this new weapon based on some alien technique.'

'What?' A chorus of surprise and horror. 'What sort of weapon?'

Potter repeated the brief description he had been given, and Natasha and Abramovitch started to talk fiercely in Russian.

Ignoring them, Radcliffe said, 'Oh, I know that, Potter. You needn't think I'm kidding myself. It's going to be tough for a long while yet. I've been wondering what in hell I can do to quiet the relidges, for example. I heard earlier that Brother Mark, the king of the angel-chasers, really was killed yesterday. Walked up to the alien which came to collect the live relics stored in his church, and—well, like you might expect, they say he was struck down by a flaming sword. Losing him means the relidges are like a chicken without a head.'

'So why not give them another head?' Congreve said. 'Before some genuine new fanatic crops up and takes charge.'

'That's an inspiration,' Radcliffe muttered. 'Are you volunteering?'

Congreve put his hand on his chest, startled, as though to ask: *you mean me?* And then, after only a few seconds' reflection, said, 'Well . . . well, why not? I'm unlikely to be any use on the scientific side, and I do want to make myself useful somehow. Okay, I'll—'

He was interrupted by an excited cry from Natasha. 'Now listen, all of you! This weapon of Buishenko—it is not from the aliens!'

'Not from the aliens?' Potter echoed in amazement. 'But where did he get it, then?'

'It is based on work by Academician Kapitza,' Natasha declared. 'When he was under house-arrest by Stalin because he refused to help make a hydrogen bomb, he did research on lightning-balls—no, you say ball-lightning, I am sorry. From his work it was discovered how to stabilize a globe of plasma in the air with power-sources from two intersecting radio beams, very tight. The wavelength is about half a metre to two metres. We had done some work to make the weapon opera-tional, but having so many nuclear weapons we did not complete many projectors. Buishenko must have had more built for him, that is all.'

'I was right,' Radcliffe announced into the subse-quent silence. 'Once you start talking calmly about the aliens, you cut them down to size.'

'Don't be in too much of a hurry,' Potter countered. 'They did explode all our nuclears—piles as well as warheads. They did drive armies insane just by waving a wand . . . If Buishenko's forces manage to reach the

Ground, I guess we can hope for a repeat performance of that, but I can't say I look forward to it.'

'Why are you so sure Buishenko will come here?' Waldron demanded.

'Where else would we logically have taken Pitirim?' Potter retorted. 'As soon as he's convinced the boy isn't at Victoria any longer . . .'

'I'm afraid it's all too likely,' Radcliffe said, glancing at his watch. 'And before it happens, there are a hell of a lot of preparations to be made. You'll have to excuse me. But I won't forget about that trial you want to run on Ichabod. Late this afternoon, maybe, or this evening. I doubt if I can organize it any sooner.'

23

As though the stars have fallen to Earth, Potter thought. *And the Day of Judgement is at hand!*

Although the preparations they had been able to make for this crucial test were minimal, compared to the scale he would have liked—with say a thousand trained scientific observers on hand—they had taken even longer than Radcliffe had predicted. Now it was dark, and below the helicopter which had been put at their disposal while their own was having the bullet-holes repaired, scores of fires sparkled fitfully on the hillside facing the alien city, surrounded by half-seen figures standing up to sing hymns or kneeling to pray.

'Has anybody counted them?' Greta said under her breath.

Potter glanced sideways at her. Their brief separation had returned them to the condition of strangers; they had not enjoyed real friendship, let alone true intimacy, during the months they had been physical lovers. He found that knowledge depressing. Given it was so easy for two human beings to avoid mutual understanding, what hope was there of eventually comprehending the aliens?

'You mean counted the relidges?' he said, though she had probably not expected an answer. 'Oh, two or three thousand, at a guess. I don't know what they hope to gain by camping out. You'd think that now the aliens have wrecked their churches they'd be having second thoughts.'

'Oh, they are,' Waldron said sourly from the other side of Greta. 'All wrong! They're convinced this is the final test of their faith. Brother Mark was really Christ born again, and in three days he will rise from the dead and lead the righteous into the heavenly city.'

'I hope it stays fine for them.' Greta leaned across him, raising her binoculars; they each carried binoculars, a recorder, and a still or ciné camera, while Abramovitch—in the co-pilot's seat forward next to Natasha, who was flying the 'copter—had assembled a scratch collection of instruments from loot found in the basement of Grady's mansion earlier today. 'I don't see any tents,' she added after a pause. 'Some of them don't even have blankets.'

'Too scared to go home and fetch any,' Potter sighed. 'In case fire descends on the shanty-towns like Sodom and Gomorrah.'

'In a lot of places it already has,' Waldron grunted. 'So most of them probably don't have homes any more. Looking at them, you know, makes me wonder what right we have to object when the aliens treat us as beneath contempt.'

Neither of them had the heart to comment on that remark. Potter, uneasy, glanced towards Ichabod, who was excitedly pointing out the fires below to Maura, his inseparable companion. Radcliffe had warned them that the boy might be afraid of flying for the first time, but on the contrary he had been delighted. Apparently his parents regarded man's flying machines as blasphemous—usurpation of a privilege reserved to the angels—

and now he was free of their control Ichabod wanted to try everything they had forbidden.

By contrast Maura looked unhappy and uncomfortable. She had been told to put on a dress, for fear the sight of her body might infuriate the relidges, and she kept fidgeting as though she had completely lost the habit of going clad.

'What became of the kid's family, does anyone know?' Greta whispered. Potter answered in an equally low tone.

'Rick heard a rumour that they were murdered by Brother Mark's followers during the riots.'

'Does he know?'

'Not yet. I judged it better to tell him later.'

'Yes, of course.'

Forward, Congreve—who was armed with a 16-mm. ciné camera to which he had fitted the longest telephoto lens Potter had ever seen—was using binoculars to study not the vast gleaming wall of the alien city, rearing up ahead and filling the cabin with shifting radiance, but the ground, searching for the party of Radcliffe's men who had preceded them in order to clear relidges away from the spot they had chosen for their landing. Looking at him, Waldron said suddenly, 'Does Ichabod have any preference about where he goes in?'

Greta shook her head. 'He says he just walks around until he finds a safe place to enter. According to Zworykin Pitirim was just as vague.'

'What kind of safe place? Does he find—well, a door, or a gate of some kind? Or simply a weak spot?'

'He can't tell us. So all we can do is take him close to where he started from last night. You know Abramovitch and I came out this afternoon and tried to reconstruct his movements. The ground is fairly soft, and we found some footprints. Beyond that, I'm afraid it's up to him.'

'We've spotted the ground party!' Natasha called. 'Going down now!'

'Fine!' Potter answered, and by reflex checked his still camera and recorder.

'What puzzles me,' Waldron said, 'is that he doesn't look in the least bit scared. You'd think after being told so often that the city is full of angry angels . . .'

'True enough,' Greta agreed. 'But he's so pathetically pleased that we approve of what he's done, instead of whipping him for it the way his parents always did. It's a hell of a thing to say, but I honestly think he's going to be better off as an orphan.'

The 'copter touched down. Beyond the glass of the nose loomed the bright bulk of the alien city. From this angle Potter found that it reminded him of something; frowning, he chased and pinned down the elusive resemblance.

Of course. A calving glacier.

But a glacier transmuted. Where the pack-ice of the Arctic would be whitish, greyish or perhaps greenish as it bent to the bitter sea and cracked off its daughter bergs, this was jewel-brilliant, more dazzling than a sunbeam, more colourful than a rainbow, more fascinating than fire. At this point the ground-hue was white with a tinge of yellow, and the bands and striations and jagged flashes which moved across the surface alternated dark red, scarlet and apple-green.

'Those colours mean something!' Natasha said fiercely as she shut off the engines. 'There must be meaning in them. But will we ever know what it is?'

From this close, the sheer bulk of the alien structure was as awesome as its radiance. Shivering—and not from cold—Potter kept feeling his eyes drawn back to it as he thanked Rick, leader of the ground party, for getting rid of the relidges; they were being kept beyond rock-throwing range by the threat of guns, though no doubt they would have enjoyed smashing the helicopter.

Its quantity, its volume, is what makes it so impressive. A human city might cover just as much ground, but it would be notched, skylined, threaded with streets and alleys. This is a unity, a single mass.

His companions were helping Abramovitch rig his equipment, makeshift as it was, apart of course from Maura and Ichabod. When Rick moved away, he took some photographs and noted the exact time on his recorder, and then turned to the boy with an encouraging smile.

'Well, son, this is your big moment, isn't it? But since you've been in there twice before, it should be easy.'

Liar. For all we know the aliens may have doubled their defences and this kid is about to die or go insane . . .

'Oh, sure, mister!' Ichabod chirped. And hesitated, with a glance at Maura, who was gazing in childish delight at the gaudy play of colours. 'Hey,' he went on, 'can I take Maura with me? I know she'd just love it in there!'

Startled, Potter could not answer at once. Waldron had told him about Maura, so he knew her personality had been degraded with dociline or a related drug— and on learning that he had revised his originally favourable opinion of Radcliffe. But did that mean she could stand the strain Ichabod endured without noticing? Sending a backward child on this expedition was bad enough; sending him with an artificial idiot for company . . .

'Oh, please!' The voice was bright and eager, so that for a disjointed second he thought it was Ichabod's again, but it was Maura's; she was showing the first animation he had seen on her face.

'I guess maybe it would be better if you took her

some other time,' he prevaricated. But Ichabod set his jaw mutinously.

'I won't go!' he threatened. 'Not if she can't come too.'

'We're all set,' Greta called, walking towards them. 'He can start off when he likes, and—Is something wrong?'

Potter explained, and then had to explain again when the others, puzzled by the delay, came to find out what was happening. Sweat crawled like insects on his face. He tried cajolery, and Greta tried candy as a bribe, and Ichabod remained adamant.

'Well?' Potter said at last. 'What do we do? Call it off?'

'And come back without Maura,' Congreve said, nodding.

'You're as bad as my pa and ma!' Ichabod exclaimed furiously. 'Telling me what I can't do all the time!' Big tears formed on his eyelids, while his mouth turned down at the corners.

'Is it really out of the question?' Potter muttered.

'Yes,' Waldron said, and the others agreed. 'He can get in and out, we know that. But she might go crazy and attack him, or get him lost, or—anything.'

'Very well. It's an abort,' Potter said angrily. 'Apologize to Mr Abramovitch for wasting his time, Natasha.'

'Oh, he quite understands,' Natasha sighed. 'Please come help pack up the gear again.'

Despondently they complied. But, just as he was about to pick up the first item of equipment, Potter glanced back and uttered an exclamation.

'Hell! They're going anyway!'

'What?' Greta spun around, and almost broke into a run on the instant. Ichabod and Maura were no longer where they had been standing; the boy hobbling in the lead, they were already a couple of hundred yards on their way to the alien city.

Potter caught Greta's arm. 'No, no!' he snapped. 'If we catch him and drag him back, he'll never forgive us. He already said I'm as bad as his pa, didn't he?' Feverishly unslinging his camera, he snapped a picture of the current colour-patterns. 'We'll just have to make the most of our chance. Mike, get your movie-camera working!'

'What do you think I'm doing?' Congreve grunted. 'But there isn't a prayer of filming them as they actually go in—there's no contrast left when you stop down far enough to get the colours right. Should have brought a spare camera with black-and-white film, might give a silhouette effect at least ... Say, Maura's taken her dress off again.'

'Probably a good idea,' Waldron said. 'She's more used to going without.'

Natasha, who had hastily assisted Abramovitch to restore his instruments to working order, straightened and stretched. 'So now we take pictures, and make notes, and wait, hm? I do not often smoke, but if someone has a cigarette I shall say please. It will be a tense time now.'

'Here.' Potter proffered a pack. And went on, 'Of all the damned stupid things, giving them the chance to run off like that! I—uh—I guess I should apologize.'

'Well, well!' Greta said with a recurrence of the mockery he had come to know so well during their time together. 'The great Orlando Potter, apologizing!'

Her tone changed abruptly. 'Oh, for heaven's sake don't make a meal out of it!'

All the colour had drained from Potter's face.

'Greta, quiet!' Waldron said. 'He doesn't look well.'

'I'm okay,' Potter forced out, and covered his moment of shock by taking a cigarette himself. 'Keep up the pictures. We want the fullest possible coverage. I'll—uh—I'll record a note of what happened.'

But behind the effortful calm of his words, his mind was in turmoil.

Doubling their defences ... Oh, I should have thought of this before! Suppose it's nothing as subtle as disturbance of the time-sense which drives a weirdo crazy. Suppose it's simply a low-grade effect of the same defence they use against an army.

It would have to be very low-grade indeed; after all, there were said to be almost a million people now living inside the limit at which armies had been affected.

But if there were two factors involved, one numerical and the other qualitative, so that the reaction could be triggered either by a great many somewhat hostile people or by one intensely hostile individual ... Natasha had said that all the Russian saboteurs went insane; on the other hand, the relidges boasted that some of their number had entered the alien city and never returned.

I must think this over. Because if it's right ...

Later, though. While waiting for Ichabod and Maura to come out again. As yet, they hadn't gone in.

'How much longer?' Waldron muttered, grinding out the latest of too many cigarettes.

'A few moments ago I asked you the same thing,' Greta countered tartly.

'Did you? Sorry, I guess I didn't hear you.' Waldron glanced around; his eyes were tired of the alien splendour and its ceaseless swirl of colour. 'Where's Potter?'

'Went to the 'copter. Said he wanted to call Radcliffe and let him know what's happening.'

'That shouldn't take him long ... I wonder what it's like in there. Did Ichabod manage to give you any idea?'

'Not much. He did talk about a long high place full

AGE OF MIRACLES ————————— 195

of coloured lights, and the shining ball he brought back was *on* something and he had to reach up for it. Might be a pedestal, might be something completely foreign to us. He did make a comparison, though. Said it was like the alley barber's. I gather that was a place with lots of mirrors and bright lights, obviously a barber-shop back in the city where his family came from.'

'Try again,' Waldron told her. 'How about a kids' Christmas show he was taken to? The cave of Ali Baba was full of jewels, wasn't it?'

Greta's jaw dropped. In disgust she said, 'Hell, why didn't I think of that? It never crossed my mind. Maybe I took it for granted his parents would disapprove of going to the theatre. But before the aliens came probably they weren't so strict—'

From behind them there was a shout: Congreve's voice. They spun round, and froze in horror.

With the dragging, zombie-like motion of a man fighting a fit of insanity and losing, Potter was clambering down the short ladder of the 'copter with a gun in his hand. He was descending awkwardly, staring towards them while he kept his balance with his free hand on the side of the door. And his face was transformed: the lips curled back in an animal snarl, the eyes wide and glaring, a shiny trickle of drool running down his chin.

The gun rose jerkily, wavered, steadied, targeted on Abramovitch—or perhaps on his instruments; it was hard to tell. His jaw clenched with terrible effort, and a sound leaked between his teeth which might have been, 'Help me . . .!'

The gun twisted, its muzzle pointed now at his own temple. Waldron moved.

Infinitely long ago, infinitely far away, a piece of the aliens' incomprehensible workmanship had lain on a table in his New York apartment. Shamefaced, he had pocketed it when setting out for the Ground, and it was still in his pocket, and he knew its weight and shape with greater precision than anything else he had ever handled, even his old police automatic.

He threw.

The heavy, stubby rod slammed the bones of Potter's upraised wrist with a noise like a hammer. The gun boomed, the flash scorched his hair, but the slug whined harmlessly away, and by then Waldron had followed his missile, arms at full stretch, to claw anyhow at Potter and hurl him to the ground. Close behind him came Congreve, who twisted the pistol free and kicked it out of reach before applying an expert wrestler's grip. For long seconds Potter strained to break loose; then, as suddenly as it had come on, the mad fit left him, and he went limp and spoke in a thin parody of his normal voice.

'My God, I never thought it would be so strong!'

'What happened?' Greta cried—and the question was repeated in a shout as Rick came hurrying to find out why a gun had been fired.

'I . . .' Potter had to swallow, 'I know now how the soldiers felt when they were driven mad. I was sitting thinking through an idea I'd just had, and I was picturing the way the world used to be—messed up, sure, but halfway to paradise compared to what it's like now— and all of a sudden I found I hated the aliens. It's very strange, you know: I never did manage to hate them before, because they always seemed so remote and— different. Maybe it's because Abramovitch said this morning they may be quite like us after all. I don't know. All I do know is that I felt this great wave of hate go through me, and then, without any warning, I knew I wanted to kill and smash and burn. And because I couldn't hurt the aliens, I'd have to hurt you . . . or myself.'

Unsteadily he rose to his feet, rubbing his bruised

wrist. 'Thanks,' he added. 'What the hell did you throw at me, by the way?'

'This,' Waldron said, bending to retrieve the heavy rod.

Potter stared at it for a long moment. At last he gave a chuckle. 'Well, well! Do you know something? I guess that may very likely be the first time anybody has used an alien product for a human purpose.'

'Corey Bennett?' Greta countered. And he looked at her straight in the eyes and rebutted her with a single word.

'Human?'

24

'The way I see it is this,' Potter expounded. He was shivering although they had wrapped him in a blanket, as a result of the shock he had undergone. But his voice was back to normal. 'If it's true—and we agreed this morning that it must be—that some of the aliens' processes can affect humans, it's worth asking what *part* of us they affect. The answer seems to be the brain, right? Weirdos go crazy, Bennett suffered a brain-haemorrhage as a result of jumping through time ... Leave the reversal aside for a moment; it's not really relevant. From that we can reasonably guess that the aliens may have cut out some of the intermediate stages we use in communication and information processing. Verbalization, for example. Alternatively, and I think on the whole I prefer this idea, they may not reason in linear terms at all, but in—oh—a matrix pattern. Or a field. Or something of the sort, anyhow.

'So it struck me that possibly they have an automatic detector in operation, set to measure the complex of signals in a human brain which associates to hostility. I visualize two inter-related curves on a graph, one measuring straightforward intent to attack, one for some quality like intelligence indicating that when the attack happens it won't just be the blind pounce of an animal; it'll be something sophisticated enough to cause the aliens actual harm. Now when the combined reading exceeds a preset limit, I hypothesize that a counter-field of some kind is generated to modify the pattern. It fits, doesn't it? All of a sudden I found the hate I thought wasn't in my mind bursting loose—what I'd accumulated over years and never noticed. Half a min-ute later, I felt as though I was under a posthypnotic command. Like I said, I needed to destroy something at all costs. And when I resisted that impulse, I found I was turning the gun on myself. Greta, you've read up on the Ground recently. Are there many suicides here?'

'Grady never let out any figures. Bad publicity. But rumour says yes, a lot. Not that that's surprising, of course. Virtually everybody here is some kind of refugee.'

'Yes, but I suspect that a lot of the deaths could be explained by assuming the victims gave way to hatred of the aliens, the way I just did.'

'Something else must be involved,' Natasha said, frown-ing. 'A numerical factor, a third line for your graph.'

'Yes, I imagine there is. Right now there are two or three thousand more or less organized relidges camped around here. If you exchanged them for the same number of troops, I bet they'd take off for an orgy of looting and burning within minutes. Our armies were affected as far away as Ball Club, I seem to remember. At the extreme opposite end of the scale, didn't you say, Natasha, that you actually managed to send in saboteurs?'

'Not completely in,' Natasha said. 'But right up close, certainly. To within a few metres.'

'It fits, Orlando,' Greta said. 'It does fit.'

'Thanks for those few kind words,' Potter countered sardonically. He glanced towards the spot where Congreve and Abramovitch were monitoring the scientific instruments and watching for the re-emergence of Ichabod and Maura. 'Natasha, would you explain my theory to Abramovitch and ask his opinion?'

'Surely.' She had been crouched down at his side; rising, she checked her watch and added, 'I do wish they'd come back!'

'So do I,' Greta concurred grimly. 'It's been over an hour, and we told Ichabod on no account to stay more than a few minutes. All we wanted to prove was that he could get in and out—'

'Hey!' Congreve's voice broke excitedly on the night. 'There they are now, I can see them! But—Hell! Didn't you tell the boy not to pick up anything?'

Scrambling to his feet, Potter called back, 'Over and over! Damn, what did I do with my binoculars? Yes, of course we told him—after the way the aliens snatched all the live artefacts yesterday, it'd be insane to take any more!'

'Then the temptation was just too much for them,' Congreve snapped. 'They've each got a whole armful of shiny gewgaws!'

'Pictures, quickly!' Potter rapped, and raised his own still camera.

As he recorded the current pattern of colours, he realized that even at this distance and on the tiny view-finder screen of the camera he could see how the two approaching figures were bathed in coruscating light to match that from the luminous wall behind them. A tap on his shoulder, and Waldron's voice, worried.

'Should I run over to them, make them drop what they've taken?'

Potter took his time over answering. When he did it was in a resigned tone.

'Too late for that, I'm afraid. Look. And keep on taking pictures.'

He pointed. In horror and dismay they watched: moving with inhuman swiftness outward from the shining city, a thing that did not need the ground to tread on, but moved as a wave moves, making successive volumes of air bloom into furnace-bright radiance. It closed on the humans, and Congreve screamed a futile warning—futile?

Not quite! Potter felt his heart leap. Maura, startled by the shout, turned her head and caught sight of the glowingness as it swooped/dived to the attack. With a cry she incontinently let fall the baubles she carried, so as to snatch at Ichabod and drag him away.

Being suddenly grabbed by the arm, he too dropped his treasures, and began a wail of complaint—cut short by a howl of alarm as he too saw the alien pursuer. Perhaps all the tales about avenging angels his parents had dinned into him rose to his mind; at any rate, he promptly forgot about everything except flight. Limping, moaning, he let Maura rush him along on feet to which terror lent wings.

The pursuer, by a miracle, was content with the booty. Above the random mound of artefacts it hovered; they were somehow drawn up into its substance, and it was gone—not visibly, along the path it had followed before, but in a trice.

'Thank goodness for that!' Waldron breathed, and set out to meet the fugitives at a dead run.

'Shall I carry him?' Congreve said to Natasha, who had picked up Ichabod and was crooning to him over his helpless sobs. 'We ought to get back to the 'copter right away.'

'Thank you—he'd be heavy to walk with. But take care. He has wet himself in fright.' Natasha transferred her burden to him. 'How is Maura?' she added, looking around.

'Shaking like a leaf, but otherwise okay,' Greta reported. She was standing with her arm around the naked girl's shoulders, comforting her. 'So at any rate we've proved what we set out to.'

'A pretty negative result if you ask me,' Congreve said. 'A couple of nights ago Ichabod stole a live artefact and got away with it, whereas this time—'

'Correction,' Waldron interrupted. 'It was taken back when Radcliffe was arguing over it with Brother Mark. No, I don't think our results are negative at all. Have you asked Abramovitch what he thinks?'

'Oh, he's overjoyed,' Congreve answered. 'Said he got a lot of "highly interesting" readings. Now he wants all the live artefacts we can provide, so that he can set them up and see if the aliens will retrieve them too.'

'Funny, the way the—the alien ignored Maura and Ichabod,' Waldron said musingly. 'Almost as though they weren't there. Hmm! I wonder if . . .'

'What?' Potter invited.

'Nothing.'

But, when they were back in the helicopter and all the instruments had been stowed and Natasha was winding up for takeoff, he spoke up again, somewhat diffidently.

'Look, I'm no scientist, and I can't pretend I've followed all the theories we've been batting around today. I feel kind of giddy, to be honest. But I've been piecing together what you said'—a nod to Potter—'with something Mike said this morning, and something you said, Greta, and . . . Well, I think I may have an idea. Mike, didn't you suggest posing as a new leader for the relidges to prevent some unknown fanatic stepping into Brother Mark's shoes?'

'It seemed like a great idea for a while,' Congreve said sourly. 'The more I think about it, the more stupid it looks.'

'Just a moment. Isn't it true that Buishenko owed at least part of this tremendous impression he made on his followers to the way he could send Pitirim into the alien city and bring him back safe and sound? Well, Brother Mark couldn't go in and out—couldn't even send someone like Pitirim. But won't it prove your sanctity beyond doubt when you demonstrate that you can?'

Congreve stiffened. 'Hell, if you think I'd take dociline like Maura just for the sake of—'

'No, no, I don't mean that.' Waldron leaned earnestly forward. 'I'm thinking of what you said this morning, remember? "Except ye become as little children . . .!" And there is a way of "becoming as a little child". I've read about it. It's a trick you can pull with hypnosis, called regression. The hypnotist tells you to act as though you were five years old again, and you do.'

'My God,' Potter said in an awestruck tone. 'Mike, he's on to something. What's more, you're a good hypnotic subject. You said you were once considered as a possible hypnospy.'

Paling, Congreve said, 'Yes, I damned nearly made the grade, too. Are you seriously claiming that I could be put into a trance, walk out in front of a gang of relidges, and publicly pay a visit to the holy city?'

'Greta, could it be done?' Potter snapped.

'You'd have to ask Porpentine,' she answered, brushing hair from her eyes. 'It's conceivable, but don't take my word for it.'

'If this works . . .!' Potter was shaking with excitement. 'Waldron, you've only scratched the surface of the idea. Mike said something else this morning, which I dismissed as just a bit of gallows humour, but now I'm inclined to take it literally. What he said was, "Rats get on ships."

In the silence which greeted his words, a sudden tremulous hope took root in all their minds.

Much to their surprise, they found Radcliffe waiting for them when they landed. Jumping down first from the door of the 'copter, Potter called to him.

'It came off! But that's only half of what we have to tell you!' In his frantic enthusiasm for the slim chance they had conceived for mankind, he found himself forgetting everything else about Radcliffe apart from the fact that he was an improvement over Grady. For a few seconds he found himself almost liking the man.

'I have something to tell you!' Radcliffe snapped back. 'More urgent than anything you've come up with! Do you know somebody called Fyffe?'

Potter sobered on the instant. He said, 'Of course. He's the acting Chief of Continental Defence.'

'He telephoned. Said Buishenko has taken Victoria and now controls the whole of Vancouver Island. The Canadian government tried to get away by air but almost all the planes were shot down. There *is* no Canadian government now. We can expect Buishenko, according to him, no later than tomorrow morning, and he'll probably begin with paratroops. And that stupid lazy greedy bugger Grady . . .!'

'What?'

'He didn't trust his own private army. Issued ammunition to them personally. Rationed it out. He had stocks okay—but they're in a concrete vault with a six-inch steel door that only he knew the combination for!'

25

The distant voice—somehow Potter could not think of it as belonging to an individual with a face and a name, and was labelling it mentally just 'Washington'—was jagged with hysteria.

'Why should anybody here give a shit what happens on Grady's Ground? Far as I'm concerned those bastards can carry on cutting each other's throats until doomsday! Damnation, don't you realize the Russians have invaded? They've taken Vancouver Island, they've wiped out the Canadian government, there's practically no organized resistance and they're flying in reinforcements as and when they choose!'

Potter tried to interrupt. The man ignored him.

'And the refugees are on the move in Washington and Oregon, tens of thousands of them, same as last time only worse because now they *know* the Russians have landed. Why should we care about your crackbrained schemes when we're in a mess like this?'

'Stop talking about "the Russians"!' Potter barked. 'I've told you, those are Buishenko's forces, and I've told you the only conceivable reason for him to invade!'

Sweat was running into his eyes; angrily he wiped it away.

'It's too big! This is a full-scale military operation, not a—a bandit raid!'

Potter felt his temper strain towards breaking point. 'What sort of man do you think Buishenko is? An overgrown Boss Tweed, like Grady? Hell, no! He's more like a reincarnation of Attila!'

'I don't have time to listen to any more of your garbage,' Washington said. 'Your last chance, Potter. Do you have the guts to come back and work to save the nation with the rest of us?'

'I'd rather put up with the aliens than a bunch of block-headed, short-sighted fools like you!' Potter snapped, his temper finally giving way. He slammed down the phone and slumped back in his chair.

Beside him, Radcliffe gave a humourless chuckle. 'So you finally realized how Washington looked to those of us who settled for Grady as the lesser evil, hm?'

'I guess so,' Potter admitted, running harassed fingers through his hair. 'What does the situation look like this morning—any improvement?'

'None at all. The best we can hope for is that when Buishenko's men get close enough they'll go out of their minds and maybe a few of us will survive to pick up the pieces.' Radcliffe uttered the words with gloomy relish.

'But I don't believe they will go crazy,' Potter sighed. 'They won't if my theory is correct. They don't have the least intention of attacking the aliens, and the aliens apparently don't care what we do to one another.'

He jumped up angrily. 'It's a nightmare! Here we are on the verge of our first real breakthrough, and it looks as though we shan't live to see the benefit. I'm going to talk to Porpentine. If I'm likely to die in the next couple of days, at least I want to go to my grave with the satisfaction of having been nearly right.'

'Yes, Zworykin and I have been over both of them from head to foot,' Porpentine said over his shoulder as he washed his hands in a stainless steel sink. A miniature hospital was among the more remarkable facilities of Radcliffe's home. 'Short of cutting them open for a direct look, we can't find out more than we know already. Apart from literally scaring the shit out of them—excuse me—the experience left them completely unharmed.'

'Fantastic,' Potter grunted. 'So what about Waldron's idea of using infantile regression as a means of deceiving the aliens' defences?'

'It's barely possible it might work,' Porpentine said, inserting his hands into a hot-air drier. 'The sort of detector I gather you're postulating would presumably register only gross mental attitudes, the overall mood and not individual thoughts. Not that I see how it could operate at all, but I'll accept it for the sake of argument.'

He dropped into a chair and crossed his legs, his expression thoughtful. 'The trouble is this, though. Congreve, as we know, is an excellent hypnotic subject. But people like him are very rare. If we make the technique work for him, all we shall have proved is that it works for him! Suppose it does work; suppose volunteers come forward who are averagely accessible to hypnosis—are we to send them off and risk them returning as hopelessly schizoid as the existing weirdos? Radcliffe roped in a couple for us to study, did you know? I've never been so depressed in my life.'

'I guess it will have to be a matter of volunteers,' Potter said heavily. 'What else can we do?'

'Yes, but if the volunteers are valuable, perhaps irreplaceable, what then? And they're likely to be, you know. Good hypnotic subjects are typically of high intelligence and strong personality.'

'You mean, is the chance of our gamble paying off good enough to risk reducing some of our key personnel to mumbling lunatics? How can I say? But I tell you this: if Mike Congreve wants a companion on his first trip, I'll go with him.'

There was a pause. At length Porpentine said with a faint smile, 'You won't have to. Jim Waldron's been here already, and I tested him. He's a highly susceptible subject, and if the treatment doesn't work on him it won't work on enough of us to be any use.'

At that moment a wall-mounted PA speaker said, 'Orlando Potter, please. Orlando Potter. Join Mr Radcliffe at once. Trouble on the way.'

'Trouble!' Potter echoed with a harsh laugh. 'More like disaster! Thanks, doctor. Though I'm afraid the whole question is about to be rendered permanently academic.'

Porpentine blanched. 'What do you mean?'

'You must have heard. We're expecting Buishenko to—ah—drop in today.'

'Come in,' Radcliffe said, not looking up from his control console as Potter appeared at the door of his underground sanctum. 'Thought you'd like to be present at the funeral. He's on his way; we just picked up the first wave.'

Potter glanced at the multiple TV screens on which one after another shots of key points were being projected. He said, 'How long do we have?'

'Thirty-five to forty minutes. Rick!'—to a hanging mike.

'Yes, sir?'

'How are the relidges today?'

'Sort of chastened. It won't last.'

'I guess not. Okay, thanks.'

'Are we expecting any help?' Potter inquired.

'Not so as you'd notice. The Canadians have promised all the missiles they can spare, but they only have about thirty within range. A few fighters have been harassing Buishenko's planes, but I only know that because I picked up a couple of clear-language calls for help on the Air Force band. Washington won't talk to us, you know. Gabe!'

'Yes, sir?'

'Making any impression on the door of that vault?'

'Two hours ought to see us through.'

'We don't have two hours. Change of plan. Mine it, and be quick. Run a landline away from the charges. Hide the terminals somewhere we can find 'em again later. If Buishenko turns up in person and takes over the Grady mansion, maybe we could at least bring it down around his ears.'

'Sir, two hours is a maximum. Surely we can stand 'em off for a while after they—'

'Okay, do both!'

Radcliffe leaned back with a sigh. 'Never thought I'd wind up doing the *Götterdämmerung* bit,' he muttered. 'But it seems like the only thing I can do. Lord knows where Buishenko got all those planes of his—we counted over a hundred already, and we're not sure there isn't a second wave. Whatever we do, whatever anybody does, he's almost bound to get on to the Ground with five or six thousand men. Suppose we have a drink. I have some English gin in that compartment there, courtesy of Grady's estate.' He pointed at a sliding door on the side of the console. Compliant, Potter opened it and found bottles and glasses and a bucket of ice.

'With tonic, half and half,' Radcliffe said.

And sipped, never taking his eyes from the TV screens.

Potter's mind filled with hopeless visions. Out around the alien city the relidges, still chanting their foolish hymns, unaware of the wrath of an all too human kind which was about to descend from heaven. On the roads to the west, hordes of maddened refugees, many of them fleeing their homes for the second time in less than a decade. And here, waiting for the storm to break, a handful of people who had deluded themselves into believing they could defy beings closer to the angels . . .

Is this a case of survival of the fittest? Are we shut out forever from the clan of the highest races, those who come and go between the stars? Buishenko and those like him care nothing about the stars, and never will. Does that mean the rest of us must be content to copy them? A rat with dreams of flying is not cut out for the life of rats!

'Think there's any hope for us?' Radcliffe said unexpectedly. 'I don't mean you and me. I mean mankind.'

'I don't know,' Potter answered candidly. 'Sometimes I get the impression the spirit is being bled out of us . . . Ever been in a country occupied by a powerful foreign army?'

Radcliffe shook his head.

'I was in Viet-Nam two or three times in the—the old days. And there were all these uneducated peasants caught up in a monstrous clash of ideologies which they didn't understand. The most advanced machines they'd ever run across were broken-down old trucks and tractors. All of a sudden, here was this war going on around them with rockets and tanks and helicopters . . . Their minds closed up. They had no—no handle to grasp the situation by. Their language didn't even have words for what the fighting was about! So the best they could hope for was to raise a harvest and keep a few kids from starving to death so they'd be provided for in old age. That was the greatest ambition they could take seriously.'

'Think that's how we're going to wind up?' Radcliffe said, and glanced at his watch. 'Ah, there's news on Far-West in a couple of minutes—and come to think of it I might as well monitor any other station I can reach ...." He flicked a series of switches and the room filled with a gentle susurrus of sound from which occasional words peaked.

'I guess so,' Potter said in answer to the earlier question. 'Oh, in two or three generations we may adjust enough to make another attempt ... but equally we may adjust so well the idea never enters our heads. Then we'll have become an inferior species. Permanently.'

The radio crackled again.

'Rick here, Mr Radcliffe. It's no use. Things are getting out of control. The word's got around about Buishenko and there are refugees coming into the west side of the Ground like a tidal wave and the relidges are turning out in force again and—oh, hell, by the time Buishenko gets here he'll just be able to walk over us!'

'Do your best,' Radcliffe said without emotion. 'What else can I say?'

'Nothing, I guess,' Rick muttered. 'Okay, I just needed to blow off a little steam.'

'Want to be evacuated?' Radcliffe said, turning to Potter.

'Rats leaving a sinking ship?' the latter countered. 'I didn't realize you had facilities.'

'Oh, I've been keeping a 'copter fuelled and ready. I just decided I don't want it. You have it. Take Natasha and Zworykin and Abramovitch—if Buishenko gets his hands on them he'll probably show them what he thinks of them, right? And I guess you'd better take the kid, too. And Maura. That's about the limit of what it can carry. I'll call the airfield and tell 'em you're on the way.'

Before Potter could say anything, he had thumbed a switch. 'Keene, you there?' he snapped.

'What? Oh! Yes, Mr Radcliffe. Look, there's something very funny going on. I just picked up a whole string of Russian, very loud. The guy sounded like he was in a panic. Mike Congreve is over at the radar desk and he speaks Russian, so maybe he knows what—Yes, just a second, he's coming this way, and . . . Mike, what the hell are you laughing at?'

'They're turning back!' Faint, as though Congreve was distant from the microphone, but perfectly clear.

'What did you say?' Radcliffe barked.

'Who's that on the radio? Oh, I know that voice. Yes, Mr Radcliffe.' More loudly. 'It's quite true. They've been recalled.'

'But *why?*'

'The Chinese! That message just now said they're invading Buishenko's territory in force.'

The Chinese! Potter doubled his fists so that his nails bit painfully into his palms. One had almost forgotten about that sleeping giant of a country, which had closed up on itself again after the arrival of the aliens, in the ancient manner of the Middle Kingdom, its leaders thinking perhaps that one day when the other Great Powers had been sufficiently ravaged they might quietly re-emerge on to the world scene . . . It seemed the day had dawned sooner than predicted.

'Age of Miracles,' Radcliffe said under his breath, and for the first time Potter felt the phrase contained a grain of truth.

26

A week later Waldron stood shivering on the same hillside from which they had watched Ichabod and Maura set off on their nearly disastrous expedition. A cool wind carried the sound of chanting; the relidges were still clinging to their beliefs, their numbers greatly swollen by the influx of refugees who had fled from Buishenko's invasion, and now the danger was past were too weary to go home ... or perhaps afraid to face the scorn of friends who had stayed put. A score of would-be successors to Brother Mark were wandering wild-eyed from group to group of them, preaching on texts from the Book of Revelation. Luckily, so far no clear-cut inheritor of his mantle had emerged.

If this doesn't work ...

But it had to work. He looked around, seeing Greta, Potter, Congreve, Porpentine, others and others. Rick had taken over the big movie camera Congreve had previously used. A short distance away, Natasha and Abramovitch were setting up a rather more elaborate array of instruments than before; during the past few days they had had time to sift through the incredible miscellany of loot accumulated by Grady, and extracted enough equipment to stock a small physics lab.

Natasha called out that everything was ready, and he and Congreve moved towards Porpentine.

'Okay!' the psychologist said briskly. 'You both know—at the moment—how this technique works. When I give the order, you'll regress to the respective juvenile ages which you can reach most completely. You'll approach the alien city and if possible go inside. You're protected by hypnotic injunctions against taking anything and against staying too long. When you come out again, you'll revert automatically to normal awareness. Are you ready? When I say "nine" . . . One, three, five, seven, *nine!*'

Waldron blinked and stared at the looming, shining marvel ahead of him as though he had never seen it before. In a very real sense, he hadn't. Somehow—he didn't remember how—he knew it was safe to go to it and see all the marvels hidden inside. Provided, of course, that he didn't go alone, but went with his friend Mike, whose mind was as full as his own with love and adoration for the beings who had devised such a miraculous edifice.

Not saying anything, gazing with hungry eyes at the glory before him, he beckoned Mike and set off across the rough ground.

Oh, the colours! Emerald and amethyst, ruby and turquoise, sparkling and gleaming! But—*mustn't touch!* Mustn't take anything. Look as much as you like, but *leave things alone!*

'I will,' Jimmy Waldron said, a good boy aged seven excited to be visiting such a wonderful place in company with his best friend Mike who was nine.

He walked at a dutiful calm pace on the rough ground that ended abruptly where transparent air turned into a riot of colour and light. Sheened and filmed with beauty, this was an elseness, not a wall. Division: here, the see-through breeze; there, the be-through frieze. It did not cross his mind to wonder how they would enter, whether there was a gate or a door or a portal. Entering had nothing to do with it. Other-going did. Some few yards distant still from the shining, which from here looked like a mist somehow prevented from drifting and not at all like a solid barrier, he experienced a pleasant shift of directions, very much like letting his body fall to full arm-stretch from a tree-bough and swinging, except that there was no back-and-forth, *only* forth.

The steps regularly measured compressed into a glide and the last/next several paces happened without being noticed. First there was a gentle sucking sensation, not applied only to the surface of his body (lowering himself into water made astonishingly viscous) but to every cell and fibre of his being: as an iron filing might feel on responding to a magnetic field. Oh, yes! Glancing back because of a last tiny tingle of alarm he saw clearly, but confusedly, as in a kaleidoscope with transfinite mirrors around it (the polygonal truth of a circle), the exterior Earth; he was reassured to know that this amazing place could be looked out of. For he was already in it. As were-in-dark into are-in-light at the touch of a switch, electricity not having been discovered yet. It made him gasp, but with delight. Everywhere happened to him, instantly! No sky, no ground, no horizon, no up, no down, but only *around*, the immanence (a word he had not learned at so young an age) of iridescence (a word he had fallen in love with and proudly boasted of spelling with the correct single *r*). Oh delicious. Blue sparkled tartly on his tongue, but on balance (over an infinite abyss) he liked better the gold which was inspiriting and heavy in all directions, especially inward.

Mike said something in a ripple of predictive pinks across which black bars glossed additional layers of meaning; he was not sure whether he heard, tasted, smelled or was hurt by the information, but he understood it and was aware that there was very much to appre-see-eat in very little Xıoshun of thyme. He tunnelled back concurrence, hot brown sand fashion, and imagined himself as a waffle-iron, which was very funny. It broke him up into about a gross of separate bits.

But that was at the surface/frontier/border/transition zone/meniscus. Click, he had feet again, hands, body et cetera. Here there was place, which briefly or perhaps for several eternities there had not been and substance, which had dissipated but now was back, and he could see Mike, friend, draped (like himself he realized) in rainbows stiff as silk and rough as butter. It was too much to reason about. It was a totality, an embracing feel/sense, beyond dissection like the sudden recent improbable interest (age seven) in the presence of girls budding into body-hair and ... (??? Age seven? An instant of confusion, if there were instants here; he found other figures like 12 and 38—24—36 and 17 washing across his mind, fraught with incomprehensible significance and ignored them because he couldn't reason about them or anything, could only experience and react.)

Fundamental, anyhow, was the number EYE. Straight ahead lay all possible directions including east, west, north, south, up, down, sideways, backwards, acute, obtuse, slow, fast, fat, thin, bronze, yellow, parabolic, paregoric and pandemonic. It was great fun.

'We've done it!' Mike exclaimed. 'We got outside!'

'And look at everything!' Jimmy cried. (That was possible from where they were.) He had to giggle.

'Mustn't touch!' (Funny, because touching couldn't be avoided. The place touched them, inside and throughout.) Paths, passageways, corridors, rooms, tracks, volumes!

Objects . . . after their fashion. Dreamwise, they moved without motion, being in a succession of localities while remaining where they were. Fairground: the engineer at the centre of the carousel, without an engine and without the world revolving because it wasn't a *round* turning . . . No use; if he was ever going to find words, that must be later. What counted was that it was happening, and it was wonderful.

They must be objects, though, surely . . . except they were not. They—they *existed*. Like position and direction. It was possible to wander among them and examine them, often making a slight effort akin to reaching out/up/into, at other times (if any) simply chancing on them. The first was a fabulous sparkling ellipsoidal shower, at least as big as a breath and nearly as light as fever-heat. Some of the sparks were capacious and smelt of probity and congratulations. Others, though, were hollow, prickly with fatigue, and incurred a sense of being remote.

Digesting that led to vague hunger, so they agreed on a spiral under their left and front respectively (they were talking all the time, of course, being overwhelmed by the variety of impingement) and invoked it until its absolute cold began to bore them. By then they were oriented—the sunrise was among the directions they were facing—and the place began to make sense to them, so they were able to start counting the hundred paces which, it had been agreed, must limit this initial incursion. In Jimmy's case the initial was W, and in Mike's it was C.

The limiting velocity here is W.

'Well, it is for me at any rate,' Jimmy said, proving it

by saying a cloud of pumpkins though not quite understanding what a limiting velocity might be. Something
at which you could expand outwards, he imagined,
doing it. A cluster of spheroids like a bunch of grapes
dangling from a hyperbolic function—well, it was curved
like a cat's tail, actually—measured him off in degrees
absolute and that tickled until he could scarcely bear it,
although he chuckled as he writhed.

Little by little, to his surprise, the tickling began to
make sense of a red fish, and the thought expressed to
him: *I ought to be wearing co-ordinates. What goes well with
red?*

Mike's answer was prompt and coarse-textured. He
had sneezed about it for a while and decided on a very
mild electric shock, the kind you get when you touch
your tongue to the terminals of a dry cell. That fitted
excellently except that it wasn't completely square, and
he wriggled around until he had altered the perspective he was viewing it from. Were the hundred paces
up, or had they turned minus? Counting backward, he
got down to about twenty-nine or possibly fifty-five, and
hesitated. The brilliance was somewhat dazzling and
the style of his friend was inadequate, lacking the middle rung.

'Mike?' he called, looking up and forth the cylindrical
platform he was groping down.

'Yes, Jimmy? Say, did you greet this one yet? It horns
us! That must be what it's here for!'

'Mike, this way—over here!' (But where am I?) 'You're
going too lofted!'

'No, I'm right here inside you! I promised we wouldn't
be too short, same as you did!'

What? What?

(But it was making more and more sense, because it
was full of echoes: age-seven echoes. On a window-
ledge, nailed secure, a box with one side and the floor

of wire mesh, enclosing two sad chickens that dropped
limy excreta to the street. A moment when, standing
at the front of a subway train, he had been sure that
this time the brakes were going to fail. In a corner
scarcely daring to breathe while his cousin three years
older and much stronger hunted him, promising loudly
and with fervour he would smash his teeth, kick his
balls, pull his hair out by the handful . . . Everything
on the sudden confining, expectant, apprehensive.)

'Jimmy? Jimmy!'

'Here comes a something!'

A *someone.*

August, majestic, awful, the crystallized sound of a
million crashing cars made him desire fromness. Flee-
shrink-absent him. He knew how.

He knew how.

It was exactly like discovering that he could wiggle
his ears, which he had never thought of until he was
fourteen.

*But I'm not fourteen. I'm only seven. Somewhere I must
have got doubled/folded/plied.*

'The last time I went through here . . .'

I haven't been here before. I didn't come here until
next time, was I? Oh, this is terrible, I can't stand it,
guts twisting, nausea churning, *where's Mike?* The entity,
the being, the personage (infinite reflections of authority from mother to master, parent to policeman): must
not catch in that gong-ring claw I felt brush the raw
nerve of my spine. Red, shock-taste, go back until it
looks absolutely square and . . .

The way out, as before in a deformed perspective, a
headlong dash down a kaleidoscope, yes. Stable light,
daylight that didn't shift insanely through irritation
into maddening thirst and back to animosity. Solid
ground with regular up and down, salvation, Earth! He
flung towards it and realized in mid-career: *No!*

Caught at the interface, he bounced on it, like a fly collided with the web-thread of a spider, and in the moment of rebound saw: pale grey rocks crowned with brownish vegetation, overhead a slate-coloured sky. Near the horizon a sun sinking, lurid red and not from sunset clouds. An old sun, chill and unfriendly.

He cried out and reversed, and was lost before the infinite choice of ways open to him. How do you invert a taste, a colour and a not-quite square?

But . . .

'Jimmy! Jimmy, come back!'

His cry. Worked. But answered from . . .? Tears streamed down his cheeks, little boy lost in the city, where's a friend to help me home? Beware of strangers who do dreadful things to little boys, always wait for the green before you cross, look out for funny cigarettes and funny pills . . .

Wait. Wait. Think. Be calm. Once, long ago, in a visited city: recollection of a sign which was not the right one, only identical, and then discovery of a threatening street, and . . . Oh, yes. He had remembered west by the sun. Used it, returned safe when artificial clues like names and neons failed. Parents worried since he was only nine—and he was seven, *seven*, and it was Mike who was nine and . . .

'Hey, Jimmy! *Jim-m-m-y!*'

Blindly, yet with assurance, he set off in the wake of that shrieking acid signal and prepared for the shock of yesterday which lay ahead. It felt as though he had to shred a million years.

But in the end there was a—form? Shape? Figure? It took hold of him, and wrenched him diagonally across aeons, and somewhere on the way he lost himself.

Stop.

* * *

'Jim! Jim!'

Bending over him, person. Fair hair, anxious voice. Greta. Others nearby: Mike, Porpentine, Natasha, Rick. He felt grass tickling, smelt air tinged with smoke. His throat was sore from half-remembered screaming.

Seeing him stir, Porpentine knelt, briskly touched his forehead, examined his eyes with a brush of his thumb to each upper lid, counted a dozen beats of his pulse. 'Are you okay?' he demanded.

'I . . . Yes, I guess so,' Waldron whispered. 'Except I feel as though I've been through a mincing-machine. Someone help me sit up. And I'd like a drink of water.'

'You're all right!' Greta exclaimed, clasping her hands. 'Mike came out carrying you! We thought at first you were dead, and then . . .' She let the words die unspoken as the others gathered around, looking as though she could have bitten her tongue.

'You thought I'd gone weirdo,' Waldron suggested, suddenly racked by shivers.

'Well . . .'

'Of course you did. Thanks'—to Rick, who had offered a canteen. He took three measured mouthfuls, savouring the stability of the clear taste which was not going to dissolve without warning into the blare of trumpets or the agony of amputation. And continued: 'I guess it was a close call. In fact for a while I think I did go kind of crazy. Mike!'

Face concerned, Congreve bent towards him.

'Mike, I—I didn't mean to scare you, but when the alien turned up . . .'

'What? What alien?'

'You mean you didn't see it? No, that's wrong. Hear it. A crashing noise. A tremendous crashing noise. I must have panicked.'

'I don't get you,' Congreve said after a pause. 'When we got to that sort of waterfall place—you know, the one we came to after the hundred steps—you seemed to become ... I don't know! What would you call it? Petrified? As though you were mesmerized. I shouted at you, and you didn't react, and in the end I just had to drag you back.'

'Petrified?' Waldron repeated incredulously. 'But I ran off. I thought I'd never find my way back. And I wasn't in any waterfall place, as you call it.'

Congreve hesitated. Glancing at Porpentine, he said, 'Doc, I guess we'd better go home. It's going to take a long while to get to the bottom of all this.'

'But I did run off!' Waldron insisted. 'And what's more ...' He licked his lips, while the others waited intently.

'What's more,' he said at length, 'I found my way to somewhere else. Bennett was right. I didn't go out, but I saw it. I saw a planet of another sun.'

27

'It works,' Potter said a week later, and looked around the table, marvelling at the optimism he could read on all these tired faces. Never, since the day the aliens struck, had he seen so many cheerful expressions in the same room.

Radcliffe said, 'You mean Jim found his way back to the same place he stumbled on before.'

'And this time I brought pictures to prove it,' Waldron said, fanning a group of Polaroids that showed slate-blue sky, red sun, grey rocks, brown plants. 'Thanks to Abramovitch. Without his analysis of the external colour-signals I wouldn't have known when and where to go in. It looks as though you can enter the alien city anywhere, but the internal relationships are constantly changing. Alien city—oh, damn! I keep trying to use a better name, but the habit's so ingrained ... Never mind. What counts is that we can apparently respond to the conditions inside. We can learn to recognize what are presumably the counterparts of direction-markings, the way a rat might cross a river on a fallen tree.'

'But when you went in the first time,' Radcliffe said,

'how was it that you thought you ran off and Mike believed you were right next to him, and he thought you were in a place with a waterfall and you remembered something different, and . . .? Come on, I want an explanation I can understand. I'm sick of merely being *told*.'

Everyone looked at Porpentine, who shrugged and leaned back.

'You're asking a lot. After all, we've barely begun to study the problem. But it looks as though Jim's analogy will hold. A dog in a city can learn to cross the street only when the traffic's halted for a red light, without having to understand electricity. Pavel is still analyzing the readings he got from the instruments Jim took on his second trip, but one or two things have become clear, so I'll do my best to sum up what we know. Natasha, correct me if I say anything completely wrong, won't you?

'Both Mike and Jim agree that when they walked up to the wall they realized it was permeable and all they had to do was keep straight on. It is not in fact a wall, and we might have learned that long ago if we'd thought of using absolutely non-hostile means to test it, like touching it with a long pole. In fact, of course, what we've tried to touch it with have been rockets, bullets and laser-beams, and anyone who was fool enough to push high energies at it was immediately driven insane.'

'So if it's not a wall, what is it?' Radcliffe said.

'Something we have no words for. For the time being we've decided to call it an extraface—by analogy with interface. Under hypnosis Mike and Jim have both clearly described the sensations they felt when they reached it. Jim says it was like falling to arm's length from a treebranch, Mike that it was like being spun around in a fast river-current. Pavel says there must be a local condition analogous to the boundary layer of a liquid, maybe even a macro equivalent of the surface tension on a nucleon; at any rate it seems to mark a change in the nature of space itself. During the transit, there's no idea of direction and the senses are hopelessly cross-connected, although willpower remains and the confusion is quite enjoyable. Mike said it was like being drunk, and Jim—who incidentally had far more vivid sensory experiences—said it was like delirium but without the pain or sickness.

'As to what's inside . . . or outside, as they both insist on calling it: well, it is a *place*. In other words you get your sense of location back. But as well as that you acquire an awareness of uncountable directions, all lying ahead of you. They're agreed on this much, even though they differ on almost everything else. But it ties into a suggestion Orlando put forward, as I recall.'

'Which one?' Potter said dryly. 'I've had lots of ideas, and most of them have turned out to be wrong.'

'You proposed that the aliens might think in a matrix mode, didn't you? And you also said they might omit verbalization when communicating data.'

Potter nodded.

'Well, we're tentatively regarding this in terms of a multiplex data situation, but not quite the way you originally phrased it; more, we're comparing it to a modern city as a bushman might see it, confused by the plethora of information making claims on your attention—advertisements, radio noise, TV, warnings, street-corner speakers and the rest. Only that's a terrible oversimplification. It does look as though beyond the extraface many, many different layers—volumes—segments—whatever you call them—many different bits of space-time, anyway, coexist, and can be perceived as simultaneous.'

'But not to the same degree by everybody,' Congreve put in. 'Once we were through the extraface, so far as I was concerned it was possible, though hellish hard, to walk a hundred paces as arranged, stop and look around, come back to the point of entry ... I interpreted my surroundings in rather conventional terms; Jim didn't. He must be far more sensitive to these space-time strata. Right, Louis?'

'I suspect so,' Porpentine agreed. 'You were convinced he never left your side on that first visit. He's absolutely certain he lost touch with you when a passing alien scared him and he fled down a direction which luckily he perceived as being labelled by—ah— some very peculiar coordinates.'

Waldron chuckled. 'Co-ordinates! Yes! I remember I was thinking about putting on well-matched clothes. Literally. I guess I must have been seven when I first learned that use of the word, and of course that was the age I'd been regressed to. Except ...' He hesitated.

'Yes, *except*,' Porpentine said. 'That brings us to an absolutely crucial point. You were right to suggest we might sneak past the aliens' defences by using hypnosis. But for completely the wrong reasons.'

Radcliffe started. 'How's that again?'

'Regressing someone to an earlier age is of course a fiction. You don't wipe out the later memories. You can't. At most you can discount them. Fortunately for us, that's quite enough, combined of course with a good deal of conditioning, orders not to hate the aliens, not to touch or interfere with anything, and so on. The point is, though, that from the regressed age you can *remember in both directions*. Jim gave some vivid examples of this. He compared some of his sensations to the tingle of excitement which went with his awakening adolescent interest in girls' bodies, yet at seven he was still pre-pubescent, and is consciously aware that his sexual urge was dormant until he was twelve, while he didn't lose his virginity until he was seventeen. All these numbers got mixed up with his attempts to count a hundred paces, as well as his concern for his theoretical mental age. And when he was struggling to find his way back from the distant exit he chanced across, he says he clearly recalls preparing himself for the shock of yesterday, but he had to wait a hell of a long time before it arrived.'

'Bennett,' Radcliffe said. 'He got turned around. Why didn't Mike and Jim?'

Porpentine spread his hands. 'Pavel is working on the assumption that whatever the device was which he restored to working order, it must have lacked some associated mechanism, or field, which beyond the extraface prevents that kind of mishap. Compare it to having an accelerator and no brakes, or no steering. If you have to compare it to something, and I keep finding that I do.'

'So it may be confusion of the time-sense which drives at least some weirdos out of their minds,' Potter said.

'Yes, it may. But we're going to have to get rid of the blanket category "weirdo",' Porpentine asserted. 'When we study them in more detail, we'll almost certainly find there are a number of different types, some affected by the defensive field, some by time-confusion, some by the cross-connection of sensory data—like someone who can't come down after an overdose of LSD—and some quite possibly by the shock of encountering an alien inside the . . .' He glanced ruefully at Waldron. 'I was going to say "city", too. I mean inside the transit nexus.'

'That,' Waldron muttered, 'is a very alarming experience. Believe you me. We'll have to work out some means of detecting their approach. Not that the chance of meeting one of them seems to be very high.'

There was a pause. Radcliffe said eventually, 'The main point is, though, that with proper preparation we humans can learn the—the co-ordinates of the system, even if we don't have the least idea how they work. And sneak quietly through to other worlds.'

'Yes, that's what we're hoping. We can't do it on the adult level, that's definite. Regression is going to remain essential, at least for the foreseeable future. The learning process is non-intellectual, like learning to swim, or ride a bicycle, or walk a tight-rope—in Jim's phrase, like learning to wiggle your ears. And it's notorious that it's best to start young when it comes to developing any talent that can't be verbalized. Music is the prime example.'

'I get you,' Radcliffe said. 'When I was a kid I used to think music was kind of sissy. When I was about fifteen I got interested in guitar, but I never became any good. It was already too late.'

'Pavel seems to have been right to suggest that in fact the aliens may not be very different from ourselves after all,' Potter said. 'At any rate we do seem to have the necessary mental equipment to make some sort of sense out of their processes. The necessary muscles, as it were—I'm thinking of Jim's ear-wiggling image. Given the proper incentive, even though we don't ordinarily have any use for them we can bring them under conscious control.'

Porpentine nodded. 'The next step I plan to take is an investigation of yoga techniques, to see if the kind of acquired skills which can reduce oxygen requirements or alter EEG waves offer any clues to what happens inside your mind when you cross the extraface. It's going to be a long project, this, but I'm confident of eventual success.'

'Given some backing,' Potter said. 'Given personnel and funds. Den, could you have those Polaroids of Jim's copied, and extra prints made of all the film we've shot? I'm going to Washington, to scream and yell and raise Cain until those purblind idiots realize what's happened. I'm going to recruit physicists, engineers, astronomers, doctors, psychologists . . . I'm going to bring you more rats than you can handle.'

'I get on best with my own kind,' Radcliffe said.

Chuckling, Potter continued, 'But before they arrive . . . Mike, you'd better add a few trimmings to your scheme for taming the relidges.'

'Mine?' Congreve said, laying a hand on his chest. 'Well, I guess by adoption. Such as what?'

'Don't stop at half-measures. Don't simply imitate Brother Mark. Go the whole hog and call yourself the Archangel Michael, and preach on the text you mentioned yourself—"except ye become as little children"— and promise that you'll actually escort people into the holy city. We'll make arrangements to screen all the disciples you acquire, sort out those who are most susceptible to hypnosis, or drugs or yoga techniques according to what Louis's researches turn up, and then we'll hold private tuition for them in secret. I don't believe the nexi give access to only one other planet. I suspect it's more like thousands. After all, they've put five nexi on this planet alone, and so far as we can tell Earth is no more than an interchange station. By trial and error we should find the way to hundreds of different worlds.'

'But they may not be fit for human life,' Natasha said. 'Suppose we send people through, and they die?'

'How many people died trying to repel Buishenko's invasion?' countered Potter. 'How many are dying right now as the Chinese take over his territory? How many were casually blotted out by the aliens when they set off our nukes? Maybe we'll have to accept that some of the people who go out will become casualties, the way we do in wartime. They'll include some of our finest individuals, but hasn't war always taken the best instead of the worst? Surely it's better to risk death in the cause of all mankind than for the sake of some stupid political squabble that's going to be forgotten in a hundred years.'

'Rats get on ships,' Radcliffe said, as though the whole argument could be dismissed in those four words.

'Yes, but whatever you say, Den, we *aren't* rats. We're human beings, with some guts, some intelligence, some capacity for planning ahead. And there's going to come a time when the aliens will wish they'd treated us with more respect!'

28

It would snow tonight for sure; the leaden overcast was threatening and the wind bore a keen edge. But Fred Johnson paid little attention to the state of the weather, like all the others standing patiently with him on the bleak hillside. His main reaction to the prospect of snow was a vague regret that he would not see how glorious the heavenly city appeared when there was a mantle of white over the surrounding country.

By then, though, he would be *in* glory . . .

He was an electronics engineer in ordinary life. Right now, however, he was first and foremost a disciple of the Archangel Michael. He had attended a relidge meeting out of sheer curiosity; afterwards he had been invited to talk privately with one of the apostles, and had agreed because he wanted to argue the guy out of his ridiculous convictions, and the tables had been completely turned on him. He had reached the unexpected conclusion, over prosaic coffee and doughnuts, that his greatest ambition was access to the angelic city. 'Except ye become as little children . . .!' the archangel had thundered—and he had obeyed. He waited passive with the rest of today's Chosen, eyes fixed in adoration on the spectacular play of colours across the valley, and never for a moment wondered why he was hung about with tools and equipment: an axe, a shotgun and shells, a first-aid kit, a portable radio, a bag of food, seeds, extra clothing, a bedroll and a cookpot, a load he was just strong enough to carry at a fast walking pace.

All the others, too, carried similar burdens, including anything that might facilitate their survival—somewhere else. But he did not notice. He would not be able to until the post-hypnotic trigger buried in his subconscious during those sessions of 'private tuition' in the mysteries of the angelc host were tripped by an external stimulus.

Then he would remember what the transit nexus really was.

A helicopter settled to the ground alongside the glass-fronted hut which overlooked the waiting group of Chosen. Radcliffe jumped out and walked—briskly, for the air was icy—towards its door.

The occupants nodded a greeting as he entered. Monitoring a screen on which was presented a continuous analysis of the colour-patterns on the nexus—their instruments were linked by landline to Radcliffe's own computer, a very respectable three-and-a-halfth generation model—Pavel and Natasha were too busy to do more. Waldron and Greta were only checking equipment manifests, and could spare time to chat.

'Come to see them off?' Waldron inquired.

'Not exactly,' Radcliffe said. 'I brought some news from Orlando. Thought you might like to hear it before it turns up on the radio.'

'Orlando?' Greta glanced up. 'I thought he was still in Australia. Is he back?'

'No, this is a message from Canberra; Washington

passed it on. They successfully infiltrated the city there at 5 a.m. our time and the reports look good.'

'Another possible?' Waldron said eagerly.

'More than possible. They call it the best yet—a sub-tropical climate, green vegetation, no large animal life in the immediate vicinity . . . Of course, it'll be a long time before we can start shipping people to it, what with that bastard Villiers-Hart trying to grab back his ground, but it does sound kind of special, doesn't it?'

Waldron stared out of the window at the Chosen. It was a big group today, nearly 800 strong.

'You know, when I got that glimpse of Exit A on my first venture into the nexus, I was scared blind. I still don't know how I found my way home. And here we are in a matter of months equipped with route-finders small enough to drop in your pocket. I thought we'd abandoned hope, resigned from the business of think-ing and decided to turn into vegetables. I can hardly believe so much has happened in such a short time.'

'Speaking of route-finders,' Greta said, reverting to her equipment lists, 'you did hear, did you, that Pavel has confirmed his guess about Type Five artefacts? People are already starting to refer to them as compasses.'

'I hadn't heard, but I'm not surprised. We thought of the aliens as being infinitely superior to us for far too long. We should have realized they had faults and shortcomings of their own as soon as we discovered they were capable of breaking things and throwing them away.' Radcliffe moved to Waldron's side and pointed at the Chosen. 'Where are they going, by the way?'

'This is the first follow-up party for Exit G,' Waldron answered. 'It's a trifle ahead of schedule, but today there's a good plain path—purple-salt-and-rubbery all the way. The advance guard has been there nine weeks, and they're very enthusiastic, and if we miss this route

we may not get another good one for several months.'
He scanned a bank of clocks on the hut wall, which
showed GMT, local time, sidereal time, corrected transit time—by which they scheduled the departure of the
Chosen—and several new rhythms derived from obser-
vation of the cyclic colour-changes on the extraface of
the nexus. 'Mike's late,' he added. 'He was due here
two minutes ago. I hope nothing's gone wrong.'

'I saw his 'copter on the way here,' Radcliffe said.
'Look, there it comes.'

They glanced at the grey-shrouded sky. All the Chosen were doing the same. The arrival of 'Archangel'
Mike Congreve was the signal they were so anxiously
awaiting. Up to the moment when he showed himself,
doubts might linger about their chance of entering the
heavenly city.

Doubting was over. A ragged cheer went up, and was
followed by the chanting of a tune they had been taught
as a reinforcement for their hypnotically-imposed orders.

'Quite a guy, our Mike,' Radcliffe said soberly.

True enough, Waldron signified with a nod. During
the past few months his mind had been stocked with
data concerning every route so far charted through the
nexus. Even without a route-finder he could lead the
Chosen through the swirling flows of colour-as-taste,
sound-as-pain and the rest, as easily as along a human
street. So far he had guided parties totalling almost
fourteen thousand to eight different habitable worlds.

Of course, 'habitable' would remain a questionable
description for generations. Some plague might spring
up, some long-term effect of alien chemicals in what
appeared to be safe soil or clean rain might depress
intelligence, some parasite or predator might emerge
from hibernation ... But there was a slim chance,
worth taking, of ultimate survival.

There had been casualties, as predicted: a few right

here, people whose hypnotic armour failed them, who returned as weirdos, and others on the far side of exits now classified as dangerous, who had ventured through and never returned. Later, with better facilities and more knowledge of what the aliens would and would not tolerate, someone would investigate their fate. Not yet. There was too much else to be done.

'It's a hell of a big batch,' Radcliffe muttered. 'Isn't it risky to send so many at once?'

'You think the aliens will be annoyed?' Greta said.

'It's a possibility.'

'I guess you're right. But since we quit pilfering live artefacts, the aliens have shown no sign of even noticing us. I suspect they can't be bothered to. We've put up with rats and mice for thousands of years, and we only take steps against them when they cause direct harm: rob the larder, carry plague.'

'Yes, but suppose we affect them in some way we don't know about,' Radcliffe objected. 'Mice stink, for example. That's regarded as a good reason to poison them.'

'We'll go on taking that chance,' Waldron grunted. 'I'd rather risk that than be in Asia, wouldn't you?'

Radcliffe shuddered visibly. 'Damned right. The way it started off, I thought the Chinese would just roll Buishenko up tidily and put him away, and the world would be a lot quieter. Then of course when the loyalist Russian forces intervened . . . How many casualties so far? Twenty million, is it?'

'Can we have silence, please?' Natasha called, and picking up a microphone went on without a pause. 'Mike, the colours are coming up to Exit G pattern now, and they should take about two minutes fifteen seconds to stabilize. When you get three green ripples moving right to left, you'll have six minutes forty seconds to complete your pep-talk, and you get moving on a recurrent flash of rust and gold.'

'Fine!' came the whispered reply. Congreve had a contact mike taped to his throat for messages he didn't want the Chosen to overhear. As for his earphones, they were concealed by a static-aura halo of a handsome electric blue which Abramovitch, laughing like a hyaena, had personally designed and built for him. It went splendidly with his luminescent robe of white and silver.

And, a moment later, he started to deliver his final address in a monstrously amplified voice that made the ill-carpentered window of the hut rattle in its frame.

His job for the moment over, Abramovitch leaned back and gave a mountainous sigh. He said something to Natasha which made her laugh, and she translated. In the past months he had learned some English, but he was still far from fluent.

'Pavel says he is like a man in a post office, or the ticket clerk at an airport, yes? Always hearing about distant places and never seeing any himself because he gets too little pay for foreign vacations. Now doubtless they will ask him to go to Australia, and he will have been all around this planet and still not have travelled properly.'

'He's right,' Waldron said. 'In fact he's so damned right I think it's painful. I'm going to quit my job. I'm not very good at it, you know.'

Radcliffe glanced at him in surprise. 'But you've made nearly as many transits as Mike, haven't you?'

'Sure, sure. I've been through Exit G and seen a bird as big as an eagle which wasn't a bird but the detachable crown of a tree. I've been through Exit K and seen a rock that wasn't a rock but a colony of creatures as hard as marble. I've been lots of places. But I'm too sensitive. I cross-refer sense-data too readily. Louis has to give me tranquillizers now—and did you know I came back from one trip with a burn on my arm because somebody shouted too loud?'

'Is that a fact?' Radcliffe said incredulously.

'Oh, yes. I had a blister the size of my palm. It's healed okay, but . . . No, I'm going to quit and join the Chosen.'

'So am I,' Greta said, putting aside her equipment lists. 'I'm going to see Louis tomorow, find out if I'm suitable for hypnosis. Not that that's so important any more, with the new drugs they're using.'

'I'll be damned,' Radcliffe muttered. 'Know something? You're turning out to be better rats than I am.'

'You're not going anywhere?' Greta suggested.

'Me? No, the project's too long-term to appeal to me. The best we can hope for is to plant colonies and creep around under the aliens' feet. Sure, it's a great scheme, because it means if they ever get sick enough of us to sterilize Earth we can hope to leave descendants elsewhere. If that does happen, though . . . Well, look at the way we've messed up this planet, even though it is our own home. We damned well can't afford to make the same mistakes anywhere else, right? So it's best to let my type stay behind.'

There was a brief silence. Then, as though embarrassed at having spoken so nakedly, he shrugged his coat tighter around him. 'Must be going. Maura and the kid are waiting in the 'copter.'

The door slammed behind him.

'Hasn't Den changed?' Waldron said in a low voice.

'We all have,' Greta said. 'We've *been* changed. It's a great thing to have hope again, even a slender hope like ours.'

'Yes, but that's not all. Maybe it's not the most important.' He frowned, struggling to find words. 'I think of it more like this. We've been desperately trying to make the world seem familiar again. We've been using comparisons and analogies: Den with his rats and mice, Orlando with his peasants under an army of occupation, Louis with his bushman in a modern city, and so on. Finally we've begun to admit that this isn't the same as anything we've run across before. It isn't even much *like* anything else. How could it be? We've been tossed without warning clear over the horizon of our own past. We calculated that the odds were against our being alone in the galaxy. Now we know we're not. We deduced that other stars must have planets. Now we can go and walk on them. It's a clean break. It's killed our past. We can't live in it or by its standards any more. All that counts from now on and forever is the future.'

He broke off, for the others weren't listening. They were staring with aching, longing eyes across the valley. One by one, following with perfect confidence in the steps of the archangel who led them, the Chosen were leaving for their appointment with destiny on a world for which there had not yet been time to coin a name.

When the last of them had dissolved into the incomprehensible web of forces which would shrink interstellar vastness to the dimensions of a morning stroll, Waldron glanced at Greta.

'Have you decided what exit you want to go through?'

'Yes.'

'Mind if I pick the same one?'

'Good idea.'

Smiling, he leaned back in his chair. And thought: *so rats get on ships . . . True. And what I'm going to do is much the same. But I'm not going to do it as a rat. I'm going to do it as a man.*

At long last the sky began to shed the first of its threatened flakes of snow.

DAW

**Unforgettable science fiction
by DAW's own stars!**

M. A. FOSTER

☐ THE WARRIORS OF DAWN   UE1994—$2.95
☐ THE GAMEPLAYERS OF ZAN   UE1993—$3.95
☐ THE MORPHODITE   UE2017—$2.95
☐ THE DAY OF THE KLESH   UE2016—$2.95

C.J. CHERRYH

☐ 40,000 IN GEHENNA   UE1952—$3.50
☐ DOWNBELOW STATION   UE1987—$3.50
☐ VOYAGER IN NIGHT   UE1920—$2.95
☐ WAVE WITHOUT A SHORE   UE1957—$2.50

JOHN BRUNNER

☐ TIMESCOOP   UE1966—$2.50
☐ THE JAGGED ORBIT   UE1917—$2.95

ROBERT TREBOR

☐ AN XT CALLED STANLEY   UE1865—$2.50

JOHN STEAKLEY

☐ ARMOR   UE1979—$3.95

JO CLAYTON

☐ THE SNARES OF IBEX   UE1974—$2.75

DAVID J. LAKE

☐ THE RING OF TRUTH   UE1935—$2.95

NEW AMERICAN LIBRARY
P.O. Box 999, Bergenfield, New Jersey 07621

Please send me the DAW Books I have checked above. I am enclosing
$_____ (check or money order—no currency or C.O.D.'s).
Please include the list price plus $1.00 per order to cover handling
costs.

Name _____

Address _____

City _____ State _____ Zip Code _____
Please allow at least 4 weeks for delivery

DAW

The really great fantasy books are published by DAW:

Andre Norton

☐ LORE OF THE WITCH WORLD   (#UE1750—$2.50)
☐ HORN CROWN   (#UE1635—$2.95)
☐ PERILOUS DREAMS   (#UE1749—$2.50)

C.J. Cherryh

☐ THE DREAMSTONE   (#UE2013—$2.95)
☐ THE TREE OF SWORDS AND JEWELS (#UE1850—$2.95)

Lin Carter

☐ DOWN TO A SUNLESS SEA   (#UE1937—$2.50)
☐ DRAGONROUGE   (#UE1982—$2.50)

M.A.R. Barker

☐ THE MAN OF GOLD   (#UE1940—$3.95)

Michael Shea

☐ NIFFT THE LEAN   (#UE1783—$2.95)
☐ THE COLOR OUT OF TIME   (#UE1954—$2.50)

B.W. Clough

☐ THE CRYSTAL CROWN   (#UE1922—$2.75)

NEW AMERICAN LIBRARY
P.O. Box 999, Bergenfield, New Jersey 07621

Please send me the DAW Books I have checked above. I am enclosing
$_____ (check or money order—no currency or C.O.D.'s).
Please include the list price plus $1.00 per order to cover handling
costs.

Name _____

Address _____

City _____ State _____ Zip Code _____

Please allow at least 4 weeks for delivery